THE ISLAND OF FOREVER

JEREMEY HARRISON

Published in the United States of America December 2025 by Jeremey Harrison.

Cataloging-in-Publication Data is on file with the Library of Congress.

ISBN: 979-8-9938684-2-4 (Paperback),

979-8-9938684-3-1 (ebook)

Author Website: www.jeremeyharrison.com

Editors: Tara Sexton, Ramona Mihai, and Charlie Knight

Cover Art: M.E. Morgan

Content Warnings

Dear Reader,

    Welcome to the island! Even though *The Island of Forever* is a YA Fantasy, I want you to feel protected while you're here. During their journey, Max and his friends deal with some heavier topics that may be sensitive to some readers. Below is a list of potentially triggering content, and I encourage you to look over them before proceeding.

Wishing you an enjoyable stay on The Island of Forever!

- **Depictions of Bullying**
- **Foul Language**
- **Smoking/Alcohol Use**
- **Depictions of Anxiety**
- **Use of Weapons (guns, swords, etc.)**
- **Descriptions of Blood**
- **Mention of Domestic Abuse**
- **Death of Animal/Creatures**

*This book is dedicated to all of the shapeshifters of the world.
On this island, you are heard, you are valued, and you are seen.
Regardless of the villains in life, you are the Hero. Don't forget it.*

And, of course, to Harper Grace.

ISLAND OF FOREVER

THE FOREVER SE

HIDDEN SPRING

Morwend's Cottage

HAUNTED MARSH

Sand Phantom La

LAKE OF
REFLECTION

Dragon's Den

MIRAGE OASIS

VALLEY OF SLEEPING GIANTS

Vane

Sand Elves

STONE GRAVEYARD

ISLE OF
THE CURS

Chapter One

A defined torso, chiseled abs, and biceps the size of grapefruits—all features Max knew he would never have. Changing in the locker room for his last class of the day has always been stressful, and today was no different. Looking at the upperclassman's toned body, he was embarrassed by his own underdeveloped frame.

Could I ever have a body like that?

Judgment overcame him whenever he entered the weight room at school. The jocks' snide looks and raised eyebrows saw right through him as they scanned his average body from head to foot. The presence of his peers made Max's insecurities flare, leading him to abandon his workouts before they even began.

An upperclassman turned and caught Max's eye. "Greenfell, are you checkin' me out?" Reaching to his shorts, he cupped the middle with his hands. "Lookin' for this?"

Max's cheeks grew hot, and blood rushed to his ears. He shoved his head through a white T-shirt before deepening his voice to respond. "I-I wasn't looking at you." Even as the words came out of his mouth, he knew they weren't believable.

A loud voice across the locker room cut through the accusation. "Come on, Reznik, do you really think he's checking you out? His girlfriend is Hannah Reeves."

Max's attention was drawn to his best friend, Rylan, who was making his way over to them. His blond hair was tousled and wild from gym class, yet it seemed to suit him perfectly. His dark green eyes narrowed as he stepped over a wooden bench and placed his palm on his friend's shoulder to give a reassuring squeeze.

Thank God Rylan's here.

The upperclassman raised an eyebrow in disbelief. "I've hit Hannah up a couple of times, and she left me on read." His eyes surveyed Max from head to toe. "She's hot...and she's datin' *you*?"

His cheeks reddened, and a sheen of sweat appeared on Max's brow. As his heart began to thump, his palms became clammy with a nervous sweat.

Rylan extended his arm and lightly squeezed Reznik's large bicep. "She probably didn't get back to you because you only have muscles in your arms." He shrugged with an eyebrow raised. "She's looking for them elsewhere."

"Get the hell offa me." Reznik tapped two palms on Rylan's chest, causing him to take an abrupt step backward.

"I'm just saying, word gets around when you promise big things and don't deliver." Smirking, Rylan watched Reznik slip through the locker room door and disappear into the school hallway. With a smug look of triumph, Rylan reached into his coat pocket and grasped a thin metal vape filled with a unique blend of his favorite ingredients: CBD and THC. Placing the end of the tube between his lips, he pressed a small button on its exterior, illuminating a small square around his thumb. Holding the vape in his hand like a baton, Rylan cocked his head toward the exit. "Let's wait for Hannah outside. I gotta smoke."

Max placed his arms into his jacket and threw his backpack over his shoulder, following Rylan outside the gym to the dingy hallways of the school. He was thankful to have a friend who understood his anxiety. Rylan helped him when he couldn't stand up for himself, but he constantly wondered when he'd find his own confidence.

"Max, you know what I'm going to say," Rylan started as he pushed open the school doors.

"Let me guess, something like, 'man up and nail her?'" He rolled his eyes and punched his friend in the shoulder. "You know how much I hate it when you talk about my sex life."

"You mean the non-existent one?"

Stepping outside, the crisp fall air and bright light had awakened his senses from the dim, fluorescent lighting that enveloped the school. The landscape was alive with color as the leaves had shed their coats of green, transforming to hues of red and yellow. Noticing a bite in the air, Max buttoned his jacket for the walk home. A large storm had been predicted for later that night, and dark clouds collected on the horizon as a reminder.

Out of the corner of his eye, Max noticed his friend struggling to put a knitted hat over his flowing blond hair. "You talk a big game, Ry, but you can't even get into that hat, let alone a girl."

"Believe me, I've gotten into a hat before, *many* hats, actually." Rylan snickered as he blew a plume of white smoke into the brisk air. "You and Hannah have been together for over a year, and every time you guys get close to doing it, you chicken out." He sucked on the end of his vape, which made a crackling noise before continuing. "Let me bring you to reality: your girlfriend is captain of the cheerleading squad. At this rate, she's more likely to get banged by the entire football team before you make your move." Rylan laughed, causing him to cough out the smoke he'd been holding in his lungs. "Even Reznik is after her, and if you don't seal the deal, he'll be sliding into more than just her DMs."

Max's friend's callous comment made his bright gray eyes roll in annoyance before he stumbled back as two arms wrapped around him. Breathing in the sweet smell of lilac, the soft tickle of his girlfriend's blonde hair wrapped around his neck. A mixture of joy and apprehension overtook his body.

"You two are so cute." Rylan scowled. "It makes me wanna throw up."

"You wish someone were *this* excited to see you." Hannah brushed her hand through Max's hair with a large smile sitting on her lips as her irises sparkled in the sunlight. "You make me melt."

Yeah, right.

Max smiled and put an arm around her shoulder. Hannah had always been a beautiful girl; he'd be lying if he said he didn't ask himself why she was with him. When she commented on his eyes, smile, or even his body, a gremlin of doubt burrowed into his mind.

What does she see in me?

A loud, shrill voice rang through the chilly air. "Omigosh you guys! Look at the leaves, they're so pretty!"

The sound of rustling leaves drew Max, Hannah, and Rylan's attention to their friend, Leona, whose cheeks were red against the brisk air, and her naturally highlighted brown hair blew in the breeze. She wore a confident smile, and her eyes circled in amazement as she marveled at the vibrant colors surrounding them.

"This is the perfect weather to practice shooting with my

dad." Her confident smile disappeared as she brandished the cell phone from her pocket. "There's only a few more months until hunting season."

Rylan raised one of his eyebrows and pointed to Leona as she walked toward them. "Why don't you lovingly throw your arms around me like Hannah does to Max?"

"Have you ever thought that maybe I'd be happier to see you if you were less of a dick?"

Max and Hannah's laughter filled the air as they listened to their friends volley playful remarks back and forth. Leona and Rylan were constantly bickering, but their true affection for each other was evident to those who knew them well.

"Max, are we picking up your sister at Ana's house?" Leona's thumb proceeded to scroll through her phone, never stopping for more than a split second before continuing on.

He nodded to his friend. Ana had been their babysitter, shaping them from children to teens, and she continued to watch over his little sister while he was at school. Knowing and trusting Ana for so long created a strong bond between them, and they felt as though she were family.

"Ella asked me to make her a princess bracelet with some of my craft supplies, so I was hoping to give it to her today."

Rylan dramatically huffed, "I really can't deal with Ella's personality without something to mellow me out beforehand. Lemme refill my vape."

"Asshole," Leona muttered, rolling her eyes. Her face was pointed downward as the endless scrolling abruptly ended. "Hannah, did you see your newest post? It's up to five thousand likes!"

"It must have been the fabulous photographer that took it." She winked and nudged her elbow into Leona as they walked.

Oh shit, did I forget to like it?

Max quickly took out his cell phone, clicked the app, and typed Hannah's name into the search bar. He navigated to her profile, tapping the tiny heart button within seconds. His eyes then shifted to Hannah's most current picture. Her thin frame stood before a backdrop of brightly colored fall leaves and her perfectly manicured fingers delicately tucked a strand of hair behind her ear, as if she was lost in deep thought while gazing beyond the camera. With her blonde hair casually thrown over her shoulder and a pair of dazzling white teeth peeking through her pink lips, the post was a picturesque reminder of the hike she'd gone on just the weekend before.

"Look at Hannah," Leona gushed. "She looks like a model."

Rylan cocked his head to look at the picture. "If you ask me, she looks more like a porn star." A sly smirk triumphantly sat on his mouth as he took a long drag from his vape, the tendrils of smoke drifting from his nostrils like a dragon.

While Leona punched their friend in the shoulder, Hannah tugged at Max's shirt. "Walk with me? I want to talk to you."

"Ignore him," he reassured her. "You look amazing in the picture and even he knows it." They eased their pace, creating a small distance from their friends. Max rubbed the back of his neck, his palms slick with sweat. "What's up? Is everything okay?"

"I've been meaning to bring this up for a while, and I don't want you to take this the wrong way." She paused and considered her words carefully. "You know I think our relationship is perfect, and you're the best boyfriend a girl could ask for, right?"

I think I know where this is going.

Having seen enough movies and television shows to know where this conversation usually led, he asked, "Are you breaking up with me?"

"No! Not at all!" Hannah's body tensed, and her eyes widened as she realized the possible misinterpretation of her words. "I just feel like we should take our relationship to the next level... I know you get nervous and uncomfortable about it, but I was just wondering when we were going to...you know..." Her fingers brushed the back of his arm as she bit her bottom lip.

Her unfinished words pierced the air and hung around them like humidity. The silence created an awkward barrier around them that seemed impenetrable.

Does she mean what I think she means?

He quickly stole a glance and noticed her eyes were alight with yearning and desire. Through the noticeable silence, she stammered, "...unless you don't want to?"

Yep, she wants to do it.

Immediately, the familiar panicked heat crept over Max's body, and he imagined long, spindly fingers wrapping themselves around his heart and bashing it against his chest, trying to escape. His breath shortened like he was underwater, sweat made his palms slippery, and his vision blurred like a murky veil covered his eyes. He wanted to make her happy, but whenever he thought about their first time, an anxiety spiral would paralyze him. "How about tonight?"

Did I just say that? It's like my mouth said it on its own.

Hannah was accustomed to his evasive answers, so when he answered directly, her mouth dropped in shock. "Tonight? Are you sure?"

Max hesitantly nodded and wiped his palms on his jeans. "My mom's working the late shift again, so you can come over once Ella falls asleep." A weight sat on his chest as his mouth dried, forcing the words in short breaths.

Leona turned around, waving her arms to Max and

Hannah. "Can you two hurry up back there? I'd rather eat my leg than spend another second with this idiot."

"Hey!" Rylan yelled. "I was trying to sweet talk you."

Max and Hannah laughed and ran a few feet ahead to save their friend from her torture. On the corner of the street was a large apartment complex which Leona, Rylan, and Max called home. The faded brick building was painted in splotches of gray and white as the birds that flew overhead used its exterior for target practice. The windows that overlooked the street were murky, with grime clouding the glass, and the cement between each brick was crumbling. A large wooden sign stood on the small lawn in front of the building with the words, 'Ocean View Terrace,' in big white letters with a splintered wave painted behind it. Max always found the name of the complex ironic as there was no ocean remotely near them.

"This place looks shittier every day," Rylan spat as they walked past the building. "I know it's low-income housing, but it looks like it needs to be condemned." Signs depicting a sleazy politician littered the lawn of the complex. The man's forced smile disappeared as the blond teen put his foot through the nearest one. "And this guy's a dick. He's trying to force people out of their homes!"

Leona jabbed his arm with her lip upturned. "Would you rather be homeless? Be thankful for what you have."

Max nodded, he remembered being homeless for a few days after his parents' divorce was final. His mother drove him and Ella around until they were too tired to stay awake, "adventuring," she had called it, stopping only to use the restroom and buy a slice of pizza from a gas station. It was a stroke of luck when Ocean View Terrace accepted their housing application, and they moved in with nothing more than one twin bed and a box filled with various odds and ends.

"The widow's house is straight ahead."

"Her name's Ana, you idiot!" Leona firmly slapped the back of Rylan's head.

At the end of the dead-end street sat a spacious Victorian house that loomed over the other residences in the neighborhood. The trees in the yard were completely bare, and the branches looked like gnarled old fingers reaching out from the trunk. An iron fence marked the perimeter, making eerie noises when the wind blew, and the grass inside was brown and withered.

"Ana has the perfect house for Halloween," Hannah commented as the gate in the fence swung shut, followed by a reverberating *clang.*

Leona shuddered and rubbed her arm. "Yeah, but it always gives me goosebumps. I always feel like someone is watching me from inside."

"Well, she *does* always say she has eyes everywhere." As if to further prove his statement, the wooden door flung open, and a little girl stumbled out from the darkness inside the house. Swaying back and forth, she acted as if she were drunk as she hugged the handrail to get down the wooden steps.

"Ella, what're you wearing?" Max asked.

A smile crossed each of their faces as they gazed upon the child and her odd assortment of clothing. In her ill-fitting red high heels, she shuffled across the creaky, old wooden deck. Her legs were covered in pink polka-dotted pants, a frilly orange shirt hung off one shoulder, and a faux pearl necklace draped down to her knees. Encircling her neck was a purple boa while a pair of black wayfarer sunglasses constantly slid down the bridge of her small nose.

"This is what princesses wear, duh!" Ella squealed, pointing to the silver plastic crown with two pigtails sticking

9

straight out of the top. "I'm the princess in the story Ana told me about."

Max smiled and lightened his voice. "I think Leona has a gift for you, Princess Ella."

The little girl gasped and shimmied out of Max's arms. She ran to the brown-haired girl, jumping up and down. "Did you bring my princess bracelet? Did you bring it?"

Rylan closed his eyes and rubbed his temples. "I'm *so* glad I smoked before coming here."

Leona reached into her corduroy bag and pulled out a bracelet with crowns and wands dangling from it. "You have to promise to keep this safe, okay?"

Ella looked Leona square in the eye and answered with a serious nod, "I promise." She slid the bracelet onto her tiny wrist and shook it, the charms jangling with each turn. Feeling satisfied, the little girl turned around, grabbed the high heels, and gestured toward the house. "C'mon guys, say hi to Ana."

As they approached the large house, the dim lighting made it appear ominous, and a musty smell emanated from within. The polished dark wooden floors gave the illusion of walking on glass, while vintage wallpaper was peeling at each corner of the room. Mirrors were fastened to every wall, big and small, while multicolored string from unfinished knitting projects lay scattered over the floor.

Ana emerged from her kitchen holding a tray of food, looking far more modern than the dingy ambiance of her home. Today, she was wearing a matching white and black striped pantsuit that looked as if she'd borrowed it from Beetlejuice and had paired it with a shiny pair of ankle boots. Her dark eyes twinkled as a smile crossed her red lips to reveal a set of perfectly white teeth. She pushed her black bangs out of her eyes as she sidled into the room.

"Is that food?" Rylan's forehead furrowed as his eyes lifted, eyeing the silver tray.

"Oh yes," Ana said softly, enunciating every word. The rumor was that Ana had been a famous soap opera star in the early eighties, but she rarely talked about her time on screen. "I just finished cutting up some apples, sliced an orange, and quartered some celery stalks as an after-school snack for all of you."

"Fruits and veggies aren't exactly my top choice for munchies, but they'll do." Rylan helped himself to a piece of apple, noticing the multicolored string haphazardly thrown across the coffee table. "When are you gonna clean this place up? I get that you're a widow, but there's yarn everywhere."

Ana's sparkling eyes glanced toward Rylan, her eyebrows raising. "I'll remember not to send you a new knitted hat this year if you're so concerned with the yarn in *my* house."

Ella tugged on Ana's pants. "Can you please please please tell them the story about the princess?"

She patted the little girl on the head and shook her head. "I don't think your brother and his friends are interested in hearing a fairy tale. I'm sure they've heard one too many of my stories throughout the years."

"I'll listen if a bag of chips is involved." Rylan lobbed a half-eaten carrot stick back onto the silver tray as he lifted one leg, dangling it over the wooden arm of a lush vintage couch.

"You'll live." Ana rolled her eyes and dramatically stole to the light switch on the wall to dim the lights. Lifting her black-and-white striped sleeves, she deepened her voice as if she were the narrator in a story. "Far out at sea, where no one from our world has ever stepped foot, lays an island. A magical island." She drew out many of the words for a more pronounced effect. "Many fantastical beings, such as mermaids and fairies, call this place home and live together in perfect harmony."

"There are princesses, too," Ella interjected, nodding at Hannah as she crunched on a celery stick.

"Yes, and princesses too." Ana smiled. "This magical place is called the Island of Forever. Everything within this island stays constant; there is no war, famine, or disease. This world always stays the same—never aging, never changing. That means there's no fighting, and no one has to grow up and be old."

"We know what it means." Rylan dramatically rolled his eyes. "We've heard this story a million times." He stood up and pushed his hair out of his face. "The bad guy comes to the island and takes control while the princess tries to find a hero to protect them. The hero shows up with a magical sword, fights the bad guy, and wins. Am I right?"

"You're so impatient," Leona screeched at him. "You forgot the hero ended up sealing Samael away inside a volcano."

"Right, that was his name." Rylan crossed his arms and stood. "Since we've heard this before, can we go?"

Ana pursed her lips as she stomped to her front door, inviting a brisk breeze inside the warm house. "Now that you mention it, there's a bad storm coming. You should be getting home." She shooed the blond boy quickly outside while her glistening eyes landed on the little girl. She put both hands on her knees and bent her body to be eye-level. "I'll see you tomorrow. Let's hope Rylan is in a better mood so we can finish the story."

"Wishful thinking." Max laughed as he exited the house.

The storm approached slowly, with dark clouds rolling in and the environment growing still as the sky turned gray. Before heading into Ocean View Terrace, they stopped on the stone pavers at the end of the road, now covered in weeds and overgrown grass.

"Do you guys mind bringing Ella up with you? I wanna say

goodbye to Hannah." Max nodded to his friends, hoping they'd catch the hint.

The question was directed toward Leona, so it was a surprise to everyone when Rylan asked, "Mind if I tag along?"

"You? Choosing to spend more time with Ella?" Max asked in disbelief. "Are you feeling okay?"

Rylan scowled and took another drag from his vape. "I don't wanna go home right now. My parents have been on my ass."

"You can come with us...but you have to play along." Leona grabbed Ella's hand with a flourish. "Shall we escort you to your palace, Princess?"

A deep breath expelled from Rylan's mouth as he silently regretted his decision, but begrudgingly held his hand out to the little girl. His eyes lingered on Max. "Don't be long. Please."

"Let's go!" Ella giggled and wrapped her hand around the teens' hands before they disappeared into the large building.

A sideways smile awkwardly hung on Hannah's face as she hooked her arms around his neck before placing her lips just outside his ear. "See you at eight?"

Her warm breath made a chill run down Max's spine as he nervously ran his fingers through his messy hair. A ball formed in his throat that wouldn't go away, no matter how often he swallowed. "Yeah...definitely. I'll text you." With his words of affirmation, Hannah vigorously pressed her lips to his, showing her excitement.

Her hands left him delicately as she gazed into his eyes. She spun, fanning her blonde hair behind her and disappeared down the road.

Max's palms became slippery, and a queasy sensation formed in the pit of his stomach. He placed his wet palm on the metal door handle that led inside the apartment building and realized that he couldn't use fear as an excuse tonight.

Oh, shit.

He walked through the small lobby area strewn with cardboard packages from online retailers and pressed the button for the elevator. As the dim button blinked to life, the realization of what he had agreed to overwhelmed him.

Shit. Shit. Shit.

Chapter Two

B*ing!*
    The sound of a newly delivered text message stirred Max from his slumber. After dinner, he put Ella's favorite cartoon on TV, and they both dozed off on the couch. Cracking one eye open, he realized a few hours had passed as he navigated to his messages. A message from Hannah roused him from sleep, and as he typed back to her, his fingers left a thin film on the bright screen before pressing send.

Shit, it won't be long now.

He rose from the couch, scooped Ella into his arms, and hoped she wouldn't notice the rapid drumming of his heart. Carrying her swiftly to the bedroom, he watched as her eyes fluttered open. Gently, he tucked her beneath the fleece blankets and laid her head on the pillow.

"Why isn't Mommy home anymore to tuck me in at night?"

Max picked up a stuffed mini giraffe and explained, "You know she works late." A forlorn look crossed his sister's face. "Princesses need to work hard to be good at what they do, right?"

"Princesses don't need to work, and neither should Mommy."

He couldn't say it aloud, but Max agreed with her. Ever since their mother divorced their father, she worked a full-time career and two part-time jobs to make ends meet. As a single parent, she was determined to make her children's lives as comfortable as she could. The downfall was that their mother was always working, leaving Max and Ella alone most of the time.

She gave a half smile. "At least I have you, Max."

"Thanks, kiddo." He smiled and placed one arm around her back, bringing her head to his pounding chest in a hug.

Ella scrunched her face and placed one hand atop his heart. "Is everything okay?"

She knows something's bothering me. Shit.

"Um...nothing. Just nervous for a big test tomorrow, I guess." He knew his voice was shaking, the tremor betraying his nerves, and hoped Ella wouldn't catch on.

"Oh, school stuff." The weight of sleep bore down on her eyelids, making it a struggle to keep them open and fight off an impending yawn. "Goodnight, Max. I love you." The stuffed giraffe's neck was pinched from her hooked elbow.

"Goodnight, you little booger. I love you, too." Max flipped the switch to Ella's nightstand lamp, which emitted a dim glow and played a soothing melody to lull her asleep.

As he exited the pink and purple room, his anxiety surged even higher, overwhelming his senses. A sudden wave of nervousness flowed through him; like his body knew and was reacting to the fact that Hannah would soon be at his doorstep once Ella was in bed. *Shit.* His heart fluttered like a caged hummingbird as he typed the passcode into his phone, letting his girlfriend know the coast was clear.

Am I ready for this?

He let out a breath of air that he didn't realize he was holding once the text was delivered.

I need to find something to spice up my bedroom and make it romantic. That's what I'm supposed to do, right?

He scanned the dining room, taking two unlit candles with faded metal bases from the table. He opened the small junk drawer with his free hand and spotted the red handle of a stove lighter amid dull scissors, pens, and tape dispensers. Wrapping his finger around the handle, he pushed the button as a test, and an orange flame popped out of the tip.

Running down the hallway, he pushed his bedroom door open with his shoulder and bounded over the mound of clothes piled on the floor. He set both candles atop a wooden dresser and surveyed the room, wincing as he recalled his mother's daily scolding to tidy up.

I don't have much time, but I gotta make this place look like I give a shit.

Max quickly grabbed the dirty clothes from the floor and threw them into his wash basket as if he were a basketball star. Looking for more items to clean, his eyes landed on his unmade bed. He was unsure if Hannah cared about this, but his mom did, so he freshened the blankets and fluffed his pillows.

I should've been more prepared for this. I didn't realize this would be happening so soon.

He slid a pile of potato chip bags, an empty lotion container, and various water bottles that were half full under his bed. For the final touch, he dispersed a can of body spray labeled Fierce Phoenix until the receptacle was empty, hoping it would give his room a subtle, manly smell.

Surveying the room once more, his eyes caught the flash of a small white stub on his dresser.

"Score." It was an old joint that Rylan must have rolled in his bedroom and forgotten about. He stuck the paper between his lips and lit it. A thought struck his mind and he paused, feeling foolish at his lack of sexual knowledge.

If I smoke this, will I have trouble getting hard?

Fear of embarrassment and insecurity crept into his mind as he contemplated lighting the small white paper. Weighing his thoughts while sitting on the floor with his back to his bed, he shrugged and clicked the lighter's button.

I don't think Rylan has ever had that issue before. I'm just being paranoid.

Max sucked on the end, held the smoke in his lungs for as long as he could, and then exhaled. The herbal remedy clouded his mind, and he closed his eyes to center and calm himself. As the joint disappeared, the tension in his shoulders and neck lessened like the weighted blanket he had been carrying had been removed. The internal dialogue that constantly played in his mind quieted as if he were in a state of unconsciousness but completely awake. Taking the joint's final hit before it burnt out, his eyes shifted to the storm howling outside, scratching at his bedroom window as if trying to break through.

Max stood from the floor and threw the nub of the joint into the trash. Grabbing the lighter, he neared its flame to both candle wicks and dimmed the lights to create as much of an intimate atmosphere as he could. Looking into the dirty mirror hanging on the wall atop the bureau, he combed his fingers through his unkept brown hair with a lopsided grin.

What does she see in me? Does she find me sexy or just cute? I mean, my mom always says I have beautiful eyes and a kind smile, but that's the kind of stuff your parents say to you.

His phone lit up and a loud, ominous *bing* reverberated through its speakers. Max looked at himself in the mirror one last time and shook his head.

Whatever she sees, I don't.

Glancing at the bright screen, he saw one simple word that made him want to throw up: Here.

It's now or never.

Taking one last look to make sure nothing was out of place, his nostrils curled at the overbearing smell of spray deodorant. Running to his small bedroom window, Max lifted it to let the stench of artificial mint and locker room waft outwards. The sound of rustling of dead leaves in the wind reached his ears as the cool air entered, signaling the storm's beginning.

"You got this." Max hoped the words of encouragement would boost his confidence as he ran down the hallway. Pausing in front of the door with his girlfriend on the other side, he readied himself by exhaling a long breath and wiping his hands on his pants.

The overhead lighting in the apartment hallway cast a flattering glow on Hannah, highlighting her beauty. With her straightened blonde hair pulled back, a touch of makeup subtly enhanced her eyes and cheeks. Her white shirt clung tightly to her waist, lightly veiling the black push-up bra underneath that assisted her in all the right places.

"Uh...hey," Max stuttered as he put his fingers through his hair, feeling a burn on the tips of his ears.

Hannah pressed herself against his chest and the scent of a candy-like sweetness filled the air from her slick lip gloss-covered mouth. Letting herself into the apartment, her eyes gleamed with excitement as she eagerly grabbed his hand. "Let's go to your room."

She's getting right to it. Am I ready for this?

Max shakily led her down the hallway and the smell of Fierce Phoenix reached his nose as it seeped into the rest of the house. He put one finger against his mouth to remind Hannah that Ella was sleeping. Nodding, she pressed her lips against his, their footsteps stumbling towards his bedroom. They went inside and closed the door behind them, their lips never leaving each other as Hannah grabbed the cloth of Max's shirt and pushed him onto the bed.

With his legs outstretched in front of him, Max wasn't focused on his girlfriend taking off her top, but was instead fixated on the high-top sneakers still on his feet.

Why didn't I take these off? It'll be so embarrassing trying to get these off with my pants around my ankles.

Pushing his toes into the heel of the other in an attempt to force it free, he soon realized the laces were tied too tight. Twisting his foot within the shoe and enacting more force to get it off, the sounds of rain pounding at his windows doubled his anxiety, further distracting him from the half-naked girl in his bedroom.

Hannah's actions spoke louder than any observation of his shoe struggle as she climbed on top of him and forcefully locked her lips with his. Their tongues danced in a passionate swirl while Hannah awkwardly squirmed against Max's pelvis, her breasts pushing against his chest.

"Do you have a condom?"

He gulped and paused for air, putting both hands on her waist. "Are you sure you wanna do this?" Max knew her answer but wanted to give himself one last attempt at prolonging the event before proceeding. He saw the lust in her eyes as she nodded with anticipation.

She's ready. This is it.

He pulled the drawer to his nightstand and fished around for the packaged condom he had received from the nurse's office at school.

Why can't I find it? Did I remember to bring it home? Is Hannah going to be disappointed if we can't do it?

Fear set into his mind as he searched the drawer blindly, the tips of his fingers grazing some loose change and an old deodorant stick. Time passed agonizingly slowly as he rummaged through the random odds and ends, trying to find the rigid foil wrapper.

Hannah laughed and reached into her back pocket. "Don't worry, I brought one. Just in case."

Shit, here we go. How can I show her I'm ready?

He reached around Hannah's back and flipped her onto the bed so she was underneath him, wafting the scent of lilac to mix with the deodorant spray in the air. The sudden movement caused the bed frame to jolt, knocking against the dresser.

Shit.

His eyes widened at the sight of the lit candle that had toppled from its holder, inches away from a heap of homework. Max jumped out of his bed, propping it up quickly to stop the fire, while the other candle lifted from its base, seemingly on its own.

"What's happening?" Hannah sat up. "Why do they keep falling over?"

Before he could respond, Max's legs quivered, and a strange sensation of weightlessness overcame him, as if he were being tossed around on a stormy sea. The floor of his bedroom shook violently, and picture frames on the wall crashed to the floor. The abrupt movements made him wonder if his apartment complex had grown legs and was walking away with them in it.

Throwing a dirty white shirt over his head, Max heard a loud banging on his door with the whimpering of a little girl. "What's happening? Where's Mommy?"

Rushing to his bedroom door, Max flung it open and Ella climbed up Max's body, wrapping her arms around his neck before hiding her tear-stained face in his shirt. The windows in the bedroom shattered with heavy rain and wind that began storming into the bedroom.

21

"Max, what's happening?" Hannah repeated. "Is it an earthquake?"

What do I do? We aren't safe here, but I can't seem to leave my room. Every time I try, it's like I'm being pulled away.

A loud bang came from the front door, and Rylan's voice called through the apartment. "Max? Max! Where are you?"

"In here!" He wrapped one arm around Ella to ensure debris didn't fly into her face. The wind howled and roared in his ears; its force was so strong that his feet slid toward the window as if a vacuum were sucking him out. A large gust of wind forced its way into the bedroom, throwing his feet out from under him and landing on the hard, wet floor. His free arm flailed until he secured his palm around the leg of his bed.

"Grab onto something stable," Max yelled to Hannah as he kept a firm grip on his sister.

Rylan appeared in the bedroom doorway followed closely by Leona, their eyes wide and faces pale. The storm heaved violently, sending sheets of rain into the room, while the vacuum-like force intensified, loosening their grip on the bedpost. They winced as the raindrops hit their skin like sharp pellets.

"What the hell kinda storm is this?" Rylan yelled as he and Leona clutched the doorframe with their fingers. Their bodies were completely airborne, and both of their shoes got sucked off their feet.

"I... I'm slipping!" Hannah's legs were flailing in the air as her fingers barely held onto Max's sliding closet door. "I can't hold on anymore." With one giant lurch, her body soared through the air and her flailing hands grasped Max's ankle.

Rylan and Leona's hands slipped from the doorframe, and the intense pull of the storm hurtled them toward the broken window. They slid down the bedroom floor, plummeting directly into Max and causing his grip to weaken. Rylan's hand brushed his face and Leona's scared hazel eyes flashed by him as they disappeared through the open window.

"RYLAN! LEONA!" Max's voice cracked as he yelled for his friends. Fear struck his body, and his muscles were tiring. "I-I can't hold on much longer," Max yelled to his struggling girlfriend in defeat. He glanced at his white knuckles, and with one last pull of the storm, his grip was lost, and they followed his friends through the window and into the storm. Ella's small hands dug into his neck along with Hannah at his ankle, but his vision instantly blurred as gravity took hold.

The raindrops pelting him scratched his skin, and the wind blew straight through him. His body was exhausted as the storm threw his body back and forth. The chaotic experience resembled being thrown into one wall, then retracted to be thrown into another. He never experienced the full impact of the whiplash until he was caught off-guard and pulled in a different direction. His body was light, as if he were free-falling and became numb to the elements throwing themselves at him.

Suddenly, everything halted.

No more rain.

No more wind.

Silence.

Chapter Three

Am I dead?

A warm breath reached his ear as his sister's grip weakened. "Max, where are we?"

It took a moment for his eyes to adjust to the brightness, but when they did, he realized they must be a great distance from their small apartment at Ocean View Terrace. Max was lying on an immaculately polished wooden deck of an enormous ship with stark white sails fluttering above him. His gaze followed the smooth espresso-colored trim that wrapped around the hull and stern, while seagulls soared through the sky above him, some resting briefly on the towering crow's nest. The ship appeared magnificent and other-worldly, as though the storm had not only taken them a distance but also transported them to another world altogether.

"Max, where are we?" Hannah's voice shook as she spoke. "How did we get on a boat?"

He shrugged before admitting, "I don't know."

Try to stay calm, you don't want to scare Ella.

Max's gray eyes met the little girl's as she buried her face into his chest, seeking comfort. "Are you okay?"

His sister rolled her head to the side, one eye peeking at him as she nodded. Max scanned the area for Leona and Rylan before returning to his disheveled girlfriend. "Do you think whoever is on this ship will help us?"

"How did we get here, Max?" Hannah's voice cracked. "How do we get home?" She crossed her arms and stomped her foot on the wooden floor. "Why aren't you doing anything to help?"

"Do you have any bright ideas? I'm doing the best I can," he snapped.

Is she serious?

Max's eyes traveled upward and he tried to remain calm. "The skull and crossbones flag is putting me on edge."

Ella's head perked up and she shimmied her way out of Max's arms, her feet landing on the wooden landing below. She snuck her hand into Max's palm, and her eyes grew wide as she gazed toward the crow's nest. "Are we on a pirate ship? I would be a good pirate and find lots of treasure." Ella jumped into the air, covering one eye and hooking one finger once her feet touched the deck. "Aye matey, let's go find the captain."

Max was somewhat grateful for his sister's lightheartedness in the situation, but hoped his role as her brother wouldn't have to be tested if Ella's excitement got them into trouble.

Hannah ran her fingers through her hair like a comb, trying to straighten the nest on her head. Her soaked clothes clung awkwardly to her chest and hips, and her black eyeliner continued to run down her face, leaving streaks resembling a community of roads over her cheeks.

The sound of a high-pitched screech started soft and became louder as a noisy blur flew by Max's head, landing on the smooth deck of the ship and skidding to a halt. A bird boasting an emerald body and wings that shimmered with cerulean, gold, and ruby red sat before him. The parrot's hooked beak was large and intimidating, and its beady black eyes studied them with suspicion.

Max's eyes were drawn to the black bicorn hat sitting on the bird's head as it hobbled on a small wooden peg in place of its right leg.

This has to be a dream; there's no way this is happening.

The bird reached to its side and brought out a small, curved sword the length of a paper clip. Its beady eyes glinted as they swiveled to look at the three. "Squaawk! Who trespasses on *The Morgana* unannounced? Do ye want to walk the plank?"

He was too stunned to speak.

Yep, this is absolutely a dream.

The sight of Hannah's wide eyes and gaping mouth made it clear that she was just as shocked as he. His body tensed up in disbelief as he peered at the bird, trying to decide if it was real or a mere illusion.

Could this be animatronic? Like at Disney World?

Max had met a parrot before, and it repeated single words back to him that he had to say multiple times for it to understand. It was astounding that this bird spoke to them in complete sentences and seemed to acknowledge them with understanding.

Ella crouched down to the bird and placed one hand over her eye. "Arrr matey, we're pirates, too. We're looking for treasure."

"I'm lookin' for the legendary treasure of Black Beak the Pirate. What treasure ye be lookin' for?"

"We *aren't* looking for treasure," Max interjected. "There was a huge storm in our town, and it sucked us out of my window...and we ended up here...on this boat."

This sounds absolutely ridiculous.

The bird's eyes widened. "BOAT? This be my *ship*, my baby, and her name is *The Morgana*; it is respectable to call a lady by her name. Ye can call me Captain Marris, what be yours?" The bird turned his beak away from Max and pointed his peg leg at Hannah and Ella.

His mind raced, trying to find a logical explanation for being on a ship.

There is no ocean remotely near where I live, so the storm either carried us miles and miles away...or this is a dream.

As much as he didn't want to admit it, a dream was the most reasonable explanation based on what he'd seen thus far. His anxious brain had conjured many strange dreams in the past to deal with his problems, but this one just seemed so much more...real.

"I'm Pink Pirate Ella, and this is Hannah and Max!" The little girl pointed to each of them.

Stepping in front of his sister for protection, he clutched her hand tighter. He wasn't sure what the bird's reaction would be and didn't want her to get hurt if it decided to attack.

"Squawk! A pink pirate, eh? I've heard of those. Fearsome little devils, aren't ye?" His green feathers ruffled like a shiver went down his spine.

A smirk crossed Ella's lips. "We're the toughest and the bravest."

Captain Marris nodded in agreement. "Between ye pink pirates and the beautiful women on *The Pirate Booty*, these seas aren't safe."

Hannah stifled a laugh. "*The Pirate Booty*?"

"Aye, that's the name of their ship. They be a crew of strong and fearless women and are a beautiful sight on the eyes." The bird seemed to get lost in his thoughts momentarily before shaking his head. "Speaking of ships, what brings ye to mine?"

"That's what I've been trying to tell you! We were at my

house one second and the next, here." He spread his arms into the air before his next question spilled from his mouth. "Where *are* we anyway?"

"My ship flies around the coast of the island looking for a secret cove that hides Black Beak's treasure. Mark me words, I'll find the rest o' the map one day, and the fortune will be mine."

"We're flying?" Max ran to the edge of the ship and peered over.

What the hell?

He expected to see waves crashing against the ship's hull but instead saw a blanket of white clouds parting as the vessel cut through. A group of seagulls lazily drifted below them, high above the expansive blue water below.

Did I take one of Rylan's edibles again?

His mind conjured logical answers to what he was seeing but refused to process the image of them flying through the sky on a pirate ship as reality.

"*The Morgana* is an enchanted ship; she can glide through the water or fly with the birds. I'd rather fly me ship in the air than the rough ocean waves. Ye never know what kind of trouble will find ye on the Island of Forever."

"An enchanted ship? The Island of Forever?" Hannah breathed as she turned to her boyfriend. "There's no way this is real."

He shook his head. "If this isn't real, how are we in each other's dream?"

Ella's response was a sudden and high-pitched squeal that made Captain Marris's feathers stand on end. Lifting his wings, he propelled himself into the air and circled the three of them. "Danger! Danger! All hands on deck! The pink pirate is attacking!"

"Ella, stop screaming! He thinks you're going to hurt him!" Max hurriedly covered his sister's mouth with his hand.

Captain Marris was still circling the ship yelling, "Danger! Danger!"

"We aren't going to hurt you!" Max yelled. "She was just excited."

The parrot landed on the trim of the ship, his eyes furrowed in skepticism. "Excited ye say? Now what is the pink pirate excited for?"

"Are we really here? On the Island of Forever?"

Max let out a breath of disbelief he had been holding in his chest.

This must be some sort of trick.

His eyes reached his sister, and he smiled at her excitement from hearing stories about the fantastical island. To her, it was as if she fell into her favorite tale full of mermaids, fairies, and adventure. Her eyes told him that getting home was the last thing on her mind; she was more concerned about finding princesses and learning magic.

Captain Marris nodded. "We're flying over the Forever Sea at the moment, but if ye look into the distance, ye can see the island for yourself."

Ella had to cover her mouth to keep from squealing again and looked at both teens with a huge smile. "Max, Hannah! Do you really think this is the place that Ana tells us stories about?"

I'm not sure if this is real or a delusion caused by anxiety, but that bird just looked at me like it wants answers.

Max threw his arms up and shook his head. "I can't believe I'm going to explain this to a talking bird, but here goes...a woman tells Ella stories about a magical place called the Island of Forever, and we thought it was only imaginary." He paused as he attempted to get his thoughts in order. "I-I guess until now."

"Squawk! Imaginary? Does this seem imaginary to ye?" Captain Marris knocked his wooden leg on the deck of the ship. "She be as real as they come, matey."

Max collected his thoughts and breathed the salty air, allowing the scent to calm his racing mind. "We had two friends that were sucked into the storm with us. Are they here, too?" Before continuing to confront the obvious questions, he needed to know that Rylan and Leona were safe and uninjured.

"Ye be the only scallywags I found on me ship. Be lucky I didn't make ye walk the plank. Hold on a minute—" As if realizing a critical detail, the green bird stiffened, ruffled its back feathers, and narrowed its eyes suspiciously at them. "If ye aren't from the island, ye be Mainlanders. Ye will put everyone in danger and need to leave this island immediately. Maybe ye *should* walk the plank!"

"W-we don't know how to get home." Hannah was trembling but managed to speak softly, hoping it would calm the bird down. "We don't even know how we got here and you're not doing anything to help us!"

"Don't know how, eh? Well, I can't get ye back. All I know is how to be a pirate." Captain Marris fanned his wing on the side of his cheek as if to tell them a secret, leaning closer to Ella. "And not to mention a pretty handsome one, if I say so meself."

She laughed and pointed to her brother and his girlfriend. "Can we be your crew to find the treasure of Black Beak the Pirate?"

"Ella, this isn't a joke. We need to get home."

"Squawk! I wish I could have ye as my crew on *The Morgana*, but Mainlanders aren't welcome here.

"Mainlanders?"

The bird nodded. "Aye, if ye ain't from the island ye be from the Mainland...and that be a problem. Look over yonder."

Their eyes followed Captain Marris's outstretched wing, and they saw a gigantic mountain planted in the middle of the island with a ring of smoke circling the top. The rock encircling the volcano was as black as polished obsidian, reflecting the sunlight like a metallic mirror. The ground surrounding it was a barren gray, devoid of any sign of life, as if it had been consumed by the volcano's power.

"That volcano imprisons the demon Samael. Any change brought to this island puts us all in danger. The seal holding him inside will slowly deteriorate and time will begin again. Ye being here weakens his prison."

"Right, the island is frozen in time." Max nodded. He remembered this part of Ana's story: it was an unchanging utopia, and any change that came would disrupt its balance. The story narrated how the island suffered when Samael was previously freed.

"We didn't even ask to come here." Hannah uncrossed her arms and flung them into the air. "Do you have any idea how we'd get back home?"

"I'm not sure. The Sofillians may be the only people on this island who can point ye in the right direction."

"Who are they?" Max didn't recall hearing of these people in the story.

"Aye. They be a settlement of children and teenagers that live within the Hesperian Jungle. I'll drop ye off on the coast of a beach nearby." Captain Marris flew onto the helm and turned the wheel, the whole ship turning toward the island as if spinning on an axis. The bird pointed its helm towards a tiny bit of sand next to a large forest. "Full speed ahead!"

Chapter Four

The massive ship soared through the clouds until land came into view, prompting Captain Marris to pull a lever beside the wheel. They hurtled toward the ground, the wind in their faces carrying the taste of salt. Eventually, they were hovering just above the small beach full of sand and rocks on the outskirts of a large jungle. From above, the trees in front of them looked much smaller than those towering over them now.

The parrot unraveled a rope ladder. "I won't make ye walk the plank."

"Thanks for that." Max rolled his eyes and bent his legs, nodding to his sister. "Miss Pink Pirate, hop on and hold tight."

As they reached the shore, Captain Marris whistled one last time before returning *The Morgana* to the sky. Ella sighed as they watched the magnificent ship ascend, her hands shielding her eyes from the afternoon sun. "I hope he finds Black Beak's treasure."

"I'm sure one day he will." Hannah smiled at the little girl's enthusiasm. Her innocent spirit kept them moving forward through the strange land they'd ended up in.

Max nodded and turned to his girlfriend and little sister. "We need to find these Sofillians and get home. Mom must be really worried about us."

They stood on the small beach, gazing at the magnificent flying ship's return to the sky until it was a speck among the clouds. The ocean in front of them seemed to go on forever, its vastness stretching for miles. The blazing sun radiated its warmth against their skin and their feet sunk into the grainy sand. The jungle behind them was alive with the sound of rustling leaves carried by the refreshing ocean breeze.

The peaceful scene was interrupted by an ear-piercing shriek from Hannah's mouth. "What are you doing? Get off me!"

Before he was able to turn around, rough rope bound Max's wrists and ankles so tight that the slightest movement would cause enough friction to create a burn. Three kids around his age caught them off guard, sneaking out from the jungle to apprehend them. Blindfolds were swiftly placed over their eyes and wadded pieces of fabric were shoved into their mouths to muffle any noise they may emit.

Hopefully by thrashing around, I can loosen their tight grip around me.

His body was held taut and completely immobilized, making any movement or escape impossible. He tried yelling to Ella or Hannah but could only mumble as the cloth gag left little room for air.

I need to get out to help my sister.

Rage burned in his chest as he hoped Ella and Hannah were unscathed. A tinge of fear crawled up his back as a bag made of leather wrapped around his body, and a durable rope was tightly knotted around his shoulders. Despite the debilitating sack tied around him, he continued to thrash his body in an attempt to break free.

If I were stronger, like Reznik, I'd be able to get free.

The forest was alive with the sound of twigs snapping beneath his captors' feet as they carried him deeper into the woods.

They better hope Ella and Hannah are safe when I get outta here or I'm gonna raise some hell.

In his mind, Max said it as a threat but knew he was too weak to fight their captors. Clenching his swollen hands, all he could do was hope they were safe. The brown burlap bag tied around his head smelled musty and dirty while droplets of sweat raced down his face with every passing second. The scratchy rope fastened around his wrists and ankles slowly cut off circulation from his hands and feet, making them feel as if they were pulsing. His breathing became shallow, and his heart was beating fast; the adrenaline from the situation was pumping through his body.

The kidnappers stumbled a bit, making Max's head bob forward, and with a quick crane of his neck, the itchy brown bag fell to the ground. Greenery sprung to his eyes as leaves and trees cascaded into view. Tied around his body was a leather sack that compressed his arms and legs, leaving only his head poking out of the top. He was strapped to the back of an unknown teenager who walked in a line of three, their skin tan from the blazing sun. Turning to his left, Max saw a small body whose head was hidden.

Ella! She's safe.

At the other end, he saw a waterfall of blonde hair poking out from the brown bag.

Hannah too. These assholes are lucky they haven't been hurt.

Their captors rounded a corner, revealing a small clearing

with a village of small houses resting in the branches of the trees within the jungle, connected by planks of wood and rope bridges. Each of the huts were built around one colossal tree, which looked to be the center of their community. Its roots stuck out of the ground as if trying to uproot itself and walk away and its trunk was so vast that it would take hundreds of people with arms linked to reach around its perimeter. The branches above stretched for miles, like an umbrella, and clusters of bright green leaves that were as big as a compact car extended from each.

The young inhabitants of the village looked at them with disgust. Everyone they passed appeared to be between twelve and nineteen. The scene was peculiar because there were no adults around, only children lounging on the grass in a circle with plants hanging out of their mouths and filling the air with smoke.

What's their problem?

The captors made their way between the tree's ascended arched roots before bringing them into its monstrous trunk. The tunnels inside twisted and turned like a labyrinth as they navigated the dimly lit hallways carved out of a hole at the base of the tree.

A set of stairs were carved upwards through the trunk, but they passed by, continuing onward until they neared the tree's center. The room the captors paused within was the biggest Max had seen and smelled like a fire had recently been extinguished. Roots snaked up the room's dirty wooden walls, and the tree's swirls created a beautiful pattern on its floor.

Unhooking them from their sacks, a flash of silver glinted and the rope binding his wrists and ankles fell to the ground as if they were strands of hair. Max ran over to Ella without a second thought to ensure she was not hurt, ripping away the brown bag covering her head.

With a worried look, he placed one hand on his sister's face and the other around her neck. "Are you okay? Did they hurt you?"

She shook her head and rubbed her arms, a scared look crossing her eyes. "My wrists are a little red from the rope, but I'm okay."

Max placed a gentle kiss on her forehead, hoping it would soothe her, even though his own heart was racing. "I'll always be here with you." He turned to make sure Hannah was okay and found her standing with a steely gaze fixed on their captors, a fire burning in her eyes.

The large, circular room was reminiscent of a courtroom, with intricate wooden furnishings and decorations strategically placed around the perimeter. The walls of the room had various carvings of animals hidden within the whorls of the wood, and all the fixtures were sculpted out of the tree itself. Situated at the head of the room were four podiums, and in the middle was an ancient stoned well that was so dark, it seemingly had no end.

Without a word, the three that captured them left down the hallways from where they came, and three others entered. Two muscular guards with their chests painted in different patterns held spears in their hands while they dutifully followed a girl wearing a dirty white tunic over her shoulders with a blue sash tied around her waist. Her luscious brown hair caught everyone's attention and her tanned skin looked as pristine as a newborn doe. The most striking feature of this girl were her eyes—one was colored gold and the other, a piercing blue.

Max blinked frantically, attempting to adjust his eyes to the dim room so he could get a good look at the men standing in the shadows behind the woman. "Who are you? Where did you bring us?"

The young girl's eyes shifted to Max. "I should ask you the

same, but all our questions will be answered in time, I suppose." She looked wistfully away as if lost in thought. "On my orders, the Sofillian hunters brought you to the grounds of our camp. I am their leader, Wintey." She gestured behind her. "This is my brother and bodyguard, Calvo."

The man stepped into the light, and Max's breath cut short. The dim lighting made his chest muscles and abs look even more prominent while his jaw looked like it could cut glass. A colored headband was wrapped around his forehead under cascading mounds of dark hair and his dark eyes glinted in the light.

Great, another jock to make fun of me in front of my girlfriend and sister.

The man's voice was low and calm, not matching his rough exterior. "Who are you, and how did you come to be on the island? Who brought you here?"

"We're Captain Marris's pirate crew, and we just got off his flying ship!" Ella answered, closing one eye and making her index finger into a hook. "We're looking for treasure!"

Max's grip tightened on his sister's arm, and he fixed her with a grave stare before shaking his head. His eyes darted towards the large ax hooked onto the animal hide tied around Calvo's waist.

We have to be smart; they have weapons and outnumber us.

Putting his hands up, he avoided the man's gaze and deepened his voice. "Sorry for my sister's outburst. My name is Max, and that's Hannah." He pointed to his girlfriend, who had a scowl pinching at her lips. "We got caught in a storm back at home and the next thing we knew, we landed on Captain Marris's ship. He brought us here thinking you may know how to help us get back to where we're from."

Wintey turned to Calvo in confusion. "Captain Marris? Is

he that pesky bird that tried to steal some apples from our tree?"

He rolled his eyes. "Yes, that is him." A smirk appeared in the corner of his mouth as he noticed Max's eyes gliding down his body.

Shit, he saw me.

Her eyes locked onto them, disbelief etched into her expression. "All Mainlanders must leave this island immediately and I have gotten word that two others have followed you here. Who are they exactly?"

"They're here? On this island?" Max's heart jumped with relief. "Those are our friends. We were separated in the storm."

"Indeed." Her lips moved silently as if she were having a conversation with herself while her eyes darted back and forth behind closed eyelids. Snapping her eyes open, they were renewed with energy and newfound brightness. "My insight is never wrong, and I trust my instincts. I see you pose no direct threat to me or anyone within my community, despite the growing problem of you being here. I will attempt to help you for the good of the island. Please follow me outside, and we can talk while enjoying the last bits of sunlight." She turned to Calvo. "You may return to your quarters."

The buff bodyguard silently nodded and walked away, flexing with each step. Wintey ushered Max and Ella to the entryway, and just as they were leaving, Max stole one last glance back at Calvo, secretly hoping they'd see each other again.

Chapter Five

Is this really happening? This is the longest dream I've ever had, when am I gonna wake up?

The girl led them through the tree's wooden tunnels and out into a small clearing, where the sunlight filtered through the branches in delicate streams. She found a patch of flowers growing abundantly and curled her feet beneath her to sit. "Join me among the sofillia."

Ella crossed her feet and plopped on the earth below while Max turned to look at Hannah. She shrugged her shoulders in annoyance and knelt to the ground, resting on her elbow.

"You know, the red sofillia only grow around the base of the tree, it's where we get our name." Wintey started stringing flower stems together, her eyes focused on the project her fingers were constructing. "When Samael was imprisoned within the volcano, everything returned to how it once was. Diseases disappeared, plentiful food options returned, and time seemed to have stopped. We achieved calling this island a complete paradise—a utopia. The only way for that balance to be threatened is if Mainlanders find their way onto the island, which is why I am so concerned with your arrival."

"What's everyone not understanding? We *want* to leave, we just don't know how." Hannah was exasperated, which differed from the perfection she always seemed to attain at home.

"Understood, but the entire island is at risk for every second you're here. You must find your friends and travel north."

"What's at the northern end of the island?"

"Yeah, what's there?" Ella repeated.

"An ancient temple," Wintey whispered, stringing flower stems together. "The last Mainlander disappeared inside and never returned. It is rumored they found a way off the island."

"How do you know they left and were able to get home?"

Wintey shrugged. "I suppose we don't...but it was our last Hero that imprisoned Samael, and once they left, the island flourished."

"Hero?"

Ella nodded. "Don't you remember, Max? The Hero beats the bad guy and brings peace back to the island."

He nodded to his sister, forgetting she knew much more about the Island of Forever than he did from the stories Ana told her day after day. In each of the tales, there was always an almighty Hero who defeated the evil that manifested on the island.

With her finger under her chin, Hannah tapped her foot. "How can we find Rylan and Leona to bring them to the temple if we don't know where they are? They could be anywhere, and we don't know how big this island is."

"That is a good question." Wintey's eyes sparkled in the dim light, and she extended her finger upwards. "Tonight, when the moon is at its peak, I will use my psychic abilities to consult with the spirits and ask them to locate your friends. Although time is of the essence, we will have our answer in the morning."

Ella jumped up and started clapping her hands. "We're going to have a sleepover? I've never had a sleepover before! What kind of pajamas do you wear here?"

"Unfortunately, we do not have any clothes for you, little one. You'll have to stay in the ones you are wearing." Wintey held two flowers in front of Ella's face. "Do you like this yellow sofillia or the red one?"

"The red!"

"Good choice." Wintey laughed as she weaved it into the crown within her hand.

Max couldn't help but look at the young inhabitants of the camp. Most of them wore animal fur clothing and had leather sandals strapped to their ankles. There was a crowd of people within the area, all ranging in age, although none seemed to be older than him.

Wintey knotted a stem and watched his eyes wander from person to person. "You have likely noticed that we are a group of teenagers who do not physically age beyond twenty years old. We watch and protect the Great Tree of Hesper, who is our mother. I assume Captain Marris brought you here because we would be the most relatable to you as our ancestors were once from the Mainland."

"The tree is your mother? Our mommy isn't a tree, is she, Max?"

Max laughed at his sister's question. "No, she's not, Ella."

"Once every few years, our mother grows beautiful golden apples and at their ripest, they fall to the ground where we collect them. Many creatures and people on the island want the Hesper apples as they are known to elongate one's life. To protect herself from those greedy and unthankful, the Great

41

Tree hides us from the rest of the island. You must be physically brought here by a Sofillian to find us."

"Is that why everyone is so young? The apples?"

"We may look and act young on the outside; on the inside, we age just as everyone else, just at a somewhat slower pace. I suppose it is a residual benefit from the apples and from ingesting the leaves that fall from her."

The area they'd been sitting in was quiet despite it being near the middle of the bustling, raised village. A sunbeam brushed Max's cheek; it was a pleasant touch that calmed him as his mind raced from the information Wintey had provided, blissfully unaware of the dangers that may come. It was like he was in a movie or video game and was going on a quest to return home.

The only time I ever left my hometown was with my dad. We went camping, and I didn't sleep at all because I was afraid a bear was going to come into my tent.

"What should we expect when we leave this camp to find Leona and Rylan?"

Wintey was finishing the flower crown, delicately intertwining the stems. "That I cannot say. The majority of the islanders will not welcome you, but Samael's followers will want to keep you here as long as they can to release their leader. With every passing moment, time trickles back to the island and begins to weaken his prison. You'll be met with obstacles, but we will equip you with light weapons to help you along your way."

"Weapons?" He knew there was a chance of danger but hadn't thought about the necessity to wield weapons.

Will Ella be okay? Will I be able to protect her?

"Oh yes, you'll need weapons in order to find your friends and get home. The Island of Forever may be a utopia, but it's not without danger." The Sofillian leader finished the crown made of flowers she'd been connecting and placed it atop Ella's head, much to her delight.

Wintey's words of warning lingered in the air, leaving an unpleasant taste in everyone's mouth. Without much more to say, Max shrugged as his mind raced. "Thank you for allowing us to stay the night."

"It's my pleasure." She nodded with a slight bow. "Just promise you'll leave this island with your friends as soon as possible and never return."

"Believe me, if we can find our way home, I can promise we'll never come back," Hannah snidely retorted. It was clear she was not processing this change all that well.

"Unless you need a princess!" Ella yelled, pointing to the floral crown on her head. "Then I can stay."

Wintey, Max, and Hannah laughed at the little girl's comment and stood, wiping bits of grass and dirt from their clothes.

"Come, let me show you where you will stay for the night."

On their way to their quarters, Max observed that the Sofillians were occupied with various tasks, dispelling his earlier notion that they were just idling around. They passed one Sofillian girl skinning animals for their meat and collected the fur to make their clothing. Another teen was working in a small garden near his hut, gathering various vegetables growing from the ground.

It seems there's no pressure to do more than what's assigned to each person, and everyone has their purpose. It's a slower, nicer change of pace from back home.

Passing the working Sofillians, Wintey paused at a small straw hut with three hammocks hanging from the ceiling and animal skin blankets draped over their side. "This is where you'll be staying for the night. Please make yourselves at home.

Then, when the light first touches the sky, we'll have an idea where your friends are."

"Why don't we get to sleep in a treehouse?" Ella stomped her feet, crossing her arms.

"You'll not be staying long, little one." Wintey smiled. "This will suffice."

"Thank you again for helping us." Max nodded and provided an appreciative smile.

"I must protect my people, and I'll be damned if harm comes to this camp." She bowed before turning to walk back toward the Great Tree.

Within moments, Ella emitted a giant yawn and stretched her arms into the air. "What a busy day."

"Tomorrow will be just as busy. It sounds like we have a lot of ground to cover. Make sure you get a good night's sleep." Max attempted to keep a tone of normalcy for Ella, ensuring she didn't become afraid or realize the dangers of being dropped into a fairy tale.

"I will," Ella said as she squirmed underneath the blanket. "Can you tuck me in like you do at home?"

Max kneeled on the ground next to the hammock where his sister was lying. "You know, I couldn't think of someone I'd rather be stranded on a magical island with than you."

A large smile graced the little girl's face, and her eyes became wet as a tired wave crossed her face. "G'night, Max. Thanks for being the best big brother ever." She reached up and wrapped her arms around his neck. "I wish we didn't have to go home."

He laughed and kissed his little sister on her forehead. "We have to leave so that the bad guy doesn't escape, remember? Plus, we don't want Mom to worry too much about us, right?"

The little girl yawned and nodded. "I just wanna be a

magical princess, but I don't want Samael to get out. Promise you won't let him take me?"

"I promise not to let anything bad happen to you on this island."

"Pinky promise?" Ella asked, holding the smallest finger on her hand in the air.

Max hooked his finger with hers. "Promise." As soon as their pact was complete, Ella turned over, and within minutes, her breathing became rhythmic, and a tiny snore emanated from the back of her throat.

Standing awkwardly to the side of the hut, Hannah turned her gaze to Max. Catching his eye, she tucked her hair behind her ear. "I can't believe this is happening, this is crazy! Do you think we're really on the Island of Forever?"

Max shrugged. "It's hard to believe, but yeah, I think so. We haven't woken up yet." It seemed unreal that they'd been whisked away to this fictional island. He was numb to everything happening because back at home, his life had been pretty unremarkable; nothing exciting happened, and he continued to wait for the bad news that seemed to follow him. "I don't want to worry Ella, but I'm scared. What happens if we can't get home?"

"At least we have each other, right?" Her voice was tired and hopeless; even her optimism sounded futile. "That's as much positivity as I can muster for today."

"I'm hoping that once I fall asleep and wake in the morning, I'll be home and in my bed." Max took a few steps toward her and wrapped his arms around her waist. Putting his head in the crook between her neck and shoulders, he breathed in the damp smell from her hair and lightly kissed her neck as she returned his embrace.

I love the smell of lilac that follows Hannah, it's something that makes me feel not so far away from home. She's someone I can hold onto while I try to hide how scared I am.

"Should we continue what we started in your bedroom?" Hannah's eyebrows rose, and a playful smile perked at her lips.

"Is that really at the top of your mind right now?" Max shook his head. "I couldn't think of a worse place to have our first time than in a hammock with my little sister directly next to us."

Hannah laughed in agreement and kissed him on his cheek. "It was a joke, dummy." She yawned and slid into a hammock near the hut's small window. "Goodnight, Max. Get some rest."

"No chance of that." He laughed and climbed into the remaining hammock and swung in the light breeze that came through the door. Staring at the straw roof above him, Max couldn't turn his thoughts off long enough to fall into slumber.

Are Rylan and Leona hurt? Maybe they found a group of people like we did, and they're being told to find us and leave the island, too? How can we get off this island, and once we do, how far from home will we be?

An uncomfortable pang stabbed his chest.

What will Mom think when she gets home from work and finds that we're missing?

As he spiraled, the minutes turned to hours, and the only sounds he could hear were Hannah's breathing and Ella's quiet snores. A faint rustling coming from the hut's entrance reached his ears, and he was unsure if it was his mind playing tricks. His ears perked, listening for the sound again. Sitting upright, he heard the crunching of leaves underfoot as someone was making their way closer to them. His hands began to sweat, and his heart raced.

Will I need to fight someone to protect Hannah and Ella?

Max slipped out of his bed and tiptoed toward the entrance

to the hut. Poking his head out of the doorway, he saw a dark figure in the shadows, slightly illuminated by the moon above.

"Max?" a voice whispered. The shadow drew closer until he stepped into the moonlight. Calvo's statuesque body came into view, his hair spilling over the headband around his forehead, each strand looking like a spider's web. His smile crinkled at his eyes, and his jaw created a sharp line separating his neck.

Max let out a sigh of relief. "You scared the shit outta me," he breathed. "What're you doing here?"

"Apologies, I did not intend to alarm." Calvo bowed. "Wintey sent me to ask if you and your lady friend would like to join us for a Sofillian tradition in praising our Great Tree?"

Max's throat went dry as he thought about the question and wiped his hands on his pants. "I can't leave Ella."

I'll admit, it would be cool to explore, but I can't afford for anything to happen to my sister.

"Probability of an outside threat is low due to Hesper's protection, but I can have two guards stand outside the hut if you'd like. We won't be too far away, and they'll let me know if there's any disturbance."

"I don't know..." Max said, remembering the promise he made to his sister. "Let me ask Hannah." He tiptoed over to Hannah's hammock, lightly tapping on her shoulder so she'd wake. Her eyes opened sleepily, and she brushed the golden hair from her face, a look of questioning in her eyes. Max put one finger to his mouth and gestured toward the large man.

"What's going on?" A sheepish smile pulled at her lips.

"We've been invited to a party," he whispered.

"Actually, our *tradition* is to praise the Great Tree of Hesper as she showers us in her leaves, which we then ingest."

"Let's do it!" Hannah's eyes were alight as her head jerked back to Max. "Would you be okay with leaving Ella, though?"

"It may not be appropriate for a child as young as her,"

Calvo explained. "But you can come back to check on her after the ceremony if you wish."

Max had been to many smoke sessions with Rylan before, and this seemed no different. Max glanced at Calvo's brawny arms, and a jolt penetrated his body as his eyes pierced through him, dispelling any doubt in his mind.

"Can't I bring her? It'll make me feel better."

Hannah huffed. "Why can't we have some time, just the two of us, for once?" She made a fist, pointing her thumb over her shoulder at the man. "If he says she'll be fine and there will be extra protection, let's just go. We won't be far."

"But we just met these people, and it's a completely new place. I don't feel comfortable leaving her."

She rolled her eyes and crossed her arms. "I didn't know that dating you meant dating *her,* too."

Did she really just say that?

Max was taken aback by Hannah's comment, although he understood why it was said. Ella was always in his life and his top priority, yet he still should make time to show his girlfriend how important she was. Hannah enjoyed spending time with his sister, but he failed to see how it was straining their relationship. He knew he had to make a hard decision to make, weighing his girlfriend's disapproval against his worries for Ella's safety.

Screw it, I could wake up any second from this dream and I need to do this for Hannah. For us.

"Do you promise that she'll be safe?"

Calvo nodded.

"Are we doing this?" A smile stretched across Hannha's face, her eyes glowing.

He let out a long breath of air and shrugged his shoulders. "Let's have a date night."

Chapter Six

The nighttime air on the island was cool and still, offering a refreshing break from the heat of the day. The trees around them stood motionless, and the only sound was the crunch of fallen sticks beneath their feet. Hannah's arm wrapped around Max's as they walked toward the center of the village with Calvo leading the way.

The boughs of the trees were dotted with tiny huts, their windows each glowing with the flicker of candlelight. As Max walked through the small village, his attention was drawn to the man walking slightly in front of them. Every time he moved, the moon shone on different muscles, highlighting those on his legs while others outlined his back and shoulders. Against the backdrop of dim light in the darkness, he stood out like a perfect silhouette. Max's thoughts turned back to the constant teasing at school, and he averted his eyes, feeling as if he'd gotten caught.

Their eyes glowed as torches illuminated a dozen Sofillians kneeling in a half circle around the large tree trunk. Wintey stood before the kids, her one blue eye glinting in the torchlight. "Sit quickly, we're almost done."

Max dropped to his knees and sat like everyone else around him. Turning to a puzzled Hannah, it was clear that neither knew their role nor wanted to interrupt the ceremony. With a quick glance, Max observed Calvo's eyes closed and his chest rising and falling with each deep breath.

Maybe if I were more like him, I'd actually have the guts to sleep with my girlfriend or know how to get us off this damn island.

Mirroring the people on each side of him, Max sat with his back erect before closing his eyes. His senses focused on the crackling of the torches and the deep breathing of the kids next to him. He practiced sharply inhaling through his nose until he couldn't hold his breath any longer, then slowly letting it out through his mouth, finding serenity in the pattern. It was almost intimate how they were each breathing in sync.

What's that thumping sound?

As if it were incorporated into the air around them, the heartbeat-like noise reverberated through their ears and into each of their bodies. He breathed in, then out. A sense of peace began to wash over him as a cloth settled onto his head and draped over his body. Peeking from behind his eyelids, Max saw a veil of green in front of him that had dark veins stemming from its center like the grid of a roadway.

Wintey's soft voice stirred them out of their meditation. "The ceremony is over. Eternal thanks to our protector, the Great Tree of Hesper."

Part of the green covering lifted, and Calvo's smiling face appeared underneath. "Hesper blessed you. This is a great honor." With a flourish, he removed the material from around him and draped a large leaf the size of a picnic blanket over his arms.

"What does that mean?"

Calvo's eyes turned to the large tree, his head tilting upward to her protective branches. "She gave you one of her leaves; it means she sees something within you."

Max raised an eyebrow. *What could anyone, let alone a tree, see in me? I'm the least remarkable person in the world. If anything, she should've blessed Hannah or someone else.*

His eyes quickly glanced at the towering Sofillian standing beside him.

Wintey strolled over with her hands clasped. "It is our honor that the both of you joined our tradition this evening. We will now cut the leaves Hesper blessed us with and ingest them to become one with her."

A woman wearing many necklaces beaded with turquoise stones and a short deerskin skirt around her waist approached, placing her hand on the leader's back. She'd weaved her thick black hair into a braid, and her thin lips were curved into a smile.

"I don't believe I have made introductions." Wintey reciprocated by placing her arm around the girl's waist before kissing her cheek. "Max, Hannah, this is my partner, Ness."

"Nice to meet you." Hannah smiled.

Max nervously smiled and nodded to her, unable to find the words to exchange niceties. His face warmed as Calvo's rough hand touched his lower back, gently nudging him to a wooden table nearby where he'd thrown the leaf over his shoulder.

Calvo spread the large leaf like a tablecloth, its edges spilling over the side. Then, grabbing the sharp ax strapped to his waist, he swiftly cut the leaf into uniform strips, his warm brown eyes focused on each intentional cut he made.

Max turned his head to look at Wintey and Ness, who were holding hands a few feet away and gazing at each other, their eyes flickering with fire and passion. He glanced at Calvo and asked, "So, Wintey has a girlfriend...is that normal here?"

A horrified look crossed Hannah's face, and Calvo's ax stopped splicing. "Why would that be out of the ordinary?"

"Well, where we're from—"

Calvo interrupted, "This is *not* where you are from." His warm brown eyes went cold as he focused on cutting the leaf. "We create relationships with the soul, so take care not to pass judgment while you're here. Otherwise, you'll start sounding like a shapeshifter."

"I-I didn't mean to..." Calvo's pointed tone sounded as if he were judging him. "What's that supposed to mean?"

Calvo shrugged and continued cutting the leaf in front of him. "Before the shapeshifter clan ended, they resembled Mainlanders: judgmental and power-hungry. They'd do anything to get their way, which is exactly how Samael was molded."

"We're nothing like them," Hannah said, giving her boyfriend a stern look.

"Let's hope not." With that, Calvo finished his project, and a stack of perfect rectangular leaves sat in front of him. The brawny man hunched himself over the table, and rolled one until it was about the size of Max's middle finger. A smirk crossed his mouth as he held it out while the white glow of the moon stuck its face through the branches above. "To light this, put it between your lips and breathe inward. The air will ignite the tip of the leaf, you'll know once the effects hit you. Give it a try."

Max took the rolled leaf and stuck it between his lips, sucked on the end, and cool air filled his lungs. The smoke he was breathing was ice cold, almost like he was swallowing a breath mint, which was the opposite of the last time he tried a cigarette with Rylan.

"Will you be joining our circle to smoke Hesper's leaves?"

Before Max could respond, Hannah spread her fingers and ran them through her tangled blonde hair. "We were hoping to have a date night tonight. Do you know where we can go to be alone?"

"No." Max shook his head, handing the leaf to his girlfriend. "I'm not going too far from Ella."

"Come on, live a little. If we're on this island, we might as well see some of it. Please?" Hannah's bright blue eyes looked up at him and her eyelashes fluttered as she exhaled the smoke from her mouth. "Calvo will make sure the guards stay outside our hut so we can do something tonight. Right?" She turned her head to the man at the table, her eyes were pleading for an answer in her favor.

"I can do that." A large smile graced his mouth as the girl's face lit up at his response. "There's an overlook nearby, just beyond our village. You'll have a great view of part of the island from up there."

"Is it safe?"

Please say no so I can convince Hannah to forget this idea.

He shrugged his shoulders and nodded. "The overlook is slightly outside of Hesper's protection, but I've never experienced anything threatening there."

"It sounds like a perfect place for a date to me." Hannah winked. "You must bring a lot of girls up there, huh, Calvo?"

Are his cheeks red?

His eyes widened as his pupils danced from Hannah to Max. "N-no romance in my life," he stammered. "I'm too focused on my duty as a Sofillian warrior."

Awkward tension filled the air and he stepped backward, nearing the path back to his sister. "Let's go back toward our hut, smoke this, and get to bed."

"Come on, Max, let's go to the overlook. Do it for me. For your girlfriend."

Her words reached him much harsher than she intended.

Ugh, the girlfriend card.

He exhaled a deep breath in defeat. "Let's check on Ella. As long as everything's okay and the guards can stay, we can check it out. But we can't be long, deal?" He entwined his arm with Hannah's, their fingers dancing with one another.

She nodded and an arc of red light caught their eye. The light seemed to be part of the air itself, jumping around like a rabbit before disappearing. They turned to one another with amusement.

Calvo laughed at their astonished faces. "Go check on your sister and enjoy your time at the overlook. I'll make sure she's safe." He bowed. "Goodnight, Mainlanders. Rest up. Tomorrow you'll set out on your adventure." He walked back to the trunk of the Great Tree with a handful of leaves clasped in his palm, where a throng of children sat in a circle around a roaring fire.

Max turned to look at Hannah, who had a mischievous glint in her eye and a smirk on her lips. "Ready to go?" He grabbed her hand, and they walked through the camp, stopping quickly to poke their head inside the hut to ensure Ella was sleeping before disappearing into the forest ahead.

Even though it was night, the sounds within the jungle were very much alive. The tree branches bounced as the wind blew through, and hidden underfoot, bugs chirped in the silent night. It was as if all of the inhabitants within the forest were finishing their daily duties before falling asleep. There was a thin line of dirt that snaked through the trees, a worn path that was illuminated by the silver moon above. The trail of bent leaves and crushed grass twisted once but was otherwise a straight shot to their destination.

"We must be close," he surmised as the ground beneath his feet inclined. In his eyes, Hannah seemed to sparkle in the moonlight as they walked hand-in-hand.

This is how it should be—just me and her. I'm excited about this? Of course, I am. It's like we snuck out together. This is so much less pressure than when we were in my bedroom.

He shuddered and pushed the thoughts from his mind.

Hearing Hannah's hushed breathing next to him, they trudged up the small hill.

I should be lucky that a girl as hot as Hannah is my girlfriend, right? Why do I make everything so hard?

More glints of neon light danced through the air around them as they neared the overlook. Hannah dropped his hand and began sprinting to the top of the hill they had been climbing. "Race you to the top!"

He loved her playful energy and willingness to have fun whenever a situation seemed bleak. He was not too far behind her when he saw an opening in the trees and leaves, signaling the end of the hill. The sticky air collected at his temples until sweat formed, and one bead ran the length of his face.

"I win!" Hannah yelled with her arms in the air.

Max laughed and brought her head close to his mouth. "I let you win." His eyes turned to the land outside the overlook, and his breath was taken away. "Hannah, take a look at this."

The hill that they stood on overlooked a large island expanse, and seeing it made them feel on top of the world. Slightly to their left was the giant volcano they'd seen on the pirate ship, but being much closer now made it seem otherworldly. A blanket of green flourished down the overlook and stopped as it reached the mountain's base to a ring of scorched earth which wrapped itself around the volcano, not allowing any life to reach it. The air around it was fraught with foreboding that wrapped itself around its craggy exterior as it sat smugly in the distance.

Stars twinkled overhead as they turned their attention to their right, seeing a patch of yellow sand and black dots littering its top. The wind rustled through the air, and the moon above cast the landscape in a still glow, illuminating just enough to make the scene look like a black-and-white picture.

Max squinted to see what was beyond the beach and only saw darkness. It was like a barrier had stopped where his line of sight ended, all unknown. He wished he could take a photograph of the scene to remember its stillness and allure.

"It's beautiful, isn't it?"

Max nodded and hugged her palm with his, reassuring his girlfriend that he was happy to be there with her. He noticed a mess of grass that sat just on the edge of the landing. The overgrown sprigs curved inward to form the shape of an egg, showing that someone had sat there recently.

"This must be the spot." Hannah laughed and winked, knowing full well what Sofillians did up here.

They kneeled and sat in each alcove; the grass cradled their bodies like a soft chair. Fireflies danced through the air and flitted through the trees like little stars that had fallen from the heavens to the Island of Forever. They sat in silence for a few moments, marveling at the beautifully strange landscape they found themselves in.

Chapter Seven

"I don't think I could've found a better place to spend time with you." Max laughed. "You know, given the circumstances." He reached into his pocket and the rolled leaf Calvo had given them touched his fingertips. Raising one eyebrow at Hannah, he asked, "You wanna try this?"

She shrugged and took the rolled leaf from Max's hand, placing it between her lips. "Why not?" She breathed inward, and the tip of the leaf glowed orange. A few moments passed before her lungs released a large plume of smoke, wafting into the sky like a ghost. She held it out to Max. "It's amazing that earlier today we were home and now, all of a sudden, we're on this tropical island, isn't it?"

Max nodded and took the leaf, holding it between two fingers. "I'd be less nervous if it were us, Rylan, and Leona, but Ella being here has me constantly hoping we can all get back home safely."

"Don't forget that when we do leave this island, our senior prom is this year."

"Oh yeah, *the prom* is the reason we need to get home." He

laughed at his girlfriend's comment. In the few years they dated, she had always obsessed over her senior prom and how magical it would be. He knew that she would be nominated for prom queen and had a good chance at winning, but it was doubtful that he would be considered for king.

A few moments went by before smoke from Hannah's mouth drifted into the air. "What do you think brought us here? Do you really think it was magic?"

Max inhaled the icy smoke as his mouth was enveloped with minty freshness and released it into the air. "I dunno, we may have somehow shifted to another world or dimension or something. I think I saw something on TV like that before, but I'm still waiting to wake up from this dream. I don't understand it at all."

He handed the leaf that was almost at its end back to Hannah and dizziness overcame his body as his surroundings changed. He was unsure if it was an effect from the Hesper leaf, but everything around him began to pulsate with color. The trees that swayed in the light wind looked as if they were moving in slow motion, pulses of green light around each leaf sprung around it. Flashes of red, blue, and yellow danced around him like he was at a concert. The colors were not bright but demanded to be seen. "Hannah, do you see this?"

"Yeah...it's beautiful, but what's...happening?"

He shrugged, held his hand in front of his eyes, and saw vibrations of blue, purple, and yellow extending outward from his palm, making it look like his hand was slightly moving, though immobile. His eyes darted to the fireflies dancing around them. The light from their bodies created a long streak of yellow that remained long after they'd flown past. Their light became interwoven with the other insects and colors around them.

"These are the same streaks of light we saw at the camp."

The stars in the sky swirled within the universe, reverberating dark hues like a Van Gogh painting, and the moon extended flares of white light like it was pulsing. The volcano that was quietly sitting in the middle of the island was giving off more energy than everything around it. Short bursts of red and purple shot through the sky at record speed like a light show.

"This is amazing." Hannah shimmied her body closer to Max and laid her head on the small of his shoulder, just above his heart.

For a moment, they both sat in silence, in awe of the colors surrounding them. The effect of the Hesper leaf was taking hold as their bodies relaxed into one another. However, their silence didn't feel lonely; they were together and experiencing this moment as one. Their thoughts lazily wandered while they marveled at the magical world that was playing out before them.

Hannah's blonde hair covered his arm like a blanket, and as the wind blew through the trees, the faint scent of lilac wafted from her and caught his nose. Her breasts hugged his chest as she wrapped her arm around his waist, their individual colors intermingling to create a new painting. He rested his chin on her head and breathed a sigh of contentment.

Max relaxed his body, allowing Hannah to nestle into him further and resting her cheek on his chest.

She wants me.

Her bright eyes gazed upward, scanning his face with desire. A light wind blew through the overlook, and he ran his fingers through his windswept hair to tame it, knowing his anxiety may spark at any second with Hannah's gaze. Turning his head downward, he saw a slight smile resting on her lips. He couldn't help but notice her face was perfectly flushed, like she was wearing makeup, and her plump lips were red and lightly wet. The look in her eyes told him all he needed, and in response, he leaned his face to hers, piecing their lips seamlessly together like a puzzle.

Engulfing one another, Max pulled her closer, placing one hand on her hips and the other behind her neck. Their lips continued to meet each other, and a burst of warm air from Hannah's nose met his cheek as she breathed a quiet moan. He felt closer to her than ever before. Poking his tongue out of his mouth and into hers, he sensed her body sighing as their tongues swirled together, making a bond of affection.

Hannah pulled away from Max for a moment to gaze at him. "I love you."

Max's eyes lingered on her expectant eyes, piercing into him like daggers about to tear him to shreds to find the truth.

Am I in love with Hannah? She's my girlfriend, and I care about her, but is that enough? This feels different than what I thought love would be. Is this the best it's going to get?

Max looked back at her and attempted to say it, but the words caught in his throat. So instead, he cupped one hand around her face, smiled, and brought her face into his to continue kissing, hoping she would take the action as his response.

They continued to kiss and squirm against one another, colors emanating and melding from them on the overlook. The entire night, the sounds of the jungle had quieted, and the overlook became silent to everything except the sound of their lips and Hannah's light moans until a creature scurrying through the leaves behind them reached their ears.

The sound came closer, startling them. Hannah put one hand on Max's chest, her head at full attention as she tried squinting through the darkness. "What was that?"

There was another rustle, much closer this time. Max carefully tapped Hannah on her shoulder, removing her from his body. He stood from the small alcove and adjusted his pants. His eyes were wide, and a pit formed in his stomach. The Hesper leaf had been wearing off, and his body became heavy, but he could still see the faint dance of colors around him. He gazed into the darkness within the forest and saw a minor blip of red.

"H-Hannah," Max whispered, unable to take his eyes off the figure in the darkness. The shadow concerned and scared him; his instincts told him they were in danger. "G-go back to the Sofillian camp and g-get help. Make sure Ella is okay. I w-will stay here and distract it so that it d-doesn't follow you."

"What about you?"

"Just go." Max squeezed his sweaty fists. "W-we aren't safe here."

"I thought Calvo said—"

"Just go."

A look of fear crossed Hannah's face as Max's voice grew stern. Her body trembled as she stood from the grass cradle, her eyes locked onto the forest's darkness as she backed toward the trail that led back to the Sofillian camp.

As Hannah disappeared into the jungle, Max's body froze, and he heard the sound of the creature running towards him. The animal's eyes glinted with wild ferocity in the moon's light as a dim ray of light trailed behind it. Quickly jumping to his feet, Max's fingers found a rock the size of his palm and tossed it toward the waning red streak.

A deep grunt returned from the darkness as the stone reached its target.

Is it a person? It sounded like it was running at me on four legs a moment ago.

Fear shifted into mystery as he raised one eyebrow. "W-who's there?"

A dark figure sailed through the sky, and a feral wolf stood before him, saliva dripping from its fangs onto the grassy ground below. The wolf's mangy hair was matted and standing on end, while its big yellow eyes targeted its prey and were full of bloodlust. The wolf snapped its jaws twice at Max, making odd noises deep in its throat.

"G-get back!" Max yelled, picking up a stick that had fallen from a nearby tree branch.

The wolf locked onto him. Its pink tongue licked its lips, a permanent smile on its face as its strong paws inched nearer. A deep growling sound emanated from its throat as its tail swished behind.

Max held the small branch with a plume of green leaves in front of him. The tip of his weapon was shaking with fear through his hands, and he watched the wolf open its mouth and latch onto the piece of wood. Max pulled as hard as he could, but realized the beast was stronger once the bark scraped his fingers and it was tugged away from him.

He dropped the stick and sprinted toward the exit to the overlook, hoping his legs could get him far enough away where he may be under Hesper's protection. Within his first few moments of running, the wolf latched onto his shirt and dragged his body to the hard ground. Fear paralyzed him instantly as he flipped from his stomach to his back; the rabid animal was at his feet, snarling and spitting at him.

The wolf lunged, its strong paws landing squarely on his shoulders. Its claws dug into his skin as their pointed tips worked to pin him to the ground. Spit from the animal's mouth dripped onto his face, and its stale breath reached his nose. He tried to move his arms, but the wolf's weight made him immobile.

The rabid dog brought its snout to Max's face, and the noise coming from its throat finally expelled from its mouth. "Save yourself...or die."

Max was shocked.

Another talking animal? How can I save myself if I'm completely pinned to the ground by a wolf threatening to kill me?

He winced at the thought and closed his eyes, ready for whatever the wolf had planned next. He wished he was stronger and had muscles that would make him unstoppable, as if flexing a bicep would make the wolf retreat and have Hannah fawning over him.

Maybe then I'd amount to something.

His chest became hot, and in a burst of energy, Max's arms were being twisted and stretched like taffy; he feared that if the sensation continued, they'd snap. Smokey, swirling black tendrils engulfed his arms like veins, shocking him every few moments. He screamed as his arms were at their breaking point, but the pain didn't cease. Then, through the tears lining his eyes from the intense pain and pressure, he saw the smoke dissipating and his arms emerge four times their normal size.

"Max, are you okay?" a robust male voice behind him yelled.

With his newfound arms, he clamped one hand around the wolf's snout and used the other to lift its body off him, throwing it backward. Max watched as an ax swung just above him and hit the wolf squarely in the chest, throwing the rabid dog out of his hands. The gray wolf sailed through the air, and in the light of the moon, disappeared into a cloud of dust, blown away by the wind that crossed the overlook.

Max turned his attention to the figure standing next to him, their body outlined by the moonlight in a confident pose. The sensation of his arms spinning returned, and his once-plump muscles reverted to their standard size. His head grew light, and his legs buckled, no longer able to support his weight. Max tried to catch his fall, but his arms refused to move, as if they were completely broken. A scowl and grunt expelled from his mouth as his head met the hard ground.

Calvo picked Max's limp body up from the ground and threw him over his shoulder. "We need to get to Wintey. She needs to know about this."

Just as they were about to return to the forest, Calvo stopped in his tracks. Max saw the man turn his head to look behind him, and he hoped the wolf hadn't returned. Instead, Calvo's eyes turned downward, and briskly walked down the hill toward the Sofillian Camp.

Chapter Eight

"Get the two Mainlanders and have them meet us in the Great Tree." The dim embers from torches within the camp met their eyes, a gray haze of smoke settling in the area. The smell of skunk wafted through the air between the quiet treehouses above.

Walking under the exposed roots and through the small doorway into the carved tunnels within the large trunk, it was clear that Calvo knew his way through the maze as he expertly turned down hallways without a thought. Eventually, he threw Max off his shoulder and deposited him on the floor of a large room. The dark wood that covered the floor and walls cast an eerie shadow in the torchlight.

"You should regain use of your arms and legs shortly," Calvo advised. "I need to find my sister." With that, he disappeared once again through the maze of tunnels.

As Max lay on the dirty wooden floor, a slight tingling traveled through his arms and legs, almost like a needle was furiously poking him.

Is the tree magically healing me?

Looking at the tip of his finger, he saw a slight twitch and knew he was going to be okay.

"Max!" a scared voice screamed from the other side of the room. He heard two sets of feet run to him, and a cascade of blonde hair swept over him while a sleepy child squatted and waved her hand in his face. "I'm so happy you're safe."

The prickling lessened, and he could slightly move his body. Then, pushing himself upright, he cleared his throat. "I-I don't know what happened. My arms changed..."

"They *changed*?" Hannah said in disbelief. "Into what?"

He shrugged, unable to explain further, and Ella enveloped him in a hug.

Did my arms transform, or was that some sort of hallucination from the Hesper leaf? How did I get the wolf off me? Did Calvo do that?

His mind contemplated the logistics, considering everything he had seen within the last twenty-four hours, and a sense of doubt crept into his mind while Wintey hurriedly appeared in the room. Calvo closely followed her, focusing his eyes and keeping his face expressionless.

"My brother advised me what happened tonight," Wintey started, her eyes shifting to her brother. "I'm sorry Calvo suggested going outside Hesper's protection, but I am thankful he was there to assist with the wolf before you were hurt."

Max shakily stood. "Did he tell you *everything* that happened?"

"Yes." She nodded and glanced back at her brother. "When he got up there, you were pinned to the ground by the wolf, and he used his ax to scare it off. You were lucky he was going to check on you."

Max's cheeks burned; he must have imagined his arms changing, though the pain of the transformation had been so real.

Maybe I wasn't paying attention because of how fast everything happened. Calvo had to have been the one who got the wolf off me, there's no way I could've done that myself.

He gazed into Wintey's curious eyes as he reasoned with himself. "I thought I saw something else, but it must have been a side effect from the leaf."

She nodded. "That would make sense. The leaves have different effects on everyone. We had one Sofillian claim he saw Hesper one year." Wintey looked to Calvo, a smile crossing each of their faces at the memory. "After our prayer this evening, I consulted with the spirits, and it's apparent that the three of you need to leave this island for the sake of all its inhabitants. Mainlanders always bring trouble, and you're no different."

"No shit," Hannah whispered, barely loud enough for Max to hear. "After what happened tonight, we want to get home as quickly as we can. Can you tell us where our friends are and what we need to do next?"

Wintey raised one finger into the air to silence her. "The spirits gave me limited information; they mainly spoke about a ripple effect of danger coming to the island if any of the five Mainlanders stayed, much more than Samael's return." A quietness fell over the room. "I attempted to obtain your friends' location, but there was an interruption within the psychic fabric I was using, and I received no guidance. This can only mean the island has integrated them with our species."

"What does that mean?" Hannah crossed her arms and popped her hip to one side.

"It's extremely complicated." Wintey shrugged. "The Island of Forever has the ability to integrate any Mainlander into its history, so they are not considered a harmful change. Your friends have become inhabitants of this island. Their minds have blocked out their memories and replaced them with new ones that only involve living on the Island of Forever, so they'll have no recollection from their lives on the Mainland."

Max squinted, trying to piece together what the Sofillian leader was saying. "You're saying Leona and Rylan are now part of this island and may not remember us? How can that even happen?"

Calvo stepped forward, and his neck stiffened. "The island chooses. There's no explanation."

Wintey shrugged. "We would have never known if your friends were integrated into the Sofillian Campsite. When the island accepts someone, it's as if they were never a Mainlander —they get written into the memories of everyone around them, sewn into the fabric of our stories."

What's the point? I hate that I'm going to ask this, but here it goes.

"If they've been integrated into the island, why do we need to find them? Can't we just go straight home without them?" After what happened to him at the overlook, Ella's safety was at the forefront of his mind.

Wintey's head lobbed from shoulder to shoulder. "You're correct, you could. Although if you leave them here, you will erase their existence from your mind and the Mainland forever."

"We can't do that, Max." Hannah looked astonished at what he suggested. "If the roles were reversed, they would never have suggested leaving without you."

"We don't even know if they're here! We could be going on this wild goose chase and wasting more time than necessary when we should focus on how to get home." He was beginning to get frustrated because his girlfriend wasn't understanding his fear of staying. "If we knew they were here and where we could find them, I wouldn't even think about leaving without them, but we don't, and it doesn't sound like anyone here is going to help us."

Calvo's eyes glinted in the light, and Wintey's dual-colored eyes peered at Max's exasperated face. "I know someone who may be able to tell you where your friends have been integrated."

Ella raised her fist. "Make me a Sofillian! I'll force the information out of them!"

Wintey's laughter danced along the walls, a pleasant change from the seriousness of the interaction. "It takes much more than looking like us to become a Sofillian, little one." Her smile disappeared as she looked toward Max and Hannah. "I know who my brother speaks of and getting the information will not be the hardest part of this task. The difficulty will be finding the one who can offer it, as we have not seen him in years."

Hannah scowled. "Then how are we supposed to find him?"

"It isn't so much that he's elusive, but more that he's difficult to pinpoint." Wintey squinted her eyes. "He's as old as the island itself and has been known to live on a beach we call Seashell Shore, which is to the east of our village. The only way to find him is to put the seashells scattered on the ground to your ear, and the one shell that sounds like the ocean is him, the Shellder."

"Don't all seashells have the sound of the sea when put against your ear?" Max remembered going to the beach with Ella, who had collected shells that washed ashore and called them her treasures.

"That is normally true." Wintey nodded and extended her arms. "But you're on the Island of Forever, not everything is as it seems. The Shellder will be able to identify exactly where your friends are and may be able to provide more details on how to get home through the temple to the north. I packed a bag filled with animal skins to sleep on and pouches of water for your journey."

Calvo stepped forward and handed Max a leather backpack he slung around his shoulder. The man's eyes looked like glassy pools of caramel, although there was something different about them; it was as if he were lost in thought.

"You will meet many enemies throughout your travels. Max, come here and accept this gift from the Sofillians."

Pulling his eyes away from Calvo, Max slowly approached Wintey. Cradled in her arms was a small metal sword that was no longer than his forearm. The blade was sharp and lightweight, while the wooden hilt was smooth and durable.

"Look at Max!" Ella was tugging on Hannah's shirt. "He just got a magic sword!"

A smile crossed Wintey's lips. "Although this does not contain magic, it is sharp and swift. It'll be useful in your journey and protect you when needed." Wintey removed herself from the podium and strapped a sheath around Max's waist. "For you, Miss Hannah, we are entrusting you with a bow. May your arrows fly straight."

Calvo walked to the blonde girl, deposited the smooth bow into her hand, and slung the leather belt holding the weapons across her chest. She gripped the bow as if it were a foreign object.

"Now that you are fully equipped, I have one last resource for you." Wintey's eyes flashed within the dim room, turning to Calvo. "Brother, I am ordering you, on behalf of Hesper, to escort the Mainlanders to Seashell Shore, and once their friends are identified, continue the journey with them to ensure a swift departure from the island. We cannot risk Samael escaping."

The room became quiet as her words hung in the air. For

the first time since they'd returned to the Sofillian Camp, Calvo looked as if he had finally snapped out of his trance. His eyebrows rose in surprise. "I am not questioning your judgment, sister, but considering the mission I recently returned from, am I the right person for this task?"

She nodded. "This journey may intersect with your prior mission, and more knowledge may be unearthed. In addition, you are the only one I trust to ensure the Mainlanders leave before the beacon lights."

He nodded, nervously strumming his fingers through his hair. "How much time do we have?"

Wintey began counting on her fingers. "If you remain on the Island of Forever for more than four days, you will ignite the beacon in the center of the volcano, signaling the opening of Samael's prison. I am counting on you to succeed—we all are." She snapped her fingers, and Calvo lowered his head, his palms at the center of his chest before gesturing to Max, Hannah, and Ella to follow him.

Leading them through the twisting hallways inside the Great Tree, Calvo was silent until a doorway of stars in the night sky reached their eyes. Slinging his leather bag over his shoulder, he tightened the ax crossways to his back. Tendrils of hair spilled from the headband on his forehead, and his voice was exasperated when he spoke. "I suppose we will get to know each other well through this journey, but please remember that my priority is the Island of Forever."

Max nodded. "Got it."

"As we walk through the jungle, please be quiet." His eyes shot to Ella. "If there's an outside threat, we don't want to draw attention to our camp."

Ella put one finger to her mouth and nodded in acknowledgment.

Max's gaze returned from his sister. "Let's go."

Chapter Nine

T he jungle was filled with towering trees that seemed to
stretch endlessly toward the sky, with vines coiling
around their trunks like serpents. The team was enveloped by
the wet, humid air with a slight hint of earthiness while the
chattering of birds hidden in the jungle filled their ears. Bugs
scattered out of their way as they trekked through the forest
and the overgrown grass brushed against their legs.

Max's eyes followed his sister's gaze as she marveled at the
lush greenery around them. Their silence as they walked
through the jungle put Max on high alert. Every slight sound,
his head turned in surprise—once to look where the noise came
from and then secondly at his sister to make sure she didn't
make a peep. He was nervous that one false move or a large
spider could trigger Hannah or Ella to scream, revealing their
location. Besides that, he wondered what, or who, they were
hiding from.

Calvo's skillful way he navigated through the jungle was
admirable. He moved intentionally, the soft pads of his feet

making hardly a sound on the mossy ground. Clearing the way with his sharp ax, he moved through the vines and bushes with ease. Max studied the man, analyzing his every move, and attempted to copy them as closely as he was able.

They trudged through the expansive forest for about an hour in silence until the smell of the ocean reached Max's nostrils. The trees in the jungle were large and lush, but as they neared the beach, palms with pointed leaves became more frequent. The salty scent made him long for the days when he was a child and spent his summers at the beach in his hometown. His mother would always complain about how hot it was; his father would collect rocks and shells while he would be in the sand playing games with the other children or swimming in the ocean. The smell brought back happy memories of his life before his father's departure, and a bittersweet smile crossed his face.

Calvo wiped the sweat from his brow and lifted his ax, slicing a trove of vines that blocked their way, and a sprawling beach unraveled at their feet. The blazing sun reflected off the ocean, making the sand ahead appear white. The waves from the ocean rolled into the shore, leaving a trail of white sea foam before retreating into the current's pull. Freckled on the beach's face were multicolored shells carefully placed as if they were constellations in the sky.

Returning the ax to his waist, Calvo's animal skin blew in the breeze. "We've arrived at Seashell Shore." Glancing upward at the blazing sun, he furrowed his brow and placed his palm above his eyes. "Do you remember how to find the Shellder?"

Max nodded. "We have to find a shell that sounds like the ocean or something, right?"

Calvo gave a slight nod in return. He scanned the warm

sand and all the shells that littered its surface. "It's going to be a hot one today. We need to make sure we're drinking water."

"We have a lot of beach to cover and not a lot of time, so let's spread out." Max wanted to sound like he knew what he was doing, but the reality is that the entire endeavor was full of unknowns.

"I'll start in the middle." Hannah pointed to Calvo, a smirk crossing her face. "And this quarterback will search the right side of the beach."

His eyes rose. "Quarter? Back? I don't understand."

Cocking her head to the right, she winked at him. "Don't worry about it."

Is she flirting with him? Am I not good enough for her?

Max's head turned to look at his girlfriend, surprised and slightly offended.

Calvo's definitely a good-looking guy, anyone with eyes can see that, but is that the type of person she's looking for? Why is she with me?

A large breath expelled from Ella's mouth. "This beach is so big, we could be here for a week!"

Max knew his sister liked exaggerating, but she was right. His eyes landed on the shells poking out of the sand, and hopelessness overcame him.

There are thousands of shells. How are we going to find the right one?

"We can't be done if we don't start." A disgusted look crossed Hannah's face as she combed her fingers through her hair. "I need to get home for some shampoo and conditioner. My hair is getting so raggedy."

"It looks almost like that time you got a perm for our semi-formal and..."

"We don't talk about that moment." Hannah's eyes were

closed and she held one hand in front of her. "I don't think I've truly forgiven Rylan for smoking in the bathroom."

A laugh was building in Max's throat, but he contained it. "You were soaked before I could take off my jacket to save you from the sprinklers."

"Let's forget that memory and get to work." She gave him a look that was both stern and playful. It may have been traumatizing but it was a story they could think back on and laugh.

Max took his sister's hand in his, and they walked to the opposite side of the beach, the shells underfoot crunching beneath his shoes. "Let's start here."

Ella kneeled and began picking up shells and placing them to her ear. Her eyes widened, and she dropped the shell back into the sand. "Max, you can hear *people* in the shells."

"What're you talking about?" He raised an eyebrow at his sister and picked up a shell at his feet covered in calcium deposits, its craggy gray exterior made it look like a fossil. Placing the shell to his ear, Max expected to hear lush waves but instead listened to a chaotic moment in someone's life.

A panicked woman who sounded as if she were crying reached his ears. "Hello? Is this the police? I came home from work, and my house was broken into!"

He removed the shell from his ear and dropped it back into the white sand. "That must be why we're looking for a shell that sounds like the ocean. These must tap into other people's conversations."

A dramatic and pained look crossed Ella's face. "Are we done yet? This is boring."

"We'll be done soon if we work together," he coaxed his impatient sister. "I'm going to go to the right. If you hear waves in any shell, let me know."

The little girl gave him the thumbs-up sign, picking up the

other shells on the beach by the handful and leaning her head onto each of them.

The sand was so soft that Max's sneakers sank with each step as he made his way toward Ella. He bent down to pick up the countless shells strewn on the ground. The shells he collected were a diverse collection, each one possessing its own individual designs, colors, markings, and shape. He surveyed the endless expanse of shells on the beach, wondering how much time they had to find the one they needed.

He stooped to pick up a shell, and his fingers closed around the cone-shaped object that was a deep shade of blue. Placing the opening at the bottom to his ear, Max heard a man's booming French accent reverberating outward. "Zut, c'est vrai! Non? C'est vrai, Jerome!" A gunshot rang out from the shell, and a yell drowned out all other noise.

Max ducked and briefly thought the bullet would go through the opening, but nothing happened, and he returned the shell to the sand. Looking to his left, he saw a charming pink shell half buried in the white sand.

If I were the Shellder, I'd wanna live here.

He picked it up, put it to his ear, and heard the quiet sounds of fabrics rustling together. Within seconds, a woman's moan and the deep breathing of a man tickled his eardrum as rustling in the shell grew more frequent. Max made a disgusted face, dropped the shell, and pushed a mound of sand over it with his foot.

I hope Ella isn't hearing anything like this.

Turning his attention back to the task, his fingers brushed a white shell with red freckles and a magnetizing aura. From the moment Max put it to his ear, he knew he was about to hear something unexpected. A smooth voice with an amused tone emanated from within. "Hello, Max. I know you're listening. Good luck getting home. You're on *my* island now and I'm not letting you out of my sight until you release me from this wretched volcano."

Uneasiness enveloped him like a blanket, and his hands began to sweat.

Is that...who I think it is? Is Samael speaking directly to me?

Max knew there was more to these shells than just over-hearing conversations, but hearing the threat aimed directly at him was concerning. He shuddered, clasped the shell in his palm, and reared his arm backward before catapulting it towards the sea. As it sailed through the air, it arced toward the ocean's depths and ended with a quiet plop.

The search continued for hours with no results. As they held the seashells to their ears, they were transported into a world of different conversations—from playful children to the tense scene of a bank robbery or the peaceful sounds of a mother and her baby. The sound of the ocean never seemed to reach their ears, possibly because they were too busy to notice or because a new shell sat on the side of their head every few seconds.

As time progressed, the sun gently moved through the sky, taunting them as the morning turned to afternoon. Their skin reddened, and their mouths turned dry as they craved a sip of water.

Max wiped sweat from his forehead. "Let's take a break and grab some water." He gestured to a shaded area near the edge of the jungle where a bunch of driftwood was haphaz-ardly thrown. He squinted into the sunlight and noticed they'd covered about half of the beach, judging from where they had started.

We could be here for days searching for the right one.

Sweat stained Hannah's shirt, and she wrapped a vine from the forest around her hair, fastening it into a ponytail. Her skin was burned pink, and tiredness clouded her eyes from being in the sun.

Max offered her a half smile as she neared. "Any luck?"

She shook her head and fanned her face with her hand as she unscrewed the lid on her water pouch, gulping down every drop she could. "I wish! I'm frying out here."

He unsheathed his sword and poked the tip through his jeans, haphazardly cutting them into shorts. The ocean wind touched his legs, relieving his body from the constraint of the pants.

He snuck a glance at Calvo and found himself at a loss for words as he took in the sight of his glistening, muscular body. Max gulped as he watched a bead of sweat roll down his chest, over his abs, and disappear beneath the animal skin at his pelvis. To make matters worse, Calvo took the canteen and dumped a handful of water over his face. Max's mouth dropped, and his body involuntarily grew stimulated.

Why am I watching him like a creep? It isn't normal how drawn to him I am, but something just keeps pulling at me. Something's there that I find so...interesting.

Max grabbed his canteen and deposited it into Ella's hands. She drank so fervently that the water ran down her chin. As soon as she finished, he took a swig. The cool liquid enveloped his mouth and reinvigorated his dry throat. He didn't realize how much his body needed this water until it reached his lips.

Ella took a break from drinking. "I'm hearing a bunch of people. It's almost like we're spying on them. It's kind of fun!"

"Yeah, me too." Hannah gulped the water and wiped her chin with the backside of her hand. "A lot of really strange ones—"

"In one, I heard a man getting yelled at by his wife for gambling all their money away in Las Vegas," Ella excitedly recounted. "I don't even know what that means, but boy, was she mad!"

"It sounds like you're getting the funny ones." Max laughed, taking a swig of cool water from his canteen. "Mine have been like Hannah's...odd."

"As have mine." Calvo's dark eyebrows sat just above his eyes, and he itched the scruff on his face.

"I'm just going to imagine I'm on a tropical vacation on this beach rather than trying to track down a shell that seems impossible to find." Hannah raised her chin in the air and closed her eyes, the warm sun beating on her face. "Let me know when someone comes around with an ice-cold pina colada."

"I'll let our cabana attendant know." Max laughed as a gleam of light caught his eye.

There's no way I can like anyone else the same way I like Hannah. She's perfect.

Then, gazing downward, he saw a shell the size of his palm sticking out of the sand, partially obstructed by the driftwood. It was pearlescent, the colors swirling like a fresh oil spill and twisting into a small earlobe-like structure.

Ella followed Max's eyes and reached her hand toward the shell, placing it to her ear. Her eyes lit up, and a smile crept along her face. "Max! Max! It's the ocean! I hear the ocean, Max!"

He grabbed the shell from his little sister and put it to his ear. To his delight, the familiar sound of water washing in and out of the shore with a bit of wind mixed into the background.

"Is it...?" Hannah's eyes were hopeful.

Max nodded to her as a smile spread across his lips. Ella threw her arms into the air, jumping up and down with glee while Hannah's tired eyes looked thankful. Calvo was stoic, but the relief on his face was evident.

As the sounds of the ocean continued in his ears, a stirring reached his fingers from within the shell. The vibration curled as if something were squirming towards the opening. Removing it from his ear, he noticed two small claws grasped the rim and from the shell's innards, a small crustacean emerged like a genie from a magic lamp. The blue crab had two beady black eyes on each side of its head, two long antennae sticking out from its forehead, and a long gray mustache that hung above his mouth.

The crustacean lifted his claws and yawned. "Haven't been out of my shell in a while! I cannot believe how long it took me to get out. Guess that means I need to go on a diet." The tiny creature patted his stomach as he let out a laugh. His voice sounded like a grandfather—old and wise but with a flavor of mischief.

Its mustache lifted a bit, indicating to Max that he was smiling. "Are you the Shellder?"

The crab nodded and placed one claw across his waist, bowing. "You're correct, sir. How did you find me? I haven't been sought out in ten, maybe fifteen years." He looked at his claws like he was counting. "Nevertheless, I need to get out more."

Calvo's body straightened, and his hips pivoted slightly forward. "Hello, Shellder, Wintey, the leader of the Sofillians, encouraged us to seek you out—"

"Ugh," the crab interrupted as the man looked taken aback. "Your sister needs to stop telling everyone where I am. She told the last person to find me, too. I don't mind the company, but everyone is always looking for something. They never come just to see how I'm doing." His eyes darted to Ella before he continued, "It certainly gets lonely here by myself."

"You don't have to be lonely; we can take you with us," Ella suggested, her eyes full of excitement.

The Shellder laughed, his breaths sounding like a seagull's caw. "No, no, little one, I cannot leave this beach. It is my duty to be the keeper of the island's knowledge." His eyes fixated on Max, a glint in each of them. "And I know that you're Mainlanders looking for two others who were separated from you on your trip here, am I correct?"

Hannah nodded. "Do you know where they are?"

"The wind that blows and the water that runs throughout the island share their stories with me. Let me look at my notes and see what I have." The blue crab disappeared back into the shell and Max could feel him stirring inside as it moved from left to right.

The trio watched intently, hoping the Shellder would give them an answer and direction to leave the island. They were desperate for answers and running out of time. The calm wind caressed their hot bodies, and the sound of the ocean a few feet away calmed their nerves.

Thank God we found him. I just hope he can tell us what we need to know and we can get outta here.

The shell in Max's hands shook once again, and two blue claws pulled the small crab out of the shell. Tucked between his pincers was a scroll of paper, and his eyes scanned the document with the occasional pause to move his mustache out of his way. "Aha, here we are. You're looking for a fiery girl with hair the color of caramel, correct?"

"Yes, Leona!"

"Hmm...my sources have recorded that she's currently in a garden full of flowers, living harmoniously with animals. I'm going to assume the fairy habitat to the north."

"Fairies?!" Ella screamed with delight. "Why couldn't I be the one hanging out with fairies?" The child stomped her feet into the sand.

Hannah swiftly moved past the tantrum and asked, "What about Rylan, our other friend?"

The Shellder's claws moved quickly through the scroll,

whispering the name under his breath. "Found him," he said and pointed to the paper matter-of-factly. "Does he have a messy mane of blond hair, eyes the color of fresh moss, and the stature of a green bean?"

"Yes, that's him!"

The crustacean shrugged. "I believe he is right behind you."

Chapter Ten

M ax swung his body around, expecting to see his friend casually smoking his vape with a smirk as if to ask him what took so long to find him, but he saw the opposite. Rylan's body was face down on the wake of the beach, the waves lapping against his immobile and rigid body. He lay on the sand with his arms spread wide while the dampness of his hair made his curls even more unruly. "Hannah, help me get him out of the water."

Their friend was lying on the wet sand, lifeless. They hooked their arms underneath Rylan's armpits and pulled him towards the shaded area of driftwood, where Ella was waiting with a canteen of water and a frown of concern. Propping his body up on a tree trunk, Max lightly tapped his cheeks, hoping that he would wake up.

"Rylan, are you okay?" Ella patted him on the back.

"Hannah, you were a lifeguard last summer, you have to give him CPR." Max pulled on his friend's legs, his back flush to the ground.

"Kiss Rylan? That's the last thing I wanna do," she spat. "Plus, I didn't pass the test to get certified."

"But you were at the beach every day."

"That doesn't mean I was a lifeguard, Max!"

"He's not breathing, can you at least try?" Max pleaded. "Please."

"Why can't you do it?"

Why can't I do it?

Max saw Calvo's eyes narrow with curiosity, wondering what he would do next. Kneeling on the warm sand, he pinched Rylan's nose. The rush of adrenaline made him dizzy and his heart was pounding in his chest. Lowering his face to the pink lips below, he took one last deep breath and closed his eyes.

I wonder if Calvo's watching.

"Don't forget to do chest compressions aft—ew!"

A burst of water shot into the air as Rylan's mouth let out a few hearty coughs, his lungs dispelling the watery contents coating his throat and stomach. A sleepy grin spread across his face as his eyes slowly opened. "Max?"

The Shellder sat atop the driftwood, its eyes full of worry and its body angled to fully see what was happening. "Very curious indeed."

As Rylan heaved the contents of his stomach, Max noticed that his friend's clothes had changed entirely from the sweatpants and hoodie he was last seen wearing during the storm. His body was covered in a mosaic of blue and green scales, resembling freckles, while a tattered mesh net made of rope hung loosely around his shoulders, ending just below his chest. Suctioned to his hips were skin-tight swimming shorts that looked like scales, clinging to him like spandex.

Rylan caught his breath, his chest heaving as he twisted his head, his long hair slapping against his face with every turn. "Who are you?"

"He doesn't remember you," the Shellder explained. "That's what the island does."

"But he said my name..."

"First thing's first," Rylan interrupted as he pointed one finger to the trio, his eyes narrow. "How do you know me?"

"Stop with the games, Rylan," Hannah shouted at him, exasperated. She locked eyes with him, their faces just inches apart. "It's us! We're going to go find Leona and go home!"

Ella looked up and met his bright green eyes, but there was no recognition in them. "D-do you not know who we are?"

"That is what I was saying," the Shellder announced as he popped out of his home. "Memories of your past life slowly begin to disappear once you arrive on the Island of Forever."

Calvo nodded in agreement with the Shellder. "It's like my sister said: Rylan has been fully integrated on this island, and while he is here, memories from the Mainland dwindle until they're completely hidden away."

"Will he still be able to leave the island?" Hannah asked, her eyebrow raised.

The Shellder's wrinkled neck bobbed. "He can, but when your friends return to the Mainland, they'll retain their memory of the Island of Forever until they choose to forget."

"Ry, you said my name a few seconds ago. Do you remember me? Max?" He could see in his eyes that the boy's mind was trying to piece everything together but to no avail.

Calvo stepped forward. "Who are *you*?"

He stood from the sand and flexed a skinny bicep. "I'm Prince Rylan, Captain of the Royal Sea Guard." His chin tilted upward, a confident smile perched on his lips. "My father is King of the Forever Sea, and I'm next in line for the throne."

Watching his friend take himself so seriously was out of

character, given his typical laid-back demeanor back home. Unsure of how to help, Max bent down and spoke directly to the Shellder. "Is there anything we can do to trigger his memory?"

"Hmm," The crab pondered as he placed a small pincer under his chin. "I believe I can help with that. I haven't done it in quite a while, but I'm willing to give it a try. Put me near his ear." The Shellder placed both claws on the edge of the shell and hoisted as much of his blue body as possible.

"Rylan, the Shellder is going to help you remember everything that happened off the island, okay?" He gazed at his friend's flashing green eyes expectantly.

He shot Max an ice-cold stare and ran his fingers through his curly hair. "There's nothing for him to do. I know who I am." He crossed his arms and turned his head away in defiance.

"This is weird," Hannah said, her eyebrows raised. "I don't blame him. I think I'd break up with you if you put a crab inside my ear."

"Noted," Max replied with a smirk and turned back to the merman. "C'mon, Ry, I need you to think. You said my name earlier, you must have remembered something, right?" Rylan's face twisted with a moment of recognition, only to be replaced with a look of surprise as he was slammed into the sand.

Ella and Hannah let out a scream as Calvo suddenly tackled Rylan, wrapping his strong leg around his waist and putting him into a chokehold. The man's bulging muscles easily overpowered the skinny boy's feeble attempts to break free.

"Get—offa—me," Rylan gasped as the man's bicep stilted his neck.

Calvo's eyebrows furrowed as he tried to keep hold before ordering, "Hurry up and let the Shellder do what he needs to do. We don't have time to convince him."

Grasping the pearly shell, Max nodded and stuck the little crustacean near Rylan's ear. The Shellder stretched himself as far as he could, placing both claws on either side of his ear, and disappeared within. Rylan's emerald eyes began to gloss over, a white veil appearing on the surface of his iris. His eyes stared straight ahead at nothing in particular, although behind his eyes reeled a personal movie connecting to his brain.

"What's happening to him?" Ella screamed in horror.

"I don't really know," Max admitted as he watched Rylan's shoulders slump forward, and his mouth hung open as if his brain had turned off. "The Shellder knows what he's doing. We'll have the old Rylan back in no time." In reality, Max wasn't sure if this would work or if the crab could fix their friend. All he could do was calm the nerves of his girlfriend and sister and hope for the best.

A few minutes passed until the Shellder popped out of Rylan's ear. "Can you put my home near his ear again so I can return without exposing myself to the world? I'd be completely naked without my shell."

Situating the cone so that it was an easy slip for the Shellder, Max swore that he saw the crab's cheeks turn a light shade of purple out of embarrassment. It was comforting to know that even this powerful, all-knowing figure was insecure about his body, much like himself.

"You may release your hold on the young boy." Calvo's arms unlocked as the Shellder crawled into his shell, slapping the side with one of his claws. "Ahh, home sweet home, eh?"

Max was hopeful that Rylan's memories had returned but noticed the same confused stare from his friend's green eyes. As the balloon in his chest deflated, a disheartened realization that Shellder's plan hadn't worked overcame him.

Seeing Max's concerned face, the small crab raised his

pincers, and his long mustache bobbed up and down as he spoke. "It takes a few moments for the brain to connect its old and new memories; it tries to place them where it makes the most sense. Give it a second. When he awakens, he will remember his memories from the Mainland and recall his interactions that happened here on the island."

Rylan blinked a few times, and his eyes widened as a sudden realization hit him. When he first looked up, his expression was one of confusion, but his eyes gleamed like the first rays of sunshine after a long, dark night. The green orbs dimmed moments later, seemingly to show they disappeared just as quickly as his memories came. He turned to look at Max and Hannah, the veil of forgetfulness still shrouding his memories.

"I know what'll trigger his memory," Hannah said with a glint of mischief in her eye. She grabbed Rylan's limp hands and cupped them to her breasts as she rolled her eyes at Max's appalled expression. "He isn't that hard to figure out."

Rylan's eyes slowly reawakened with their familiar mischievous glow. Trying as he might to hide it, a sly smirk crossed his lips. "Would you mind if I put my face between them? Maybe it'll help my memories return?"

Hannah threw his hands away from her body in disgust and smacked him upside the head. "Maybe if I hit you hard enough, your memories will come back!"

"You kind of sound like Leona," Rylan muttered as he scanned the beach. Finally, his green eyes landed on Max like a laser beam. "Did you finally get it on with Hannah?"

"Even here, you're still a perv!" Hannah shook her head and closed her eyes in frustration.

A smile spread across Max's face. Rylan's perverted comments didn't bother him, even though they were made in front of his little sister. A wave of relief rushed over him, thankful that Rylan's memory lapse was resolved quickly. Wrapping one arm around his friend's neck, Max smiled. "We're so glad you're back."

"Speak for yourself." Hannah crossed her arms.

"Max, there's actually one problem," Rylan said as he held his head in his hands. "I don't have my vape. What the hell am I gonna do?"

Ella yelled at him with one eye bulging, "How are *we* going to put up with *you* without it?"

Max laughed at both of them. It seemed like a typical conversation they'd have had back home, and the sense of normalcy gave him strength to continue their journey. "Rylan, wait until you try the Sofillian's Hesper leaves. You'll love them."

The Shellder's craggy voice whispered, "A person from the sea is now on land; quite curious indeed..."

Rylan's head turned to look at the small blue crab and nodded. "This hasn't happened in a long time, but my father gave me these legs to cease the change that will come if the Mainlanders don't leave." He waved his legs in the air to prove his point and put two fingers under his chin. "Although I suppose that makes me one of them, too..."

"You're one of them," Calvo confirmed. "The island has much to lose if Samael is freed."

Rylan shifted his shoulders backward and gave the Sofillian a sideways look, raising his eyebrows as they looked up and down, assessing him. He put his palm to the side of his face and snidely asked, "Who's the jock? Reznik's brother?" A scared look crossed his face as he reached to his back and started frantically touching his body, searching for something. "Wh-where is my trident?"

"Trident?" Max punched his friend in the shoulder. "Who're you? Percy Jackson or something?"

Rylan dropped to the ground and began sprawling in the sand, waving his arms and legs like he was trying to make a snow angel. "I-I can't find it." His eyes began to glass over as if he were about to cry. "I'm Captain of the Royal Sea Guard and was gifted that weapon specifically by the King himself."

"Maybe it didn't wash ashore with you?"

Rylan winked at the three of them and placed a finger to his lips. Closing his piercing green eyes, he began to knead the air in front of him, his hands moving in a fluid motion. As he moved his wrists in opposing waves, his forearms flexed and strained against an invisible force, making it look like he was performing a graceful dance.

"What's he doing?" Ella whispered.

In response to the little girl, Max shrugged and put one finger to his lips. His body twisted, and his stomach gurgled in anticipation; he was unsure what Rylan was doing, but the air surrounding him seemed to be at full attention. He heard the sound of boiling water and turned toward the ocean, where he saw bubbles rising to the surface as if something were stirring beneath.

The water rippled and churned until a thin stream of greenish-blue ocean hovered just above its surface, crawling its way through the air to Rylan's outstretched hand. A glint of silver shot through the trail of water and placed itself within his palm. As the current in the water ceased, the stream dropped from its suspended state in the air. A line of wetness reached from the ocean to Rylan, almost like a carpet rolling out for him.

"Aha, here you are!" Rylan held a silver three-pronged trident in his hand. The points glinted in the sunlight as they collected into the staff's body. He grabbed the handle and jabbed the air. "Lightweight yet deadly, perfect for combat."

"Rylan, what the hell was that?" Max asked, gesturing to the wet sand in front of him.

Fastening the trident onto his back, droplets of ocean fell onto Rylan's abs. "All merpeople can manipulate water, it's in our nature."

Ella's eyes grew wide like she was a child in a candy store. "You're a mermaid?"

"Mermaid, merman, call it whatever you want."

"Can I be a mermaid?" Ella's eyes twinkled as she clasped her hands together.

Rylan put his palm on the little girl's head. "Sorry, kid. The King of the Forever Ocean can give merpeople legs, but it's a bit more difficult for us to return to the sea. The only people who could easily go from sea to land were shapeshifters, and they aren't around anymore. Even if they were, they're banned from stepping foot in our water."

Noticing Max's mouth open and close a couple of times, Hannah raised an eyebrow. "When you were in the ocean, did you have a tail?"

"I had the *biggest* tail anyone in the ocean has ever seen." Rylan winked at his friends and squeezed Max's shoulder.

"Rylan's officially back," Hannah huffed. "And his innuendos haven't gotten any better."

Max winced as a sharp pain shot through his hand, the Shellder's pincers clamped onto the center of his palm. "Please put me back near the driftwood, I think my work here is complete. You three must get going before any more change happens."

Gently placing the small shell onto the lush sand, Max turned to his friend. "What's it like having two sets of memories? Is it weird?"

Rylan shrugged. "I have memories of my life here and ones from back home, it's kind of like I've lived two lives my whole life. Remember when I used to get really baked and would tell you I remember things that never happened? Maybe those were my island memories."

I wonder if the Mainland and the Island of Forever are more connected than we know?

"Where are we going now?" Rylan asked. "Get me up to speed."

Despite the merman's attempts to lighten the mood, Calvo's face remained serious, conveying his annoyance. "My sister told us that the temple to the north is your way home. We must find your last friend so you may leave together."

"Sister schmister," Rylan spat. "Who else is here with us?"

"Leona came with you, and the Shellder said she's in a fairy garden." Hannah paused and threw both arms in the air. "It's crazy to think that I'm actually saying the fairy garden like it's normal."

"Of course Leona is here. She's always trying to ruin my fun." Rylan laughed and nodded. "I know where she is: The Garden of Bliss. My father has dealt with the fairy queen on many occasions."

Max raised an eyebrow. "I know everyone's memories have changed, but is your dad here the same person from the Mainland?"

"Thankfully, no." Rylan shook his head. "They're completely different people altogether."

Max's mind was trying to make sense of the island's integration when Hannah interrupted his thoughts. "So, you know where the garden is?"

He shook his head. "We've only communicated with her through the water. This is the first time I've actually been on land."

"Time is of the essence!" the Shellder yelled as Max carried him back to the driftwood. "The quickest way to the fairy haven is through The Rift at the end of this beach. It may not be the safest, but to go around will add days onto your journey."

"What's The Rift?"

"It's a huge gorge that was created when Samael was imprisoned in the volcano, and it's overrun by goblins. They're nasty little balls of flesh but dumb as a box of rocks." He craned his neck over Max's shoulder. "Remind you of anyone, Calvo?"

The man behind Max furrowed his eyebrows with a blank look in his eye. "I'm not sure I understand?"

Seeing the large smile playing on Rylan's lips, Hannah threw her canteen. "Stop being such an asshole!"

"It was a genuine question!" Rylan feigned innocence as he eyed their weapons.

"The only time goblins are a threat is when they're in a horde because there are too many to keep track," Calvo explained and unclasped his ax. "I haven't seen a horde in years, so your sword, Hannah's arrows, and your friend's trident will be sufficient."

"Yeah, I'm sure we will be fine, don't worry!"

Max reasoned that if Rylan and Calvo, who knew the most about the island, were not concerned with the goblins, he'd believe them. "I trust you."

"Do you mind if we grab some of this driftwood to use for a fire tonight?" Calvo asked the Shellder. "If we leave right now, we can set up camp in the gorge and make our way to the garden by tomorrow afternoon."

"Take what you need but make haste! Since you've already been here for one day, you have only four left to find your friend and figure out how to get back to the Mainland through the Temple of Harper at the island's northernmost point."

Max nodded in understanding and gingerly placed the

Shellder where he'd found him. Once their satchels were stuffed with the dry wood, he slung the bag around his shoulder and clasped Ella's hand with his. He stuck his sword straight ahead and announced, "To The Rift!"

"To Leona!"

"To mermaids!"

Chapter Eleven

"Ugh, are we there *yet?*" Ella dramatically threw her hands into the air and breathed a tired sigh.

It was hard to believe that hours prior, their feet were shuffling through the beach's foamy waves that washed ashore and were now walking through a gorge of rust-colored rocks. The Rift, a magnificent canyon, had a stream rushing through its center, splitting the land down the middle. Ledges of different sizes protruded from the tall walls with black caverns scattered throughout. The thought of what could be hiding in the shadows constantly put Max on edge.

Calvo noticed him eyeing the caves. "Goblins live in those holes." During their initial descent into the gorge, he had suggested they travel along the stream as it would bring them to an exit, leaving less chance of getting lost.

Rylan lifted his arms and gestured to the gorge's walls. "Legend has it that the final fight between Samael and the Hero ripped open this part of the island. It stretches from Seashell Shore all the way to the meadow beyond. There's a path that diverges to the west and stops at the base of the volcano."

"Must have been a pretty harsh battle if the island split apart," Max remarked.

Calvo rolled his eyes. "It's a myth. Don't believe everything you hear."

Ella's impatience was evident as she repeatedly asked the group, "Are we there yet?" every few minutes while walking through The Rift. She was tired from the sun sapping her energy, but the rest of the team knew that they had to carry on. Instead, she decided to walk with her fingertips touching the wall, leaving lines of dust in the stone behind her.

As the sun began its descent, the sky transformed into a canvas of colors with pink clouds ablaze against a backdrop of lavender and orange hues. It reminded Max of hot summer nights when he was younger, and his parents used to take him for ice cream after dinner. They'd sit outside on a picnic table and bask in the cool evening air.

Rylan had been carrying Hannah's satchel and swung it off his shoulder, plunging his hand into the stream. "Let's stop here. The flow of the water is telling me we're a little more than halfway through the canyon, and it's getting late. How about we set up camp, start a fire, and make some dinner?"

Max nodded and set his backpack next to Calvo's, stealing a glance at the man next to him. The area Rylan had chosen was comfortable; a smooth ledge separated the stream from the ground, making it a perfect place to set up camp.

"Max, you and Calvo gather kindling we can add to the driftwood to start the fire and keep it going. Hannah and I will catch some fish in the stream for us to eat."

"What do I do?" Ella whined, crossing her arms.

Rylan rolled his eyes at the little girl's dramatics. "How

about you take out the animal skins and set up a place for us to sleep?"

Calvo hooked his arm around Max's neck and clapped him on the chest. "Guess it's just you and me, bud. Why don't you try to find some twigs and underbrush, and I'll try to start a small fire with what we have?"

Nodding in agreement, Max scanned the area, looking for anything that could be added to the small amount of driftwood they'd brought from the beach to create a sufficient fire. Scattered around the area were small twigs and dried leaves that blew in the wind. Max recalled two protagonists on a television show that he'd seen had started a fire by creating friction between two sticks. He wondered if Calvo was using the same method, and his eyes wandered toward the shirtless man squatting toward the ground, setting the wood in a tent-like formation. His crouching raised the animal skin around his waist, exposing his well-defined thighs.

I've never met someone like him before. He looks like a jock from school, but he's so nice...it's weird.

He secretly wished for the squat to be a smidge lower or for a breeze to blow through the area.

"Hey Max, stop gawking and gather what we need for the fire!"

He spun around and dropped to his knees, hastily picking up the small twigs that were scattered around him. His cheeks burned with embarrassment, keeping his eyes focused on the ground.

Ella fanned out each of the blankets on the dusty ledge circling the makeshift fire pit that Calvo was assembling. As the sun descended, the walls of the gorge cast a shadow, making it appear later than it was. Yawns escaped each of their mouths as they continued to work to prepare for their night.

Max's eyes drifted over to Rylan and Hannah and watched

as his girlfriend readied an arrow, let go of the bow's string, and struck a fish through its side. Rylan stood beside her, manipulating the water with his hands until a small ball lifted into the air and deposited a fish on the ground, where it squirmed helplessly.

He gazed at Hannah. Her stance was open and powerful as she focused on the flowing water, waiting for a fish to swim by. She looked beautiful in the rising moonlight, her golden hair messy yet carefree and her shirt revealing a sliver of cleavage just below her collarbone.

She's really jumped into this adventure headfirst. I'm so lucky to have a girlfriend who can see something in me that I'm not able to find in myself.

Rylan laughed and raised his eyebrows at Calvo, who was sitting on the dirty ground, rubbing two pieces of wood together. "Do you really think that'll work?"

"I've done it before," Calvo grunted. "Why don't you worry about catching fish, and I'll get this fire lit."

"I can help you, but you seem pretty confident in yourself—"

"I can do it."

Rylan combed his fingers through his hair and rolled his eyes before turning to Max. "We're almost done at the river, but if he still needs help, use this to start a fire." He dug into the satchel and retrieved a white lighter, which bore a striking resemblance to the one he kept for lighting joints before he began vaping.

"Of course, you'd have that, even on a magical island."

Rylan shrugged. "I found it in a grotto one day and held onto it. Weird that it looks like my lighter from back home, huh?"

Max nodded, finding the parallels between the island and the Mainland strange. He set the wood so that three pieces leaned on one another and situated many dried leaves in its center. Striking the lighter with his finger, an orange flame sprung out of the small hole. Bringing it closer to the leaves, their brittle and brown edges quickly clothed themselves in the ember, creating a warm glow around the campsite.

Calvo stepped backward, trying to conceal his upturned lip by crossing his arms. "I could've done it."

Hannah and Rylan made their way back, hugging dead fish in each arm. "Ella, can you find us four long sticks that we can use to cook these bad boys?"

The little girl nodded and rummaged through Max's wood pile before returning with four spear-like twigs and handed them to the merman. He snatched them within his palm and stabbed two fish onto the ends of each.

Calvo put his hand on one of the sticks before Rylan propped it into the fire. "Aren't you going to clean them? What're you trying to do to us?"

Slapping the large hand away, Rylan turned to his friends. "Normally, you'd have to descale the fish for them to be safe to eat, but these just fall right off over an open flame." He twisted his head toward Calvo and narrowed his eyes. "Leave the fish stuff to me."

"How many times have you said that before, eh, Ry?" Max thought a joke would break the tension in the air, but it only grew thicker.

As the blue-toned scales of the fish fell into the fire, its skin sizzled, and the smoke tendrils danced into the air. The first bits of stars were just beginning to twinkle in the beautiful, inky blackness of the night sky. The sound of the wind blowing softly through The Rift filled the air as a silver half-moon illuminated the dark clouds in the night sky. The area was quiet, except for the melodic sound of the stream flowing nearby.

The fish at the end of each stick began to turn black from

the fire, and Max removed them from the heat. Holding them like kebabs, he sunk his teeth into the cooked meat, and the delicious flavor flooded his mouth. The sweet tanginess of grilled pineapple burst over his taste buds and activated his salivary glands.

"They're good, right?" Rylan nodded as Max's eyes went from expectant to amazement. "These are sweetwater fish; their flavor comes from the algae they eat in the stream. Paired with the smokiness from the fire, I'd say this easy meal is chef's kiss." He collected his fingers atop his thumb and put them to his mouth.

"I didn't realize these were sweetwater fish," Calvo admitted. "Otherwise, I wouldn't have said anything."

"But you did."

Max noticed the tension in Calvo's shoulders, the way he kept his posture rigid, and a slight frown on his face. It seemed Calvo was annoyed at Rylan's snarky attitude and defiance toward him. Ella's stick was licked clean and sat at his feet; the child lay on her back with her eyes gazing into the sky. "Are you okay, El? I know this must be a lot for you."

Ella laughed as she stared into the dark sky. "Look at the stars, they aren't like the ones we have back home."

Max was amazed that his sister seemed unbothered by all the traveling they were doing because earlier, she'd been complaining for what seemed like hours. Nevertheless, he turned his gaze upward and saw the stars directly above them resembled a horse with a spiral horn on its head. "A unicorn constellation, cool! I wonder what the story is for that one."

Calvo laughed. "The island itself has the ability to add new stars and constellations to the sky if your story is worthy enough." He turned to Max and winked. "That unicorn constellation you see memorializes a famous being that once walked the Island of Forever's shores, Flickerhoof. Back when unicorns lived on the Mainland, they were hunted for the healing properties of their horns. Flickerhoof found a way to the Island of Forever and traveled between both worlds to assist with their remaining brethren' safe passage."

"Is that why there are no more unicorns back home?"

He nodded. "I suppose there may be some hiding. Flickerhoof collected as many as he could and brought them here to escape the hunters."

Max took a bite into the last lukewarm fish that Hannah and Rylan had caught, watching Calvo direct his sister's gaze into the sky, regaling her with another story of how the unicorn constellation came to be.

He isn't bothered by Ella's questions or her enthusiasm like most people are. This is a softer side of him that I haven't seen before. Maybe he picked up extra patience from living with the Sofillians. But either way, his personality has layers.

As the myth of Flickerhoof finished, Ella's eyes grew heavy, and a yawn caught in her throat. She shifted her body and rested her head on Max's shoulder. "Can you tuck me in?"

"Yeah, let's hit the sack." Rylan nodded. "Tomorrow will be just as long of a day."

"I'll go and try to find more kindling for the fire. We're almost out." Calvo stood from the dirty platform and grabbed his ax, hooking it to his waist.

"D'you need help?" Max asked in a hopeful tone.

He shook his head and walked until his body disappeared down The Rift's river.

"He'll be fine," Hannah assured Max, noticing him watching the man leave alone.

He nodded and picked Ella off the ground, carrying her over to the blankets she'd laid out hours before. Max lightly tucked the blanket under her back and legs, cocooning her securely.

A quiet yelp quickly jumped through the air, making everyone jump in surprise. Hannah's face turned ashen, and her eyes bulged out of their sockets as if she'd seen a ghost. Max and Rylan's hands immediately clasped their weapons, ready to jump into action.

Max squinted his eyes to try to see through the darkness, but couldn't make out any intruder. Holding his sword over his shoulder like a baseball bat, his gaze didn't leave the inky darkness. "What did you see?"

Short and quick breaths released from Hannah's mouth, trying to get her fear to stabilize. "S-s-s-spider!" Her finger was trembling as she pointed into the darkness outside the campsite.

Max and Rylan let out a relieved breath of air and rolled their eyes; they knew Hannah was afraid of spiders but didn't expect her to be so dramatic after seeing one. Given that they were in the wilderness, she should've known that encountering spiders at some point on their journey was a possibility.

Max fixed on the point where Hannah was staring, her eyes flashing wide with every lick of fire in the pit. A big black hole was situated on the side of the rocky walls, which Max hadn't noticed before. He cocked his head to look as he picked up one of the sticks they used to cook the fish and held it near the blazing fire. A small flame jumped onto the wood, its body crackling in Max's ear.

"No, Max, d-don't go over there." Hannah's voice shook with each word.

With his makeshift torch in hand, he approached the wall, casting light on what she'd seen above them. As the light reached the darkness, a bulbous body with black and white stripes came into view, its eight spindly legs clutching the stone wall of The Rift.

Max stopped in his tracks as he realized the hole in the

gorge's side was, in fact, a giant spider—so large, it was the size of an automobile. The light flickered on the rocks, and the creature turned its face towards him. Small beady eyes glinted in the torch's light, and two white fangs rested on its lips, upturned into a smile. Max's breath became labored, and his hands began to sweat as he tiptoed backward, hoping the spider wouldn't attack. He could hear his heartbeat in his ears, and a ball formed within his throat.

The spider moved its front and back legs, scurrying up the side of the gorge, and disappeared onto a ledge above them. Once it was out of sight, the group let out a collective sigh of relief after thinking there was a great possibility that they'd be the spider's dinner.

"Max!" Hannah screamed. "Are you okay?"

He gripped the torch and ran back to the camp, the darkness retreating from his body as the warm orange glow invited him. Rylan's eyes were wide, and Hannah's face was still devoid of color.

He nodded. "I think it went away, but we may need someone to keep watch tonight to make sure we're not spider food. I'm tired, but I'll go first. Once Calvo returns, I'll tell him what happened. I'm sure he'll be okay with taking the second watch to give you three more time to sleep."

"Hannah." Ella sniffled. "Would you cuddle me? We will be safe because Max is watching out for us."

She smiled and allowed the little girl to wiggle under her blanket before each of them closed their eyes. The soft sounds of the wind blowing through the rocks and the river rushing downstream were lulling them to sleep.

Sitting on the ground, Max unsheathed his sword and placed it beside him while his friends slept behind him. The worn blade glinted as the fire danced behind it, reflecting the stars in the sky. Despite the dry heat blowing through the gorge, the air turned cool, offering a refreshing gift with every gust of wind.

The river running through the center of the rocks had calmed its current as if it were going to sleep with the rest of them. The lilting sounds of water gave Max a feeling of tranquility, and he closed his eyes to listen to his surroundings.

Calvo will be back shortly.

He heard insects chirping into the night and the branches of the barren plant life scratching together when the wind blew through. Listening to the sounds emanating from The Rift, a wave of exhaustion ran through his body. He didn't realize how tired his body was until he had this moment to himself.

He leaned onto the rocks, and his back and feet were instantly relieved. Max rested his head, making sure his neck was against the cool stone as he realized they'd been awake for over a full day without sleep. His body relaxed, and his eyelids grew heavy. His mind slowly shut down, and he could no longer muster the energy to lift his tired eyes. Feeling himself fading into slumber, he knew he was expected to keep watch and would jerk back awake periodically.

Calvo should be back any second, so even if I fall asleep, it won't be for long.

Eventually, his body succumbed to its need for sleep, and he exited his watch to the land of dreams.

Calvo will be back soon.

Chapter Twelve

His eyes felt like they had only been closed for a few minutes when one hand grabbed his shoulder and the other around his mouth. "Calvo?" Max cracked open his tired eyes to see Rylan with a frightened look next to him. His friend put one finger to his lips and pointed down The Rift, where they saw a faint light of a torch coming their way. The sound of snorting echoed throughout the gorge as ominous shadows danced on the rock walls' jagged exterior.

"We need to hide," Rylan whispered. "I'll douse the fire, you wake the girls. Tell them to find a good hiding spot."

"What are those things?"

"Goblins!" Rylan twisted his wrists to begin manipulating water from the stream. "Hurry!"

Max took note of the fear in his friend's eyes and ran to Hannah and Ella, who were sound asleep. He nudged both of them, and their eyes sleepily flitted open. Putting one finger to his mouth, Max glanced at the impending shadows. "Hide."

A grunt, followed closely by a cry, sounded from the river, and Max ran toward Rylan to see what had happened. Milky white orbs of light shone through the darkness, and spindly arms slowly crawled closer.

"They're here," Rylan breathed, rubbing a light cut on his arm. "They nicked me with one of their spears. I couldn't put the fire out."

"Hannah, grab your bow and arrows. I think we're going to have to fight them." He picked up his sword from the rocky ground, the hilt cool in his hand.

As much as I don't want her to be alone, Ella has to disappear to remain safe.

He put one arm on his sister's shoulder. "You like to play hide and seek, right?"

She nodded as fear filled her eyes.

"Perfect, I want you to hide so well, no one will be able to find you. Don't come out until you hear me calling for you."

The little girl nodded in understanding, her eyes wet as she ran in the opposite direction before disappearing from sight.

The snorting and forced breathing grew closer. The goblins' earth-toned bodies were a mottled mix of brown, green, and gray, with some walking on all fours and others only on their hind legs. Each of them had a flat nose and two small, cat-like ears folded atop their head. Their wide mouths were accentuated by two deep wrinkles on each side, revealing their jagged teeth. Tightly held in their knobby hands was a collection of spears and knives made from makeshift sticks and rope.

Max looked to his left and saw Hannah had put her golden blonde hair into a ponytail and had an arrow ready in the bow, her hands trembling. To his right was Rylan, who looked like he had battled goblins many times with his feet positioned in a strong stance, grasping the handle of his trident.

Adrenaline and fear pumped through his body like a raucous parade, vibrations encapsulated him as they traveled up his spine.

Shit.

His gaze turned upward toward his hand and saw a faint glow of black smoke twisting around his fingers and crawling up his arm.

This happened at the Sofillian Camp and it paralyzed me afterward. I don't want anyone to know I can do this.

Max's thoughts lingered in the air until a spear pierced through the darkness, narrowly missing his shoulder. Seeing this, Hannah removed her fingers from the bowstring, releasing the arrow into the crowd of goblins. A disapproving hiss sounded from the throng before loud yelps traveled through the area.

The dark gorge lit up before them; the goblins had touched their torches to the dry and lifeless plants, the blaze illuminating the night. The toad-like creatures began to run at the three friends with malice in their eyes.

"Shit!" Max yelled with his sword ready. "It's a horde."

The area was filled with the scent of burning wood, and Max had only a split second to defend himself before a goblin attacked him. With a swift motion, he swung the sword in front of him, slicing the green skin and causing red blood to pour from its body. As the goblin was launched through the air, its screams echoed off the rocky walls before it hit with a resounding thud. Max glanced at his hand to see the thin smoke had disappeared and breathed a sigh of relief before returning to his friends.

Rylan's legs were slightly bent, almost crouching, and he swung his trident in a half circle, piercing the horde of goblins around him with its barbs. Once they were hurt, he then stabbed at their overgrown bellies. "This would've been easier if there weren't so many of them. I could ask the river to rise and drag them downstream."

"You said they were dumb. They seem pretty organized to me!"

"Instinct is all they have!"

Two nearby goblins leaped at Max, each dragging their sharp nails down his arms. Despite the pain, he managed to swiftly slash one of them in the neck and impale the other with the tip of his sword. The impaled goblins made one last hiss before its milky white eyes lost their glow. Using the heel of his shoe, he scraped the creature off the end of his sword, and a sharp pain shot through his ankle.

"Max, watch out!" Hannah yelled, firing her bow.

The pressure of the goblin's sharp teeth dissipated as its soft triangular ears brushed against his legs. It fell to the ground with a thud as Hannah's arrow lodged itself through its temple.

Its mismatched teeth penetrated Max's skin so deep that he could not shake it off. He kneeled and hooked his fingers into the roof of its mouth, slowly removing the teeth from his leg. Bits of glass and sharp stone were stuck in his ankle where its teeth had been latched moments before. The wound throbbed, painful and grotesque, but knowing he had to continue fighting to keep Ella safe kept his adrenaline pumping.

"Are you okay?"

Max grunted. "Yeah, just be careful, their mouths are filled with glass and rocks. I don't think they have teeth of their own." He swung his sword at a nearby goblin and gazed at the sea of green in front of him. "There are a lot of them, do you think we can make it out of this?"

"We have to try." Rylan swung his trident and pierced three incoming goblins.

Max nodded and began waving his sword at the creatures that came his way, trying to shift his weight to his better leg. Throughout the battle, Max only heard his own grunts, the sound of Hannah's arrows whizzing by his ear, and the snorting of the goblins around them. A sound he didn't anticipate made him pause—the piercing screams of a young girl. The sight before him caused an immediate pit in his stomach and a sharp pain in his chest as if a goblin spear had struck him. He turned to where the scream emanated and began limping away from the army before him.

Rylan's hand reached Max's shoulder. "We need to have Hannah make sure Ella is okay; you're in no shape to find her quickly."

He shook his head. "I need to go. She's my sister! I can't let anything happen to her."

Rylan forcefully clasped his hand around Max's shoulder, his fingers digging into his skin. "You can't go if you truly want her safe." With his free hand, he swung his trident at a goblin soaring through the air toward them like a baseball bat; its wails echoed as it sailed through the air. "With your mangled ankle, you won't be able to catch up with Ella, she's had too much time to run away or climb. Plus, Hannah and I can't hold them off with just my trident and her arrows. You and I have to stay to give Hannah time to find Ella and get her to safety."

I hate this and I just want to scream because I feel so helpless.

"I need you to listen to me for a second: you can't help her if you're dead. Hannah can do it." Rylan kicked one foot in the air, round-housing a jumping goblin.

"I'll go, Max, I can do it."

He looked at Hannah, his eyes full of defeat and hers wide with concern.

I don't like it, but they're right, I can barely stand on my ankle right now. There's no way I'd be able to find her, let alone protect her.

Max looked at his girlfriend with an intense stare and clenched his jaw. "Go find Ella." His voice trembled. "I need you to do this for me. Get her home if I don't make it out of this."

"I'll make sure she's safe." Hannah's bright eyes grew wide with fright as more goblins ascended upon them. Without leaving Max's eyes until absolutely necessary, she turned and ran in the opposite direction, searching for the little girl.

Max said a silent prayer before turning around, his arm outstretched and his sword gleaming. "You bastards better hope my sister is okay." With his sister's scream ringing in his ears, adrenaline pumped through his veins, giving him the strength to swing at the creatures that surrounded him. Dead goblin bodies surrounded the two friends as blood pooled beneath their feet.

He and Rylan battled on, swinging their sword and trident at any oncoming creature that neared. Hope grew in his heart. They were holding them off. Not one of the creatures had snuck by them or had chased after Hannah. He hoped their stamina was strong enough to continue fighting until Ella could reach safety.

A second scream rang through the gorge, causing any hope Max had to completely dissipate. He and Rylan looked at one another as surprise and fright vibrated throughout their bodies —it was Hannah. Max's body twisted as he looked up, searching for the origin of the cries for help echoing off the gorge's cliffs.

"Max, watch out!" Rylan jumped in front of him, swinging his trident like he was trying to shoo mosquitoes away.

Max and Rylan were suddenly thrown to the ground by an immense weight, their limbs completely immobilized. A heavy net ensnared them, and the goblins descended like a pack of wolves on helpless prey. Hannah and Ella's screams reverberated throughout the air amid the gnashing and clawing of the creatures on top of them. The net coiled around Max's body, and he thrashed about, but the horde that leapt onto him made it impossible to move.

It's all over. We're done.

A deep yell that sounded like it came from a wild animal filled the gorge, causing the goblins that were piling on top of Rylan and Max to freeze and revert their attention to the oncoming attack. Terror filled the goblin's milky white eyes as they shrieked to try and get away. A new shadow appeared on the gorge wall that was holding a blazing ax with a flag of fire that burned deep orange.

The creatures were frozen in their spot with their ears twitching back and forth. Their milky eyes were aglow as their thin legs slowly backed away. One by one, the goblins retreated, their cries sounding like abused dogs.

A booming voice sounded around them, "Return the girls to us or prepare to die!" The man who had saved them slowly walked by Max's head, his legs pulsing with every step. With one swift motion, he swung his arm, and the blazing blade of the ax sliced through the goblins, leaving behind a trail of burnt flesh and severed limbs.

Upon seeing the damage caused by the man's few swipes, the goblin army screamed and scrambled up the walls of the gorge, racing back in the direction they came from. Within seconds, the campsite was void of any living goblins.

The rope net flung off of Max and Rylan, allowing them to escape. "Are either of you hurt?"

Max glanced up into the concerned eyes of Calvo, his jawline looking sharper than ever as the fire shadowed it. The man held out a rough hand to help Max get to his feet. "Where's Hannah and Ella?"

Max didn't have the words to explain what had happened. *Why did I let Hannah go? I should've gone myself because maybe—maybe they'd both still be here.*

A hollow feeling overcame him, like his emotions had turned off. He was empty.

A few moments of silence passed and Calvo scanned their eyes before the realization flooded his mind. "They—they were taken?"

"We need to go and get them."

Calvo shook his head. "The goblins have disappeared inside the tunnels throughout The Rift. They're an interconnected labyrinth that only they know how to navigate. If we went inside, we'd surely meet death."

"No, that can't be right. We have to do something!" A sudden rush of heaviness clouded his head, and his surroundings spun.

How did I allow Ella to get captured? Why did I let her leave my sight and protection? It's my job as her big brother to make sure she's safe.

I've failed her.

Chapter Thirteen

A fearful Ella haunted Max's thoughts as he tossed and turned on the lumpy dirt ground. After the attack, Rylan and Calvo suggested they continue to utilize their existing campsite, both to recoup and for Max to make a plan to get his sister back. They suggested he sleep, but a mixture of adrenaline and regret kept him awake and on full alert to any noises in the gorge.

He rolled onto his back, watching the last bit of smoke dull his view of the stars. As time passed, Rylan's breaths went from quiet to a boisterous snore and was the only sound in the silence, punctuated by the occasional crackle of the dying fire and a faint whistle of wind through the ravine. It reassured him that Calvo was keeping watch and got lost in his thoughts, gazing at the inky black sky clouded with smoke.

I should've gone to save Ella; I could've protected her. Even with my bad ankle, I could've done something to help make sure she was safe. Why'd I listen to Rylan?

The weight of his questions made his palms sweat and his heart thud against the ground beneath him. His hurt ankle throbbed with every movement, keeping him awake for longer than he would have liked.

On the other side of the ashen campfire, there was a stir. The stillness of the scene was suddenly broken by a figure lurking in the shadows, concealed by the hazy darkness and departing from the campsite.

Max turned to Rylan, who was still sound asleep.

Where's Calvo going? Why's he leaving us?

Throwing his dirty shirt over his shoulders, a sense of determination washed over him as he set off to find the answers he sought.

I shouldn't leave Rylan, but I need to know what's going on.

He winced at the pain pinching his ankle from the goblin bite and hobbled after Calvo. Max caught up as quickly as he could and moved stealthily along the rocky trail so as not to alert him.

Is he going to try and find Ella and Hannah by himself? But why would he sneak away?

As Calvo approached a dead end, he glanced back, causing Max to duck behind a large tree that offered protection. A few moments of hiding passed, and when he peeked back toward the trail, there was only darkness where the rugged man stood moments before.

A strong breeze blew through the gorge, causing loose dust from the ground to blow into Max's face. Swirling dirt particles in the air caused him to tilt his head downward and shield his eyes with his hand. The gust of wind died down, and he saw a trail of footprints outlined in the dirt where Calvo had stood just moments before. He winced at the pain in his ankle as he followed the outline of toes. Max's gaze led him to the base of a giant boulder resting on the side of The Rift.

Scanning the footsteps, Max sidled over and discovered a small gap between the rock and the gorge wall. The space was hidden well, and he wouldn't have found it if Calvo's footprints had not led him directly to the entrance. A dusty handprint was outlined on the tunnel's entrance.

Should I follow him? Maybe he found out where Ella and Hannah were taken and is going to save them. Why wouldn't he tell me?

Dropping to his hands and knees, Max attempted to shimmy his way into the hole, but his shoulders were too broad.

I need to know where he's going.

His heart pounded in his chest, and a warmth spread throughout his body as he struggled to push his way through the hole. Swirling black tendrils circled his neck until a sharp dagger-like pain struck his shoulder blades. He winced, and with one final push, was able to enter the hole.

Did my body just change?

The dry air inside the tunnel made him thirsty, and the rocky ground dug into his hands and knees like sharp glass. Thankfully, he was able to scurry after Calvo with his knees, rather than his pained foot. After some time, he lost track of how long he'd been crawling. He had lost all sense of time in the pitch-black surroundings, his mind racing with every possible danger that could be waiting for him.

What if this tunnel is home to a rabid animal? I won't even be able to see before it attacks. It's so dark, what if I fall into a hole and can't get out?

Turning his head to see how far from the entrance he was, Max only saw darkness behind him. Ignoring the pit forming in his stomach, he took a breath and crawled onward, hoping the long tunnel would end without one of the life-threatening results spinning through his mind.

Just when his hope was waning, a small white speck appeared in the distance. Max wasn't sure if the dot was a trick of the dark or if there was light up ahead. He crawled faster, but the white speck remained stubbornly small.

As Max shimmied his arms and legs through the tunnel, praying for an end, he turned his mind to Calvo and what he could be doing.

How did he know this tunnel was here? Where does it go? Is this where Ella was being held hostage?

Just as the thought popped into Max's mind, the dirt walls around him opened, and the rough soil beneath his knees gave way to smooth stone.

A slight hum reverberated through the air as if his presence brought his surroundings to life. The darkness that clouded his eyes lifted and was replaced with a soft greenish-white glow. Max's eyes darted back and forth, hoping to take in as much of his environment as possible before the darkness returned. Instead of fading away, the light persisted, illuminating a cavern filled with vibrant rocks and stalagmites.

He raised his arms, his bones cracking with the ascent as if his shoulders were relocating themselves and knelt to inspect the wall of stones. He flinched at the pain that shot through his leg as he crouched. Upon closer examination, he discovered that the light was coming from the cavern itself. Reaching his hand to touch one of the glowing rocks, it became as bright as a light bulb, but it dimmed when Max moved his hand away.

The small pebbles that made up the path at his feet glowed with the same light as the cave around him, creating a twisting trail that never lost its illumination. The path sharply turned to the left, and the green-white glow intensified around the corner. He slyly poked his head around the turn, expecting to see Ella and Hannah held hostage in makeshift cages by a tribe of goblins with bared teeth, but instead found an ornate room that was hidden within The Rift.

A large breath of warm air reached Max's face as he peered

around the corner. Squinting, he saw the cave open into a sizable room shrouded in dense fog. A rectangular pool of water dominated the room's center, sending out waves of steam that filled the air. The thin, white mist formed tendrils that snaked across the surface of the water, dissipating into the air above. White statues surrounded the room, each holding a pot that gently poured water into the pool.

A deep voice reached Max's ears. "Why are you following me?" Calvo stepped into his line of sight from behind a stalagmite near the chamber's entrance.

He questioned whether the warmth on his cheeks was from the room's temperature or his own embarrassment. He stepped out from around the corner to face Calvo and responded with a sheepish smile. "Why are you sneaking away in the middle of the night? Did you think I wouldn't wake up?"

"You think I was sneaking away to save your sister and your girlfriend, don't you?" Calvo folded his arms and narrowed his eyes. "Do you think I would risk my life and go into a goblin's nest by myself?" He had a stern look in his eye, like he was being defensive and playful simultaneously. A slight smirk drew his right lip upward like he was winning at a game.

"Yeah, I guess it wasn't one of my smartest suspicions." Max walked toward the Sofillian in front of him, trembling. "If you weren't sneaking away, where were you going? What is this place?" The pool area was characterized by a minimalist aesthetic, with white benches placed between rows of statues and a small stone hut situated at the far end of the cavern. The room was lined with pillars, each one meticulously crafted with intricate details and perfect spacing.

"Let me show you." Calvo put his arm around Max's shoulder and led him closer to the water. "I wasn't sure it was here, but this cave holds one of the many hot springs hidden throughout the island. The water is constantly warm because of tunnels that expel pockets of heat from the volcano and has healing properties. The first time I came here was when I was on my mission before you turned up. It's a good place to rest and re-energize."

"What was your mission?"

Calvo paused, weighing the decision to release the information before answering. "There have been reports of missing people throughout the Island of Forever," he admitted, "and Wintey tasked me with finding out if it's related to a plot to release Samael. Thanks to the protection of the Great Tree, we've been able to keep the Sofillians safe."

"From what you know, do you think the missing people are part of the plan to free him?"

The man solemnly nodded. "From the research I've gathered, if he escapes the volcano, his powers will only return if he removes the youth from another."

"Youth?" Max's ears locked onto every word he was saying. "So, he's looking to kill Hannah and Ella?"

"Not necessarily," he answered. "I believe the vessels will age once he takes what is needed. He seeks out younger individuals because he believes they have more vitality to drain, leaving them aged and frail when he's finished."

I can't believe this. If Samael takes Ella's youth, will she not be a kid anymore?

He couldn't bear to think that his sister's life could so easily be tossed away. "Will you help us get them back?"

Calvo's eyebrows rose in acceptance. "My original mission was to find out if that's his plan and to prepare to combat it. My new task is to help you get home." He stopped speaking as he looked at the boy next to him. "Mainlanders finding their way to the island was the first crack in his prison. The next is collecting enough people to regain power. All the kidnapped individuals, I suspect, are being held within a castle to the north, which is right near the temple from which you must leave."

"Does that mean Ella and Hannah will be there too?"

"Just from my knowledge and assumptions, yes. Samael wants nothing more than to leave this island, and your arrival sets it all in motion." Calvo paused and placed a finger under his chin. "Do you remember what you suggested at the Sofillian Camp?"

A pit formed in his stomach as the shameful memory resurfaced. "About leaving Rylan and Leona here?"

Calvo nodded. "With your limited time, would you consider heading directly to the temple if you knew your sister was there?"

Max's head sharply turned toward him in disgust. "I'm not leaving anyone behind." To him, they were not just his friends but his chosen family. He knew that without them, he wouldn't be the same person. "Leaving now would be the easy choice, and I thought about leaving without Rylan and Leona at the Sofillian Camp because I was concerned for Ella's safety. I couldn't leave here without my friends." He paused, giving a definitive end to the conversation. "Promise me that what I said will remain between us?"

Calvo's eyes narrowed. "Of course."

A sense of relief flooded through him, and Max knew he had to distract his thoughts from going wild by surveying the room before them. "What do you do here? What's the purpose of the spring?"

"The water within the pool is infused with herbs and minerals then filtered through the barrels the statues are holding." He pointed to the white stone basins around the pool. "Mixed with the warmth of the water, the concoction soothes any aching body."

"So, you just...relax? It's like a big hot tub?" Max asked.

Calvo laughed. "I'm not sure what a hot tub is, my friend, but yes, you simply relax." He led Max to one of the white benches and pointed to the small hut. "I'll deposit my clothes and grab my bag in the bathhouse. While I do that, put your belongings on this bench and meet me in the pool."

"I can't do that." Max shivered despite the warm temperature of the room. "I'm not going to relax in a big tub when my sister and girlfriend were just kidnapped."

"It's up to you."

He watched as Calvo walked to the far end of the pool and disappeared within the small hut.

I'm leaving, this is stupid.

He hobbled a few steps toward the exit and looked over his shoulder.

I can't continue to walk for days on this bad ankle, so any relief will help. My body hurts from sleeping on the ground, maybe I'll go in for just a second.

Bouncing on one foot, he untied his shoelaces and removed the sweat-logged socks from his feet. His fingers pulled the dirty shirt he'd been wearing over his head and draped it over the bench next to him.

He unbuttoned his pants, peeling them off and leaving them in a heap around his ankles. Memories of the gym locker room at school came flooding back to him, and he quickly reached down and hoisted them over his hips.

Nope, shorts on.

"Plus," he reasoned aloud to himself, "they need to get clean after rolling around in the dirt."

Making his way to the pool's edge, Max lowered his feet into the spring. He braced himself as the hot water hit his skin, stinging like needles, but he focused on taking deep breaths to adjust. He entered slowly, feeling the temperature change as it covered him until only his head remained above water.

The warmth hugged him like a tight blanket, instantly soothing his muscles. The water had a floral scent mixed into its layers of earthy undertones; he assumed it was due to the mineral infusion that Calvo talked about. No matter how low he sank, his feet could not touch the floor of the pool. He laid his arms outside the pool, allowing his body to float effortlessly.

Calvo's voice rang throughout the empty room. "Sorry it took me so long, I was experimenting with the spring's salt levels."

Max turned to reply but couldn't articulate the right words to come from his mouth. The hot steam curled around the man as he made his way toward the pool, but it did nothing to hide the scene before him. He watched in disbelief as Calvo approached him with a smug look, strutting confidently and shamelessly while exposing his naked body.

What's he doing? Is he really going to strut around like that? With everything hanging out?

He breathed and no matter where he moved his eyes, they continued to land on the guy walking toward him.

Okay, it's fine. I'll just not look because I don't wanna make it weird.

Turning his head before his eyes traveled too far, he hoped that Calvo didn't notice the quick glance. He wiped his brow with the back of his hand, his face flush from the warm spring. He winced as Calvo's footsteps drew closer and closer, stopping right in front of him.

Calvo raised an eyebrow. "Have I offended you?"

Max's cheeks turned red and burned his face so intensely that he swore they'd be able to start a fire. "Where I'm from, we don't stare at another dude's junk."

"Another dude's junk?" Calvo had an amused smirk on his face as he lowered his calves into the pool. "You don't have to feel weird around me. And if people are concerned about someone else's body where you're from, I am glad I live on this island."

Max stole a glance at the man and with every inch of descent, the water seemed to swallow him. He cleared the lump in his throat as Calvo's naked body slowly disappeared under the hot mist that lay on the water, its surface hiding everything but nothing at the same time. He deepened his voice. "Yeah, uh... I guess you wouldn't understand what it's like back home."

"Why do you do that?" Calvo's eyes bore into Max, looking directly into his soul.

"Do what?" Even though he asked, Max knew what Clavo was referring to.

"Actually, let me ask you a question. How many versions of yourself do you think you've lived throughout your life?"

His stomach dropped once the question was asked. He made a conscious effort not to think about his past too often, but he knew that he had different personas depending on who he was with. He tried to blend in with the jocks at school, has a distinct playful demeanor for when he was around Ella, and another when he was alone. All existed within him but were different variations of who he was. "Too many."

Calvo's eyebrows raised, and he nodded in understanding. "Much of what you do, like deepening your voice, is a survival technique. You flex toward who you're around." His amber-colored eyes looked inquisitive; the pools of yellow and brown swirled into Max's soul. "Speaking of those you surround yourself with, you've recovered one of your friends already. Are you interested in him?"

Taken aback by the question, Max snapped at him. "I don't like guys. Hannah's my girlfriend and Rylan's my best friend." Even in the water, Max could sense his hands sweating and his face flushing further. He'd never had someone be so direct about this before. Usually, the conversation was masked with jokes in the locker room at school. "I know Wintey has a girl-friend, and sexuality means nothing on this island, but where I'm from...it's just not normal."

Calvo's questioning eyebrows showed his curiosity. "On this island, we fall in love with people and their souls—who they are, what they stand for—not their body parts. If you have a connection with someone, why wouldn't you pursue them simply because of their gender?"

"It's not that easy, okay? You don't know what my world is like. There are stupid standards and old ways of thinking that make...well, that makes what you're saying not possible for some people." Max was exasperated.

Although it would be easier if all that didn't matter.

The man stared at him in silence, trying to formulate some-thing to say that would not escalate the conversation further. "We are a product of our environment, I suppose." Tension permeated the steam-filled air, and he pushed himself off the edge of the pool, propelling his body towards the center. With nothing to hold his body up, his head bobbed just above the water. The mood in the room shifted, and an awkward silence filled the space.

A sharp pang in his heart caused Max to cringe because he realized Calvo was attempting to change the conversation so it didn't upset him further.

I shouldn't have snapped at him like that, but it's frustrating trying to talk to someone who doesn't understand. He was born here, on this island. There's no way he could relate to me even if it was true.

"While I was changing, I adjusted the salt levels so we could float in the pool."

His embarrassment was evident and he was thankful for

the change in conversation. "I don't have to hold on to the side?"

Calvo shook his head. "Give it a try."

Max let go, and his anxiety flared instantly. He frantically began flailing his arms and legs, gasping as if he was drowning. Once his body began to shut down, it was impossible to exert the energy to keep himself afloat. Grasping the pool's edge as if it were going to disappear from under his arms, he breathed a sigh of relief. "Uh... I'm good over here."

Calvo laughed at the boy's panic-stricken face. "*Are* you okay over there?" Swimming back, he situated himself right next to Max. The warmth from his body radiated between them like electricity. "What's wrong?"

He shook his head. "Don't worry about it. It's just me."

"C'mon, let me in. I'm a good listener."

Max looked into Calvo's golden eyes and found himself speaking before he could stop. "Sometimes I get anxiety," he admitted. "It comes and goes; there's no telling when it will affect me. When it does, it's crippling to the point where I have to rest until it's passed."

Is he going to think I'm a freak?

"I see." Calvo nodded, his eyebrows nearing his hairline. "This spring soothes and re-energizes, so you shouldn't need a rest after a strenuous event. My people used to rest in these waters after constantly fighting monsters when Samael first wreaked havoc on the island." He rose an eyebrow, looking at Max with a mischievous smirk. "Do you trust me enough to let me try something?"

I don't normally feel this comfortable around people I barely know. It's weird how Calvo puts me at ease, like I can tell him anything. Do I trust him?

To answer his own question, Max nodded, unsure what the tan man next to him was about to do. His nervousness heightened as Calvo swam closer, his eyes fixed on the water lapping against Calvo's athletic arms.

"I can tell that at this very moment, you're uneasy." Calvo laughed, his chest dancing just above the water line. "Do me a favor and lean back so your hair is partly submerged. I want to show you what this spring can do."

Max hesitated, his heart pounding, afraid that the man would force his head underwater. Looking down, he couldn't help but notice the small stream of water trickling between their chests, highlighting the stark contrast in size between him and Calvo. *Do I trust him?*

His lips parted into a reassuring smile. "Trust me." He took his rough hands and cradled the back of Max's neck, urging him to give in and lean backward.

It was as if the man's piercing eyes and dazzling smile had hypnotized him. As he leaned into Calvo's security, he relaxed and allowed the tension to dispel from his body. Taking a breath, he turned to putty under the effect of Calvo's rough hands, tilting his head backward slowly. Max quickly glanced at the abs next to his head and closed his eyes as he exhaled the air from his lungs.

Breathe.

Out of nowhere, a weight appeared behind his eyes almost like a migraine. The pressure in his head was accompanied by a sharp, stinging sensation that made it difficult to concentrate. Calvo slowly moved his body around the pool, making sure never to remove his hands from him. One thick drop of water brushed his lips, gradually evaporating the heaviness behind his eyes until it was lifted entirely. With each layer that was peeled away, it was like he was shedding a part of his anxiety.

After drifting together in silence for what seemed like forever, Calvo's deep voice whispered to him, "How do you feel?"

Max's eyes re-opened as he couldn't formulate his thoughts into words. He was different, not just in his body. Calm. His mind was relaxed, a sensation he'd never experienced prior. It was as if the thoughts that constantly ran through his mind decided to nap; the dark veil that plagued him had been lifted. Quiet. "What did you do?"

Silence.

"The water in this spring has special powers. All you have to do is put a drop on your forehead or tongue, and the water siphons whatever ails you—in your case, anxiety. It's also a good remedy for migraines and brain freeze." Calvo laughed, making the light in the room vibrate. Seeing the amazed look on Max's face, he winked. "I've already put a small vial of the water in your bag for later."

"Th-thanks." It amazed him that there was a cure for his severe apprehension. He wished he could always feel like this. The calm allowed his thoughts to converge in one place rather than all over, a clarity he'd scarcely been able to access.

"Now that you've calmed down." Calvo smiled mischievously. "Join me out here." He pushed himself toward the middle, his body bobbing on top of the water.

Instead of doing this, I really should get back to camp. What if something has happened to Rylan?

Max's eyes drifted from Calvo to the seemingly never-ending pool below. He tried reasoning with himself to gain confidence: *I know how to swim, that's not what I'm scared of. It freaks me out that I can't see the bottom. Do I trust that the water will keep me afloat?* The only difference was that while swimming in a pool, he could see the bottom, but here, he could not. He knew this sudden fear was his mind causing unnecessary anxiety, but the fear began to lessen.

His fingers grasped the side of the pool and instantly had

the urge to push off. It was an impulse, like he wasn't scared anymore.

I'm going to do it.

Each digit tingled at the thought of throwing himself off the edge toward Calvo.

I have to show him I'm not scared. Maybe he'll be impressed by me?

Before he allowed another shard of doubt to cross his mind, he pushed his body away and extended his arm, reaching out for Calvo. He glided through the glistening water without fear, feeling infinite, like nothing could stop him.

Calvo wrapped his fingers tightly around Max's hand and pulled him closer to his chest. His face lit up with a big smile, almost as if he was beaming with pride. "See? I knew you could do it. You're braver than you think."

He took note of the sensation of floating in the water. His body was weightless and buoyant as if a bubble were carrying him. Calvo's strong arms reached around him, cradling his back. "Yeah, I guess I am."

His voice softened. "Do I make you nervous?"

"I—no, it's just, Rylan is out there alone, and we have so much to do. I'm nervous around everyone, you know?"

His head bobbed from side to side. "Right, your anxiety." He hesitated before admitting, "I want you to feel safe around me. If you're nervous around me and us being close makes you uncomfortable, you're welcome to return to the pool's edge." Calvo began to release his arms from around Max's body.

Anticipation churned in his stomach like a butterfly that was delicately flapping its wings inside of him. "I...I do feel safe with you. I don't think I've ever been this comfortable around someone so quickly." It surprised him at how effortlessly these words were leaving his mouth. Calvo's embrace loosened, but Max's arms remained latched around his neck.

"So, this is okay." Calvo put his index finger on the side of Max's cheek and swiveled his head, so they were looking into each other's eyes. Their bodies were radiating heat as he wrapped his arm around Max's lower back.

Calvo's knee wrapped around his leg, and their bodies intertwined as they floated just beneath the water. Max could feel himself inching closer to submission with each passing second as his eyes glowed with enthusiasm and his breath became hushed.

His heart was beating furiously, but not because he was anxious like when Hannah had been in his bedroom. It was almost comical to think it had only been a couple of days prior and how much had changed since then. This was different. His eyes never left Calvo, noticing his eyelids begin to close and his mouth slacken.

Do I like this?

As much as he tried answering the question, he couldn't deny feeling safe and wanted. It was something he hadn't felt in a long time, if not ever and it was nice. His body was paralyzed as he gazed at the man inching closer to his face, his lips pursed in slow motion.

A small drip of water fell from the condensation above and landed on Max's forehead. His vision swirled, and his body began expelling heat as if he were boiling. Calvo's brows were taut, and his mouth was half-open as their irises briefly lingered on one another...until eventually, everything went dark.

Chapter Fourteen

The smell of dirt and old campfire ran across Max's nostrils as he groggily stirred. Blurred vision clouded his eyes, and after a few blinks, the clearing where they'd made camp came into view.

How'd I get back to the campsite?

The sound of the rushing stream filled his ears as he scanned the dusty ledge, his eyes falling on the empty square where Calvo's blankets should have been.

The events from the night prior flooded back into Max's brain. "Ella! Hannah!" The sound of his voice reverberated through the gorge, bouncing off the walls until it faded away into silence.

Damn, my body's heavy. Maybe it's an after-effect of the water from the spring?

He looked around and realized he was alone. Rylan's area was deserted, his messy blankets sprawled over the ground, and Calvo's area looked like he had never been there.

Did he leave without so much as a goodbye?

Silence met Max's ears, and his chest tightened, making his breath shallow.

A faint voice yelled from the trail a bit further, "Max! Is everything alright?"

He sprinted to the area his friend's voice had called from and, as he rounded the corner, saw Rylan holding two pouches of water. "There you are," Max breathed, his heart thumping in his chest. Relief quieted his anxious mind once he was able to see Rylan's wild blond hair. "Where were you? And where's Calvo?"

Rylan shrugged and handed him one of the satchels. "He was gone when I woke up this morning."

A pit grew in Max's stomach when he realized Calvo wasn't there to discuss his fragmented memories of the night prior. A thought struck him, and he looked at what he was wearing.

Did Calvo put my clothes back on me once we came back? What happened last night? Did he leave because of me?

He brought the pouch of water to his lips, and the cool liquid slid down his throat as his body yearned for water. Within seconds, Max had drained the satchel and dipped the opening back into the river to refill.

"There you are!" Calvo's voice boomed through the gorge. "I thought you both left without me."

Rylan scowled. "Tried to."

He threw two full leather satchels at the boys and smiled. "If we leave right now, we'll make it to the fairy garden by mid-afternoon."

Max slung the bag's strap around his shoulder and walked with his friends. He wanted to discuss what happened in the spring, but not in front of Rylan. Inside, his mind was in turmoil as he thought about his conflicting emotions from just a few hours ago with Calvo. Part of him believed he'd done something behind his girlfriend's back, even though he knew it wasn't true. Breaking the awkward silence, he asked, "Do you think Ella and Hannah are alright?"

Rylan put his hand on Max's back. "Don't worry, we'll find them."

Calvo's eyes roamed over the top of The Rift, where the sun's rays cast a brilliant cascade of light. "But we have to be quick, there's only three days left before the beacon lights."

He nodded, wetness pricking his eyes. "I hope that's enough time to find them and stop Samael from escaping." The timeline made him uneasy as every second seemed to count. "I-I just hate myself for letting them get taken because back at the Sofillian Camp, I promised Ella that she'd be safe, and," he cleared his throat, "nothing can happen to her. I'd never forgive myself."

"Nothing *will* happen to her," Calvo reassured him with a pat on his back.

"Yeah, Max, don't forget that Ella and Hannah are together. They'll look out for one another. She promised you." Rylan placed his palm on Max's shoulder, giving him a reassuring squeeze. "Before we leave this gorge, do you wanna try venturing into the goblin caves to find them?"

"They're likely at the castle to the north, if I had to venture a guess." Calvo pointed his ax toward the blue sky ahead of them.

Max shook his head. "He thinks Samael is holding them to help him once he's freed. It makes sense, so even if we went into the tunnels, we'd never find them."

Rylan's eyes widened as he sneered. "That dirty shapeshifter must be confident that he'll escape."

"Indeed he does." Calvo nodded and tightened his grip on the ax at his waist.

Everyone seems to despise the shapeshifters.

Rylan pounded his fist against his palm. "If Ella and Hannah have been taken to the Temple of Harper, that's exactly where we will go once we find Leona. It's our only way off this island, so it's a win-win."

What would Rylan and Calvo think of me if I were a shapeshifter? Would we still be friends or would they abandon me?

They walked silently for about an hour, each lost in their thoughts until sprigs of green grass began to cover the orange stones in the canyon like a thin film. Two colossal stone pillars that looked as if they could crumble at any second stood as an exit marking an end to The Rift.

Calvo lifted his arms above his head to stretch as warm sunbeams reached his skin. "The Garden of Bliss isn't too far from here. It'll be straight ahead as soon as we leave."

The transition from rocky gorge to the green and grassy meadow was drastic. Stepping into the field before them, insects flew into the air from underfoot, circling the plant life surrounding them. The trees, which looked bountiful and healthy, were surrounded by multicolored patches of flowers growing in droves around their trunks. The gorge seemed like a completely different world, separated from the outside field by an invisible border created by nature.

Watching Max's eyes question the clear line between The Rift and the meadow, Calvo pointed at the change of terrain. "When Samael was at full power, this area was a wasteland of dead plants, but after the Hero imprisoned him, the island's magic helped the nature in this area return. Once the balance was restored, it caused some places to separate, like oil and water. I assume the gorge extended into the field before, yet now there's a clear line from one to the other. Seeing that change tells me this area was impacted negatively during the land's restoration."

Nodding, Max crossed the line from The Rift and walked through the stems of leaves as they kissed his bare legs. Ever since the negative experience in the gorge, he had been constantly on edge, anticipating the next attack from goblins. The lush meadow in front of them hid their worries in a grassy sense of safety.

Rylan crouched with his elbows on his knees, eyes scanning dozens of gray mushrooms with red hats perched on their stems. "The fairy garden should be straight ahead. The clusters of mushrooms tell me we're close."

"What do mushrooms have to do with anything?"

"The Garden of Bliss is a magical reserve specifically dedicated to the fairy population," Calvo explained. "A circle of mushrooms indicates recent fairy activity within an area, and great magic can be drawn from that circle. A wide circle of mushrooms surrounds the garden, shielding the fairies from outside threats. I haven't seen one in years."

"Ella would be so excited that we were going to meet fairies." Max's voice quivered as he solemnly gazed at the cluster of fungi in front of him.

"I can't even imagine how excited she'd be." Rylan put his head into his hand and shook his head, stifling a laugh. "But these fairies are different from the ones in children's books."

Max took a deep breath and noticed the air around him smelled like sweet honey. "Do they not grant wishes or help you fly with pixie dust like some kind of Peter Pan shit? What's different about them?"

Rylan's eyes widened as he turned to Max, stopping them in their tracks. "That's exactly what you *don't* wanna say to them. It is extremely offensive, and their leader is a bit touchy with subjects like that."

"Noted."

"Fairies are generally very nice, but don't let their allure distract you; they're also some of the deadliest."

Max laughed. "Deadly isn't the word I thought you were going to use to describe fairies."

"Yes, deadly." Calvo's eyes grew wide. "They're some of the most technologically advanced beings on this island. We think it's because they have ways of seeing what's going on the Mainland to gather intel. Rumor is they found a bridge and can travel there at certain times, too."

A smile crossed Max's face as he thought of woodland creatures driving cars and playing video games. "Will they have a cell phone I can use to call Hannah?"

"We don't get proper cell phone service here." Rylan shrugged, and his lips turned upward. "Oh, there's one more thing I need to warn you about, but there's no point in telling *you.*"

"C'mon, Ry, I know you're baiting me right now."

"Me? Never." A sly smile painted his face as he glanced at Calvo. "But no matter how much they try, don't sleep with any of the fairies."

"You're a real dick, you know that?"

Rylan shrugged before admitting, "They make it hard to not make the most of their advances. Emphasis on hard." He snickered. "Every single fairy I've ever seen is drop-dead gorgeous, extremely flirty, and constantly horny. They get pregnant easily, and once the mother bears children, the father is killed. My merman uncle found out the hard way."

Calvo's laugh rang through the meadow. "Rylan's right. When fairies openly roamed the island, I saw them charm many innocent people before killing them."

Max's palms began to sweat as he quickly glanced at Calvo. "I'd sleep with one to spite you if they wouldn't kill me directly after. Talk about a bad first time."

"I think this is it."

At the tip of their toes were a line of mushrooms, but only meadow stretched before them. Max's eyes shifted back and forth as confusion burrowed into his mind.

"You'll see." Rylan firmly grasped his trident and latched onto Max's wrist with the other. "Step inside the circle and you'll see the fairies, but be careful, we don't know what's waiting for us."

Max lifted his foot and stepped inside the perfect line of mushrooms. A pressure instantly rested in the space between his eyes. He expected to see a few plants and flowers, based on what he'd seen in cartoons with Ella, but was pleasantly surprised by the vibrant array of colors and textures surrounding them. Beyond the line of fungi was a beautiful garden that looked as if it had come straight out of a picture book. A kaleidoscope of flowers stood tall, their petals pointed upward as if sunbathing. Bushes and shrubs bore multicolored fruits and berries that poked out from their green boughs, and a beautiful stone fountain spouted water just beyond the entrance. The world around him appeared as though he was viewing it through a crinkled, pearlescent cellophane veil.

He rubbed his eyes and saw a woman standing before him, holding a wooden gun with a firm grip.

"We come in peace," Rylan breathed as he stared down the firearm's barrel. "We came to find our friend."

The woman in front of him wore a knee-length skirt made of golden straw that swayed with each step, and her torso was covered with a corset of tightly bound green maple leaves. Each woman inside the circle wore very little clothing. It was impossible not to notice the stunning appearance of the fairies, who all looked like they had just stepped off a Victoria's Secret runway.

"Wow," Rylan whispered, nudging Max in the ribs. "I've

never been here, but now I don't wanna leave. Look at all the beautiful women! I wish there were such things as condoms here."

Calvo's head whipped toward Rylan so quickly, it was a wonder he didn't suffer from whiplash.

"Dude, shut up!"

A shared expression of disgust passed between the women as they looked at each other. The fairy closest to them narrowed her eyes. "If you come in peace, why disrespect us so?"

Calvo opened his arms and bowed his head. "Forgive the Prince of the Merpeople, I assumed he would know proper etiquette, but his mouth often works faster than his brain." He looked disapprovingly at Rylan before straightening his back and gesturing to the two boys. "I am from the Sofillian Camp in the Hesperian Jungle, we come in peace as I've been tasked with ensuring these *Mainlanders* leave the island immediately."

A gasp sounded throughout the assembly of women, and all the animals within the garden stiffened at the mention of the two being new to the island. It was as if their words had validated the women's suspicions that something was wrong.

The sound of wind chimes blew through the air, and a tall woman walked through the crowd of ladies. Her lovely brown hair was gathered in a bun, which was adorned with crystals that looked like tiny dewdrops. The way she moved was fluid, almost as if she were gliding above the grass instead of walking. "Everyone, please calm down. I'll handle this."

Chapter Fifteen

Max stood motionless, observing as the woman navigated her way through the swarm of fairies, a sense of awe washing over him. The air in the garden seemed to have gone still, and the only sounds were the whispers of the fae around them.

The woman's golden complexion radiated under the sun, and her eyes were deep pools of honey with thick, long lashes. Pointing her upturned nose at the two friends, she loudly asked, "What brings you to our garden?" She sounded as if she were an authoritative figure and was giving a speech—soft but very stern.

Rylan bowed slightly, making sure not to take his eyes off the multitude of guns pointed at his head. "I'm Prince Rylan of the Merpeople. You must be Queen Aeryth, is that correct?"

With a critical eye, she looked him up and down, then glanced at the other two before giving a nod of acknowlededgment.

"You've been an ally to my father, and I'm hoping you can

help me." Rylan's voice was unwavering and confident. "We're looking for someone who came from the Mainland. The Shellder advised us she's here, but has likely been integrated as a fairy. We need to find her so we can return home."

"H-her name is Leona," Max stuttered.

Queen Aeryth looked as if she smelled something foul. "The air has been tainted with a strange smell, and the garden's animals have been chattering much more than usual. I knew Mainlanders had made their way to the island. It was only a matter of time before you found your way to my garden."

"On our way here, a band of goblins kidnapped two of us." Max's chest tightened as he re-lived the scene in his head.

"It sounds as if some changes have already started to occur, and you're no closer to reuniting than you were when you arrived." Queen Aeryth rested her head in her hand, the crease between her eyes deepening. "The only reason goblins choose to kidnap instead of kill would be if someone they fear had ordered them to."

"Do you think it was Samael?" Rylan asked with a slight quaver in his voice.

"There have been rumors that the shapeshifter's spirit walks among us, biding his time before he's released from prison." The sunlight disappeared behind a cloud, darkening the garden as a shudder ran through the crowd. "Nevertheless, the goblins know you're Mainlanders and are trying to prolong your departure. The longer you're here, the more change will come to the island, and the sooner he can escape."

"You're correct, Queen Aeryth," Calvo said, his eyes darting towards the women holding guns around them. "During my recent research, I found evidence suggesting that Samael's followers are abducting islanders, but I couldn't determine their exact location. However, I suspect that they are being held in the castle to the north unless his followers found a way to access the temple."

"We need to find Leona before we go to the castle. Do you know where in the garden she is?" The castle was the final destination of Max's journey, and all he needed was to retrieve his friend to embark on the last leg of their adventure.

Queen Aeryth shook her head. "I don't know of a fairy by that name and if she was integrated within my home, it's unlikely anyone else will. As it's nearing the end of the day, I will allow you to stay the night and search for her, but once the light rises, you must leave. I cannot put my garden at risk by having Mainlanders inside for too long."

"If I may ask." Rylan put a finger up. "Every creature on the Island of Forever has a reason they don't want the change to come. For most, it's the fear of Samael, but I know that his reign didn't affect the fairies before his imprisonment, so why are you concerned?"

"Change brings consequence." Queen Aeryth opened her arms to gesture to the fairies around her holding their guns. "The women in this garden are fairies of nature and light. We're protective of one another and the beings on this island, but the male fairies weakened once the Hero gained the upper hand on Samael. We took advantage of their weakness and locked them in a tomb on the outskirts of our garden."

"Male fairies?" Max whispered and raised an intrigued eyebrow.

"What will happen if they get out of their tomb?"

"Chaos," she breathed. "We will no longer be safe. Think of them as the fairy version of Samael. We're just as scared of them as you are of that demon."

"I remember." Calvo nodded. "They were the first of Samael's supporters."

The queen nodded in concern before gliding away, her

regal presence fading into the distance. The fairies in the clearing stopped pointing their guns when she retreated and returned to their previous tasks.

"I think we were able to turn that around well." Despite the tense situation just moments before, Rylan found himself laughing as he watched the fairy who had held him at gunpoint now engaging in playful antics with a pack of young bunnies. "This garden's enormous. Let's get looking for Leona."

"Keep in mind that she may not initially remember us." Calvo's eyes darted back and forth between the girls, scanning their figures. A naked woman ran one finger down his muscular arms and giggled. His eyes never left her.

Why do I feel this way toward him if he's interested in these women?

Max remembered that the only way Rylan's memory returned was because of the Shellder's magic and nodded in understanding.

Starting their adventure within the Garden of Bliss, Max and Rylan looked at each fairy as they passed. The trance-like state they were in was evident from the carefree smiles on their faces and the relaxed, happy look in their eyes. The air was thick with the sweet aroma of fresh flowers and honey, accompanied by a gentle hum that seemed to be coming from the trees themselves. It was clear that the garden was designed to put all inside at ease, but Max couldn't be sure whether this was for genuine comfort or a false sense of security to make one vulnerable.

A beautiful blonde fairy held out a couple of yellow and blue colored berries. "Would you like some food? You must be starving." Her almond-shaped eyes glinted in the waning sunlight, and she giggled. "Go on, take a few. You handsome boys need your strength."

The fruity scent from her palm made Max's mouth water

as he gazed at the vibrant colors of the berries that looked like candy. His eyes lit up with excitement as he reached out eagerly to grab a few of the multicolored balls but pulled back with a sharp intake of breath when a sharp sting rapped his knuckles.

"Don't touch those berries," Rylan said, slapping the back of Max's hand once again. "Don't eat anything."

"Forgetting in the garden is a normal occurrence that can cost you your life. Now stay focused and look for your friend." Calvo's hand was firmly grasped around the wooden handle of his ax, yet his eyes never left the beautiful naked women that surrounded him.

Max couldn't lie. Every time he passed by a fairy asking if he wanted to try a different kind of food, he found it hard to resist. The smells emanating from each of the offerings made his mouth water, and their constant flirting made it more challenging. In addition to their ploys, many of the women were nearly naked, causing his eyes to wander rather than look for his friend. They learned to keep their distance from each of them because if they drew too close, the fairies would seductively wrap their arms around their shoulders or lightly kiss their bodies as they walked by in an attempt to lure them in.

Hours slipped by as they explored every inch of the expansive garden in search of Leona. The Garden of Bliss was like a slice of paradise, with abundant fruit trees, verdant foliage, and a clear waterfall that spilled into a stunning blue lagoon, drawing many women to its banks. Every shade in the garden seemed to be turned up to the maximum, making the blues even bluer and the greens even greener. Small, gleeful woodland animals played with the fairies, chasing them around the flowers or playing games around a tree. Max's eyes were wet as they scoured the area. Ella wouldn't want to leave this place.

Every time they passed by a beautiful woman, Max's eyes

lingered for a moment, wondering if he was attracted to them or if they possessed a magic that made their allure undeniable. His mind ran with questions, trying to find answers within himself. Their beauty was clear, but he didn't necessarily experience desire like he thought all guys did when they saw a naked woman.

Is there something wrong with me?

They neared the back of the garden and saw a group of fairy girls dancing in a circle near a bed of tulips.

Rylan nodded to the dancers. "Let's see if they know where she is."

Max turned his head to catch a glimpse of the girl's features. One had blonde hair—not Leona. Another had skin the color of snow—not Leona, and another had breasts busting out of her dress—*definitely* not Leona. As he followed each of the dancing girls in the large circle, one wearing neon green banana leaves with vines of pink and purple flowers entwined throughout, making her stand out as the brightest fairy in the whole garden. "I think I found her!"

Calvo followed Max's gaze and grabbed the girl garbed in green by the arm, pulling her aside. "Can we talk to you?"

Leona stumbled as if she were drunk, and the fairy girls swiftly pulled guns from their holsters, their wooden barrels pointed directly at the three boys. Her thick eyebrows raised in anger. "What do you want?"

"We'll tell you as soon as you talk to us."

Her eyes filled with lust once she gazed upon the shirtless man before her. "Who's this hunk?"

Lifting his strong hands, Calvo cupped his palm to the side of her face, just under her jawbone. "Let's chat and get to know one another."

Max was taken aback by his friend's demeanor and rose one of his eyebrows in surprise. He couldn't help but sneer in disgust at Leona's lovesick expression being so over-the-top; it was like something out of a cartoon.

Before he could put an end to the flirting, the fairy compound was surrounded by a mysterious cloud of darkness, which blew in like a plume of smoke and shadowed the rising moon. The eyes of the fairy girls grew wide with fear, and their hands immediately sprang to their holsters before hastily departing the area.

"Oh no," Leona whispered looking into the sky.

A film resembling a thin cloth stretched over the top of them with whorls of smoke weaved throughout. The moon was muted outside the veil, and a dark mist ran underfoot of the frantic fairies.

"We need to talk to you," Max spat at Leona amid the frenzy surrounding him. A small yelp emitted from her mouth and her warm breath brushed against his neck as her heart raced against his shoulder blades. "What're you doin—"

"Shh!" Leona covered his mouth with her palm.

Following her line of sight, he saw a cluster of yellow eyes creeping at the garden's edge. They were different from the ones he saw in the darkness at the outlook days prior. The yellow orbs looked crazed with hunger, enough to raise all the hair on Max's body. He glanced back at Leona, whose hazel eyes were wide in fright and her mouth closed shut, barely letting breath escape.

Almost as if someone had flipped a switch, all hell broke loose. The silence in the garden had turned to frantic chaos, and Queen Aeryth was shouting over the commotion, "Attention all fairies! We're under attack!"

What was once a peaceful, lulling sanctuary turned into a chaotic war zone within seconds. Fairies ran through the area as if their houses had caught fire, and their screams of terror sounded like they were in a haunted house. Jets of darkness flew by each of them, like laser beams zipping through the air. Within the smoky darkness, only piercing yellow eyes could be seen, encircling the garden like a menacing cat.

Everyone in the garden heard Queen Aeryth's voice boom over them. "Attention all fairies! Replenish your weapons and gather around the fountain to join your sisters in attack formation. We need to remove these beings from our home."

Leona urgently grabbed Max's arm. Her eyes lingered on his sword at his hip. "We need your help, the three of you. We can talk after." She looked at them with frightened eyes and furrowed brows.

Max and Rylan nodded to one another, and Calvo's biceps bulged as he held the handle of his ax with both hands. The surrounding air stiffened as the moon bathed the garden in a silver light. The three ran to the fountain towards the entrance to the garden and stood in line with the other fairies awaiting Queen Aeryth's orders.

The yellow eyes swarmed around the fairy retreat, biding their time to attack. The creatures were shrouded in darkness, and they moved so quickly that no one could catch a glimpse of their true form.

Max peered intently into the glowing eyes surrounding the garden's perimeter, hoping to see a sign of movement, but it was as if he was staring into an abyss. The air became motionless, and the usual sounds of nature were replaced with an eerie silence.

The tension in the air put everyone on edge, giving the impression that an explosion could come at any moment. Max's stomach churned with anticipation as he tightened his grip on the sword, its cold metal sending shivers down his wet hand. His heart pulsed against his chest, each beat drumming in his ears.

Oh no, not again.

With the darkness surrounding him, Max almost missed the black veins crawling over his body.

Go away, he willed the dark lines. *If Queen Aeryth sees, she may send us away without Leona or worse...order me to be executed. Would Leona and Rylan save me if they knew?*

Just as they crawled up to his elbow, they retreated back within his skin as if they were never there.

The darkness surrounding the garden was shattered by an ear-piercing scream, followed by trails of yellow beaming eyes streaming inside. As the creatures neared, Max could finally make out their faces. They looked like a fusion between a monkey and a bat, and their dark fur made them almost invisible in the darkness. Max could see their white fangs glistening in the dim light. The creatures were incredibly stealthy with the combined help of their large feet and rubbery skin-like wings that stretched across their back.

"Ladies!" Queen Aeryth yelled from the garden. "We're being attacked by a clan of imps! Form a circle and ready the protective barrier." As if on cue, the beautiful fairy women on the outskirts of the garden outstretched their arms while the others within the circle had their pistols pointing toward the yellow eyes encircling them.

"It's weird being on the other side of the pistols now, huh?" Rylan nudged Max with a grin.

The women surrounding Max amazed him, they appeared to be so confident as their stance was pointed and unwavering. To an outsider, the fairy army looked solid and unfazed by the attacking imps, a sisterhood of women who stood collectively and were ready to fight for their protection.

Each of the women on the perimeter of the garden raised their free arm and cupped a nearby fairy's hand. The air around Max felt electric, almost like lightning could strike any moment. A flash of white light erupted around the fairies, forming an impenetrable shield that sent the imps tumbling backward.

Attempting to rebound, the imps tried to raise themselves from the ground and their legs shook like they were drunk.

"Ladies," Queen Aeryth yelled. "The shield has partially paralyzed them. Now is our chance! Protect our home."

Chapter Sixteen

G unshots reverberated throughout the garden, and a thick plume of smoke flowered throughout the masses. Max unsheathed his sword, and Rylan raised his trident, running at the creatures before they regained their bearings.

A loud, angry screech from the imps shook Max to his core. The air was filled with the continuous sound of gunshots, and the fighters were enveloped in a web of danger as white bullets whizzed by. Each woman held her ground, standing with their chins held high and only moving if it was to refill their holsters.

Max watched as Leona narrowed her eyes at a rabid imp running directly at her. With a slight twitch at the corner of her lips, she pulled the trigger of her pistol. A white bullet sailed through the air, and planted itself directly into the beast's chest, spurting black liquid over the grass below. A howl came forth from its mouth as it lay twitching on the ground until death came to collect its newest addition.

The white bullets whizzing by reached many of their targets, but the imps that persisted were unscathed and sprang at the fairies as if they were on a bloodthirsty mission. Leona barely had time to react before a nearby imp launched itself into the air, its wings flapping madly. Its webbed feet kicked her wooden pistol out of her fingers and it fell to the grass as the imp then sank its teeth into her arm.

Hearing Leona scream in pain, Max's mind instantly snapped to attention. As a trail of blood dribbled from his friend's arm, he swung his sword through the air. A hollow thump reached his ears, and he knew that he had delivered a finishing blow to the creature. The imp's head rolled past his shoes before its body crumpled to the ground. A pool of black blood oozed from its neck, dampening the green grass below.

Leona turned to Max, clutching her damaged arm as her mind struggled to comprehend what had occurred. He knew that, to her, a stranger had jumped to action without knowing who she was but could see the truth just below the surface of her mind. Watching her scan him, a smile peeked at his lips as recognition slowly washed across her face. It was as if her brain was downloading a large file as bits and pieces came together to form a clear picture.

The veil that covered Leona's brain slowly lifted until a single name remained. "Max?" She bent her legs, picked up her gun, and aimed it at his shoulder, firing off a shot in one fluid motion. The white bullet sailed through the air, nearly missing Max's ear, and found a home between the eyes of an imp lunging at him from behind.

He winced at the warm sensation of black liquid splashing onto the back of his legs.

Seeing his astonished face, Leona gave a knowing smile and winked. "I got your back. Let's finish this."

They shared a look of understanding before Max began swinging his sword at the group of imps surrounding them. He shifted his gaze towards Rylan, who skillfully skewered an imp in the chest with his trident's prongs, then turned to see Leona, exuding confidence while shooting her gun. He was whole with his two best friends by his side, the only people who were missing were Ella and Hannah. Turning his attention to the imps that hadn't fallen and with a newfound sense of strength, he began waving his sword with much more precision, piercing the attacking imps to ensure they didn't make their way to the inside fairy circle.

With a swift slash, he wounded the arm of an imp when the voice of Queen Aeryth suddenly echoed in his ears. "Join me in producing one more protective light barrier as the majority of the imps have weakened. Return to your station around the fountain."

In his adrenaline-fueled spree, Max didn't realize how many of the fairies had been hurt by the imps. The remaining women were now gathered around the fountain, tending to battle wounds. On the dark, wet ground lay many broken bodies of imps and injured fairies, their screams pouring into the night.

The women touched hands once more, and the odd electric sound grew around them. A burst of light lit up the sky as the white barrier spread throughout the garden, lifting the dead imp bodies and the paralyzed creatures lying helplessly on the garden floor.

"Max! Help!"

The deep voice calling his name stopped him in his tracks. He turned and saw Calvo attempting to push an imp off the top of him. Its claws latched into his shoulders and drops of blood dribbled down his chest. "Queen Aeryth, stop the shield!"

Despite his efforts, his words were in vain. The white light picked up the remaining imps, along with Calvo and pushed them through the entrance and into the meadow outside. The last thing Max saw before Calvo disappeared were the whites of his eyes, scared and helpless, knowing that his strength couldn't help him at this moment.

"We did it!" Queen Aeryth yelled as the fairies around the fountain cheered. "I've locked the barrier so those disgusting creatures will not find their way back inside again."

Max turned his attention to the garden entrance. Imps sprung at the light barrier that covered the entrance, only to be pushed away. The imps' ferocious yellow eyes gleamed as they sprung forward, only to be thrown backward by an invisible shield that seemed to surround them.

"Queen Aeryth, open the barrier!" Max begged. "We need to help Calvo, he was taken by them!"

"Sacrifices must be made for the greater good," she answered with a definitive shake of her head.

"Wait!" Leona cried, spinning her body in a circle. "Where are Alette, Marin, and Rosette?"

All eyes circled the fountain before their attention turned to the horde of imps still attacking the barrier, their teeth gnashing as they hit the bubble of light.

"There they are!"

All attention turned toward the entrance and three fairy girls were latched in the beast's claws, struggling to fight. Several fairies released their guns from their holsters, hoping they could save the kidnapped individuals.

Where's Calvo? Surely he could have fought them off?

Queen Aeryth jumped in front of them. "Do not leave the protection of this garden. If you do, each fairy will face certain death. Those imps will feed on you to satisfy their hunger."

The queen's words halted their advance abruptly, and the sound of a deafening screech rose through the night as the imps quickly retreated, vanishing one by one into the shadows along with their hostages. The shriek was a frightening sound that lingered in their ears, as if it was laughing at them.

They know what they did.

Queen Aeryth retained her confident exterior, though it was clear that something within her had cracked at the thought of three fairies being taken by the imps. They stood still, watching her eyes flicker with her jaw locked. A shiver overcame their bodies as the woman's eyebrows narrowed toward Max and Rylan with a fire burning in her eyes.

"You two!" She trudged through the group of fairies as if she were a bull looking at a red cape. "This is *your* fault! This never would've happened if you two were not on this island! Now, three of our kin will be killed all because of *you*."

"It's partially my fault," Leona said in a defeated voice. Her head hung low as she faced the queen, and a gasp escaped from the remaining fairies. "I'm from the Mainland, too."

A heavy silence fell over the area as everyone tried to comprehend what they had just heard from Leona. The queen's eyes widened, and she focused intently on a point in the distance, lost in thought. "The three of you must leave this garden immediately. It's my fault for allowing you to stay as long as you have, but I will no longer allow anyone under my protection to be hurt. You're no longer welcome here."

Leona whipped around to look at Queen Aeryth, who had turned her head away. "Th-three? Even me?" Her eyes grew wet as she realized she was being thrust from her home.

The queen nodded and quietly proclaimed, "Yes, Leo, you're an outsider to this island, which threatens all living beings. You caused three of our own to be kidnapped and sent for death. You're hereby banished from the Garden of Bliss."

Leona's eyes grew wide, and unshed tears welled in her eyelids. "Wha...what? But this is my home."

"Come on, Leona, you have us," Rylan spat. "These fairies are all losers anyway. Who wants to stay in a weed-infested garden?"

Queen Aeryth's eyebrows furrowed as she reached for the gun at her waist. "Why, you little..."

"Wait, wait!" Max yelled with his hands in the air, moving between Rylan and the queen. "If we rescue the fairies that were taken, could Leona return? Our friend also was taken by the imps, so we have to save him, too."

"You mean Leo?" the queen corrected and folded her arms with a thoughtful look. "Knowing how primitive the imps are, it is likely that those shameless beings have already eaten Alette, Marin, and Rosette. You must leave the island before any more harm comes to us."

"I'll leave the island because it is my duty, but I'll still try to save the girls." Leona straightened her spine and her eyes softened. "Even though I am from the Mainland, I have memories spent with all of you and would hope you'd do the same for me."

A small smile crossed Queen Aeryth's face before pursing her lips. "Bring them back, and all will be forgiven." She turned slightly toward Max. "How long have you been here?"

"Three days, and once morning comes, we will be heading into our fourth."

The queen's face paled and she whispered, "That means we only have one day before the beacon lights. Once that happens, we'll have limited time before Samael has a chance to escape. You must hurry." She turned her back to them and took a few steps before speaking over her shoulder. "I'll prepare a fairy army to be on standby should they be needed."

The queen doesn't have much confidence in us.

Max's arms erupted in goosebumps, and his hair stood on end as the fairies around him parted, revealing a path leading straight to the exit. All eyes were on the three of them as they made their way down the aisle to the dark field outside.

Standing underneath the archway, Leona looked back at

her fairy family and saw nothing but disapproving stares. They stepped onto the precipice of the mushroom circle, and Max looked toward his friend, feeling her emotions of abandonment from the home that had rejected her. Once they stepped outside the archway, he put an arm around Leona's shoulder as she wiped a tear from her eye once her fairy friends disappeared behind the magic of the veil.

The light from the garden faded behind them, and their feet touched the meadow as they stepped outside the mushroom circle. The meadow was completely empty, with not an imp in sight. Each leaf of the overgrown grass outside was coated in dew, making it resemble a delicate work of art. The forest was alive with the sounds of insects stirring from their sleep, their whizzing adding to the early morning orchestra that was punctuated by the muffled sniffles of Leona.

Rylan held a hand to his face so only Max could hear. "I'll break the silence." He nudged Leona in the ribs with a sly smile. "Do you think that once we rescue these fairies, your friends will wanna ravish me with their naked bodies?"

She wiped the remaining tears from her eyes with the back of her hand. "I forgot how annoying you are."

Max laughed heartily at his two friends who were bickering like old times, bringing back memories of walking home from school together. "Let's find the fairy girls and rescue Calvo. Where do these imps live?"

Leona pointed straight ahead of them, across the rolling meadows. "There's an abandoned village that leads to a castle that's on the outskirts of the meadow called Berylon. When Samael was in charge, the imps gained power, created an army, and took over. As a reward for their loyalty, that nasty shapeshifter gave the imps complete control over the fortress and cast it into darkness. The people who lived there either died in a battle or vanished without a trace, and the creatures have remained within the castle walls ever since."

Until today.

Max's throat went dry as he thought about Samael. He couldn't help but wonder if all shapeshifters were like him or if there were others who were more peaceful.

"We have our crew back together." Rylan threw his fist in the air. "Call us the imp exterminators. We can get rid of all your imp-festations."

A sense of shame crossed his body.

How could I have ever considered leaving them? This just feels right.

"I think I prefer your vulgarity over your puns." Leona rolled her eyes.

Everyone laughed at Rylan's positivity, although Max couldn't help but silently acknowledge the pit in his stomach thinking about the attack on the Garden of Bliss and what may await them inside the castle.

Chapter Seventeen

They traveled through the meadow for hours, and the sky slowly brightened, creating a mesmerizing blend of blues and oranges. The stars disappeared, and the expansive field was illuminated by the first rays of sunlight. As the sun rose each day, their task seemed more and more impossible as time continued to slip away.

The overgrown grass underfoot concealed any trace of the once-existing road, leaving them to forge their own way. The rustling caused by the trio's movements prompted the grasshoppers to jump from leaf to leaf and the burdocks to cling to their clothing in thick clusters.

Leona turned toward her merman friend. "Isn't it weird to have two sets of memories? It's like my brain is totally full of information."

"Yeah." Rylan nodded. "I guess that's why if you stay long enough, you begin to forget."

Max continued to have trouble understanding how the island's integration operated. "If I stayed on the Island of Forever, I'd eventually forget my life back home?"

Rylan pursed his lips and gazed downward. "It'd be like you never existed, the memories fade from one world to the other."

Silence enveloped the friends with the ominous answer. Leona pushed her way through the tall grass that surrounded them. "It's strange that Rylan brought down the mood, but I've had something on my mind since I saw you in the garden."

"What's that?"

She paused, a smile dancing on her lips. "Let's talk about your friend, Calvo!" Leo put her hand to her heart. "Ohmigod, those muscles! His eyes! Can we trade Rylan for him?"

"You'd replace me with that dummy? He's the definition of a himbo," Rylan huffed and put his fingers through his blond hair. "Even if he didn't get taken by the imps, I can guarantee he still wouldn't be into needy girls."

"C'mon, Calvo's not dumb. He's helped us a lot since we got here." His friend's intense gaze burned through him, and Max was so anxious that he imagined his ears would burn if he dared touch them.

"Stop defending him, Max," Rylan spat. "I don't know why you do whatever he says. It's like he's become your best friend or something."

"He's my friend and I'll defend my friends when someone's talking shit about them, just like I'd do for you." His face grew hot, and he shifted uncomfortably. "What're you even saying?"

"Whatever he says, you agree with. You're always sneaking looks at him, and wherever he goes, you follow. When he's around, it's like I'm the third wheel. It's like you're his puppy or —or his boyfriend—and I'm not losing you as my best friend to someone like that."

Rylan's sudden accusation caught Max off guard, leaving him bewildered and struggling to find the words to defend himself. "You don't know what you're talking about."

"Do you think I give a shit?" Rylan tapped his forehead with his palm in annoyance. "Stop hiding things from me. I can't be your best friend if I don't even know who you are." He paused, his breath heavy and the whites of his eyes blazing. "Or has someone else taken that role?"

Is he serious?

"What're you even talking about?" The words stung because he knew there was truth and hurt buried in each syllable. Max pointed to the two people with him. "*You're* my best friend and no one is coming between us. Period." He gazed at Rylan's stiff posture and timidly opened his arms to embrace. His arms reached around his friend's body, and he didn't let go until he felt Rylan loosen with the light return of the gesture.

"You two needed that." The tense air evaporated and Leona threw her arms around both of them. "We're stuck with one another, whether we like it or not!"

"Our friendship isn't going anywhere, Ry." Max left their embrace and collapsed one hand around his friend's neck, looking into his eyes with sincerity. "I promise."

Rylan smiled and exhaled a long breath of air. "I believe you."

Sheepishly, Leona asked, "Not to break up this moment, but neither of you have explained to me why Calvo was with you. Who is he anyway?"

"He's been babysitting us since we left the Sofillian Camp." Rylan rolled his eyes with a scowl.

"Rylan's a *big* fan." Max nervously laughed, testing the waters. "His sister told him to help us get home before Samael gets out. He made sure we were safe after Ella and Hannah got taken."

"Taken?" Leona stopped in her tracks and grabbed Max's shoulder. "Where the hell are they now, Max? Did something happen to them?"

He looked to the ground and shook his head. "Goblins kidnapped them. We've been told they were likely taken to the castle within Berylon."

"This isn't good," Leona stated, kicking her feet through the dirt. "Samael is growing stronger and he better hope I don't get a hold of him."

"Why?"

She took out her gun and held it in front of her. "Because the last thing he'll see is a bullet between his eyes. You know Ella and Hannah were kidnapped to assist in his escape, just like the three fairy girls, right?"

Max nodded but didn't want to discuss the grim outlook further. He was warm and uncomfortable as a sticky liquid from milkweed clung to his clothes. Bugs bit at his exposed arms and his body was tired from the walk.

"Question for you." Rylan turned to Leona and raised his eyebrow. "Why does everyone in the fairy garden call you Leo?"

She knelt and picked up a small acorn, running her fingers across its smooth surface as her cheeks turned pink and shrugged. "That's just what they've always called me. It's just who I am here." She squinted one eye at the acorn. "I kinda like it."

Max had never heard Leona verbalize this in all the years he had known her. "Do you want us to start calling you Leo?"

As she considered the suggestion, her eyes flickered with interest. "Yeah, that would be nice. I think it fits me better than my name from the Mainland." A slight smile peeked at her lips as her eyes re-focused on the seed in her hand.

"What're you doing?" Max asked as he watched the odd behavior.

She placed the seed between her thumb and forefinger. "Fairies can craft bullets from natural elements, like seeds and berries. All we need is a little pressure." To demonstrate, she closed one eye, and the oval-shaped seed turned round. "Once it's made, we use our fairy powers to infuse them for a stronger impact."

"What do you mean? I know Rylan is a merman, so he has the ability to manipulate water. What extra powers do you have?"

Bending at her hips, Leo grabbed a handful of acorns littered on the ground, placing each one between her fingers. "Originally, the fairies were made from powerful magic, which allows us to infuse natural elements with our own. For comparison, imps are made from darkness, so they constantly hunt and try to eat us for a small burst of light magic. Apparently, we taste like candy to them."

"If fairy girls taste like candy, I *definitely* need you to set me up with one of your friends," Rylan quipped sticking out his tongue.

"I'll never understand how even on a magical island, your first concern is your dick," she huffed and rolled her eyes, turning her head solely to Max. "Anyways, back to what I was saying—we take the seeds or berries and turn them into bullets and then instill our light magic in them, which can create a paralyzing effect when it reaches the target." She briefly placed her palm over the acorns before presenting them to him, showing that their once-brown shells had turned white.

Max examined the acorns. "Back in the garden, the fairy magic made the air still, like lightning could strike at any second."

"It does when there are large amounts, like the shield the fairies had produced." She nodded, dropping the acorn bullet in her gun's chamber. "Rylan, stand there so I can show him."

"Hell no! Are you trying to kill me? I'm from the water, which doesn't mix well with electricity."

Leo laughed and holstered her gun. "I was only joking...just don't piss me off again, or I might shoot a small seedling at you, just as a reminder."

They reached the top of a small hill and saw a faint dirt path form at their feet. The rocky road snaked down the hill and hugged the cliff, giving a breathtaking view of the ocean below. The light became progressively dimmer as the sky turned a deep gray, making it difficult to see even though it was still late morning. It was as though the clouds were strategically placed to prevent any sunlight from breaking through. The silhouette of a large stone castle looked like a shadow painted across the sky, its magnificence standing grandly erected in darkness.

Max, Leo, and Rylan followed the dirt path, their cheeks getting kissed by the slight mist from the water. The salty scent of the sea was carried by the wind, and speckles of water dotted their faces with every crash of waves against the cliff.

"Oh look," Leo yelled and pointed toward a small dot floating miles above the ocean. "There's the Temple of Harper."

"The Shellder told us that's how we can return home." Max squinted at the small speck resting above the clouds. "How do we get there?" They had only a day and a half left, and the vast amount of tasks ahead of them began to seem hopeless.

"The only people who are granted entry to the Temple of Harper are those given strict permission by the King and Queen of Berylon who once lived within the castle up ahead. Maybe we'll find a clue on how to enter the temple inside the castle. Let's focus on rescuing the fairies and our friends right now."

The closer they came to the fortress, the more the surrounding nature seemed to wither away, leaving only a desolate path leading to its gates. It was as if the progressive darkness had sucked the life out of everything it touched.

Leo and Rylan continued to bicker with one another behind Max when a faint noise reached his ears. Placing a finger to his lips, he turned to face his friends and scanned the horizon ahead. As they walked down the path, a piercing screech rang out, making them stop in their tracks.

"D'you think we can do this?" Max's voice shook as he asked, the screams of the imp intensifying and causing him to doubt himself even more.

"We're gonna have to." Leo sighed as she walked toward the castle. "I made a promise."

"C'mon, man." Rylan slapped Max on the back. "We are all pretty badass. Remember, we're the imp exterminators."

Max feigned a smile at his friend, but his mind gave him every excuse not to progress up the path. The metal hilt of his sword was reassuringly cool in his hand as the familiar sensation of wetness developed in his palm. He gulped down the water from his canteen, but the ball in his throat remained stubbornly in place. He didn't know what they'd be facing in the castle, but he was nervous. Reaching into the leather satchel at his waist, a sense of reassurance washed over him once he felt the cool glass of the vial filled with water clasped between his fingers.

As they approached the wall that circled the town, they couldn't help but notice the cracks in its walls and the vines that had taken root in the decaying structure. The crumbling stone barrier towered above, too tall to climb, yet looked as if a gust of wind could topple it like a house of cards. The murky brown moat encircling the wall was disturbed by bubbles pushing through the green bits of algae, indicating the presence of creatures swimming underneath.

"How do we get in?" Max asked, looking across the water.

The fortress was only accessible by a large bridge that shielded the entrance. The cracked brown platform was held tightly in place by rusted black chains.

Leo turned to Rylan and nudged him in the ribs. "Well, mister merman, why don't you jump in the moat and swim around and try to find an opening through the sewers?"

Rylan peered over the side of the river, looked at the thick brown water, and raised an eyebrow. "I wouldn't be able to breathe in that polluted water, but nice try, Leo."

She folded her arms while looking exasperated. "Well, what good are you?"

Raising his arms, Rylan waved his hands in a circular motion with his eyes closed.

"What's he doing?"

"I'll get us in. I just need to concentrate," Rylan snapped. "That's my way of kindly telling you to shut the hell up."

"Since when does Rylan tell us anything kindly?" Leona whispered, nudging Max in the ribs as they stifled a laugh.

They were mesmerized as he waved his arms, his wrists twisting and turning. After a brief pause, a meager stream of murky water rose from the moat and penetrated the crevices of the drawbridge. Rylan's nose wrinkled, and his eyes fluttered before he made a swift, jerking motion with his hand.

Max's attention was drawn to the drawbridge as it shuddered slightly and slowly descended. "Ry, you did it!"

"I'm impressed," Leo admitted, clapping her friend on the back. "I guess you're not useless after all."

"Women are usually impressed with me and my performance."

Max and Leo didn't stroke his ego, for the eerie atmosphere of the deserted village struck them both as they entered the fortress. Dirty cobblestone streets were lined with abandoned houses with broken windows and doors hanging off their hinges. The streets were empty, and the buildings stood silent, as if the town itself was grieving. Every step Max took was calculated in fear that he might break the silence, and he found himself treading slowly and carefully, afraid of disturbing the peace.

While cautiously tiptoeing through the town, the three friends noticed the remains of children's toys scattered throughout the streets and a once-vibrant stone mural now dull and faded in the square. The castle stood before them, its towering peaks casting an ominous shadow against the sky. From within, they could hear blood-curdling screams and agonizing wails.

The trio stopped at a locked set of metal double doors at the entrance to the castle. "Well," Max whispered as the animalistic sounds grew more vibrant. "I think we found the right place, but how do we get in?"

"Look over there." Leo pointed toward a window to their left with a small flickering light that seemed to shine through the darkness. The desolation around them was so complete that the slightest flicker of light seemed like a beacon in the darkness. "What's that?"

Hugging their bodies against the castle wall, they stealthily ran to the window. "Let's peek inside." Rylan crouched to the ground, balancing on the balls of his feet.

"Ugh, why me?" Max whined as he straddled his friend's shoulders. He grasped onto Rylan's head as his friend attempted to stand, wobbling as if they were going to fall.

"When did you get so heavy?" Rylan asked as he unsteadily wobbled.

Calvo wouldn't have an issue holding me up.

Moments passed while Rylan found his footing, allowing him to balance his friend atop his shoulders. As Max was lifted toward the window, he peeked into the dim room. Inside, the walls reached to the roof of the castle and had books upon books resting on dusty mahogany shelves that hadn't been touched in years. Expensive-looking furniture was placed throughout the room, and an unlit fireplace sat at the far end. Abandoned desks and tables were arranged in clusters, adorned with neatly placed pens and blank sheets of paper, eager to be used for research.

"What's in there?"

"Books...lots of them."

"Just books?" Rylan asked.

"Obviously it's a library, you idiot!" Leo yelled into Rylan's ear. "Do you see where the light is coming from, Max?"

As Max shifted his focus back to the dirty window, he was startled to find himself face-to-face with a girl holding a candlestick. He was taken aback by the sudden surprise, causing him to jump and Rylan to lose balance. They fell to the ground and huddled together, their eyes fixed on the flickering flame of the ominous girl's candle in the window.

Chapter Eighteen

"Who the hell was that?" Rylan yelled as he collected himself from the ground.

Max glanced back toward the window, and the girl had disappeared, although the faint glow of candlelight flickered in the shadows. "I dunno, let's try to get inside again."

Rylan nodded and crouched down once again, allowing him to balance on his shoulders. As Max leaned in the window, a yellow flame flickered and danced in his peripheral vision. Craning his head, he saw a small girl perched on top of a towering stack of books. In her hands, she clutched a solitary candlestick, its body marred by hardened wax tears. The flame flickered softly, casting dancing shadows on the wooden floorboards, illuminating the small girl hunched over a book.

He pressed on the window, and it didn't budge. "It's locked," he whispered to his two friends below, "but I see that girl. Should I knock and ask her to let us in?"

Rylan grunted beneath Max's weight. "Does she look possessed or like she's gonna murder us? I need to know which kind of little girl in horror movies we're talking about."

Max glanced back at the little girl innocently turning a page of a book and shook his head. "Neither, she's unarmed. She might be around twelve or thirteen?"

"Knock on the window and get us in!" Rylan yelled impatiently.

Max tapped his finger on the dirty, glass window quietly, then with a bit more force. The little girl was lost in thought until the fourth tap caught her attention. As she walked toward him, he gave her a small wave, noticing the furrow of her eyebrows as she approached him.

Her hair was a wild mess of curls that seemed to have a life of their own. The plain white dress around her shoulders gained a touch of elegance with the addition of the golden sash tied around her waist, while constellations of dark freckles on the bridge of her nose twinkled like stars at twilight.

"I thought my eyes were deceiving me when I saw you," she whispered, scanning the three friends with her deep green eyes. "I haven't seen people in a long time. Who are you?"

"Friends," Max whispered to her and gestured for her to unhook the clasp that kept the window closed. He hoped that flashing an innocent smile would help him with his case.

She squinted at him and nodded, clicking the lock free from the window. A warm breeze blew through the library, reviving the dust that had settled on the floor from years of not being used. Max jumped into the fortress and leaned his body out the window, his arm outstretched to pull his two friends inside. Their feet struck the hard, wooden floor, and he realized that despite the fireplace not being lit, the library's atmosphere was warm and cozy.

"Who are you? Are you real?" There was a serene quality to her quiet voice that made them feel at ease. She had a slight accent that made her words sound rich with knowledge.

Leo crouched to the little girl's eye level and introduced all of them. "I'm a fairy from the Garden of Bliss." She pointed to the two boys. "That's my friend, Max, and the other boy who smells like rotten fish is a merman named Rylan."

"Hey, I live under the sea. Not everyone can lie in flowers all day!" Rylan interjected.

The little girl looked entertained by Leo and Rylan's banter and laughed heartily. "You fight like a married couple. How long have the two of you been together?"

The two of them looked at each other with wide eyes, their backs straight. "We're *absolutely* not dating," Leo and Rylan yelled in unison, cheeks blazing.

With the little girl by his side, Max joined her in chuckling at his friend's unwavering stance, finding it both endearing and comical. He turned to her and asked, "What's your name?"

"Reina." Her voice cracked as her large eyes became glassy with unshed tears. She tried to hide them, but a sniffle betrayed her as she wiped her cheek. "I'm sorry, I'm constantly in a state of grief. You see, it was my duty as princess to protect Berylon and everyone in it. Once Samael stormed in, too many people died trying to protect me." The tears welled in her eyes, threatening to spill over at any moment.

Leo provided a kind smile and softened her voice. "Tell us what happened and how we can help."

"We're here to kick some ass!" Rylan exclaimed.

"You came to my castle to get rid of the imps?" A look of hope glinted in her eyes, and she exhaled a large breath of air in an attempt to compose herself. She nodded to them and spoke in a hushed tone, her voice shaking with emotion. "Long ago, Samael came to Berylon and demanded that I give him permission to travel between worlds whenever he wanted. I refused his request, and that turned him completely mad."

"The beginning of the end," Rylan interrupted.

Reina nodded. "A while passed until another Mainlander

came to the Island of Forever, requiring an audience with me. The person asked for my blessing to find the Hero, who is prophesied to emerge in times of great danger on the island."

"The Hero will rise with a gleaming sword, right?" Rylan asked.

"Correct." Reina nodded. "It had been weeks since I last saw or heard from them, and I began to wonder if something had happened to them. Samael's army grew, and fear spread from shore to shore. One day, he launched an attack on my castle, and many of my subjects died while protecting me. I remember sitting in my bedroom, praying for the Hero to show and put an end to all the fighting, but they never did. Having taken control of Berylon, Samael became determined to use his army to conquer the island and eventually the Mainland."

"Lemme guess," Rylan interrupted. "Then the Hero showed up?"

"But only after the castle had fallen to the imps and most of the island had been destroyed. The Hero fought Samael for days until they learned that imprisoning him was the only way to ensure he couldn't spread his evil. By sacrificing themself, the Hero created a holding cell that imprisoned the demon in the center of the island, bringing an end to the chaos and restoring normalcy."

"How haven't the imps found you?" Leo asked.

"When Samael seized Berylon, I thought all hope was lost so I placed a spell on myself. Its purpose was to ensure that someone would remain behind to restore the land if the castle ever fell and has been passed down by my family for generations. While my body remains in an untouchable slumber, my spirit is free to wander the island, waiting for the day someone will wake me."

Hearing that this little girl was a spirit, Max took a moment to take note of the details he'd missed prior. Her body appeared solid, yet as she moved, he noticed a faint translucence he hadn't seen before. "It looks like your spell worked because the island has been completely restored, and life has returned to normal."

Leo smiled at the little girl's relief before turning to her merman friend with her forehead wrinkled. "How did you know parts of the story before Reina told it?"

"You clearly don't pay attention." He scoffed. "Ana has told us this story so many times, I think it's ingrained in my brain."

"I'm surprised you remember that story, Rylan." Leo laughed. "I thought you were always too stoned to comprehend what Ana was saying."

"There was food and a story. I was high and interested."

"Like your pathetic love life," Leo said under her breath.

Max's gaze fell upon the little girl standing before him. "You said your spirit was free to roam the island. You look pretty real to me. Why haven't you left to find help?"

"I am real, but I'm not in my physical body. In this state, I'm limited to basic movements, such as picking up items and talking. If I dared to leave the castle walls, Samael's spell of darkness would consume me, leaving me lost and unable to return to my physical body. Once the spell was complete, I ran to this library and locked the door. I found solace in books, which allowed me to explore far-off lands and embark on new adventures while I waited."

"You must get lonely."

"At times...yes. I hope my little sister was able to get out of the castle and is safe." A look of sadness filled Reina's eyes. "Apologies, I got so wrapped up in my regrets I forgot to ask what you three are doing in *my* castle?"

Leo laughed. "It's a long story, but we're from the Mainland and were brought here by a storm."

"My sister and girlfriend were kidnapped by goblins, they're our first priority."

"What about lover boy?" Rylan snickered.

Max jabbed him in the ribs. "And our friend, Calvo, was taken by imps. He told us everyone was likely brought to this castle," Max explained. "Before you say anything, we're aware that we must leave the island as soon as possible. We just need to save our friends and get to the Temple of Harper so we can go home."

"And save the three fairies!"

"Yes, you all must leave. Otherwise, that disgusting shapeshifter risks freedom." Her nostrils flared, and her upper lip grimaced like she had eaten rotten fruit. "The goblins and imps have been frequently bringing people and have held my people hostage, so you may be in the right place."

The dancing shadows on the walls grew longer and more twisted as the flame on the candle burned lower and lower.

"The fairies are likely being held in the throne room, that's usually where the imps feed." Reina shivered. "I've heard their screams too many times."

Max was stunned by Reina's nonchalant tone, as if this were a regular occurrence. Leo had told them that the fairies tasted like candy to imps, but he wasn't ready to hear the reality.

"That's messed up." With a look of disgust, Rylan shook his head.

"What about the hostages?" Max asked.

She paused, considering for a moment before shrugging. "They're probably close by. The castle is the gateway to the temple, which Samael is keen on reaching."

"According to Calvo, they're probably being held here unless they've found a way to get inside the temple," Max replied

"Then let's get going!"

Reina shook her head and held a finger in the air, pointing to the wooden double doors at the room's far end. "The library doors must remain closed, as the imps have infested the castle. Making any noise will only attract more of them, and you won't be able to make it to the throne room. The imps are rogue creatures driven by hunger but will always protect each other in the attempt of danger. If you want to save everyone, you must sneak into the locked throne room where there's a limited number of imps."

"How did they get into the throne room in the first place if it is locked?" Rylan asked.

Reina pointed above her. "They fly in through the west tower, go down the turret stairs, and can reach the throne room through the royal study. If you can make it inside, the imps outside the room will not know of anything happening. Back when my father was king, the room was used for confidential meetings, so if you can sneak in, the imps in the rest of the building will be none the wiser."

Rylan cocked his head to the side in sarcasm. "How do you expect us to get in there? Scale the castle walls and climb to the top of the west tower? That won't be obvious at all."

Reina turned to Leo and rolled her eyes. "I can see why you're always fighting with him."

"I thought I asked a legitimate question!"

The little girl reached to her neck and unclasped a chain. Sitting in her palm was a golden key that was bright against the darkness in the library. While the object had a rough, jagged end that indicated it was meant for practical use, the intricately looped handle gave it a sense of elegance and sophistication.

Reina walked to the unlit fireplace and ran her fingers over the rough surface of the mantle, the coolness of the stone sides, and the gritty texture of the sooty back of the hearth.

"What are you looking for? Can we help?"

"Isn't it obvious?" Rylan interjected. "A keyhole, dummy."

"In the firepl—"

"Here it is!" Reina's voice rang as her fingers found the hole hidden in an old brick. Her small hands inserted the key to reveal a hidden door that opened in the brick. "This is a secret passage only known to the royal family. Far below Berylon are tombs that hold each generation of leaders. To reach the crypt, you can use one of three entrances: a secret passage in town, this hidden door...and guess where the third is." A smile crept across the girl's face.

"The throne room!" Leo breathed.

Reina nodded as a smirk pulled at her mouth. "The secret tunnels throughout the castle were made to escort the royal family to safety if there ever was an invasion, but we're beyond that now. Following this tunnel to the crypts, you'll find yourself at an intersection. Choose the path that leads right. There will be a stone wall with a lever which will lead you to the study outside the throne room."

"What does it look like?" Max asked.

The little girl's shoulders lifted, and she scrunched her face. "Admittedly, I've never been on that side of the wall before. You will know that you're in the correct area if you find yourself at a dead end." She took a moment to think. "To enter the tombs from the study, you must push the lever, so I assume you must pull from the crypt to activate the door?"

The three of them nodded in understanding.

She held up one finger. "Before you go, please do me one favor."

Max nodded to her as they developed a single file line into the fireplace.

Reina placed the small golden key in Max's palm. "Take this with you. If you're able to drive the imps out of this castle, go to my room in the east tower, and wrap my fingers around the handle of this key. It'll wake me up."

Max's fingers closed around the cool metal before he slipped it into his pocket. "We'll get the key to your body."

The girl flashed a bright white smile. "Thank you and be safe in the crypt. There are a few surprises down there."

"Great," Rylan said sarcastically. "Dead people and surprises, just what everyone loves to hear. I can *barely* contain my excitement."

Chapter Nineteen

M ax stumbled through the secret door and grabbed a wooden torch on the wall. Leona swiftly drew her gun from its holster, pulled the trigger, and the infused bullet caused the tip of the wood to burst into a bright orange flame. He shook his head in wonderment. "Well, that's one way to do it."

Leo stepped into the passageway and nodded to him with her eyebrow raised. "It looks like the island gave *you* some magic, too."

Max stopped in his tracks.

How does she know?

His heartbeat raced, and the wood from the touch became wet from his hands. "Wh-what do you mean?"

"Look at you—you're leading us into a crypt. There's no way you'd do this at home." She smiled at him with genuine amazement in her eyes. "It's like since being here, you've turned into someone else, someone more confident."

"Uh...nope. I haven't turned into anything but myself. I just wanna get Ella and make sure she's safe."

I haven't changed at all, what does she see?

"Yeah." Rylan squeezed his shoulder. "Bring this kind of ego back home and you'll never leave the bedroom, believe me!"

"Ohmigod, Rylan, shut up!" Leo yelled, her voice echoing off the stone walls.

Although his fear and anxiety were still evident on the island, he was mentally making an attempt to be more assured in his skills and capabilities. The strangeness of the adventure heightened his courage and pushed him to take risks he never would have before. He wanted Ella to see that her big brother, who always doubted himself, could make more confident decisions. It also helped that he knowingly had a cure for his unease tucked away in his backpack that he could use at any time.

The trio walked along the passageway until they reached a flight of stone steps that led them around a corner and deeper into the crypt. The stones in the secret passage seemed to be decaying, which gave the walls a sickly green hue. Old and stagnant air reached the trio's nostrils as they delved deeper.

Reaching the bottom of the steps, a large open room spread out in front of them. Max's hand gripped the torch tightly, the only beacon of light in the impenetrable darkness that lay before him. The eerie crypt was so silent that the only thing that could be heard was their shallow breaths.

Hesitantly stepping forward into the room, their eyes fell upon the evenly spread stone caskets. The dim torchlight illuminated one of the large stone boxes adorned with precious stones and gems of various colors and elegance.

"What is this?" Max asked, running his hand along the top of the box. Etchings carved into the stone ran beneath his fingers. He brought the torch closer and squinted to make out the letters his fingers were tracing.

"Queen Beatrice," Rylan read aloud with his nose atop the casket.

Leo shivered, a chill going down her spine. "Let's just get out of here as fast as we can."

Max quickly pulled his arm away, and his heart raced as the stone slab beneath his fingers trembled ever so slightly.

My mind has to be playing tricks on me.

The scraping sound of stones echoed around them until there was a sudden, loud thud. Just as he was about to look around, a loud noise echoed through the room, and his friends let out a terrified yelp as the coffin began to open.

"I'll say it again—let's get out of here!"

Max, Leo, and Rylan were caught off guard as the stone slabs fell around them, causing them to instinctively huddle together for safety. In the light's din, they noticed the outline of a figure rise from a coffin nearby as the shadow neared and entered the torches glow. With dead eyes and a twisted grin, a gray skeleton loomed before them.

Voices could be heard around the room, each saying the same thing: "Evil must leave this place." The skeletons of past kings and queens were ascending from their coffins, their heads focused on the trio.

Are they talking about me?

"L-let's find a way out of here," Rylan stammered. "Reina said to proceed straight until we reach a split, then take the passage on the right. Let's split up and meet at the entrance to the passage after making our way back to the far wall."

"Split up?" Max asked as his entire body shook in fear. "That's how everyone dies in horror movies."

"As much as I hate to say it, Rylan's right," Leona begrudgingly admitted. "We need to find the way out, and splitting up will allow us to cover more ground."

"Say it again!" Rylan laughed before squeezing Max's shoulder. "Just stay away from the skeletons."

Rylan dashed to the left side of the tomb while Leo sprinted towards the right, dodging the caskets that were coming to life.

Max's stomach sunk as he focused his attention forward, realizing he was directly in the path of the approaching skeletons. With sarcasm dripping from his voice, he charged toward the army of bones and called over his shoulder, "Thanks, guys!"

He ran through the crypt, circling around the coffins like a child playing hide-and-seek. Each skeleton had their bony arms outstretched, their old fingers curled from decay. Max turned to look behind him, and every hair on his body was standing at attention once he realized that most of the skeletons were focused on chasing only him.

It took Max less time than he thought to reach the back wall. Swinging the torch to his right, the light caught Leo's eye while Rylan hurried to keep up behind him. "Down here." Max pointed to the dank stone hallway that curved around a bend. Despite their slow start, the skeletons began to gain traction, their army growing with each passing moment.

"Ow!" Rylan exclaimed, rubbing his shoulder as he ran into a dead end. "I think Reina told us the wrong way to go. The Walking Dead back there are getting closer to us. What do we do now?"

"She said there would be a lever, but I don't see anything." Max brought the torch closer to the wall, hoping for an answer. His palms brushed against the wall, and he noticed the stark difference from the exterior walls of the tomb. Here, the stones were arranged vertically, while throughout the rest of the tomb, they'd been laid side-by-side.

Max squeezed the tips of his fingers into the cracks of the

foundation. "The study outside the throne room is behind this wall. I think the lever is connected to these stones."

Max froze as a cold hand touched his shoulder, and he slowly turned to find a grinning skeleton inches away from his nose. His heart reverently pulsed in his chest, and the sword clasped in his palm was trembling from his nerves as the skeletons closed in on him and his friends. The voice emanating from the skeletons was getting louder. "Evil must leave this sacred place."

Leo yelled over the group of skeletons and clasped her hand around the gun at her waist, "Max, are you wearing corpse attracting body spray? They're all over you."

"It's actually called Fierce Phoenix, but I doubt the deodorant my mom got me attracts dead people!"

Is it me?

Unhooking his trident from his back, Rylan held it to his side. "Get outta here, you bag of bones." With a vigorous swing of his weapon, white bone fragments scattered through the air. "Can you two find that lever *any* slower?"

"Let me do it," Max declared. "Ry, you have smaller hands than me, so it'll be easier for you to find the lever."

"These small hands will punch your lights out!" Rylan gave Max's shoulder one last squeeze. "Be safe."

Max nodded to his friend, unsheathed his sword, and swung it at the oncoming skeletons. "You're not getting near my friends!" As his arm veered left and right, he noticed it was fairly easy to dismantle the enemy. The moment his blade hit their midsections, the sound of bones hitting the floor reverberated like a hollow baseball bat. The bones were scattered about, each piece trying to attract and connect with the others like a magnet.

Out of nowhere, Max's body ached, and wetness made the

sword's hilt slick. "Oh, no," Max said aloud as hopelessness overtook him. "Please don't let this happen right now."

I can't let Rylan and Leo down again, but I don't have time to reach into my bag for some spring water. What if we don't survive this? What'll happen to Hannah and Ella?

He shook his head.

No, that's not going to happen, we'll get outta here, even if I die trying.

Noticing his hesitation, the skeletons beelined for Max in waves, which only made his anxiety grow with each swing of the sword. They'd closed in on him, and their stale breath wafted on his neck with every turn he made. "Can you guys find that lever a little quicker? I'm not sure how much longer I can hold them off."

As he swung his sword, three arms quickly grabbed it, halting his attack and leaving him vulnerable. He glanced at his friends in defeat and thought of his sister. His body was paralyzed, and for the first time on this journey, he was on the precipice of giving up. With a sudden jolt, Max was being lifted into the air by the pairs of bony fingers that had latched onto his ankles and wrists, hoisting him over the bare skulled heads. "Guys, you better find that door quickly, they're taking me!"

No words came from Rylan and Leo, and fear gripped him. His heart raced as he thought about his friends being outnumbered by the skeletons now that he was no longer defending them.

Two skeletons detached their hands, fingers twitching and wriggling as if they had a will of their own. Max was completely paralyzed as the skeletons skillfully attached the severed limbs around his wrists and ankles before placing him in the nearest coffin.

The smell inside made Max gag as decay and death filled his nostrils.

They're trying to bury me alive!

Max's anxiety was at an all-time high, leaving him completely crippled. He could hear the skeletons surrounding the coffin lift the stone slab, readying to close it once more.

A small gap of air was left before they completely submerged him in the casket. Max heard an audible bang followed by silence, and the powerful skeletal hands that held him fell off.

Max shook out his wrists and feet, and the sound of feet against stone reached his ears. He looked up to see Rylan peering down at him through his mop of hair.

"You okay, dude?"

"Man, am I happy to see you." Sweat dripped from his forehead, and he realized he was breathing like he'd just run a race. He sat up and tried catching his breath. "Th-they were going to close me inside of this casket. How'd you stop them?"

Leo shrugged. "We didn't do anything. We found the lever, and as the door opened, the skeletons dropped."

"You know I'd never leave you behind, right?" Rylan clasped Max's hand, pulling him out of the casket.

"Why do you think they were only after you?"

"I don't know," Max responded, feeling like he was keeping a secret. His whole body was shaking with fear. "Let's go."

The trio walked up to the wall that had a small hole in it, big enough for an average-sized man to fit through. They shimmied through, shuddering at the memory of the crypt they'd just left and bracing themselves for the trial ahead: a throne room full of imps.

Chapter Twenty

The large study boasted a magnificent mahogany desk, which stood in the center of a smooth yet dusty stone floor. Shelves filled with books lined the exterior walls, and the furniture around the room begged to be sat in. On the wall behind the desk hung two elegant paintings, one of a large man with a stern face hidden under a curly gray beard and the other of two little girls in beautiful white dresses with rosy cheeks.

Max attempted to calm his breathing as fear crawled up his spine from their most recent encounter with the undead. He sat on the edge of the smooth desk and turned his attention to the large portraits. As he sat, his hands shook like a leaf, and his heart pounded in his chest, making it hard to breathe.

"Is that Reina?" Leo breathed, gazing at the stunning painting.

"I think so." Rylan nodded. "The little girl posing at her side must be her sister, and the angry guy must be her father."

The painting depicted Reina wearing a jeweled white dress, a sparkling tiara nestled in her curly hair, and a smile that curved at the corner of her mouth. The little girl in the library seemed like a distant memory compared to the regal and mature figure in the picture. In contrast, the other girl in the painting looked to be her twin, although much shorter, with a look of silliness in her eye.

"She looks so happy."

"She does." Max nodded as his body began to normalize. "It's been years since the castle was taken over, but there's no denying it's her."

Leo shook her head. "It's unbelievable that they're the same people. Losing Berylon must have really taken a toll on her."

"Well, let's help her get it back!" Rylan smiled and grabbed his trident, swinging it haphazardly. "Once we're in the next room, the plan is for Leo to create a barrier to protect us, just like the one he used in the garden when the imps were taken out."

She shook her head and let out an annoyed sigh. "You really don't understand, do you? In the Garden of Bliss, all the fairies held hands, and the culmination of their powers created a chain of power and light. Individual fairies themselves aren't powerful enough to create that barrier."

Rylan shrugged and rolled his eyes. "What do we do? Maybe we can casually knock on the door and ask the imps nicely to return their dinner?"

Leo rolled her eyes at the dramatic merman. "My bullets will paralyze them. You and Max will have to fight using your own weapons."

After hearing what Leo had just said, Max's stomach began to churn. While he had killed a few imps, he rationalized it as self-defense as they had attacked first, but invading their territory gave him a sense of guilt. It didn't help that he was exhausted, anxious, and losing hope with each new obstacle. Reaching into his bag, he brought out the small vial of water that Calvo had given him. The moment the liquid hit his tongue, its effect rippled through his body, and all his worries had washed away. Taking one long breath, he centered himself; his body and mind were stronger than ever.

Rylan watched as his friend tucked the glass vessel back into the leather bag and put his hand on Max's shoulder. "Sacrifices need to be made to get back home and save Ella."

Max turned his thoughts away from his dilemma, nodding. "For Ella. Let's do it."

The trio stood before a large green door that led into the throne room and breathed one last calming sigh. Leo reached to her waist to replenish her gun with bullets while Max unsheathed his sword and Rylan clutched the staff of his trident.

Nodding to his friends, Rylan nudged the door with his shoulder and walked ahead of his peers. The trio marveled at the enormous, intricately decorated room as they entered. The stone walls were adorned with tattered tapestries perfectly placed between each window, but the once-gorgeous marble white walls were now soiled with dirt and grime. A shabby floor runner, stained and faded, ran through the center of the room. It led to three plush thrones, all lying on their sides, with a bat-like imp sleeping soundly in between. It was apparent that this room was once full of grandeur, but since being taken over, its elegance was diminished.

There was a screech in the corner of the room as two creatures rolled on the floor with one another, either playing or fighting. The room was filled with dozens of imps, some lazily picking fleas from their matted fur while others dozed on the tarnished floor with their arms crossed.

One of the creatures stood directly in front of the trio with its back to them as they entered the room. Leo held her arm out, gun extended. As soon as the door opened, the imp turned its body, but a gunshot quickly silenced any noise it might have made. Its body stiffened and fell to the ground, alerting the room to their presence.

It almost seemed as if time stopped. The cacophony of imps in the room watched as the dark blood from the imp pooled below it. They were all frozen and silent as their striking, yellowed eyes slowly widened in anger.

Leo tightened her grip on her weapon, Rylan assumed a fighting stance, and Max stood frozen, his sword hanging by his side. Though they had been fighting for days and his confidence had increased, they were in the crux of the castle now, approaching the last obstacle between Max and his sister.

I can't fail.

"You okay?" Rylan asked, holding his trident in front of him. "Get ready."

Anger crossed each imp's malicious yellow eyes as they followed the trail of the dead imp to the three teens standing in the doorway. Left and right, the creatures began springing at them, and Max's body froze as he watched their reaction. It was as if the pause had lifted, and the imps surrounding them started running at the trio, fangs and claws baring.

Thankfully, Rylan's concern snapped Max out of his fear and focused his mind on getting through the castle and reuniting with Ella.

I won't fail. I promised Ella.

It was then that he could feel the spring water rushing through his body and any fear that he once had, dissipated.

I can't believe I found a cure for my anxiety. My brain is quiet, but I'm stronger and more confident, too.

He nodded to his friends and brandished his sword at the oncoming creatures.

Leo shot two bullets at the imps running at them, stopping them in their tracks. Rylan slashed one with his trident, and

Max struck the other with his sword. The two beings let out a loud screech and retreated, leaving more imps in their place.

"I don't know if I can fire enough bullets to paralyze all of them before they reach us," Leo yelled over the sound of the gun being fired.

Max slashed the arm of a nearby imp, its blood dripping onto the floor and writhing in pain. "Let's just hit as many as we can. If we go down, we go together."

"That's the Max that I like to hear!" Rylan yelled, and he speared one to the floor through its chest.

The imps came charging towards them, their movements so fast it was almost impossible to keep up. In his mind, Max was the main character of a video game, swinging his sword at every yellow eye he saw. The sound of the imp's scream confirmed his attack had landed. He just wished that, like a game, he had three lives to spare.

Making his way to the middle of the throne room, they hit several imps, injuring them along the way. As Max swung his sword from left to right, he heard Rylan grunt, impaling the creatures with his trident, but noticed the gunshots had ceased. Wondering why Leo had stopped firing, he quickly turned and saw a pile of imps gnawing and slashing at a pile of leaves on the ground.

They ran over to the cluster of imps with their hearts pounding, wildly thrashing their weapons to see what had happened to their friend. Leo was pinned to the ground with imps covering her mouth, rendering her helpless and immobile under their thin fingers as their beady eyes glared at the intruders.

"Get off of her, you flea-infested monkeys!" Rylan's face was red, and his eyes were angry as he took the handle of his trident and swung three imps into the nearby wall.

A loud squeal came from the opposite side of the room, and

the imps on top of Leo stiffened, their ears perked on top of their head. They dispersed and ran to a large green door opposite the one Max and his friends had come from.

Leo didn't move from the ground, seemingly unconscious. Her face and body were injured as Max saw various gashes from teeth and claws that had punctured her skin. He shook her. "Leo, are you okay?"

"What do we do?" Max asked.

"I-I'm fine," Leo breathed. "I can help, just give me a second."

Max got an idea and, with trembling hands, opened the leather satchel strung around his body. He fished inside until he found what he was looking for. Brandishing the glass bottle half full of liquid, he lifted Leo's head and placed two drops into her mouth. "This will heal her, but it'll take a few minutes."

In response, a loud and excited cry rang through the throne room. The imps tore open the large green door and made way for what was on the other side. Claws the size of porcupine quills sunk into the castle walls as it pulled itself into the throne room. The gargantuan creature jumped into the air and hooked its hand around one of the various sconces hanging from an intricate diamond chandelier. The jewels intertwined within the chandelier tinkled as the creature swung back and forth.

Max's heart raced as the enormous creature soared above him, its bat-like ears and furry body silhouetted against the ceiling. It dawned on him that the creature he faced was not just any imp but one the size of a gorilla with a crazed look in its eye.

The creature swung on the chandelier as if playing on a jungle gym until its eyes were fixed on the two boys. It let out a deep, guttural roar and jumped off the light fixture, soaring through the air until landing on its feet, shaking the ground below.

Rylan ran to a nearby window, gripping his trident with both hands and smashing it through the glass. The fragments tinkled as their jagged edges met the stone floor.

The large imp in front of Max scooped Leo up with one of his snow-shovel-sized hands and threw her on the chandelier. Her body landed haphazardly within the various arms that branched off, and the candles surrounding her cast a soft glow.

Rylan had his back to Max and was focusing on something outside the window. "What're you doing?" He couldn't believe he was transfixed on something other than the deadly imp in front of them.

He pointed to the ocean far below the castle. "I'm trying to manipulate the water so I can use it against these imps, maybe even wash them out or drown them. It might be our only chance, but the water is at the bottom of this cliff, so I need to focus. Keep the big one occupied."

Max raised his arms above his head. "How the hell am I going to do that? If this were a game, this thing would be a boss level."

As soon as his words left his mouth, a large hand reached around Max's waist and hoisted him into the air. The imp let out another throaty roar, baring the sharp, jagged teeth that lined its mouth. Max gritted his teeth as the hairy fingers constricted around his waist and thrust the sword into them with a forceful jab. With a precise strike, the blade pierced the imp's gray skin, leaving a clean cut directly into its knuckle.

Roaring in pain, the imp's fingers relaxed just enough for Max to shimmy out of the beast's hold. Jumping to the ground, he quickly darted between the animal's legs, watching as it searched for him in a confused frenzy.

Max ran from his hiding place between the imp's legs and

ran to the opposite side of the throne room. As soon as the creature's yellow eyes caught sight of movement, it let out an ear-splitting cry and began sprinting towards him like a runaway truck.

The imp bound its way to Max and cornered him against the wall. Its yellow eyes gleamed both crazed and ferocious as it ascended on its prey. The slight orange hue around its pupils thickened in delight as it noticed Max was trapped.

Being only a few feet away, he knew the grizzly creature would descend upon him with one more jump and prepared for the worst. The ground trembled with every step the imp took toward him, the vibrations matching the beat of his frightened heart.

Max winced as its warm breath reached his nostrils. All he could do was hold onto his sword for dear life.

The smell of sea water filled the air, and the beast's stench disappeared from Max's nose. With tremendous force, a large wave came crashing through the open window, hitting the imp and hurling it into a marble pillar. The column shattered in thousands of directions, and the lifeless creature lay buried beneath the rubble.

Dust flew around the room, and the cries of the smaller imps echoed throughout the chamber after seeing their leader downed.

"You okay?" Rylan asked.

Feeling as if he were about to have a heart attack from the close encounter, Max wiped the sweat from his forehead and lowered his sword. "You're *so* lucky you did that at the right time."

Rylan laughed. "Whatta ya mean? You didn't wanna be an oversized monkey's dinner?"

Chapter Twenty-One

Max scanned the throne room, bracing himself for an attack from the remaining imps, but to his surprise, the room was deserted. Unease spread through his body as his mind repeated the same question: *Why did the imps retreat? Rylan hadn't defeated all of them with that wave.*

Watching Max spin frantically in circles with his sword outstretched, Rylan shrugged. "They must've gone to the east tower, where that big gorilla was being held." He glanced up at the giant chandelier. "Let's get Leo down." Rylan's trident gleamed in the sunlight as he pointed it toward the water, which slowly enveloped their feet and began to form a shimmering blue pool around them. The water lifted them into the air like they were standing on top of an elevator.

The room had a strange quiet about it as the rushing water pushed them toward the light fixture. A voice rang through the throne room from the ceiling. "Max, Rylan! Jump!"

Turning his head upward, he saw Leo holding onto the large metal chain that held the chandelier in the air, her brown eyes scanning the space below them. He quickly followed her gaze and saw the large imp, groaning in pain, slowly crawling out from under the rubble.

"Stop waiting and jump!" Leo gestured to the light fixture, which held a single candle that branched out from a curved, golden arm.

Without another second to think, Max grabbed Rylan's hand and leaped, hoping his legs were strong enough to reach. Max outstretched his hand to reach for the golden arm looped under the chandelier. The water under them fell back to the floor, and as they soared through the air, he realized they weren't going to make it—his hand was about an inch or two too short. Once the realization set in, it was as if gravity acknowledged and took over, dropping both boys to the ground below.

"Not today!" Rylan stuck his trident prongs through the arm of the chandelier, giving them just enough length to halt their descent and leave them dangling in midair.

"Oh great," Max yelled sarcastically, praying that his hands wouldn't get sweaty. "We're teasing ourselves as its dinner: two humans roasted on a spit."

"Fall to your death or be eaten. Those were the two options!" Rylan yelled back. "I chose to be dinner!"

"Will you two stop?" Leo yelled from above them. She stood on top of the chandelier with her legs squarely apart and her hand on her pistol, looking as if she were ready for battle.

"Uh...what're you doing?" Rylan yelled, seeing an adventurous glint in her eye.

The imp was on its feet and stumbling as if drunk toward the two friends hanging in the middle of the room with a deadly look in its eye. Without a word, Leo curled her lips into a smirk and unsheathed her gun, holding it straight in front of her. "Don't mess with my friends, asshole!" She shot a single bullet, leaving a small plume of smoke from the gun's muzzle.

The white bullet whizzed through the air and missed the

enormous imp, landing in the three inches of water covering the ground.

"Great job, you missed!" Rylan yelled. "I thought your aim was better than that."

"I'm sure you've heard that before," Leo retorted with a wink. "Besides, I wasn't aiming for the imp." Not another second later, the air grew warm, and the white light from the bullet created a light mist on top of the water. "Get ready for some fireworks, boys!"

A white electrical current swam through the shallow water like an eel. The imp let out a squeal like a frightened child. It wasn't a roar of fury, but one of agony. Its hair stood on end, and its body stiffened before falling to the ground. Convulsions caused its body to flop and twitch on the floor, rendering it helpless.

"Is it actually dead this time?"

Leo jumped off the chandelier with ease and precision, landing unharmed. Nudging the limp imp body with her foot, she nodded. "You can come down. Everything's okay."

Max let go of his friend's hand and stumbled as his feet touched the throne room floor. Rylan gracefully fell behind Max and ran over to the fallen imp, holding the trident over his shoulder. He prodded the greasy fur with his weapon until he was certain it was never getting back up. "This thing is a dead doornail. That's the phrase, right?"

"Finally." Max let out a breath of air he didn't know he was holding.

"It's 'deader than a doornail,' you idiot!" Leo laughed and combed her hair with her fingers. "Either way, it doesn't make sense to me, a doornail was never alive to begin with."

Rylan rolled his eyes and shook his head. "I've never understood why girls always overthink things. That's probably why you've never had a boyfriend."

"It's too bad that my bullets don't kill brainless imps with big egos because you'd be in a world of hurt if they did!"

Max hid his laughter behind his palm and let his friends banter back and forth, knowing they could go on like this for hours. "We're so close to Ella, I can feel it."

"How do you know?" Leo asked. "She might not be here."

Max shook his head. "I just know she's somewhere nearby. It's a big brother-little sister connection."

Rylan grabbed Max's shoulder. "Well, let's go get her, buddy. While we're at it, let's kick Samael's ass, too!"

The trio made their way to the busted green door from which the gorilla-sized imp had emerged, carefully stepping over various pieces of broken wood and stone. They looked around the throne room one last time and imagined how spectacular it may have looked prior to being demoted to a rundown room that looked as if it held nothing but untrained dogs.

"This place is going to need a lot of love to get it back to its old shape," Leo breathed.

"I'm sure that Reina will be up to the task."

Max, Rylan, and Leo retreated into the door and saw a room, somewhat smaller than the study, with a set of stone steps leading upward to the east tower. Leo grabbed a wooden torch from the wall and ignited an orange flame on its tip, aiding them through the dark stairway.

The staircase twisted and turned, leading the trio higher and higher until they finally reached a landing. A large golden tapestry was draped alongside the stone wall, and a metal door with a unique insignia inscribed on its center stood before them.

"Do we knock?" Rylan whispered.

Leo shrugged and carelessly pushed the door open, peering into the dark room. The wall fixtures in the room added accents of mature hues such as silver, ruby, and lavender, which contrasted beautifully with the eggshell white walls. It was clear that no one had been inside for years; dust covered every-thing from the canopy bed to the bureaus. A large white balcony, accessed through a set of double doors, let in some of the late afternoon sun, casting a hazy glow over the space due to the thick darkness beyond.

Max, Leo, and Rylan walked to the large, plush bed and pulled back the hanging canopy cloth, revealing the slumbering body of a little girl. With her palms folded on her stomach and her eyes closed, she slept soundly in the center of the bed.

"Wow," breathed Leo. "Reina looks absolutely beautiful." The little princess was wearing an elegant, baby blue gown with various jewels sewn into designs, sparkling in the light. The perfectly tousled brown curls on the pillow gave her a look of effortless glamor as if she'd just left a royal ball.

Max slipped the key inside the fingers of Reina's hands and stood back, waiting for her to awaken. The trio stood for several minutes in silence, waiting for a flicker of her eyes or a tremble of her hand, but nothing came.

Rylan poked the little girl in the arm and craned his neck. "Hello? Are you going to wake up? We did what you told us to do."

As if the girl heard him, there was a stirring in the bed. No one could pinpoint where the movement occurred, but it was noticeable to everyone in the bedroom. The key clasped in her fingers started glowing with an intense white light before lifting her a few inches above the bed.

"I hope this was what we were supposed to do." Rylan gulped. "Because this is starting to look like an exorcism."

Leo drew in a sharp breath, and Max raised his eyebrows. Their eyes were fixed on Reina as a bright ring of light surrounded her, expanding until a sudden force blew through the room, leaving them feeling as if they'd witnessed something incredible. As the bright light dimmed, the little girl was slowly lowered back onto her bed by an invisible force, and the only sound in the room was the hushed breathing of her three friends.

"That's it?" Rylan asked, throwing his hands in the air. "If we wanted a light show, we could've stayed home and waited for the New Year."

A shard of yellow twilight radiated through the balcony window, which surprised them as the dark veil ensured that sunlight couldn't make its way through. Gazing out onto the balcony, they watched as the dark clouds that painted the sky around the village slowly evaporated, allowing streams of light to penetrate through like victory banners from a battle.

Leo punched the air. "We did it!"

"But what about her?"

"I'll wake up." The trio turned and saw the spirit of the little girl they had met in the library sitting on an armchair on the other side of the room.

"Reina, how'd you get up here?" Max asked.

"Once the darkness lifted and the imps retreated, I knew it would be safe to access the castle again. Let me express to the three of you how grateful I am."

With the classic snark in his voice, Rylan crossed his arms. "Yeah, well, we almost died trying to help you. An imp the size of a gorilla constantly tried to pulverize us."

"I knew it wouldn't be an easy task, and I thank you for your service. Once my physical body awakens, I'll repay you."

Leo looked to the sleeping body. "Is your physical body alright?"

Reina shrugged and flashed them a reassuring smile. "I'm fine. It'll take some time for my body to catch up to my brain. I've been asleep for years, and as my body awakens, it needs to make sure everything still works properly. I can sense my consciousness awakening; it should only take a few hours."

"What happens now?"

"Once I'm back on my feet, my top priority is to regenerate Berylon and restore it to its former glory. After that, I must reestablish my kingdom and power throughout the Island of Forever."

"Sounds like you have a lot of work ahead of you," Max said.

"I do, but it's work worth doing." She hesitated before speaking, her gaze shifting downward. "I regret to inform you that you friends aren't here. There are no Mainlanders within my castle at this moment."

"What about the fairies?"

The shimmering girl shrugged with a look of unknowing strewn across her face.

The yellow light illuminating the room was waning, making room for night. Max turned to the spirit girl beside him. "Calvo said that if they weren't being held in the castle, they must have found a way inside the Temple of Harper. You said earlier that this castle is a bridge there. Can we go right now?"

"Patience," Reina whispered, her hands moving in a fanning motion. "Anyone without powers can enter the temple, but only my bloodline can grant access to those with magic. In all these years, I've only allowed the Hero to step inside, as the temple is the portal between worlds. Since you suspect your friends are being held at the Temple of Harper, I believe someone evil is attempting to access that portal and bring more than change to this island."

Max clutched his chest. "My sister's safety is the most important to me, I don't care if it's a trap. I'll do anything to make sure she's in my care again."

Leo looked thoughtfully at the princess. "Goblins took Ella

and Hannah. If only your family can grant access to the temple, how did they get inside?"

A gasp escaped from her throat as her fingers clasped over her mouth. "My sister must have been kidnapped." Reina turned to the trio with her eyes full of empathy. "I am sure you have seen on your travels that change has already come to the island with your arrival. I am not strong enough to open the portal right now. Tomorrow morning, my body will have regained its full strength, and I'll grant you access to the Temple of Harper. Until then, please spend the night. There are many spare rooms that each of you may use."

"Thank you for your hospitality." Max bowed. Quickly, he did some calculations in his mind. "We have less than a day to leave before Samael can attempt his return."

She turned to them with a calm exterior. "Both of our families are counting on you. Take this opportunity to rest. You'll need your strength because I'll be sending you to the temple first thing in the morning."

Chapter Twenty-Two

Max threw himself onto the firm bed and sighed in relief. His body had grown heavy once the spring water's effects had worn off. Though the blankets under him smelled musty, like a grandmother's attic, he was thrilled to finally be sleeping in a bed again. The castle had transformed with the arrival of night as candles lit up around the room, casting flickering shadows on the stone walls.

Thinking about his time here, Max couldn't believe his journey was near its end. Despite the kidnapping of Ella and Hannah, he found himself proud of the way he had overcome the island's obstacles and believed that each one helped him gain a deeper understanding of himself. A smile crossed his face as he recounted the adventures he had embarked on since landing on Captain Marris's ship. It was only days ago, but it felt like an eternity had passed.

A knock came from the wooden door, and a small head poked inside. "Hey, Max, do you have some time to spare?" Leo's nose was wet, and her eyes were red and puffy.

Max nodded. "What's up?"

She stepped into the room and sat beside him as she fidgeted with her hands. "I know tonight is supposed to be relaxing because we're walking into a pit of goblins tomorrow, but I was wondering if you could help me explore the castle a bit?"

Max looked at her with arched eyebrows, unsure why she was nervous. "You know you don't have to be nervous to ask me things, right? Of course I'll explore with you."

"Great, let me grab my gun, and I'll be right back."

"Is everything okay?" Max genuinely asked. "You seem bothered."

"Well... I admit that I have an ulterior motive to explore the castle." Her big, brown eyes glistened with unshed tears as she combed her thin fingers through her long, brown hair. "We had come here to find the three fairies and were told that they were likely eaten. Part of me thinks they might be alive and hidden somewhere in the castle. I would never feel like I'd done my due diligence to the queen if I didn't at least try to look."

A wave of realization came over Max. Their journey to the castle hadn't just been to save Calvo, Ella, and Hannah; it was also Leo's personal quest to Queen Aeryth. His ears grew warm as selfishness and embarrassment dawned on him. He couldn't believe that he was so focused on getting to the Temple of Harper that he had forgotten. "I got so caught up in trying to find Ella, Hannah, and Calvo, I forgot. What a shitty friend I am. Of course I'll help you look."

A large smile grew on Leo's face as she ran out of the room and returned seconds later with her wooden gun clasped in her hand. "Let's go!"

"Should we have Rylan come too?"

She closed her eyes and rubbed her temples with two fingers each. "I don't know if I can mentally deal with him right now." She snuck a glance at Max and sighed. "Yeah, I guess we can include him. Let's go to his room next."

They took a right down a dimly lit hallway where Rylan's room waited. Leo clasped her fingers into her palm and loudly struck her knuckles against the wooden door. The only response they received was a deafening silence.

"Maybe he's sleeping?" Max shrugged.

She rolled her eyes and shoved the door open with her shoulder. "Get up, Rylan! We have fairies to save."

With her ferocious knocking, the wooden door slowly opened into a large room resembling Max's. A bed was on the eastern wall, while various bureaus and dressers covered in dust were scattered throughout. A handwoven rug was placed under the bed, and tapestries hung on the walls.

"Rylan? Are you here?" Max's hands were sweaty as he became anxious that something sinister may have happened to his friend because this was the first time since Ella was kidnapped that the two of them were apart. "Where do you think he is?"

Leo walked to the other side of the bed and rolled her eyes at the empty bottle lying on the floor. "A wine bottle... I'll give you one guess where our friend may have found himself."

"Of course." Max shook his head. "The wine cellar."

"Well, at least it's on our way to the dungeons."

The duo exited the bedroom and made their way down the hallway. Max's mind raced as he imagined what the castle looked like in its prime: majestic, well-maintained, and full of secrets waiting to be uncovered. The fortress in real life was much more impressive than those he imagined when he read books or played video games. Gazing at the castle's architecture, his imagination conjured up images of the grandeur it might have held in the past. Each room within the castle had very high ceilings with large windows at each end caked with dust and dirt. Faded tapestries clung to the walls, and the shine from various shields and swords used for decoration had dimmed.

"It's almost as if this castle is screaming for someone's time and attention to bring it back to what it once was," he remarked.

"I feel it, too." Leo shivered. "Reina's determination will restore this castle and the village. I know we're leaving the island, but I wish we could glimpse into the future to see what she does with all of this."

Nearing the end of the hallway, his heart rate quickened, and they both gasped as they pushed open the large wooden double doors. Max and Leo found themselves atop a double staircase overlooking the castle's grand foyer. Floor-to-ceiling windows lined the western and eastern walls, providing a view of the once beautiful landscape now choked with overgrown trees and plants. Large stone pillars separated each window, and a curved ceiling revealed a beautiful mural inside the dome.

Max walked down the closest staircase, descending into the grand foyer. The sound of his footsteps bounced off the white-marbled floor, filling the once-empty room with the eerie presence of a ghostly echo. Down a vast hallway were two large doors leading to the castle's entrance.

"What happened here?" Leo commented, glancing at her feet. Shards of wood littered the ground at the bottom of the staircase as if it had been blown to bits.

Their eyes followed the trail of wood until they landed on a double doorway between both staircases. One door had been ripped off its frame, whereas the other was hanging on by a sole metal hinge.

Max and Leo walked to the door and peered inside, seeing familiar portraits hanging on the walls. "This is the room that we snuck into from the tomb. The throne room is the next chamber."

Looking at the broken lock on the door to the room, Leo pointed at the blown hinge. "The imps must have busted through the locked door once they retreated."

The sound of someone whistling in the next room was barely audible, but they both heard it. Max and Leo turned their heads to look at one another, wondering who it could be.

Hesitantly, Max pushed the door open and stepped forward, his hand firmly gripping the hilt of his sword. The throne room was still as grand and marvelous as he remembered, but now it was a peaceful sanctuary without any threats of death. Pools of blood had stained the stone floor, and leathery imp bodies lay scattered throughout.

The whistling had come from the far side of the room, on the dais where the thrones lay. The imps had knocked over and thrown the thrones about during their previous visit to the room, perhaps as a protest to what the chairs represented. A throne had been turned upright, and a boy was sitting in it with his feet draped over the chair's arm, clutching a bottle of wine.

"Rylan, what the hell are you doing?" Leo called out, trudging up the faded red carpet.

The boy's head was thrown backward, and he returned to a sitting position once he heard his name being called. Rylan's movements were slow, almost like his body was moving a minute behind the real world. His eyelids were half closed, and it took a moment for his mind to recognize his friends. "Leo and Max! What're you doing here?" His words were a slurred mess as they passed his smiling lips.

Leo swiftly smacked the merman's head. "You've got some nerve getting drunk right now! The safety of this island depends on us, and you're incapacitated."

Rylan closed one eye and ran his fingers through his blonde curls. "Chill, fairy girl. I only drank a couple bottles of wine."

"What if a few stray imps were hiding in the castle, and you got so drunk that you didn't see them, and they beheaded you? What then, dummy?"

Rylan shrugged and laughed. "I guess that would mean there was one less person you'd have to worry about getting off the island?"

"You're such an idiot!" Leo screamed, stomping her feet. "C'mon, Max, let's find the dungeons. I don't know why we were looking for this imbecile in the first place." She turned away from Rylan and trudged down the faded, regal carpet in a huff.

"If you're trying to get to the dungeons, you're going the wrong way," Rylan said in a singsong voice.

Leo whipped around with her index finger sharply extended. "You don't even know your name right now. How do you know where the dungeons are?"

Max observed as Rylan tilted the bottle to his lips and took a long gulp. The crimson liquid dribbled down his chin and stained bits of the rope shirt draped around his shoulders.

Wiping his mouth with the back of his hand, he shrugged. "When I was trying to find where the booze was held, I accidentally stumbled upon the dungeon. If you're *really* nice to me, maybe I'll tell you where it is."

Leo swiftly latched her fingers around the collar of Rylan's shirt and brought his face inches away from hers. "Tell me where the dungeon is, or you won't have to worry about an imp beheading you because I'll do it." She maintained eye contact with him, trying to intimidate him with her unwavering gaze.

His face went from calm to scared in seconds, almost as if he'd sobered up completely. "L-let me go, and I'll show you."

Leo brought Rylan closer to her face before throwing him

back onto the throne, and he let out a large sigh of relief. "Quick tip for you: lightly grab the neck if you're into choking."

"If I grabbed your neck, you wouldn't be standing," Leo muttered. "Now, tell me where the dungeon is."

"Okay, okay! Sheesh." Rylan extended his arm to the back corner. "It's through that door, just head down instead of up to the west tower." Rylan's fingers were wrapped around the cold metal handle of a lantern. "You'll definitely need this."

Without a word, Leo seized the lantern and took hold of Max's arm. The pair marched to the back of the throne room, where Leo threw open the door to the dungeon. With the door closing behind them, Max stole a final glance at Rylan, who had thrown his head back and was now holding a wine bottle in the air as droplets of alcohol fell to the floor like rain.

The landing where Max and Leo stood was so tiny that it could only fit around three people at once. To their left, a set of winding stairs illuminated by the moon led up to the west tower, while to their right, a dark, windowless staircase led downward.

"Well, this isn't ominous or anything, is it?" Max laughed. "Down to the depths of hell we go."

Leo pulled out her gun and shot one of her light bullets into the lantern. The glass from the fixture shattered, tinkling as it hit the floor, but the wick inside the lantern flourished and cast an orange light on the dark walls. "Let's go."

They descended the stairs in silence, each consumed by their thoughts. Leo hoped that the young fairies were in the dungeon alive, and Max was nervous about what the next day might bring. The steps seemed to spiral endlessly, as if leading to the depths of the underworld. They could only see inky darkness in front of them—until the steps finally ended.

A long stone wall loomed ahead of them, lined with metal shackles that clinked and clattered with each gust of wind. The wall had a greenish tint under the dim light, and there were several areas of discoloration, particularly around the shackles.

Leo wrinkled her nose as she neared the wall. "Ugh, dried blood... That's disgusting."

Max shrugged. "It's a dungeon, what do you expect?"

"What's behind this wall?" Leo touched the stone with her hand and followed it down the hallway until she reached an archway. "Here we go, a door."

As they opened it, the sound of water became audible. They feared the worst: the prison might be flooding, and they wouldn't be able to escape.

Chapter Twenty-Three

The light from the moon illuminated the area behind the wall. Metal cells ran the entire length of the room, as well as the opposite wall. There were bars on the small windows and wooden beds with thin blankets haphazardly lying on top. Loose straw filled with bones littered the floor like confetti.

Max entered the first cell across from him, jumped on the bed, and gazed out of the window. "That's where the sound of water came from." From their high vantage point, the sound of the crashing waves against the rocks below was incessant. The rhythmic sound of water rushing in and out filled the jail. "I think the dungeons were constructed into the side of the cliff where the castle sits on top.

Jumping onto the bed frame beside him, Leo put her mouth to the window. "ALETTE! MARIN! ROSETTE!" Turning to Max, she shrugged. "If these cells span the entire side of this cliff, they're bound to hear me, right?"

They sat in silence, straining their ears to hear the slightest sound of someone yelling back to Leo, but all they could hear was the sound of the waves colliding against the cliff.

"Let's look around some more." Max attempted to keep hope for them both. "Maybe they're sleeping, or we can get a clue to where they may be even if they're not here."

They returned to the hallway of cells and peered into each one, looking for clues to the girls' whereabouts. Each of the cells was similar in layout, but nothing was more adamant than the thick layer of dirt and grime spanning every inch of the cells. As Max and Leo made their way down to the second level, the crash of waves against the rocks below grew louder and more constant, and the air grew increasingly damp.

"Max, I found something," Leo yelled while standing at the far end of the hallway.

Rushing to her, he noticed that the first jail cell was distinct from the others. The metal cage was massive and empty, and the sound of its scraping against the stone ceiling made the room even more desolate. A small table with wooden guns on its surface was tucked away in the corner of the room.

"These are fairy guns," Leo breathed as she held one in her palm. "They *were* here. I knew it."

"We scared all the imps away, so if your friends were here, where did they go?" The heaviness of Max's words lingered in the air like the saltiness of the ocean air after a storm.

"Not just my friends," Leo whispered as she brandished a small bracelet pinched between her fingers and revealed a wooden ax leaning against the wall.

Max's heart raced as he saw the magic wand charm glinting in the moonlight on the bracelet, and he knew exactly who it belonged to. "Do you think Ella was taken with the fairy girls?"

They looked around the room for clues before stepping into the metal cage. The base of the structure was surrounded by a thin layer of dirty straw, which gave it the appearance of being built over a large nest. Max brought the lantern closer and saw the outlines of toes huddled together toward the back of the cage, etched into the dusty floor. He climbed into the metal prison, feeling like a trapped animal. The lantern illuminated three sets of footprints on the dirty floor—two pairs pointed at the door and the third at the wall behind them.

Bringing his lantern closer to the back wall, just under the barred window, Max found the clue they'd been looking for. "Leo, over here."

"What did you find?" Her eyes were wide with worry as she stepped into the cage.

"I saw these footprints were all facing the same way except for one pair facing the window. Take a look at the wall." As Max pulled his lantern closer, a faded drawing of an arrow pointing outside the window came into view. "Do you know where this is pointing to?"

Leo's eyes widened as the answer trickled into her mind before breathing it into existence. "The Temple of Harper. Reina was right."

"At least we know imps didn't eat them." In the dim light, he could see pools of tears building in his friend's eyes as she twirled her dark hair around her finger, deep in thought. "Don't worry, we'll get them back."

"Let's rest up for tomorrow. I'm sick to my stomach thinking about what Ella, Hannah, and the fairy girls may be going through."

Max nodded, and they left the dungeon, circling the staircase back to the throne room. Upon entering, he observed Rylan's disappearance and the pile of empty bottles next to the throne. They exited the grand room and ascended the staircase in the foyer, turning through the wooden door to the hallway where their bedrooms waited. Max reached his door and waved to Leo. "Goodnight, rest up."

She smiled at him. "We're going to kick some goblin ass tomorrow, right?"

He nodded and turned the doorknob to his room. A smile crossed his face at her infectious positivity and unwavering determination. Sitting on the bed, he released a heavy sigh, exhausted from the day's events. He then removed his ruined sneakers and unbuttoned his soiled jeans, carefully peeling them off his tired legs. He pulled his T-shirt off his body, wincing at the sticky fabric against his skin, and tossed it onto the pile of clothes already scattered across the floor.

Laying with his eyes closed, the soft pillows cradled his head, and the lush blankets hugged his body. Max lay on the bed, wondering if it was actually comfortable or if he'd just grown accustomed to sleeping on the hard ground, and the change felt like heaven. He tried remembering the last time he slept and realized that in three days, he had only relaxed after he blacked out at the spring with Calvo.

Max was on the verge of falling asleep to the soothing sound of the waves outside when he heard a knock at his door.

He jumped at the sudden noise and pulled the blankets over his exposed body. "Come in?" Confused about who could be at his door at this time of night, he posed the statement as a question.

The door slowly crept open, and Rylan stumbled into the bedroom. His legs wobbled through the doorway, and he had a glazed look in his eyes. "Didja find the fairies?"

Max shook his head. "Damn, Ry, how much wine have you had?"

"Too much." He laughed. "They have some good alcohol in that cellar. I wish I could take some home with me."

Max noticed that his friend's speech was fine. He was no longer slurring his words and was holding his body upright. The telltale signs of a drunk Rylan were clear as he'd seen it too many times: stumbling, vomiting, and the need to be pulled away from reckless choices fueled by his liquid bravery. Tonight, he didn't seem as inebriated as he had been historically.

Making his way over to Max's bed, Rylan sat on the corner. "You know, this whole adventure has been kind of fun, hasn't it? I've learned a lot about myself."

"Like what?"

What the hell is going on? Why does he want to have a full conversation right now?

Rylan shrugged. "I dunno, just things that I kept bottled up inside me. I feel like I know more about myself now, like when we get home, I can make things better."

"What do you mean? You always seem so sure of yourself to me."

Flopping onto the bed next to Max, Rylan's blond hair cascaded over the white pillow. "Back at home, my confidence was almost nonexistent. I carried myself well, but it was all a mask I hid behind." He let out a long breath and paused momentarily. "You know how religious my parents are, right? My dad, not so much my mom."

Max nodded, seeing the look of uncertainty in his friend's eyes. *Where is this going?*

"I've never really told anyone this, but he gets violent whenever I do something that doesn't fit his version of who I should be. Remember when all those social media influencers wore those dangly earrings in one ear, and they looked so cool?"

Max nodded and smiled at the memory. "You got your ear pierced and thought you were the coolest guy at school."

"Correction." Rylan smiled. "I *was* the coolest guy at school." His fingers started fidgeting. "Once my dad saw what I did, he literally ripped it out of my ear. I even have to hide my vape, or I'll be forced to go to confession or spend more time at church. He's been doing this shit since I was a kid, and every time he does, he and my mom get into arguments. I just go to my room or leave the house when a fight breaks out." He took a deep breath and shook his head. "Once it's over, I do what he wants to keep the peace, but I won't keep changing myself to appease my father or listen to his bullshit religious excuses anymore."

Max turned to Rylan with wide eyes.

I knew his dad was strict, but I didn't know his home life was so controlled. I can't believe I didn't know this.

Despite Rylan's carefree demeanor, Max was shocked to discover that his friend was dealing with this problem, and guilt overcame his emotions once he realized that Rylan wasn't comfortable confiding in him. He put an arm around Rylan's shoulders. "You know my mom and dad used to argue a lot before he left. Why haven't you talked to me about this before? You know I'm here for you, right?"

Rylan's cheeks turned a light shade of red, and he gave Max a half smile. "I may not say it enough, but you and Leo are my best friends. Without the two of you, I'd be a mess."

"Well, who else would put up with you?"

Both of them looked at one another and laughter erupted from each of their mouths. Max was unsure if they were laughing to ease the tension in the room or because it was the truth.

"I've learned a bit about myself, too," Max admitted. "I'm not exactly sure how to navigate it when we get home, but being on this island has made some things clearer to me." *Do I tell him?* Rylan's eyes were a glassy greenish blue, like waves

210

from the ocean, and a slight smirk sat perched in the corners of his mouth.

Their eyes caught, sending an electric reverberation through the air that only the two of them could sense. He'd never been so vulnerable as he did under Rylan's piercing gaze. They communicated without words, their unspoken understanding filling the silence.

"Between us...I think this is the biggest thing I've learned while being here." Rylan leaned in, his eyes shut tight, and pressed his lips softly against Max's.

Rylan's lips met his own, and he savored the faint taste of salt that left him wanting more.

I never imagined myself doing this with anyone but Hannah, but this is nice, different. It feels...right. It's like my entire life has been hidden in a fog, but now the clouds have been lifted.

Max leaned closer to Rylan, reciprocating the kiss, craving more. As their lips touched, they eased into one another, timidly moving closer until their bodies were almost touching. Rylan slipped one arm beneath Max's neck and the other around his waist, cradling him while their tongues fought against one another in a battle of passion.

"This was why I was jealous of you getting close to Calvo," Rylan whispered against Max's lips.

Something that had never seemed okay before was suddenly perfect; everything was clicking into place. Despite his attempts to suppress his feelings, Max found himself kissing Rylan, relishing in the moment of happiness and relief. A tingly and calm sensation crawled over his body as if the air in the room had become electrified.

Have I been so into Calvo that I didn't see what was right in front of me?

Rylan pulled away, his lips glistening with saliva. He

brushed his thumb alongside Max's face and whispered, "You're my greatest weakness."

Max closed his eyes and savored the moment, relishing Rylan being so close to him. With one final kiss, he uttered a grateful "thank you" before they both drifted off to sleep in each other's arms.

Chapter Twenty-Four

Max's peaceful slumber was rudely interrupted by his internal clock, jarring him awake from his serene dreams. The light from the morning sun hit his eyes as the rays illuminated the bedroom. He looked right, hoping to catch a glimpse of Rylan sleeping, but instead found an empty and disheveled nest of blankets.

Was last night all a dream?

He slid from under the covers and wrapped a linen robe around his shoulders, tying it at his waist. Crossing the bedroom and opening the balcony doors, Max filled his lungs with the warm, salty air. Looking outside, he was amazed at the wispy stratus clouds delicately spread on the azure canvas and the strong rays from the sun pricked his pale skin. Max was immersed in a tranquil scene, the rhythmic sounds of the waves from the ocean below adding to the ambiance.

A smile came to his face as he thought of the castle and the village below, cast in darkness for all these years, finally experiencing the sun's warmth. The brown-roofed houses below were glowing in the sunlight and the dull stone mural imprinted within the center of town appeared brighter than ever. Everything the light touched seemed happy, like a blanket of depression had been lifted.

The weight of reality crashed into him like a speeding train —today was their last day before the beacon lights. Samael's return was imminent if they didn't get to the temple and off the island immediately. A light knock came from his bedroom door and Leo's light brown hair peeked through. "Max, get ready and meet us in the throne room."

Nodding to his friend, he left the balcony and hastily picked up his clothes from the floor next to his bed. He grabbed his sheathed sword leaning against the nightstand and fastened it around his waist. Before exiting, Max passed by a dusty mirror and patted his messy brown hair. Despite his best efforts, running his fingers through each strand was not enough to tame his stubborn bedhead.

He gave himself one final glance in the mirror before making his way down the hallway, through the foyer, and into the grand throne room where Leo and Reina were waiting. The princess's skin radiated a glow that seemed to emanate from within, as if her very presence could heal the kingdom with light.

Leo's eyes were dark and one messy braid hung over her shoulder. "My nerves didn't let me sleep at all last night."

Reina turned her brown eyes to Max. "And how did *you* sleep?"

Max's cheeks grew hot. "Uh...good, I'm very rested." He gulped and looked around the room. "Where's Rylan?"

As if on cue, a familiar voice suddenly filled the air. "Hey all, didja miss me?"

"Seriously? Can you ever be on time?" Leo screamed down the enormous room towards the large double doorway.

Rylan rolled his eyes. "Missed you too, Leo."

Reina chuckled. "And how did you rest last night, Sir Rylan?"

He ran his long, thin fingers through his curly golden hair. "I guess pretty well. That wine really messed me up. I don't remember anything after I finished that last bottle."

Max's heart was heavy as if it had fallen into his stomach.

He didn't just say that, right?

He looked at Rylan and confirmed, "You don't remember *anything* from last night?"

He crossed his arms and shook his head. "I think that wine was roofied or something because I don't remember a thing. I don't even know how I got to my room."

Max winced and stifled a laugh with a lump in his throat. "I could hear you snoring down the hallway." His mouth had become dry as a desert and his hands were slick. Last night he felt understood and safe, which was now replaced with foolishness and embarrassment as his mind began spinning out of control.

Does he actually not remember or is he embarrassed? Am I the reason he chose to forget last night?

"I wanted to thank you three again for your assistance in waking me and freeing the castle from the imps." Reina put her hands to her heart. "As a reward, I'll open the path to the temple, which will be your transport off the island."

"I just hope Ella's there."

"Follow me." Reina turned her body and walked the carpeted trail leading to the throne. She spun and regally sat in the oversized chair. "Please, stand inside Berylon's crest."

Max bowed his head and noticed a white circle with an illustration directly beneath his feet. The mural was split into three quadrants, each showcasing a different sparkling insignia in a unique color. The top of the hill was a gradient of green, blue, and purple, and at the center sat a familiar castle.

"Is this your castle, Reina?" Max asked, pointing to the turreted fortress with a gleaming white diamond in its center.

The princess nodded. "This crest represents a legend that the royal family has handed down for years; we don't have time to get into the specifics." She tucked a lone hair curl behind her ear and unclasped the key necklace from around her neck. "As soon as the keyhole inside the arm of this throne is activated, you will be teleported to the temple. Once you take this mode of transportation, there's no turning back."

"To make sure Samael remains imprisoned, we'll leave the island as soon as we get over there and find out how," Max confidently replied.

He reached into the bag slung over his shoulder and took out the small vial filled with the water that Calvo had given him. Taking a deep breath, he popped the cork and took a swig, feeling it reinvigorate his body. He couldn't help but notice that there was only a small drop of water left. "We're ready."

"It's strange. I usually detect the Sage's power coursing through me like a tidal wave," Reina whispered to herself. "Now, I have to search for it, like a small lifeboat. I hope this works." She plunged the golden key into the arm of the chair and the jewel in the center of the crest encircling the three friends emitted a bright white light.

"Please do everything in your power to leave the island, regardless of the hurdles that may be placed in front of you." The princess clasped her hands and closed her eyes. "Sages of the Island of Forever, assist me in opening the portal to the Temple of Harper."

The white light around them grew brighter. Max latched his hands with both his friends, trying to catch Rylan's eye to no avail and watched as the throne room faded away like rain erasing a newly painted canvas. A tempest of wind flew around them, whipping their clothes and hair.

The world around them transformed from a drab throne room to a lush green paradise, the colors returning to their surroundings. The white light dissolved into the circular shape and the sensation of movement stopped abruptly, indicating they'd arrived at their destination.

They were surrounded by clouds and their feet rested on a small stone dais with Reina's crest intricately carved into the top. Max leaned over the edge of the platform and the wind rushed past him and played with his hair. They were on a piece of land suspended high above the ocean. In front of them, a grassy area stretched out, with a stone walkway cutting through its center. The walkway led to a large, enclosed temple, while an old tree leaned precariously to the right. The white building's beauty was enhanced by the grassy plateau surrounding it, where a network of roots wriggled their way around the base like a trapped serpent.

Upon stepping off the stone base and onto the grassy landing, they were surrounded by a scene of destruction, with rocky debris and broken pillars covered in moss scattered about. One eye from a fractured stone bust was visible, peeking out from the blades of grass as they walked through the area.

"What do you think happened here?"

Leo shrugged as her eyes landed on the statues. "I don't know, it looks like there was a fight or an explosion that caused everything to break."

"Do you think this happened when the Hero was here last?" Rylan speculated.

A long wooden stick with a knife fastened to its end with rope flew out of the sky, planting itself into the ground next to Rylan's feet.

Max and Leo immediately reached to their waist to wield

their weapons. Max held his sword straight ahead as his eyes scanned the area while Leo's palm grasped her gun moving her arm in a semicircle.

A flash of green reached their eyes as a goblin darted from behind a large tree trunk that had fallen near a white pillar. With his trident in hand, Rylan swiftly pulled his arm back and threw it with precision. The three prongs sailed through the air before piercing the bulbous target's belly. "Gotcha."

A final hiss escaped from the creature's gaping mouth before it fell to the ground. Snorts and grunts echoed throughout the area as the goblins emerged from their hiding places. With a rustling sound, the creatures crawled out from the safety of their hiding places behind logs, statues, and pillars, brandishing their makeshift weapons. Their mismatched teeth glinted in the sunlight as they gasped for air.

"We have to fight them to get inside the temple." Max's stance got wider to have more breadth from his sword.

Leo discharged her firearm, and the white-hot projectile flew through the air, piercing the goblin closest to them. Meanwhile, Max strode forward and brandished his sword, cleaving the side of another creature before rappelling down and plunging the blade through its abdomen. Rylan's trident spun around, and the barbs dug into a brown creature nearby, causing him to grin in triumph. He flung the creature off the edge of the flying island with a powerful swing.

Slashing the arm of a goblin off, Max looked at his friends, who were barely breaking a sweat. "They're much easier when there aren't hundreds of them coming at you all at once."

"Or biting your ankles off!" Rylan yelled, skewering one through its eye.

The back of their feet touched the stone steps that led up to the temple. Despite the goblins relentlessly attacking them with spears and spiked clubs, and even launching darts with slingshots, the trio exchanged a determined nod. Turning their backs to their enemies, they sprinted up the steps toward the large door.

Reaching the top, Max wrapped his fingers around the handle and the door groaned as he leaned against it, opening just enough for them to slip inside and shut behind them. They leaned against the wooden surface to catch their breath, amazed that they'd made it inside without any additional attacks.

A rainbow of light danced around the structure's innards, making it feel like they'd stepped into a kaleidoscope. Max's eyes were drawn upward to the source of the dancing colors, which was revealed to be a large, stained-glass mosaic spanning the entire ceiling. As the sun caught the shards of glass, rays of colored light rained down onto the white landscape.

The sound of feet shuffling came from their left. With his trident ready, Rylan turned, and Leo had her hand glued to her gun. Their eyes darted towards the origin of the sound but found no one in sight.

A line of pillars made a pathway to the head of the temple and in each corner of the temple were four large statues of animals, all looking regal and wise. The pathway ended at a rectangular rostrum, which was elevated by three stone steps. The landing was decorated with a circular stone table and at its center was a large cup filled with water that resembled a birdbath. Towering at the end of the temple was an enormous door made of pure gold, shining brilliantly in the light.

"Do you think the other door goes outside?" Rylan asked as he took in the scene in front of him.

"I think it's our ticket home. We just need to figure out how."

The sound of feet running could be heard to their left again. Rylan positioned his trident over his shoulder and after hearing the sound, threw it, successfully pinning the person to a nearby pillar by the collar of their shirt.

"Hey, get me down from here!"

Max's face lit up, and he sprinted towards the nearby pillar, determined to free the little girl from the trident that held her captive. "Ella!"

Her clothes were ripped and tattered, hanging off her body like she'd run through a farm of rose bushes. She no longer wore shoes on her feet and her perfectly combed hair was matted. Dirt covered her face, but her bright eyes still shone through.

Ella jumped into his arms. "I knew you would save me, Max. Can we go home now?"

Rylan's eyebrows rose as he watched Max and the little girl's reunion. Something was not adding up in his mind. "Ella, how are you here? Where are the goblins that kidnapped you?"

Her eyes rolled and her smile vanished when she faced the merman. "I snuck away from them, duh." She turned her eyes back to her brother, pleading. "Please bring me home, I miss Mommy."

Rylan and Leo exchanged a look, raising their eyebrows.

"Where's Hannah?" Rylan asked.

"We were told everyone was being held against their will. Where's everyone else?" Leo pressed.

Ella stiffened in Max's arms and emitted gravelly breathing from her nose as if she found it hard to breathe. "They're being mean to me."

Relief flooded him as he embraced his sister, yet he couldn't ignore the validity of Leo and Rylan's argument. "Ella, how *did* you get here?"

The little girl emitted a loud shriek and pushed herself away from Max. "Open the damn door and let's go home." Her hand flew to her mouth, eyes wide with surprise at the words that had just escaped her.

Ella's malicious outburst caused Max to drop her from his embrace, and he was horrified to see tiny pin-sized bubbles appearing all over her skin. The bubbles began to burst one-by-one, causing pieces of her flesh to fall off and land on the ground with a sickening splat.

Chapter Twenty-Five

He watched in horror as the skin melted from his sister's body and a green toad-like mass emerged. In front of him was a hunchbacked goblin with squished nose and floppy ears lying on its bulbous head. Its eyes had a milky glow, and its teeth were crooked and jagged, like a child's baby teeth. Max and his friends were confronted by a goblin, whose snorting sound immediately brought back a rush of memories. The feeling of a blossoming hope of saving Ella was quickly replaced with a never-ending dark hole inside of him. "Where the *hell* is my sister?"

"She's closer than you think." The voice sounded almost as if every word were part of a song, yet masculine and confident. "Look above you."

Fear crept into his mind as Max's gaze shifted upward to see a blanket of transparent hexagonal pods shimmer into view. People of every age range, from children to adults, were curled up in the fetal position in each of the linked pods as if they were fast asleep. Scanning each face, Max found his sister and yelled her name, hoping she might wake up.

"I see the fairy girls, too," Leo screamed behind them.

Max couldn't help but feel anxious as he scanned the crowd of people above him, hoping to catch a glimpse of Hannah and Calvo and ensure their safety. "Release them!"

A cocky laugh echoed along the walls of the temple. "Do you like my collection? These people are going to help me return to power once I'm released from this damn volcano. The final piece to my puzzle was the delivery of the three fairy girls and guess what?" The voice softened but still had a tingle of amusement. "There's nothing you can do to save them."

Leo let out a small gasp before covering her mouth and Rylan's eyes widened in fear. They all knew whose voice it was without ever hearing it before. Samael.

He was here.

"My friends aren't your toys, you asshole!" Leo whipped out her gun and started shooting. Each bullet that reached the crystal pods disintegrated upon contact.

Max raised his sword into the air with rage burning in his chest. "If I have to fight you to free them, I will. Come out and show yourself."

"Let me enter my vessel to join you. I'd like to negotiate in person."

Goblins flooded the temple, encircling Max and his companions, but Max couldn't tear his eyes away from the dark figure silhouetted against the blinding light outside. His body was frozen in place as the man strode into the temple, his muscular legs carrying him confidently through the throngs of goblins, a smug smirk on his face.

"I knew this guy was a Grade A asshole." Rylan scoffed through gritted teeth.

"C-Calvo...wh-what are you doing here?" The magical water that cured his unease instantly wore off and his heart began furiously vibrating like a drum.

The man bowed with a flourish of his hand above his head. "It has been a pleasure watching you traipse across this island while I kidnapped people to plot my return." The once warm eyes of Calvo turned toward Max. "The first night you came to this island, my spirit was freed. You were there, don't you remember?"

Max clasped his palm over his mouth.

Samael was the wolf that attacked me in the Sofillian camp.

He couldn't believe how close he was to him this entire time.

A smug smirk crossed Calvo's lips. "Of course, you do. It was at that moment I realized you were going to be an asset in freeing me. My spirit possessed a nearby wolf and once you threw me off, I separated from the beast and found," he paused to flex his abs and pump each bicep, "*this* gorgeous new vessel."

"You're despicable!" Leo pointed her gun. "You kidnapped innocent people in order to free yourself from your prison. Release them, all of them."

"You see, I picked this vessel carefully." Calvo ran his hands over his body, ignoring the fairy girl's threat. "I wanted someone strong but also strikingly good-looking to...seduce those I may gain from."

Calvo's light brown eyes darted to him.

This can't be possible.

"I may be inside this big buffoon's head, but his physical body is still his own. Deal a blowing strike and he will die. Fortunately for me, my spirit can move to someone else until my own body is released."

"We won't let that happen," Max vowed.

"If you were smart, you would." Calvo's laugh echoed through the temple, which made the goblins rowdier. "Once I am freed and my power is restored, I can resume control over this island. Don't fret, I do have a deal to offer you." He cleared his throat, a smirk still pulling at his lips. "I'll release your sister if you open the portal to the Mainland and join me in conquering both worlds."

"Where's Hannah?" Rylan yelled. "Her and Ella need to be returned without a scratch."

"Your friends are extremely rude, Max. I'm surprised you wanted to take the time to find them." His eyes glinted with knowledge and ferocity, every word calculated.

Max's ears burned.

He's going to tell them that I thought about leaving them. They'll never look at me the same again.

"Join me, Max." Calvo's voice softened, and his eyebrows rose in concern. "Think about it—no one will poke fun at you again. Your mother and even your father will be proud of you. Open the portal and accept the deal of a lifetime."

Leo and Rylan gasped in unison, and the grunting of the goblins progressively grew louder around them. Max was shaking in anger and his knuckles turned white from clutching the hilt of his sword every time Calvo uttered a word. He was lost and didn't know what to do. He was aware that coming to the temple could be a trap, but it turned out that they played into Samael's hands.

"Why can't you open the portal yourself?" Rylan asked. "You're supposed to be this big bad guy, full of power, right?"

"That's precisely why I need Max." Calvo cocked his head and pursed his lips, pointing to the far end of the temple. "Look at the writing above the door. Can you read it?"

The symbols were written in a foreign language Rylan and Leo couldn't understand, so they shook their heads. Max squinted, hoping to make sense of the squiggles. Before his eyes, the alien language rearranged itself into words he could understand.

"What do you see?" Calvo's gaze never left Max, penetrating his thoughts.

I can't let them know.

He shook his head and shrugged. "I can't read it."

"Don't lie!" Calvo yelled, making the goblins jump. "Tell me what it says."

Rylan squeezed Max's shoulder, hoping to give him a sense of comfort. "Can you read it, Max?"

Leo's gaze bore into him, and he realized he could no longer keep denying it. Max let out a defeated breath of air and slowly nodded. He turned his eyes to the newly formed words above the door. "To see new worlds, grace the cup with the blood of a shapeshifter and turn time to release the lock."

Shit.

"Exactly." Calvo smiled as his eyes filled with light. "That is why I lured the three of you here. I cannot use my blood since this isn't my body."

Leo crossed her arms. "The only shifter in recent history on this island was you, so it looks like this door's gonna stay closed."

Shit. Shit.

"You are partially correct, fairy girl." Calvo flashed a bright, white smile as if he won a game. "Because my vessel doesn't have shapeshifter blood running through his veins, I can't open the door. I need someone from the same bloodline as myself to assist."

"I thought you were supposed to be smart?" Rylan scoffed with his chin in the air. "I'm from the ocean and Leo is a fairy..."

Shit, here we go.

Rylan's voice grew quieter as they talked, as if he'd stumbled upon a crucial realization. Max's friends turned to look at him, their eyes wide with fear. Seeing their reaction, he felt exposed, as if all his secrets had been laid bare before them. The air grew thick, and sound had disappeared from Max's ears as he breathed, "Does that mean that I'm...?"

"A shifter?" Calvo finished for him, his eyebrows raised. "If my theory is correct, yes."

"Stop manipulating my friend!" Leo yelled, shaking her head. "You must be lying, shapeshifters are evil."

Calvo put one finger in the air. "While it's true that I'm often considered deceitful and calculating, I assure you I'm being completely honest. From my calculations, and I'm hardly ever wrong, your friend Max is from the shapeshifter blood-line." He walked closer to the boy, bringing his sturdy body into better view. "Let me ask you something we both know the answer to—have you ever transformed your body or shifted into another form to protect yourself?"

A memory surfaced at the top of Max's brain, flashing before his eyes. He remembered hallucinating at the Sofillian overlook. His arms were covered in black vein-like lines and transformed to four times their normal size to assist him in defending himself and Hannah. "What does this mean?"

"It means you're part of the most elite beings on this island, just like me." Calvo's arms fanned into a semi-circle. "Shifters used to dominate this island and were the most powerful beings before everyone else got scared and started a war."

"Everyone got scared? Good one." Leo laughed. "The shifters were ruthless, they enslaved fairies for their enjoyment and tortured merfolk by infecting their waters."

"Yeah, they were disgusting, don't believe a word this twat says!" Rylan urged.

He turned to his friends and lowered his head. "I don't wanna believe him, but I think he's right. I'm a shapeshifter. I know it, but I don't want to be." Saying the words aloud created a cloud of realization over the beings within the temple. It was as if speaking it had made it true. After all this, Max came face-to-face with the monster he'd been trying to escape. A deep sense of shame and embarrassment burrowed into his brain, knowing that his friends discovered the truth and that he would now be seen as evil in the eyes of many.

The goblins surrounding them let out a triumphant roar as they wielded their makeshift spears over their heads. Rylan and Leo's mouths both dropped in disbelief at Max's declaration.

He extended his finger at Calvo. "Even though we're from the same clan, it doesn't mean I can allow you to leave this island."

"I thought you may say that." Calvo smiled and snapped his fingers at the hexagonal pods, causing them to disappear. "But that's where you are wrong. I will obtain your blood to open this door, even if I have to tear you limb from limb to get it." Calvo stood tall, his shoulders squared. He pointed to the three friends and yelled, "Goblins, attack!"

The sound of the goblins' battle cries echoed through the air as they charged toward them with their makeshift weapons. Rylan's trident jabbed at the nearby goblin, and it emitted a high-pitched yelp like a dog getting its paw stepped on, and Leo's bullets were being fired at the speed of a revolver.

Max, on the other hand, was sandwiched in the middle of his two friends, limply holding his sword. A strange vacancy left him hollow, but his heart burned as if all his energy had been sent to his center. His body was overwhelmed by the sensation of being pulled in multiple directions, causing him to shut his eyes tightly and cry out in pain. As he opened his eyes, he realized that he had grown taller, and his hands and feet had transformed into hooves.

Calvo's eyes were sparkling like he was watching a beautiful firework display. "My, my, you *are* special."

Dark fur cascaded down Max's body and his mouth was seared with such pain, he feared he would soon start tasting blood. He was in so much pain that he thought he might faint, but the throbbing ceased just as suddenly as it began. He blinked away the tears and was met with the shocking sight of long tusks curving upwards from his mouth.

Once the pain subsided, Max was able to take in his surroundings and saw that the goblins had formed a tight circle around them with their weapons aimed. Rylan and Leo had done an excellent job at fighting them off, but there were too many to attack at once. With a fierce determination, he lowered his tusks and charged at the horde of goblins, sending them flying into nearby walls or pushing them away from his friends. The nearby creatures lunged, clinging to him with their teeth, but his outer layer of skin and fur protected him.

Leo sprang into action when she saw the goblins attacking Max. She aimed her light bullets at their round bodies, causing them to freeze and drop to the ground with a thump. Grabbing onto his fur, Rylan and Leo hoisted themselves onto Max's back. Leo made sure they were secure between his shoulders and replenished her ammunition while Rylan frantically waved his arms above his head, conjuring rain droplets from the moist air.

"Let's give Samael a major ass-kicking!" Rylan yelled from Max's back. "If it worked for that imp gorilla, it'll work for these dumb goblins. Leo, are you ready?"

Max gave a hearty grunt and reared his head towards Samael, who was standing on the stone platform with the cup near the golden door.

Leo nodded to her friend and Rylan released the water

from the air, almost as if a light rain cloud was hiding inside the temple. Droplets spread throughout the room, covering the ground and everyone inside. Leo aimed her gun at the wet floor and fired a single shot. The white bullet soared through the air and caused the ground of the temple to become fused with electricity, just like at Reina's castle.

The goblins seemed unfazed as the current spread, but as soon as it reached Max, his body became tingly and all the hair on his body stood at attention. By trying to electrocute the goblins, Leo had forgotten that Max was grounded as well. Suddenly, the power that had transformed him into this almighty beast left his body. Rylan and Leo tumbled from his back, and the thick fur encircling them vanished.

"What's happening?" Leo screamed as she toppled to the ground. A horde of goblins jumped on top of both of them, wrapping rope around Rylan and Leo's hands and feet so they couldn't escape.

Max lay on the damp ground and completely changed back to his original body. The clothes he wore prior to his shift were ripped and tattered, saving him the embarrassment of being naked.

Calvo let out a loud laugh. "Nice try, kids, but goblin skin works the same as rubber, so your little trick was amiss."

Rylan grunted as he tried to escape from the goblin's grasp. "Max, are you okay?"

He couldn't move his body or even muster the strength to answer Rylan. Max's ears caught a faint clicking sound in the distance and wondered where it was coming from. His vision blurred and soon, his body gave up. He closed his eyes and released everything he'd been holding onto.

"Goblins, please bring the shifter to me immediately."

A few moments passed and Max sat helplessly with his eyes closed. The sounds within the temple soon dissipated from his ears and were replaced with silence. His body carried a weight he could not lift and once the goblins sat him upright, he was nervous that he may collapse within himself. It was like all his bones were broken and his brain was not allowing himself to react.

I've failed them.

Chapter Twenty-Six

The sound of goblins' snorting disappeared, and Max opened his eyes, immediately feeling a sense of familiarity. There was a faint smell of rain wafting through an open window and the fluorescent light bulbs cast a yellow hue on the stained wooden floor. He was lying on the old couch in his living room with his sister snuggled into his arm.

How'd I get here? What's going on?

Seeing the darkened sky through the window, he realized the storm hadn't happened yet. Confusion clouded his mind as he looked around his bedroom, a space he knew so well. Having had such a grand experience on the island, the abrupt transition back to his normal life felt jarringly surreal.

Was the Island of Forever a dream I made up after hearing Ana's story?

Max brought his ear to Ella's face, hearing a small snore emit from her mouth. He breathed a sigh of relief that his sister was safe with him and was now sure that the island was just a strange and vivid dream.

Was I asleep longer than I thought?

A prick in the center of his palm startled him as there was no mark, but the light needle-like pain constantly reminded him it was there.

Picking Ella off the couch, Max held her in his arms as he carried her to the bedroom. Max laid her head against the soft pillow and tucked her small body under the blanket. Pushing the island to the back of his mind, he recalled what this night in the real world was meant to entail. "Shit, I'm not remotely close to being ready for Hannah to come over." He couldn't recognize how real his dream had appeared and needed time to process all that he'd learned about himself while in his slumber.

A vision appeared in his head, almost like a flashback. Leo appeared, just as she had in his dream, wearing a stunning dress made of an array of plants and flowers, while aiming a wooden pistol straight at him. Her eyes squinted and her lips were moving, but no sound came out. A faint pain punctured his palm once again. The skin in his palm was pink, and he tried rubbing the area to make the pain disappear.

Max stumbled into the hallway as the fragmented dream disappeared from his vision. "What's happening to me?"

With his hand on his head, he returned to his bedroom to prepare for Hannah's arrival. The howling wind outside made the nearby tree sway back and forth, and a small branch brushed against his bedroom window with a light tapping sound.

"That must have been the tapping I heard earlier." He scanned his small bedroom and didn't see the joint he remembered smoking from his dream. He looked under his bed and in the trash but couldn't find any trace of the paraphernalia. "Am I going crazy?"

Something was strange, but he couldn't exactly pinpoint what was wrong. He rubbed the palm of his hand as the splinter-like pain continued.

Sitting on the edge of his bed, Max took in the essence of his room. Perfectly lined posters hung on his wall, his dirty clothes were neatly placed in his wash basket, and his bed had been made seamlessly as if he were staying in a hotel room. Everything was well kept and was in its place. "At least everything is picked up for when Hannah gets here." He surveyed his room with a growing sense of unease, as suspicion slowly took over his thoughts. He scoured the small area, hoping to catch a glimpse of anything unusual. His mother constantly nagged him about cleaning his dirty room and it just seemed too perfect to be true.

Another person appeared inside his mind, but this time, it was Rylan. Max saw his friend with distressed rope netting wrapped around half of his chest and his metal trident tightly held in his grasp. With his trident at his side, he positioned his scaly feet ready to attack as he snarled fiercely.

He heard a voice scream: "WAKE UP!"

It was like a lightbulb turned on within his brain. "None of this is real."

As he walked to his bedroom wall, he knew what he had to do. He balled up his fist, hit the wall with all his might, and watched as the plaster reconnected itself. He let out a scream and with a sudden burst of strength, lifted the computer chair and flung it through the bedroom window. The room was restored to its previous state as the window fixed itself and the chair returned to the desk, all within seconds.

"Get me out of here!" Max slammed his eyes shut and clenched his jaw. The storm outside his house howled and the ground shook like an earthquake.

If I remember correctly, the glass in my bedroom window will shatter next.

As the thought left his brain, there was a blast of wind and a tinkle of glass hitting the floor. The pain in his palm grew and suddenly, the storm had disappeared.

Am I going to wake up back on the island? On Captain Marris's ship?

The sounds at Max's house were replaced with the snorting of goblins. Opening his eyes, he was greeted with a parade of fallen creatures and saw his friends running across the temple with their weapons ready. Despite the hectic situation, Max was relieved to be back. The illusion he had been in was too strange and unnatural for his liking.

Calvo held Max's outstretched arm in his rough hands, forcing his palm to hover over the large birdbath-like bowl. He fixated on the droplet of blood pooling at the center of Max's palm, and his honey-colored eyes darkened with thirst.

"Move your hand away from that bowl," Rylan yelled through the goblin's struggling breath. "He was tricking you into thinking you were somewhere else so he can force you to open the portal."

Max tried to move his feet, but his entire body was incapacitated. "I can't move." His eyes fell on the slow pool of crimson blood in the center of his palm. "Samael's going to escape."

The sound of high heels clicking against the floor echoed throughout the room. Leo and Rylan skidded to a stop as they caught sight of a massive silhouette looming behind Calvo, who was staring intently at the blood dripping from Max's hand into the murky-white water basin. As the shadow neared them, Max could see a seven-foot black-and-white striped spider come into his view. The spider looked familiar, and he realized it was the same one that had scared Hannah in The Rift. The spider's glowing red eyes honed onto Max and lunged toward him, sinking its pincers into Calvo's neck.

The man let out a blood-curdling scream, clutching the area where the spider had bitten him. Max withdrew his hand from the bowl, a sharp twinge of pain shooting through his fingers, and a single droplet of blood spattered into the basin below, its crimson hue dispersing like tendrils of smoke.

The floor of the temple began shaking and there was a sudden lurch from the island in the sky. The crack that split the temple in half started from the golden door and zigzagged all the way to the entrance, swallowing the few remaining goblins on its way.

"We need to get out of here, the island's going to fall into the ocean!" Leo grabbed Rylan's hand to ensure they wouldn't be separated.

A sudden tremor ran through Max as he stepped on a newly formed fissure, causing him to quickly shift his weight to regain his balance. The exit to the temple was across a deep crevasse that separated him and Calvo. "I need to close the gate so he can't leave!"

If Samael found a way to get across the large crack in the ground and twist the cup, the gate to the Mainland will open. The rumbling grew louder as Max and Calvo were separated by the widening gap. The basin and circular table it sat on fell through the hole, plummeting into the depths of the temple.

"Max, let's get out of here!" Leo cried.

"Interesting that your friends wouldn't leave *you* behind, isn't it, Max?"

"Shut up, Samael!"

Rylan's eyebrows raised as he yelled over the commotion. "What's he talking about?"

The temple gave another loud lurch and the pillars within the temple started crumbling and falling over. As the rumbling intensified, the stained-glass ceiling gave way, leaving a shower of colorful broken glass falling through the sky.

Clutching his neck, Calvo used his strong legs to jump across the temple to a nearby window and hoist himself onto the sill. "When he first came to the Island of Forever, your friend Max suggested coming directly to this temple without both of you. He wanted to leave you on this island, never to return to the Mainland."

"You're a piece of shit if you think we'd believe that," Rylan shouted.

His amused voice rose in question. "Am I lying, Max?"

The hurt in Rylan and Leona's eyes made Max's heart ache.

I never wanted them to find out. They're looking at me like they don't know me anymore.

"You're my best friend." Rylan locked eyes with him and the answer was conveyed without a word. "How could you even have considered that?"

He looked toward his friends, his eyes filled with regret, as another tremor shook the ground. The island within the sky began to descend, like the strings that held it afloat were severed.

"The temple is unraveling, and you'll soon plummet to your death. The destruction of the Temple of Harper means my freedom is imminent. Once the beacon closes, I'll have enough people to regain my full power." With a cocky laugh, he put two fingers to his head and saluted a goodbye before disappearing through the window.

Max turned to see Rylan and Leo making their way to the temple's entrance. "I can't get to you! The crevasses are too wide."

"Try using your shapeshifter powers," Leo yelled back.

The tone in his friend's voice made him wince, but nevertheless, Max nodded and closed his eyes to search within himself to find the burning power he'd summoned in his chest while battling the goblins.

Focus. I need to transform into a bird of some kind.

As he was trying to center himself, pillars crumbled to the ground and pieces of ceiling banged onto the surrounding floor. His nerves were so frayed that he found it impossible to concentrate.

What if I can't summon my powers? They've always been unpredictable. How will we get out of this alive?

Another lurch came from the temple and this time, it was like they were on a roller coaster. Max's stomach was in his throat, and he knew the temple was falling from the sky.

"I can't do it," Max screamed to his friends, who were attempting to remain upright.

I'm a failure. First my sister gets kidnapped and now I can't even save my friends. I'm the only person who's able to get us out of here. I can't protect anyone I love.

He shook his head at Leo and Rylan. "Go without me—see if you can use the teleport back to the castle."

The temple shook once more and the ceiling caved in, completely separating Max from his friends. He yelled over the commotion, hoping they could hear him, "Rylan, take Leo and leave this place before this island crashes into the sea. I can't make it over to you, but I'll try to get out of here and find a way back to the island." After these words, he heard nothing further and prayed that his friends left without him.

Looking for a way to escape, Max realized the only way he was getting out of the temple was through the window opposite the one Samael disappeared through. He reached the wall and latched his fingers into the frame, pulling his body up to sit within the window. The temple was falling out of the sky and plummeting toward the ocean, every second getting closer to the foamy waves below.

Max peered out the window and immediately realized that jumping wouldn't be an option due to the distance to the ground. The old, twisted tree on the outskirts of the small island was right in front of him. He could see the ground below was crumbling and ready to detach at any second.

This is a stupid idea.

He crouched on the windowsill. The cool breeze brushed against his face and his fingers were poised to launch him forward.

Here goes nothing!

With a deep breath, he jumped. His fingers dug into the rough tree bark, and with a sudden jolt, the tree was uprooted, sending him careening toward the ocean.

Chapter Twenty-Seven

I *think I blacked out.*

Max's eyes regained sight as the waning afternoon sun met his face. He swayed back and forth with the ocean's waves as he clutched the twisted and dried trunk of the tree. Licking his dry lips, he winced at how they stung as they regained moisture, a salty taste enveloping his mouth.

Max unclasped his fingers from around the bark and stretched them, each cracking from their stiffness. Straddling the tree trunk, foamy sea water lapped at the soles of his shoes as he had washed up on a sandy shore. Seaweed lined the outside of the beach, creating just enough friction so that the tree trunk didn't dislodge from the coast.

Max gazed around the area, hoping to see a multitude of colored shells to indicate he was in familiar territory. Instead, the beach wrapped around a small island, and ahead of him was a lush patch of overgrown vegetation. Planted in the middle of the leaning palm trees and snaking vines was a rocky cave, almost hidden by the moss that brushed over it like a waterfall.

"Wh-where am I?" Max whispered to no one in particular. He sidled off the tree trunk and brushed his dirty pants. This island was tiny; he could walk its entire circumference in at least ten minutes. The island was uninhabited, with nothing but a small plot of greenery.

I'm stranded here.

He trudged through the fine sand and stood at the mouth of the cave. The grass on the small island had turned to dirt and stone as the cave sloped inward. A quiet hum echoed from its depths that seemed to draw him in.

Pulling back the mossy hair that covered the entrance, his eyes caught a flash of red light to his left, and fear struck his core. He turned to see that, in the distance, a bright red beam of light shot into the heavens. A shiver ran through his body as the sky turned pink, and dark clouds curved around the beacon like a great force had pushed its way through. He knew the light was coming from the middle of the island and was shocked at how far away he was.

The beacon had been lit. Time was up—this was the beginning of Samael's return. His prison was slowly weakening, and a sense of helplessness hung in the air because Max knew there was no quick way to reach the island.

"This isn't good."

Why am I drawn to this cave? It's like there's an invisible string attached to me, pulling me inward. Hopefully it leads me back to the island.

Letting out a breath of air, Max readied his sword before descending into the mouth of the cave.

"Hello?" Max called out, and his voice echoed back to him, the hum within the cave staying constant. He placed one hand on the left side of the wall to steady himself as the light inside grew darker and darker. "There better not be any Indiana

Jones-type booby traps in here," Max whispered as he inched forward. "I can barely see."

The humming that bounced off the walls grew louder, and he ventured further into the cave. "Is anyone there?" Max's hand caressed the cave walls until he found his hand in front of him.

"Is this a dead end?" Max whispered aloud. "Where do I go from here?" Failure crept into his mind.

This is just a cave, not a tunnel leading back to the island. How am I going to get back to my friends and Ella before the beacon closes and the prison opens?

He removed his hand from the wall, and the humming intensified. Shards of light began blinking around him, glowing brighter until a flash of white reached his eyes.

Black spots from the harsh light disappeared from his view to reveal crystals illuminating the dead end of the cave. The walls, the ceiling, and the floor danced with light and color from the gems. It looked like a rainbow had been imprisoned, and the light finally let it out, allowing it to swiftly envelop him. A smile pricked Max's face as he was filled with a sense of internal warmth and comfort.

A female voice boomed throughout the crystal cave. "Welcome, Max. I've been expecting you."

Turning to his left, he saw a large crystal jutting from the ground, glowing exceptionally bright. Four thin, black sticks appeared inside the crystal, latching around the outside as if something were pushing its way out. He placed a hand on the sword at his hip, preparing for a fight if necessary.

A gigantic spider emerged from the crystal and stood a few feet away from Max. This large being, a few inches taller than Max, had a small round face and a bulbous backside. Its body had black and white stripes starting at its waist and continuing downward. Perched at the top of its head were several black, beady eyes that looked as if they were made of glass, and a smile adorned its red mouth.

Max's hands began to sweat, and a lump appeared in his throat. "I-I need t-to get b-back to the island." He pointed to his left and noticed his finger trembling.

"Relax. I will not harm you," the spider cooed as a pair of fangs poked out from its upper lip. "You've had a long journey here, haven't you? Where are your friends?"

This spider's voice sounds weirdly familiar; her words are very particular, like you can hear every letter she says.

Max's eyes fixated on the glistening fangs every time the spider opened its mouth. "I-if I need to f-fight you, I will."

The spider made a tutting sound with her mouth. "I see you looking at my teeth. Don't you think if I wanted to use them, I'd already have ripped your head off and sucked the blood from your veins?"

In an attempt to sound as confident as possible, Max' trembling hands unsheathed his sword. "T-try it."

The spider put two of her front legs under her chin and let out a small laugh. "That wasn't a threat, I was just trying to explain to make you more comfortable, and now I realize I failed." Her eyes returned to Max, and she tilted her head. "Do you know who I am?"

The thought had been nagging at Max's brain since the spider began talking. He had heard this voice before but couldn't connect from where. The voice was deeper, although feminine, and every word spoken was exaggerated, like each sentence was part of a story. "Th-the spider from The Rift?"

"Yes, but who else do I remind you of?" Seeing the puzzled look on Max's face, the spider threw her arms in the air. "You will make the connection in time. I know you're apprehensive about telling me anything, but I need to know what happened to your sister."

Max's eyes pricked with water. "She...she was kidnapped by a horde of goblins and is now in Samael's possession."

The spider's eyes grew wide, the light dancing in its orb-like eyes. "The beacon has been lit, and if what you say is true, Samael must have the proper amount of souls needed to escape the volcano and return to power. The beacon is the indicator for everyone on the island that there isn't much time before his prison is opened. If that's the case, you need to reawaken the Hero."

"The Hero?" Max recalled what he knew of this person. "But he's been missing since Samael was first locked up."

"You're correct," the spider agreed. "They're in a deep slumber, waiting for the day that the Island of Forever is in danger and needs to be reawakened." The spider shot a sticky white web into the air and propelled herself onto the ceiling of the crystal cave, her legs scuttling to the other side of the room. "Deep inside the center of this cave."

Max's eyes widened at the revelation and watched as the spider used her eight legs to stick to the ceiling. As each of her legs hit one of the crystals jutting overhead, it sounded like she was tap-dancing.

"I've heard that sound before," Max said, realization dawning. "You were in the Temple of Harper with us—you're the one that bit Calvo."

The spider craned her neck from the ceiling with a sheepish smirk. "I'd do it again, too. It was the only way to ensure the gate didn't open." Slowly descending from the ceiling, she hovered just above a white crystal jutting from the floor near the back of the cave. "Join me over here."

Against his fearful body's judgment, Max walked towards her with his hands trembling. Below the spider was a crystal that looked as if someone had cut off its pointed top, sanded it down, and scooped out a hollow bowl. A pure light pulsed from its center like a heartbeat.

The spider gestured to the crystal below her. "This will assist you in finding the sleeping Hero."

"How?"

"This bowl is the key to delving deeper into this crystal cave. Not just anyone can reawaken the Hero. A series of trials guard them."

"What do I have to do?" Max asked hesitantly.

"Activating the portal is easy. You must deposit a drop of blood from a shapeshifter into this basin."

Max's eyes veered downward. He didn't want to be a shapeshifter. He tried to suppress all feelings of revealing who he was until he could return home and be a normal kid.

Everyone hates the shapeshifters. I don't wanna risk being this spider's dinner.

"Judging by the orange sky outside, we have little time to save your sister. Do you have access to a drop of shapeshifter blood?" Her question made it sound as if she knew the answer and was waiting for him to admit it. "The decision is yours to make, but I think if you use it in the basin, you'll emerge from these trials a stronger person."

Max didn't expect this softness from the spider. She sounded almost motherly and like she had his best interest at heart. This exchange unlocked a memory within his mind, but he still couldn't place where he knew the spider's voice from. The memory dangled on the tip of his tongue. Although he couldn't recollect who the spider reminded him of, he knew in his bones she was trustworthy. "Let's do it."

The spider smiled wide, fangs overlapping her lips. "Excellent! You only need a little drop, then deposit it into this basin, and the crystals will guide you to the first trial." It extended a long leg towards Max's face. "Be warned, you'll be tested physically as well as emotionally."

Max wiped his sweaty palms on his jeans and wondered if he had made the right decision.

How will I be able to complete these trials if thinking of them makes me anxious?

So many questions were unanswered, and at this point, he didn't know if he would ever reunite with his sister, his friends, Hannah, or even return to his normal life.

He took the blade of his sword and made a light swipe on his palm. The cut was clean, and bits of red filled the line within seconds. He made a fist and stood over the basin, waiting for one drop to pool and fall into the bowl below.

"Oh, and one more thing." The spider flung a sticky web at Max's waist. "Weapons and accessories are not allowed." With her words, she tugged on the web, pulling the sword clear off his waist and the leather bag from his shoulder. Her spindly arms reached into his leather bag and pulled out the crystal vial of spring water. She uncorked it and dumped the last drop into the basin.

Max's palms went into full hyper-drive. He was lost without the reassurance that he could protect himself and had nothing to quell his anxiety. It was reminiscent of being in the gym locker room again, and the guys were making fun of him. He felt naked. Exposed. Alone.

The spider watched as Max continued to wipe his free hand on the outside of his pants. A sly smile crossed her face as she tapped the top of Max's hand, causing a lone drop of crimson blood to fall into the basin below. The blood pooled at the bottom of the small bowl and merged with the water, the liquid growing with each moment that passed until it was close to overflowing.

"Good luck and be true to yourself." The spider jumped

across the crystal cave with Max's sword and bag clutched in one of her eight hands, disappearing back inside the crystal from where she came.

The small pool inside the basin began bubbling and screeching like it was boiling in a teapot. The crystals along the walls and roof of the cave strobed all around him, like he'd entered a club. He stumbled. The crystal was drawing him closer as if he were inside a vacuum, just like the storm that brought him to the island.

Max's feet slid on the ground, and once he blinked, he found himself in a new room. The surrounding walls looked to be made of glass as everything around him resembled a mirror, but somehow, his reflection was too far away to see. Starbursts hung in the air, and a white hazy glow laid upon the area.

Am I inside the crystal?

Chapter Twenty-Eight

"Max!" A voice echoed throughout the room. "Grab your sister and go inside the house."

He knew that voice—his mother's tone had a tinge of fear woven within. He turned his gaze in the direction of the voice and started walking towards the shimmering crystalline wall. A sheet of milky mist enveloped him, and he found himself on an impeccably kept lawn under a blue sky. A two-story house with curtains billowing out of the windows on every floor stood before him. The front door was open, and a woman stood on the wrap-around deck, watching two kids playing in the front yard.

Blood ran to Max's face because he knew this scene perfectly. It was the last day he'd seen his father. A sharp jab pierced his heart and pressure built behind his eyes. Ella was in a playpen set up in the shade of a tree, and a khaki bucket hat kept falling in her face. Max had just thrown a yellow tennis ball and laughed as their dog furiously chased after it.

The scene replayed as he heard his mother's tone become

harsher, shorter. "Max, grab your sister and get inside the house. Now."

He watched as a younger version of himself picked up the slobbery tennis ball the yellow-haired dog deposited at his feet and threw it across the yard. As the dog darted away in a blur, he grabbed his sister under her armpits and held her securely, with one arm under her bottom and the other resting on her back. Ella's big smile and bright eyes lit up once she came face-to-face with her brother.

In his present state, Max ran to the younger versions of himself and Ella. "Just get in the house." Neither Ella nor the younger Max in front of him heard him and continued their slow pace. He ran to them and stood on the edge of the crushed rock path that led to the deck's stairs, knowing that this was as far as they'd get.

Ugh, what the hell. I wish I could warn him.

He and Ella neared the steps to ascend onto the deck where their mother had been standing when their father appeared in the doorway. His gaunt face was outlined by shadow, and a suitcase on wheels was perched next to him. There was something different about his father's face, something strange that didn't exist in his memory—his eyes were missing, and two black and hollow craters sat just above his nose.

He turned to glance at his younger self to see if he noticed the difference in his father's eyes, but his expression remained unchanged.

"Move," Max's father grunted to his wife, his voice deep and angry.

His mother stepped aside, her bruised wrist clutching the railing of the steps. The thumping of the suitcase reverberated through the thick air as it descended on each step.

"Ella, stop." He heard his younger self whisper to his sister as she shifted in his hands once she saw their father.

Max stared at the lifeless black eyes the others didn't seem to see. The pools of black never seemed to end and showed no emotion as he gazed at the two kids at the bottom of the steps.

Ella kept wiggling, arms outstretched to shift from Max to her father. In response, their dad lifted his hand and gently pushed Ella back into Max's arms.

"Don't touch them."

Max winced as he watched his mother fly down the stairs, knowing the interaction would soon end. He turned to look at his younger self and saw a wide-eyed look on the frozen child. He recalled how fast his heart was beating, and how wet his palms were as he struggled to hold Ella.

Their father whipped around, narrowing his eyes at Max's mother, who had taken her place in front of her children. "You don't have to worry about that ever again."

The dog had dropped the tennis ball at their father's feet. He pushed it aside and wheeled his luggage down the lawn. They watched as the dog picked up the ball in its mouth and circled their father, looking to play.

"Sparky," their mother called, "come over here."

Halfway to the black SUV parked in the road at the end of the lawn, Max watched his father stumble as Sparky shimmied between his legs.

"Get this damn dog away from me!" He picked up the tennis ball and threw it as hard as he could in the yard, and Sparky disappeared in a yellow blur. His father trudged down the lawn, opened the trunk of the car, and threw the luggage inside before walking to the driver's side door.

He could swear that an invisible pair of fingers were constricting around Max's neck as his breathing became shallow. Watching this scene replay made his anxiety go through the roof as he remembered how his younger version felt in this moment. He looked to his left at the little boy with a mop of light brown hair, his eyes wide and glassy, like he was about to cry.

As he turned the key in the ignition, their father took one last glance at his family on the lawn before placing his foot on the gas, eager to get away from the house, from all of them.

Max clenched his jaw, watching as the black SUV sped off. Within seconds, Sparky began running toward the car, and a loud *thump* reverberated throughout the family's ears. The car paused for a moment before continuing to speed down the street, leaving the body of their beloved pet lifeless in the street.

Sounds of screaming and crying filled Max's ears, and his cheeks became wet before the sounds were drowned out, and silence took its place. Through blurred vision, he found himself back in the crystalline chamber, the air cold and stale. He brought his shirt to his face to wipe his eyes dry and shook his head. It was odd to be standing there as if the trauma he had just relived hadn't happened. He knew this was part of the trial, but he didn't expect to be watching scenes from his past.

"Wipe your eyes, Max." A gruff voice reached his ears. "I didn't raise you to cry like a sissy."

He lifted his head to where the voice had come from and saw his father standing a few feet in front of him. The man looked as he did the day he left the family, not a day older, and his eyes were still dark, hollow sockets. "Wh-what are you doing here?"

"I'm here because I've been hearing some things about you," his father mumbled. "I hear you've been having thoughts...unnatural ones. Do you not care what this will do to your family and friends?"

Max's mind instantly turned to Calvo and then to Rylan. Embarrassment from the night prior coursed through his veins.

He became concerned smoke may pour from his ears as the blood running through his body could have been two hundred degrees. "Funny that you are worried about hurting the family, yet you're the one who walked out on us. Call me whatever names you want. Your power over me left when you did, and to be honest, I don't care what you think at all."

A smirk tugged at his father's lips. "That's where you're wrong. You care what I think. You care what everyone thinks. Why else would you hide yourself?"

Max's ears began to burn, and his palms became clammy. "I-I don't hide myself."

"Answer me, son." His father's voice grew sterner. "Why do you lie to everyone when you know those lies will hurt people?"

Is he talking about being a shapeshifter...or something else?

Max was going to have a full-blown panic attack. His heart was thumping out of his chest at a hundred miles per hour, his hands were so slick he could fill a pool, and the lump in his throat was the size of a soccer ball. He knew what he needed to say...he just didn't know if he could say it.

"Are you going to keep lying to everyone you love?" Max shook his head, and his hollow eyes narrowed in response. "Then tell me."

Before he could stop himself, Max exclaimed, "I keep everything to myself so I don't let everyone down...so I don't end up like you."

Silence followed Max's statement as the air grew thick and dense. The burning in his ears began to decrease, and his shoulders slightly lifted. He was relieved to get it out; it was something he had been holding onto for a long time, and the person he needed to say it to was right in front of him.

The silence seemed like it had lasted hours before his father finally spoke, "Why do you think I left that day?"

Max made it a point to sound very matter-of-fact before he

spoke. He didn't want to show his father that he was getting to him. "Because you're selfish and don't care about your family."

The dark sockets in Max's father's head moved, and his eyebrows drooped. "I can agree with you on one thing: I was selfish. Not caring about my family? That's where you're wrong." He paused to cough in his hand. "I left to protect my family. If I stayed, you and Ella would be more messed up than if I left." He put a hand behind his head, scratching his scalp. "I had a lot of demons, Max, and the only way to protect those close to me was to leave. You were old enough to know some things that were going on. I was becoming a monster."

Max nodded, remembering the bruises on his mother's body and the bottles of alcohol littering their house. He had forgotten these details. His mind blocked the events leading up to the day his father left, but now that he was hearing these things from his father's mouth, the memories unlocked.

"When I left, I was in a bad place and continued to be there for months afterward. I lost everything until I checked myself into a hospital to get better." He paused to clear his throat. "After years of recovery, I was ready to see my family again. I pulled up to our house and you weren't there."

Max nodded. "Mom couldn't afford the mortgage by herself, so we moved into a small apartment complex, but you knew that already, didn't you?"

"I knew you saw me that day." His father smiled. "I needed to see how my family was doing, but I couldn't get out of the car. I was ashamed of who I was and how I handled everything, so I put my car in reverse and left."

"It's probably better that you didn't," Max whispered as he looked into the empty eyes of the man before him. "If you loved us, why couldn't you get better? Was our love not enough for you?"

His father's eyes turned downward, and he shook his head.

"Love stopped me from getting better because I didn't want to face all the hurt that I caused my family. It wasn't until I got help that I realized everything I'd missed out on. The cycle of guilt and hurt that I carried weighs heavily on me."

I thought he left because of me—because I wasn't good enough.

"Due to my issues, I watched from afar as you stepped up and became the strong person Ella and your mother needed. I would never be that person. You can stand on your own two feet, and for that, I'm proud of you."

Max's heart became so full and heavy, he feared it was going to fall out of his chest.

He's...proud of me?

He'd always thought that he was partially why his father had left and had held onto that emotional baggage throughout his years. Hearing that his father was proud of him quieted the voice in his head, making him feel stronger and more confident. A balloon swelled within him, and it pushed against the hollowness he had felt for so long, finally filling the emptiness. A wave of emotion surged from his chest, coursing through his body until he used the sleeve of his shirt to dry his eyes. "I can't forgive you for leaving us, but I'm stronger because you did."

The crystals in the room started glowing brighter, their white-hot light illuminating the area. The light grew so bright that Max had to shield his eyes, and right before they all went dark, Max heard one last statement from his father. "Keep listening to your heart."

His words disappeared with the light in the crystal chamber, and Max was left in empty darkness, though he felt completely whole.

Chapter Twenty-Nine

M ilky white mist engulfed Max's feet in the darkness, and the air around him shifted. Though he couldn't see, and his feet were planted firmly on the ground, the room seemed to be spinning around him. He was lightheaded, and his legs were weak and uncoordinated, making it hard to stand upright. Dropping to one knee, Max cradled his head in his hands, waiting for the sensation to be over.

Beneath his eyelids, a warm light penetrated the darkness, and he slowly drew his hands away from his face. As he stood in the cavern, mist lingered around his feet, and the air took on a yellow hue, like the glow of old fluorescent bulbs.

Three metal doors loomed in front of him, each secured with a large circular lock adorned with sharp spokes. The spider's voice echoed throughout the room. "Use your heart to choose a door and its contents will be yours."

He walked to the door on his left and noticed an indented metal square with a sliding latch placed outside. He slid the metal square to the right, revealing a window for him to gaze into the room behind.

Max saw himself giving Ella a piggyback ride on a sprawling green lawn. Their smiles were full of joy, and their mother stood in front of a beautifully landscaped house. A brand-new Rolls Royce sat in the garage with MAX printed on the license plate, and two new cars sprinted up the driveway. Leo and Rylan emerged from each vehicle, garbed from head to toe in designer clothes.

Everyone seemed so joyous and relaxed within the scene. "What is this? Is this what I want?"

As if to answer his question, the scene faded from view, leaving one person standing before him: his mother. Her brown, rust-colored hair looked well-kept, like she'd just come from the salon, and her bright green eyes twinkled in the cave's light. To Max, this woman seemed like a completely different person compared to the one he saw at home. His mother's hair was always pulled back into a ponytail, and dark circles over-shadowed her eyes from working long hours and not getting enough sleep.

"This is the Door of Wealth," his mother said, her voice happy and renewed. "If you choose to open this door, our finan-cial struggles will be a thing of the past once you return home. You will live comfortably for your entire life, giving you the freedom in the future to pursue your dreams and giving me more time to spend with my children."

His family not having enough money had always been the cause of many issues, so opening this door could drastically change their home life.

If I choose this door, my mom won't need to work three jobs anymore. We wouldn't have to worry about budgets, buying generic brand food, or even about college.

Logically, this would be the right door to open, but some-thing was nagging inside him to see what the other doors held.

His mother saw him weighing the pros and cons of opening

this door. "Take a look at your other options. I know you'll make the right choice."

Max nodded to his mother and closed the window, shuffling to the similar metal door to his right. He took a breath before opening the window to gaze inside the next room.

He saw a two-story house with a large wrap-around deck and two little children playing in the front yard. He instantly recalled this scene from the first trial. It was the day his father left. "I don't need to relive this for a second time."

He began to slide the window closed when a booming voice reached his ears. "Max, wait! Don't close the window."

His arm froze as he heard the voice.

Is he here to help me again?

Trembling, he pulled the closure to the window back open and peered inside to see his father standing on the lawn, a mere few feet away from the door.

The man looking at Max smiled as he wiped the sweat from his forehead. "Whew, I'm glad I caught you." He turned and outstretched his hands to the house behind him. "This is the Door of Change, which would allow you to alter fragments of the past, and those changes will become reality once you return home." Hope gleamed in his father's eyes. "Let me show you what I mean."

Max noted his father's appearance. Like his mother, this man looked completely different from the person from the first trial. His face was light and full of life. Unlike the prior trial, his eyes were not dark caverns. They were bright and ocean blue, twinkling in the cavern's light. His smile caused wrinkles to perch like birds at the corner of his eyes.

"Remember when I left? If you open this door, I'll stay and work through my struggles so our family will remain whole." His father snapped his fingers, and the scene changed to show Ella, his mother, his father, and Max all having a picnic outside their house with grins on their faces. "You can change any parts of the past you want. Look at this, for example."

The scene of the happy family changed to Max preparing himself to sleep with Hannah for the first time. His face was anxiety-ridden, and his hands kept shaking. Max's father once again snapped his fingers, and before him was a different version of Max, chest held high and a horny smirk on his face. In the scene, Hannah opened the door to his bedroom, standing in nothing but delicate, lacy lingerie. When she spotted Max, a wave of emotion washed over her, and she moved toward him with a gentle sway.

The image behind his father changed to when Ella was being dragged away by goblins. "Or even going back to save your sister from being kidnapped." With a snap of his fingers, the scene changed again to Max brandishing his sword with a determined face and slaying the reptilian creatures. Running through the carcasses, he was rewarded with a big hug from Ella.

Max's thoughts were racing. This door could also change his life for the better.

If I had to guess, most of my low confidence and anxiety came from things that happened in the past and my response to them. If I could change those moments, maybe I'd never develop these issues, which would be a huge relief.

"So, what'll it be? If you want to open this door, turn the spokes on the lock outside."

Max's breathing increased, and his mind ping-ponged the options. "I'm not sure...let me look into the last door, and I'll weigh all my options." He considered opening the wealth door first, but after seeing what lay behind the current door, he hoped the final door would provide the clarity he needed to make the right choice.

His father nodded as Max closed the window. "Take a look

at your last option and decide which door entices you the most. I know you'll make the right decision."

Max furrowed his eyebrows.

It's weird how my mom and dad ended their conversation with me using the same phrasing.

Max pulled on the final window and peered inside the new room to see only darkness. A dim spotlight illuminated the area a few feet from the door, casting eerie shadows on the walls as whispers echoed in the background. The circle of light grew brighter, and Max was shocked to see hundreds of people he recognized from the Mainland. He saw his most recent teacher, his mother, Ella, Rylan's parents, and Leo's mother. Was every person he had ever met in this room? Who was beyond the light?

"Thanks for joining us." Rylan was pushing through the crowd of people and centered himself in the middle of the light. A lump formed in Max's throat once he saw his friend, and his heartbeat began racing.

I'm still so embarrassed from the other night, and I know he hates me for thinking about leaving him behind. I hope he doesn't say something about it in front of everyone.

He watched as Rylan threw his mop of blond hair backward, revealing dark holes where his eyes had been, much like his father from the first trial.

"This is the Door of Truth," Rylan's voice boomed over the surrounding whispers. "If you open this door, you can ask one person, anywhere in the world, a question and have it answered in complete honesty."

Max's face flushed as he considered which person to choose and what question to ask them. He began balancing the three doors in his mind: wealth, change, or truth. Lost in thought, he silently walked to each door with his hand on his chin. The spider's words reverberated through his mind.

"Use your heart to choose a door and its contents will be yours."

What guarantee do I have with any of these doors? Will they actually come true? I know which door will help me, but which one does my heart choose?

Max's ears turned warm, and he wiped his brow as he made his decision. Placing both hands on the spokes of the lock, he turned the wheel that opened the door. A metallic clanging sound echoed through the cavern, indicating that the levers were retracting. With a final twist, the spokes stopped moving, and a sliver of the door opened.

As soon as the inky blackness in front of him spewed, his mind raced.

I'll never know if I made the correct choice, but this was the right decision for me.

He stepped into the room behind the door, the darkness pulling at his clothes and obstructing his view. Max's eyes strained to adjust to the darkness as he made his way towards the spotlight, where his friend had been standing moments before. The darkness surrounding Max was dispelled by a bright white light, and an unknown voice instructed him: "To reveal their heart, speak their name."

There was only one person who Max had in mind. The question had been nagging at him since the incident happened. Would the other two doors have helped his life? Yes, but choosing this door would help him answer the burning question in his heart and mind, which neither wealth nor change could impact.

One thing that I've learned since being on the island is that I need to take better care of myself, and facing my anxiety is a huge part of that.

His father's words echoed in his mind, and he chose with his heart.

"Rylan!" Max yelled into the darkness.

Max was mesmerized as the white light shimmered and colors began swirling before him. He squinted as the shapes swirled in the bright light, slowly coming into focus until he could see Rylan's face in the scene before him.

"When was this?" Max whispered to himself as he watched the sequence in front of him unfold. Rylan was underneath the Great Tree of Hesper, fashioning weapons out of sticks and stones while he directed Sofillians on their next tasks. On the screen, a woman garbed in vines appeared, showing Rylan a basket of arrows that she had sharpened. His friend nodded to Leo with a determined smile on his face.

"Is this what's happening right now?" Max breathed a sigh of relief to see that his friends had safely made it out of the collapsed temple.

A pulsating red light right near Rylan's chest rippled within the video. "Speak one question." The voice didn't seem to come from Rylan's mouth but rather from deep within his chest.

Max's mind was a whirlpool of thoughts, questions, and doubts, but he knew he had to decide carefully when asking the one question. Many of his inquiries were around that night at the castle.

Was Rylan really too drunk to remember them sleeping together? Did he leave before morning because of me? Did he mean everything he said to me that night?

Going over the options in his head, he finally answered, "Can you tell me your true feelings about the night we spent together in Reina's castle?" Max's hands were wet with sweat and his ears pricked with warmth. The fluids in his stomach swirled, and a lump formed in his throat as he anticipated the answer.

The scene before him continued playing through the dark room, the red thumping heart being the only sound in the area.

Rylan turned his head to the right and let out a joyful laugh, illuminating the area with his stunning smile. Max could almost hear his friend's lighthearted laughter as he watched him run a hand through his dangly blond hair.

It seemed to take hours as he watched the scene, but it only lasted a few minutes. The thumping ceased and was replaced with Rylan's voice. "After we fell asleep, I woke up in the night, scared and confused. You're my best friend, but I've always wondered if we could be more. I knew that leaving you that morning, you'd be upset, that's why I had to lie to you. I was also protecting myself."

The voice paused, allowing Max to digest what he was hearing. He would be lying if he said that he hadn't hidden his feelings for Rylan for some time, but he was unsure if they were real until Calvo came along. He was still confused about girls, but he couldn't deny his attraction to men.

The voice interrupted his thoughts. "Once I returned to my room, I couldn't stop thinking about how scared I was for our friendship and didn't know if things would ever be the same if I told you, but I finally realized that..."

Max took a sharp intake of breath, partly hoping he was wrong about the words that came next and the other half hoping he was correct.

"Well... I think I love you."

The spotlight disappeared, leaving Max surrounded by darkness. The words hung in the air like a humid day. His palms stopped sweating, and his mind eased, Max's anxiety disappearing as quickly as it came. He smiled, and his shoulder longed for a familiar squeeze, letting the warmth of Rylan's words envelop him.

"I think I love you, too."

Chapter Thirty

A sense of satisfaction and contentment overcame Max as he returned to the crystalline chamber. When the large spider told him that he needed to complete three trials to reach the Hero, he didn't expect to learn so much about himself. In the first task, he rid himself of the guilt of his father leaving their family, and in the second, he realized his love for himself and was willing to share it with others. In his entire life, he could not think of a time he was more confident and happier being in his own body.

He was content.

"Onto the third task," Max breathed. "I hope I'm doing okay." He wasn't sure what would happen if he didn't pass, but he knew that the large spider eating him was a possibility. As there was no pass or fail indicator during each trial, he assumed that his continuance meant he was doing well.

The white mist began circling Max's feet again, its tendrils pulling at his shoelaces. The ground rumbled and shook as if something was trying to push through. Large stone pillars emerged from the floor around him, creating a perfect circle that looked like fingers reaching from the ground. Shards of glass collected on each pillar and multiplied, each piece fitting perfectly into the other like a puzzle until a mirrored wall surrounded Max, dozens of his own reflection staring back at him.

"Welcome to your third task," a male voice rang through the area.

Max swiveled his head to see where the voice had come from, but his reflection was the only person looking back at him. Several versions of himself looked back as the light from the crystal chamber refracted within the mirror. "Who's there?"

The voice rang in Max's ears. "For the third task, you will be fighting against a rival and the first to surrender, loses."

After the first two trials, Max's confidence was emanating from head to toe, but he knew that whoever he'd be sparring with would make all the difference. "Who is it?"

The only person in the mirrored enclosure was himself. His eyes scanned the faces of the many versions of himself surrounding him until he noticed one with dark, sunken eyes, reminiscent of his father and Rylan from the prior trials.

The Max in the mirror curled his lips into a mischievous smile. "You found me." Passing through the mirror, his body created ripples like a stone in a pond, with droplets falling from his clothes and disappearing into the glass. The person who emerged was a replica of himself from the casual windswept light brown hair to the high-top shoes on his feet. Everything matched except for the darkness in his eyes.

"I'm fighting...myself?"

"Watch out!" The Other Max's arm formed into a fist and extended from his shoulder all the way across the arena as if it were elastic.

Max jumped to the ground, narrowly missing the attack and landing on his shoulder. He scowled as the pain seared up his arm and planted itself squarely in his bicep. He jumped to his feet and began running at his reflection, fist clenched, hoping to take him by surprise.

Dark lines crawled up the Other Max's body, his arms and legs began flailing in the air. He keeled over, clutching his stomach and within seconds, a large bear jumped from where he'd been standing with its arms outstretched. The bear ran toward Max and wrapped its arms around him, pulling his body to the ground.

As the bear lay on top of him, the bones in his body creak under the pressure. He pictured himself as a character in a cartoon, with his body completely pinned down by the beast, leaving only his head exposed. With each passing moment, Max found it harder to catch his breath, his lungs aching and burning with each inhale.

The bear brought its head towards Max, its warm breath puffed in his face. "Do you remember the things your father used to call you? How you weren't good enough for him, and that's why he left your family?"

The truth of what was asked was stronger than the physical pain he felt pinned by. Max wriggled his arms and legs, hoping to escape from under the bear, but the weight was too much for him to handle. "I'm not talking about this." As the years passed, he became adept at suppressing these memories and emotions.

"Keep struggling. I'm not moving until you answer my question."

Max's chest burned as the memories of his father's words replayed in his mind. His body went numb like his brain shut everything down and focused on the pain in his heart. He tried calming his mind before his anxiety fully took over. "I found out that my father didn't leave because I wasn't good enough... it's because *he* wasn't."

The icy tendrils of black crawl through his veins and his

chest burned with an intense heat that seemed to spread throughout his entire body. His head got yanked upward, yet his feet pointed down and pushed back as if they were trying to break his ankles. His arms and legs felt like an invisible force were taffy, constantly pulled in multiple different directions. Water filled his eyes as the pain was at its highest point. Max wasn't sure if he could handle another second—until it all stopped.

Suddenly, the weight that was pressing down on him disappeared, and he was rising at least seven feet higher than his usual height. The bear was flung into the air and landed with a sickening thud, its face making contact with the hard ground. As the black tendrils spiderwebbed over his body, his skin was being consumed by darkness until he was back to his normal height.

"W-what just happened?" Max said aloud.

The bear's body lay with its little tail flopped into the air. Its body writhed and twisted until a boy appeared in its place, looking remarkably like Max. "Interesting way to move me. I'm impressed. We've inserted the key, now it's time to open the door!"

The left side of Max's chest bulged slightly, and a mass slowly moved up towards his shoulder and then turned towards his neck. He watched in horror, wondering what the Other Max had done to him and what this lump was.

"Open up," the Other Max taunted with a maniacal smile as he extended his hands.

Sitting on his tongue was a small ball wrapped in a slimy texture. A slight gag formed in the back of his throat as the warm and moist surface filled his mouth.

The Other Max shoved his hand through his lips and grasped the item that sat on his tongue. His hands retreated to their owner, holding a small, pink-colored object in his palm. "Wondering what this is?"

"What did you do to me?" There was something missing within him, as if he had lost a vital part of himself. Max was used to feeling helpless when his anxiety took over, but the hollowness in his body was something new.

"This is your heart." The Other Max held it in the air. "There are a few fun things I can do with it. I could squeeze until you die." To emphasize his point, he first gave the ball a short clutch, causing a sharp pain to sear in Max's chest. "Or I could hide it away, so you'll be cursed to never be able to offer it to anyone."

"Give it back!" Max yelled and began running at his dead-eyed counterpart. He lunged towards the thief's hand, reaching out to grab the glowing red ball, but his enemy vanished in the blink of an eye, leaving him grasping at thin air.

"Did you really think it would be that easy?"

Max pivoted on his heel and charged toward the boy who had his heart, but just as he was about to reach him, the Other Max moved once more. A dribble of sweat pricked at his temples as he wondered how he was going to get his heart back. Fatigue and anger filled his body.

He's toying with me.

"If you come within a few feet of me, I have the ability to move myself to another area. You can surrender right now and end this."

Max shook his head.

There's no way I'm giving up, but I can't get to him. I wish that there was a way that I could copy him. If I could disappear and reappear, I could just show up next to him.

Despite the heat that surged through his chest and the dizziness that overtook him, he bolted towards the Other Max. As he watched the Other Max disappear and reappear across the room, his body spun like it was on a roller coaster corkscrew.

Turning his head from side to side, The Other Max looked around in bewilderment. "Maaaax," he taunted. "Where did you go?"

Confusion clouded his mind as he was on the opposite end of the arena and hadn't moved from the spot where he stood. When he turned to look at one of the mirrored walls, he was surprised to see that his body was no longer visible in the room. Moving closer to the mirror, he found a change in appearance looking back at him. He no longer looked like a boy but took on the guise of a housefly; his translucent wings fluttered behind him, and his bulbous eyes were set on each side of his head.

Max knew this was his chance to get close to his heart without his counterpart instantly disappearing. He buzzed through the air until he hovered a few feet over the Other Max's head. With his tiny housefly wings flapping rapidly, he aimed himself towards the pink ball held by the Other Max, hurtling towards it like a bullet.

As his little body flew through the air, he caught glimpses of change happening to him. He stretched out his arms, and for a brief moment, two fingers were visible before they transformed into blurry sticks. As he was inches above the Other Max, his housefly body completely glitched and returned to his normal teenage self.

His shoulder collided with the Other Max's head, toppling both to the ground. The small oblong ball pulsed in his hand before he held it to his chest. The ball melted into his shirt and through his skin, disappearing back into his body. He was complete; his heart had returned home.

I did it.

Before Max could celebrate, he was thrown onto the ground. As he tried to understand how he got into this position, his eyes scanned the ceiling until the face of Other Max suddenly appeared above him. He had never been this close to one of these hollow-eyed individuals and noticed that the sockets had skin in them, almost as if a spoon had scooped out his eyes.

The Other Max sat on his chest, leaning over to pin his wrists to the ground. "Admit what you've been hiding."

Max's entire body stood at attention. "Hiding? I don't know what you mean." He wriggled his body, hoping to get enough leverage to throw the Other Max off him.

"Don't lie, you know what I'm talking about." The Other Max's breath was warm and stale. "What have you been keeping to yourself since you arrived on this island? Whenever there's chatter, you turn quiet because you're hiding something."

"It's because I have anxiety."

"No, it's not. Throughout your life, you've constantly hidden and shifted who you are to appease the company you're around. You have lived several different lives and you've done this since childhood. Say what you are or surrender."

Max knew what he was getting at. It was something that he'd tried to hide from the outside world and himself. Throughout his journey, Max had become more comfortable in his own skin, and that had eased the exhaustion from his growing anxiety. There had been many breakthroughs that tore down the walls within himself, and he was happier and more confident being who he was.

"Your father used to call you names, and so did the people in school. You know what you need to say, so just say it!"

A swarm of black tendrils cascaded over Max's body and, within an instant, realized his body was wrapped around the Other Max's arms and legs, leaving him unable to move. Looking down at himself, he saw that his sleek torso was covered in hunter-green scales. Glancing at the mirrored wall, the face that looked back at him was that of a snake.

The Other Max's laugh vibrated throughout the mirrored room. "It's becoming easier for you... Tell me what you're hiding, and I'll surrender."

Max brought his coned mouth to his opponent's ear, and his forked tongue escaped his lips. "I'm a shapeshifter."

As soon as the words left his mouth, a weight had been lifted off his body. Even though Samael had outed him within the Temple of Harper, he still felt ashamed to admit it. After finishing the trials, he had an overwhelming sense of empowerment and self-acceptance, having come to terms with his true self. He felt this version of Max was the person he constantly hid away in the shadows. But now it was time to let him bathe in the light.

In an instant, the Other Max's body disappeared, dropping Max's snake body to the floor. As Max's body twisted back to normal, he noticed a small bird with faded red feathers sitting inside the arena. He made a beeline for the bird, hoping to catch it before it flew away. The bird flapped its wings frantically as Max approached, causing his arms to tingle with excitement. His elbows stretched out further than they ever had, and the small bird flew directly into his palm.

Max clenched his fingers, snatched the bird out of the air, and pinned it to the ground. The bird twisted until its body elongated, turning back into the Other Max, who was still enrapt by his hand.

A smug smile spread across his lips. "You've done well, Max. By speaking your truth, you've accepted yourself. Most people don't get this far, but when they do, their lives are changed forever. You have successfully passed the trial." A look of defeat glazed over his face as he gazed toward the ceiling. "I surrender."

The Other Max stood on both feet, slapping his pants to remove the dust that had befallen them, and walked to one of the mirrored walls. He placed one hand on his reflection and turned to look at Max with a smile on his lips and forehead furrowed. He gave a peaceful nod before stepping back into the mirror from whence he came.

The ground shook once again, and the mirrored walls began descending into the floor, leaving Max in an empty room with no exit. He found himself back inside the crystal with rainbow streaks of light passing through the chambers above him. The strobing lights filled the room once again, and a sudden tug that caused his hair to stand on end suctioned him upward.

Chapter Thirty-One

M ax's eyelids lifted, and he was greeted by yet another small room as the sensation dissipated from his body. Opposed to the trials, he found himself surrounded by crystals instead of being encapsulated within one. His back was to a stone wall, and he glanced behind him, noticing that he was on the other side of the wall where the trials had begun. "This must be like a one-way mirror." He scanned both areas. "Where's the spider with my stuff?"

He turned deeper into the cavern, beams of light bouncing from crystal to crystal as if it were running a marathon. Max's eyes darted around the room in search of the Hero, but instead, all he saw were the grand obelisks of large crystal pillars jutting from the floor. He walked with his left hand against the wall, tracing every bump and crevice, hoping to uncover a secret pathway, but the room led to a dead end.

"You passed the trials, I'm impressed."

He pivoted to where he heard the familiar voice and watched as the striped spider crawled out of one of the nearby crystals.

"Where's the Hero? I need to help my friends. I'm running out of time."

"Relax." A sly smile framed the spider's mouth as she narrowed her eyes toward him. "You look different. How do you feel?"

"Different...changed," Max answered confidently.

The spider nodded and pointed to the end of the crystal cave. "If you tread this way, you'll find a window. All you have to do is look inside, and the Hero will re-awaken."

He nodded in understanding and before moving his feet, took one last look at the spider.

I am changed because of her.

"Thanks...for everything." He meant what he said. He *was* thankful that she had pushed him to take the trials.

Max inhaled deeply, readying himself before venturing through the towering pillars of crystals. Some stood tall and straight, while others were scattered and uneven, but all glowed with a gentle warmth at their core. Upon reaching the dead end, his eyes were drawn to a small rectangular window, and he found himself gazing inside without a second thought.

From the light in the cave, his reflection stared back at him as he peered into the room. He couldn't help but notice his more prominent jawline and the glint of confidence and knowledge in his eyes—he looked more mature. He shielded his eyes from the glare and cupped his hands around the glass, trying to see inside. However, his breath fogged up the window, obscuring his view.

"I-I can't see anything," Max stammered as he turned to face the spider. He took the bottom of his shirt and wiped the window free of mist. "All I see is a mirror."

"If you look close enough, you'll see the Hero."

Max lifted his toes to face the small patch of glass once again. He put his forehead to the smooth surface and held his palm just above his nose so the steam couldn't cloud his view. His eyes tried piercing the glass mirror, but he ultimately only saw himself staring back.

A wave of realization washed over him before turning to the spider. "I found the Hero."

The spider's smirk allowed her fangs to poke out from her top lip. "Did you?"

Max nodded and began fidgeting with his fingers.

The spider began moving her long legs toward him. "Only the Hero can complete the trial...and here you are. There have only been a handful of others that have made their way through this cave."

As soon as the spider finished speaking, a few of the pillars began pulsing with light. Three silhouettes, lacking any defining characteristics, stood at the center of each crystal.

The spider, with her bulbous black and white behind, waved her arm at the furthest left crystal. "This is the Island of Forever's very first Hero: Harper."

The first pillar lit up to reveal a short woman framed inside. Max couldn't help but smile back at her infectious ear-to-ear grin, looking down at her diminutive stature. Her saucer-like brown eyes were filled with emotion, while her hair was a unique blend of blonde and black braids. Her nose was the feature that was most surprising to him, it looked like it had been pushed inward.

"She was the first and only islander born from the goblin clan. After discovering the bridge between worlds, Harper took it upon herself to stop time on the island to keep it safe, which is why the temple bears her name."

Max nodded and his eyes widened. He didn't expect to hear that the first Hero was of goblin descent. "I bet she has an amazing story."

The spider's six eyes turned to him and nodded. "Indeed

she does." She scuttled to the next crystal that was alight with a man inside. "The next Hero's name is Phillip. He's from the Mainland, much like yourself."

Moving his sight from Harper, Max's eyes were invited to a dark-skinned man with no shirt on but a pair of Levi jeans slouching around his waist. His eyes were kind, and he had a glowing smile that seemed as bright as the crystal itself.

"Phillip was the first to jump between worlds using the portal that his predecessor sought to protect. He revealed how to activate the portal and how to return to the island at will." The spider turned to the next crystal, and her eyes turned downward. "This is where everything went haywire."

Looking towards the third pillar, Max saw a woman with a stunning freckled complexion and shoulder-length brown curls. Her bright green eyes danced in the crystal's light, and the laugh lines around her mouth made her look even more joyful. The woman's appearance struck Max as that of a motherly figure, with her kind demeanor tempered by a hint of strictness.

"The third Hero was named Rieshe, a shapeshifter from this island...who also happens to be Samael's mother."

Max's ears perked up. It surprised him that Samael's mother looked to be so kind as he would have assumed that he'd lived a tortured life. He'd always assumed he was an orphan, but the possibility that he had parents intrigued him, especially if it could help him uncover a weakness.

"When Samael was around sixteen, Rieshe found out that he had been going to the Mainland through the portal to visit a girl he fancied, causing suspicion from her parents. They eventually found the portal that Samael had been using and devised a plan to use the island's magic for their own greed."

Max rolled his eyes and stifled an unsurprised laugh. "Typical."

"One day, when Samael came back from seeing his love, Rieshe knew she had to protect the Island of Forever from the outside threat. To do that, she sealed the portal, making sure only a shapeshifter could activate it. She lifted the Temple of Harper into the sky, safeguarding it from any shapeshifter who dared to trespass without permission from the Sages."

Max remembered Reina calling upon the power of the Sages to open the portal. "So, anyone can get inside the temple?"

She nodded. "Yes, precautions had to be taken, and that is where her genius comes in. Anyone on the Island of Forever has access to the temple if they're able to reach it, but only a shapeshifter can activate the portal."

Max cupped his hand under his chin as his mind recalled their journey. "I guess that makes sense. Samael lured me to the temple using Calvo's body, so technically, he wasn't a shapeshifter entering, and I was granted entry by the Sages. Samael planned on using my blood to activate the portal."

"You got it," the spider affirmed as it crawled to the final crystal.

The fourth stone stood empty, with no Hero silhouette emerging, despite the bright light shining from within. "Care to take one final guess on who I am?"

He shrugged with confidence in his eyes. "I'm going to assume you're the final Hero?"

She put her front left leg to her forehead and shook her head. "You're really not connecting the dots, are you?" Scuttling into the crystal, her body shifted from the gigantic spider to a woman with short black hair. Her eyes had heavy eyeshadow, and bright red lipstick was painted onto her mouth. Her body was slender, and she wore a black-and-white striped jacket around her shoulders.

Max's mouth dropped when he saw the final Hero. He couldn't believe it. "Ana?"

She laughed. "I guess I had to spell it out for you, didn't I? I thought you'd be able to tell it was me by my pronunciation of my words since Rylan always poked fun at me for it."

Seeing his sister's babysitter here, on the Island of Forever, came as a shock. "What're you doing here? Why are you a spider?"

"As I've been showing you, I'm the fourth Hero and take the guise of that spider when I'm able to transcend to the island." A wave of sadness crossed her dark, caring eyes as she looked down at him from the pillar. "I was the woman Samael was in love with on the Mainland, and once Rieshe closed the portal, locking him away from me, I made it my goal to find my way back to him."

Since Max has been on this island, everyone shuddered when Samael was spoken of, some even spitting his name. They'd all been adamant in telling him he must leave the island in fear that Samael could escape prison. "How could you fall in love with someone so evil?"

Ana's smile turned into a frown, and her eyebrows furrowed. "He didn't always have the reputation he has now. When we first met, it was love at first sight. He was the most handsome and loving man I knew, but once his mother sealed the portal and he couldn't see me anymore, his thoughts turned dark until madness consumed him."

"But you found your way back here, right?"

She nodded. "I was too late. He was hellbent on destroying the island, hoping the Sages would give their consent to him so that he may enter the Temple of Harper, but seeing his path of devastation, they refused. Not only did he want to rule the Island of Forever, he wanted to go to the Mainland to extend his power."

"So that's why it's important that he can't access the portal or leave the island because he'd destroy the Mainland, too."

"Yes, it's better to keep him contained here than go to your world where his power would be too great for humans," Ana breathed. "When I finally found my way back, his destruction was in full force—the land was desolate, plague spread throughout all residents, and his army extended to all corners. I made my way to this cave, completed the trials, and became the Island of Forever's newest Hero, but I knew that the title came with a price."

"To defeat him."

"When it came down to it, I couldn't do it. I imprisoned him within the volcano, but the spell could only hold him for five days. I created the beacon to alert the Island of Forever that there was one day remaining before he was able to escape, if it ever came to that. To save the island and keep him locked up, I used the power inside the Temple of Harper to freeze time. I assumed by closing the portal and stopping time, a Mainlander wouldn't be able to sneak in, and everything would remain how I had left it. But clearly, I was wrong."

Chapter Thirty-Two

The light from the four crystal pillars illuminated Max's face as he listened to the backstory of each of the island's Heroes. Rainbows flitted around the room, each of them bouncing from one crystal to the next. A fire burned within his body and mind as if a newfound sense of purpose had been instilled since completing the trials. He had a clear line of sight on who he was and what his goals were.

"So, what is my role as...as a Hero?" The title still felt odd to him. Never would he have labeled himself as a hero in any sense of the word.

"To accomplish that which I was unable to: defeat Samael once and for all and bring normalcy back to this land."

Max shook his head. "But how do I do that?"

"All four of us are shapeshifters." Ana gestured to the other crystals, each lighting up with her gaze. "We all had issues with allowing our powers to emerge. The trials of this cave are designed to be a simulation to free our minds to awaken the Hero within ourselves."

"Wait a second." Max threw one finger in the air. "Simulation? You're telling me those trials took place in my head, and none were real?" He couldn't believe what he was hearing. It all seemed so real and healing. "What about my conversation with my dad?"

Ana closed her almond-shaped eyes and pursed her lips. "The trial gave a physical form to your anxiety and allowed you to speak to the people causing the blockage. Everything that you discussed with manifestations were topics you already knew but refused to accept. So yes, in some ways, it all came from your mind, though the conversations were just as real. You needed to delve into what you already knew to overcome, and once you did, you could break free from the tightly bound chains of your past."

Her words hit Max, and his immediate reaction was not to believe her. Realizing that everything his father had said to him in the task, he truly had already known. The fight against the Other Max was an internal struggle with himself, and all the fighting words were the things he said to himself.

Seeing Max's perplexed face, Ana craned her neck to ask him a question. "When you saw your younger self the day your father left, what did you want to say to him?"

"I-I wanted to tell him to run, to protect himself and Ella." He winced, trying not to relive the experience. "That, in the end, everything would be okay and all the bad things that will happen in life aren't his fault."

She nodded with a knowing look in her eyes. "The trial allowed you to see yourself and empathize with what he was going through, allowing you to be more understanding and kind to that child. Why do you believe that a younger version of yourself deserves compassion, but not the person you are today?"

Her words hit Max like a brick wall had been thrown at him.

It's because I knew what was coming, but she's right. Maybe I'm so protective of Ella because I see her as a younger me. Someone who needs to be shielded from everything and understood.

The revelation made the cogs in his head spin until the second trial crossed his mind. "But what about Rylan?"

She lifted a long, knobby finger. "The second trial was the only truth as you looked into the heart of someone you had been pushing away."

"So, I really found out what was in Rylan's heart?" Max was reassured once the spider nodded her head.

Rylan does have feelings for me, but they're just as confusing as my own.

There was comfort in knowing that the conversation was not made up in his head like the one with his father and that they'd be able to discuss that night at the castle.

Ana extended her long spider arm to his shoulder. "Sam can only be defeated by a shapeshifter, so you must use your newfound powers to save this island." She gestured towards a large crystal directly next to hers. "Place your hand inside."

He stepped over the smooth crystalline floor, making his way to the large crystal sitting directly to the right of Ana. Its center was radiating a powerful glowing warm light. Despite his expectation of hitting a hard rock, Max was surprised when he immersed his arm and it felt as if he'd punched a wall of Jell-O. His hand was inside the crystal all the way to his elbow.

Ana's eyes glowed in the white light, and a warm smile crossed her lips. "This will be your crystal, Max. You're now a Hero of the Island of Forever, and like all heroes before you, you'll be summoned back one day to educate the next in line."

A heavy object was pushing its way into his fingers, like an invisible string connecting them. Pulling his hand from the crystal, the sword bestowed to him from Wintey and the Sofillians sat gleaming in his hand. Though it was the same weapon, it was as if it had been imbued with new strength.

"Your sword is now infused with the crystals from this chamber, it will shatter any prison Samael creates and repel all creatures that have taken the path of darkness. In order to imprison Samael, you must insert the sword into his body and push him into the volcano. The sword now has the power to anchor him for eternity and extinguish the beacon. If you perform the task correctly, a small portal will open between dimensions, allowing you to return home."

He wondered how he'd defeat the evil shapeshifter, but his questions had since been answered. A thought crossed his mind. "What'll happen to Calvo and his body?" Even though he was possessed, his body was still his own.

The spider's eyes softened. "Calvo will join him in the volcano. It is a small sacrifice for the protection of this island and the Mainland. These are hard decisions but are ones that the Hero must face."

Max's chest hurt as he heard her words, but he understood why it had to be done. He regretted that Calvo would not be able to continue his life as a Sofillian and had no say in what was to happen. He now needed to devise a plan to get close enough to Samael to stab him with the sword and push him into the volcano. "How can I do this if you couldn't? He always seems to anticipate my every move."

"One can never be a step ahead of death." A lilting smile crossed her face as she shook her head. "I simply pushed Sam inside and trapped him, hoping that one day he and I could be together and happy again. I couldn't implant the sword, but the crystals in yours will block his power. His spirit will not be able to roam free or inhabit the bodies of others as it did this time."

Max gazed at the magnificent sword clutched in his fingers. The sword's hilt now glimmered with a polished gold finish, and its blade was a masterpiece of white steel and crystal fragments seamlessly pieced together. It was radiant and powerful in Max's hand. Retrieving his leather bag from under her crystal, he secured it over his shoulder and returned his sword to its scabbard at his waist.

"How can I do this without the water from the spring? It calmed my anxiety. It made me stronger...and you took the last bit I had."

The spider closed her eyes once more and shook her head. "Don't you see, Max? The water didn't do any of those things; you did that on your own. You've had the power within you this whole time."

Did I? Every time I drank the spring water, I was different. The loudness in my mind quieted. There's just no way.

"The water assists in relaxation and allows you to find a way to control your stress. Now, after passing the trials, you should be more adept at understanding who you are. There is no cure for your unease, but there are ways of coping."

Maybe she's right. The trials helped me to understand that a lot of my anxiety was from hiding who I am.

Seeing the look of realization in his eyes, Ana smiled. "You're ready for this."

He concentrated on his body and heartbeat as it pulsed through him. As he pictured a great albatross soaring through the sky in his mind's eye, he immediately sensed his body undergoing the transformation. He saw black spiderwebs crawling down his legs and up to his head. In a matter of moments, his arms were replaced with two powerful wings on each side. Shifting was no longer involuntary and no longer caused him great pain; he had accepted all pieces of himself. Before taking flight, he turned back to Ana and gave her a quick nod of thanks.

She smiled and winked at him as he started running and

flapping his feathered wings to catch a breeze. Before he exited the cave, Ana's voice rang in his ears, "Make sure you bring Ella and your friends over for cookies tomorrow!"

The briny air was thick and humid as Max flew through the golden clouds. The sun hung low and was nearing the horizon, only a couple more hours until night would fall. Hues of pink, orange, and purple that blended into one another like a water-color painting. Its elegance demanded to be seen by those who were able to capture it before its canvas faded to black. The sea below was calm as the waves lightly lapped upon one another. Max's feathers wicked away moisture with every flap of his wings.

Bursts of air currents pushed him higher once his wings drooped too low. Although he'd never flown before, he gained the ability with ease. Soaring through the sky was freeing; there were no distractions besides the rhythmic flapping of his wings. He turned his eyes ahead and saw a plume of black smoke circling the volcano and a thinning red beacon in its middle. Tensing his wings and dropping his shoulder blades, Max sped through the air like a bomb being dropped.

I have to hurry and get to the base of the volcano before the beacon goes out.

The first landmark to come into view was Reina's castle, where it sat on a cliff overlooking the ocean. Flying closer, he could see the prison windows carved on the side of the cliff and small lights twinkling in the castle's library, giving hope to all who may see. He veered to the left and continued straight towards the volcano.

If the second trial is right, the Sofillians are preparing an army to help Rylan and Leo.

Cocking his head, he caught sight of an expansive tree sitting in the center of the jungle below. From above, Hesper's branches and leaves looked like an interwoven blanket for the beings that lived beneath.

Tilting his wings to descend from the sky, Max glided just above the treetops as he scanned the forest. A swift movement caught his eye, and he curled his feet around a tree branch, waiting to see who would emerge.

Moments passed before the sound of rustling through the leaves reached Max's ears. Rylan's bob of wavy blond hair pierced through the sea of green, leading a pack of Sofillian soldiers. The teens followed him with dark paint strategically smeared across their faces and each of them were clutching wooden spears and axes in their fists. Max quickly shifted back to his human form and sat with his legs dangling as he waited for them to reach him.

"We're nearing the base of the volcano," Rylan shouted to the pack. "Be ready for anything. I don't know what we'll encounter."

A collection of acorns grew on the tip of a branch that Max was sitting on. Scooting over to them, he secured a handful and waited for the right moment with bated breath. Rylan neared the tree, and he drew his arm backward, throwing the acorns at his friend's head.

"What the hell?" Rylan screamed as he was being pelted with the small bullet-like nuts.

Max laughed and jumped out of the tree, his legs buckling under the impact from the ground. He thought this would've gone more smoothly as he collapsed beside his friend. Giving a sideways smile to Rylan, he asked, "Miss me?"

"At ease." Rylan held his hands upward to the army behind him, a smirk pulling at the corner of his mouth as his crystal green eyes sparkled in the sunset's light. "It's just my idiot friend."

He reached down and clasped Max's hand, pulling him to his feet.

I'm relieved that he's safe, but something's off. This entire interaction feels forced.

"Where've you been?"

He laughed. "It's kind of a long story. Let's just say that I figured out who I am." To demonstrate, he shifted his body into a bird and flew around the area.

Rylan's eyes were wide in disbelief, his mouth agape. His pupils moved slightly up and down as he watched the bird, who had been his friend moments before, fly around the area. "M-Max, you're not...not a...?"

His feet touched the ground, his body returning him to his original form. "A shapeshifter? I thought you may have known when you saw me change in the Temple of Harper."

"I did, but I didn't wanna believe you're one of them. You're my best friend, not one of those disgusting—"

"*Samael* is evil," Max interrupted. "But shapeshifters are like everyone else; they determine their path and choose between good and evil. The Heroes from the Island of Forever choose the path of good." He unsheathed the gleaming sword at his waist, its beauty blinding all who looked upon it.

Rylan's eyes widened as his mind began connecting what Max was telling him. "D-does that mean you're...you're...the Hero?"

Chapter Thirty-Three

The sounds in the forest had gone quiet, and Rylan's eyes glowed as his eyes landed on the crystal-infused sword. "You...*are* the Hero, Max. That's the legendary sword!" A big smile spread across his face as he squeezed his friend's shoulder.

Max's chest started thumping, and the reassuring grasp was comforting. Returning the sword to its sheath, he turned to Rylan and the rest of the Sofillian soldiers. "Where's Leo?"

"She traveled back to the Garden to recruit Aeryth's fairy army. She'll be here." He turned to Max with his back to the Sofillians. "What's your plan?"

Rylan looked at him expectantly, and it was at that moment Max realized he didn't have a plan outside of what Ana told him. Beads of sweat itched at his temples. "I need to get to the volcano before that beacon dies." He pointed to the red line in the sky. "If I can reach the top before the time runs out, I'll trap him inside."

Rylan nodded, noticing him begin to play with his fingers. "If time is our enemy, let's get going." He turned to the Sofillian army and gestured to his friend. "We need to get Max to the top while protecting him at all costs." The merman waved his arm forward. "Let's go!"

Max led the Sofillian army with Rylan at his side, walking in silence until the ground began changing color. The lush, green grass became increasingly yellow and thin until a clear line cut between the forest and the gray, rocky landscape of the volcano.

The army behind them fanned out, the front line just at the edge of the forest. They turned right and were met with a group of women dressed in vibrant plant life. Leading the pack was a girl who held her head high with a smirk, her caramel-colored hair sparkling in the twilight.

"Leo!"

"About time you got here," Rylan quipped.

Her eyes sparkled as she ran to them. "Max, I can't believe you're here! We didn't know if you were okay after the Temple of Harper. Where did you..." Her eyes turned to Max's waist. "I recognize that sword. Does that mean that you're...?"

"It does." Max nodded. "It's a long story, but for now, let's save this island."

His two friends nodded with determination blazing in their eyes and a mutual understanding that time was of the essence. Each of them returned to their respective army and stepped out of the forest and onto the broken, cracked terrain ahead of them.

"Let's go!" Rylan yelled at the teenagers behind him, and they all began running toward the slight incline of the volcano.

The Sofillians waved their weapons in the air, and the fairies lifted each of their wooden guns as they stormed the hill. Beneath their feet, a slimy green substance began to secrete from the volcano's porous exterior. The odd liquid resembled thick mucus, the kind you would see when you have a cold in winter, and it began to completely saturate the volcanic land.

Max twisted his nose at the smell of the odd liquid and continued running. With every step up the hill, the thick slime clung to his shoes, making them heavier. The sound of gasps and screams filled the air as the Sofillians lost their footing and slid down the volcano's slope. He tried to take another step but lost his balance, slipping and sliding into a heap of teens at the bottom.

As he looked to his left and right, the screams of the teens and fairies echoed around him as they slid down the steep sides of the volcano. "What do we do to get through this...stuff?"

"I think the slime is the least of our worries." Rylan pointed toward the mountain, his eyes wide.

Transparent circular lumps resembling fish eggs sprang up around the volcano, completely drenched in the wet slime. Clusters of the sacs adorned the side of the mountain like flowers, although they were anything but.

"What are those things?" Leo screamed to her friends, her face scrunched in disgust.

The sacs synchronized their movement, undulating like they were performing a dance until they burst open with a sickening sound that made Max sick to his stomach. The goo flew into the sky, and as it did, it left a slimy residue on everything it touched, including the horde of imps and goblins that emerged from each egg-shaped lump.

The army at the foot of the volcano recoiled in terror as the creatures emerged from the sacs, their grotesque forms twisting and turning in the dim light. The imps shook their fur like wet dogs, sending droplets flying in all directions, while their counterparts snorted constantly, the sound echoing through the air. Within seconds, the midsection of the volcano was filled with a sea of Samael's followers who were ready to fight.

"W-what do we do, Max?"

He looked ahead to the army of crazed imps and goblins. "I need to reach the top. We can do this." Max unsheathed his glistening sword and held it in the air as he turned to the children and fairies behind him. "You joined us here to protect your loved ones, your home, and this island. No amount of imps or goblins will stop us. This is to protect the Island of Forever!"

Slowly, the beings around Max lifted their arms, and a collective scream of "Protect the Island of Forever!" reverberated through the air. The team ran up the side of the volcano, wielding their axes and shooting bullets from wooden guns.

An arm hooked around Max's neck. "Maybe next time you'll have something more motivational, but that wasn't half bad," Rylan said.

"Alright you two." Leo rolled her eyes and removed her pistol from its holder on her waist. "Let's get Max to the summit before that beacon dies. Otherwise, this will all be in vain."

The arm that was wrapped around his neck slithered away and now held a gleaming, three-pronged trident. Max threw Rylan a sly smile and was given a wink in return, making his chest feel like it was filled with a thousand butterflies.

Peeling his eyes away from Rylan, Max gazed at the red beacon coming from the middle of the volcano. Concentrating his mind, tendrils enveloped his hands and feet as the familiar sensation of shapeshifting took over.

I can't believe how easy this has become, he thought as his body hunched over. *When I first came to the island, my body was exhausted after shifting, and now, I can do it without a second thought.* Tufts of brown hair sprouted over his body, and a searing pain reached the corners of his mouth as tusks emerged from his teeth.

Rylan and Leo's eyes were wide, unsure if they should be worried or in awe at the sight of him transforming.

"Take us with you," Rylan breathed.

Max shook his head. "No, you need to battle with everyone else to keep the imps and goblins at bay. I need to face Samael myself." He lowered his head to the ground and let out a battle cry, hoping that his squeal that echoed throughout the battlefield reached the ears of the person on top.

Max nodded to his friends, who swiftly wielded their weapons and began running toward the sea of imps and goblins ahead of them. He caught a glimpse of Rylan and Leo in his peripheral vision as they fell back to fight alongside the Sofillian and fairies. The sounds of Max's hooves matched his heartbeat as he pushed his way through the crowd.

As a makeshift spear thrown by a goblin connected with his skin, he was surprised to find that it bounced off as if he had a layer of armor protecting him. The goblin reached to his side and brought a small black funnel to his lips, which emitted a whistle-like sound.

Continuing to run, Max realized that once the goblins heard that sound, their small floppy ears perked up, and their attention turned to the boar. Spears and arrows began pelting at him from all angles, but it was as if his flesh and fur were protecting him, not allowing the weapons to slow him down.

Seeing the arrows break as soon as they touched him, Max confidently ran through the horde, feeling invincible. The cracked ground beneath his feet was stained with different types of blood—some green, some oil black, but the dark red pools sent a shiver throughout his body.

Making his way up the volcano, he passed fallen goblins, their bodies looking like deflated leather bags, before an imp jumped in front of him. Its yellow eyes were feral, and its short hair stood at attention like a scared cat. A smile perched on the imp's dark lips as it ran directly towards him, claws outstretched.

Do I fight or continue onward?

He lowered his neck as if answering himself, pointing his tusks directly at the oncoming imp. Oil-colored blood splattered Max's face as his tusks went directly through his enemy's stomach, its lifeless body hanging from the two strong teeth jutting from his mouth. He whipped his head to the side, throwing the lifeless creature at a group of nearby enemies.

The ground became more brittle as he neared the apex of the mountain. His hooves pounded the barren rock, and he swore that the volcano itself was pulsating along with him. His body was a muscular shell that was unbeatable, and as the throng of imps and goblins waned, he could sense his body shift. Glancing at his feet as he ran up the volcano, he saw two human hands and feet grasping at the ground. The speed of his body lessened until he was nothing more than a seventeen-year-old boy once again.

The mouth of the volcano was a few feet away. Max unsheathed his sword and took a breath of the stale air surrounding him. The crystals infused within the blade created a dim white light within the bleak landscape, and the volcano's innards lurched, almost as if it were rejecting the weapon's shine.

Walking to the craggy mouth of the volcano, he balanced one foot on the rim while gazing inward. It was a mesmerizing sight, the way the sea of burning lava blended in a chaotic dance of red and orange as it crashed into the side of the mountain like unruly waves. If Max didn't know better, he would've thought a battle was happening directly under the burning mass. Though he couldn't feel its warmth, white smoke emanated into the sky from the depths. He squinted, looking for some sign of Samael or his sister, but saw nothing but hues of red and yellow.

"Be careful, Max," a familiar voice boomed from behind him. Catching him off guard, Max jumped, and his spine tensed. "You wouldn't want to fall in now, would you?"

With his sword outstretched, his eyes immediately fell upon a familiar face. Calvo's almond-shaped brown eyes looked back at him, his muscles protruding from his shirtless torso. His hair that stood up from the headband wrapped around his forehead blew in the breeze. A smile perked at the corners of his mouth as his gorgeous, honey-colored eyes bore into the depths of Max's soul.

Chapter Thirty-Four

A few days ago, seeing Calvo would have made Max's stomach light and queasy in a good way, but now his heart was burning with white-hot anger. The realization that Samael had possessed Calvo for their journey made him feel tricked, as if he were being used by him the entire time he'd been on the Island of Forever. He pointed the gleaming sword directly at Calvo, whose eye twitched as the light reached him. "Let my sister go. And everyone else you kidnapped, too."

His eyes were drawn to the sword. "I see you're the new Hero, bravo." He clapped his thick, rugged hands. "That must mean that you've harnessed your shapeshifting powers, but don't forget, I've been one since birth and have perfected my abilities. Once the beacon closes, I'll be free, and you'll be no match for me." His neck craned forward, his chin extended. "What's your plan? Did you expect me to hand over my tributes with a simple threat?"

"If you don't, I'll make sure you never leave."

Calvo was balancing on the volcano's rim like he was walking a tightrope. "You'll do what? Imprison me again?" His body shifted, and he lost his balance. His arms rose into the air before falling into the volcano. His large body swayed back and forth, and his arms rose into the air before falling into the volcano.

Max was dumbfounded seeing him disappear into the depth below.

Was it really that easy?

Max's heart was pounding as he ran towards the mouth of the mountain. He arrived just in time to see Calvo re-emerge, his body gently cradled by a cushion of molten lava before being deposited back onto the cracked ground.

A maniacal smile was plastered across his face as the burning liquid safely deposited him on the cracked ground. "Since I have been imprisoned, I learned how to manipulate the lava. If you're looking to throw me in and seal me away like the last Hero did, you'll sadly fail."

The dark clouds were being pushed aside by the red beacon shooting into the sky, and he noticed it appeared much larger than when he was far out in the ocean. He had more time, albeit not very much.

"Maxie boy, let's make a deal." Calvo stood erect, like a man doing business. "How about I release your sister and girl-friend and let you live on this island forever?"

He raised an eyebrow and wrinkled his nose at the pet name. "What's in it for you?"

Calvo extended his arms with a flourish. "The sword in your hand, along with your acceptance and loyalty to join me in my quest to rejoin the Mainland."

He glanced at the gleaming weapon clutched in his palm and contemplated the offer. Ana's words seemed to dance on the wind around him, entering his ears and taking refuge in his mind. Max shook his head. "I-I can't do that."

Calvo raised his hands into the air, and from the dark

clouds encircling the beacon, two crystalline pods descended, floating behind him. In the first pod was a gorgeous blonde-haired girl with delicate facial features, her eyes closed, and her head tilted to one side as if she were sleeping.

A shift in Max's hand startled him. The hilt clutched within his palm trembled ever so slightly; the vibration was so minimal that only he could recognize the sudden shift.

What's happening? My sword was fine until Ella and Hannah came out of the sky.

Ignoring the quivering in his hand, his eyes moved to the second chamber, and his heart began pounding once he noticed the little girl inside. Her arms were wrapped around her legs, which were tucked tightly to her chest, and her eyes were closed as if she, too, slumbered. Her face was relaxed, and a small smile peeked at her lips.

Calvo noted Max's eyes gazing upon Ella and Hannah. "Will you reconsider my offer?" he asked, his voice soft and calm.

Max detected a change in his tone, which grew softer, suggesting that he was trying to make his offer more enticing. He shook his head in defiance of the bargain. "Release them."

The crystal-infused blade hummed in his hand, and the vibrations coursed through his body.

Calvo's eyes narrowed, and his tone became dry. "Accept my offer and your wish will be granted."

"Let them go!" Max lunged at the man with his sword in hand.

When the blade sailed through the air, Calvo's reflexes kicked in, and he tumbled to his left, anticipating the attack and dodging the blow. The tip of Max's sword missed its intended target but collided with the dark chamber that encased his sister. A small chip appeared in the smooth glass enclosure, and within seconds, a map of thin lines spiraled throughout the pod from the strike. Pushing harder into the crystal chamber, shards of dark glass rained from the sky.

Max watched as Calvo's eyes widened in disbelief. Triumph blossomed in his chest as he knew that there was a miscalculation in his foe's master plan—the pods weren't impenetrable. Taking advantage of his surprise, Max turned and stabbed his sword into the chamber that held Hannah. The sound of tinkling glass encircled them as the teenage girl fell to the ground.

"Max, watch out!"

Rylan's voice pierced his ears as he tucked an unconscious Ella against his chest. A loud clang pierced the air behind him as he raised one arm for protection. An axe was caught within the prongs of Rylan's trident, and Max realized that Calvo had attempted a surprise attack on him.

Rylan just saved me.

Pushing Calvo backward with his weapon, Leo emerged next to them with her gun pointed toward the possessed teen's bulging chest. A group of Sofillians formed a circle behind her, waiting for direction.

"You're outnumbered, Samael," Leo announced, eyes narrowed. "With Ella and Hannah removed from your captivity, you can't use them as tributes, and you won't have enough people to restore your power."

Calvo held the ax downward as his black hair obstructed his eyes. Raising his head, a confident smile full of bright teeth grazed his face. "As you know, I need people to sacrifice, so those two would've been perfect. I knew you'd do anything to save them, but in doing so, you delivered an entire army to me." With his arm extended and his palm outstretched, he effortlessly lifted several Sofillian boys into the air.

The screams from the crowd surrounded them as the hexagonal crystalline shells suddenly encapsulated the boys, causing their weapons to clatter to the ground and their bodies to freeze in place. The chambers lifted into the sky and rejoined the sea of others that circled the lighted beacon.

"My return would've been so much quicker if that damn tree didn't shield these kids from me, so I had to resort to stealing from the fairies and the people within Berylon. Now that I have all the tributes I need, the seal *will* be broken." With his words, the pods in the sky ceased moving and, one by one, began hurtling into the center of the volcano.

"Stop!" Leo shouted and fired her gun, the white bullet sailing through the air with precision.

With a quick flick of his wrist, Calvo brushed the bullet away as if it were a mosquito.

Max swallowed the ball forming in his throat and turned to his two best friends. "I need the both of you to get Hannah and Ella to safety. This is between me and him."

"Max, no," Rylan shouted at him. "We aren't leaving your side."

Max deposited his little sister into Leo's arms. "I'm the Hero on this island, and it's my duty to protect it, but my top priority are the people I love." His eyes fell on Rylan as his heart began thumping in his chest. "I was told that once my sword goes inside the volcano, a rift between worlds will occur. When this happens, I need you four to go through it and return home." He glanced at Calvo, who was impatiently tapping his foot and casually glancing at his wrist.

"We're not leaving without you."

"I'll meet you at the base of this volcano once I'm done with him." In all reality, Max didn't know if he would be meeting his friends to return home. He could only wish the battle with Calvo would be successful. He held his chin high while instructing Rylan and Leo to look as confident as possible.

I need them to believe I have a plan to defeat him. As much as I hate lying to them, I have to do it to keep them safe.

Leo turned to look at Rylan, her eyes wide with worry and uncertainty. He picked Hannah off the ground and nodded to his friend. "We have to trust him."

Rylan stopped and looked at Max with heavy eyes. "I have some stuff to talk to you about when we get home, so don't die on me, okay?"

Max gave a knowing smile and a quick wink. "Don't worry, I know." His eyes lingered on his friends as they turned their backs to him and retreated.

The sound of a slow clap came from Calvo. "Very noble, Max. Very noble indeed." He brought one finger to his face and feigned wiping a tear from his eye. "Your love for everyone almost made me emotional." His mocking laugh penetrated the area as he moved closer. "I just loathe being bored to tears, don't you?"

Asshole.

Max's sword whistled through the air as he swung it at Calvo, who expertly deflected it with his ax.

"Once the sacrifices have been made, I'll return to power and take that sword from your dead, lifeless fingers." With a swift movement, he jabbed his ax towards Max, narrowly missing his arm. "The beacon is closing, and I'm detecting some of my shapeshifter powers returning."

Max's heart was racing, the sound of his pulse pounding in his ears like a drumbeat. His eyes turned to the waning light extending into the sky.

I can't give up. I need to fight Samael long enough to lure him closer to the entrance of the volcano. I dunno what'll happen once we're there, but to make sure everyone is safe, I'll stab him, and we'll fall in together. It's the only way I'll know he can't get out.

Despite his best efforts, the swing was deflected by the man he was fighting. Calvo made a swift strike, but Max was quick to react and caught the blade with his own, forming an X with their weapons. Only a couple of days ago, Calvo's proximity would've thrilled him, but now, he couldn't recognize the person he once had feelings for. His eyes caught sight of Calvo's arms as black veins spiderwebbed across his body.

Within the blink of an eye, his enemy shapeshifted to resemble someone else. This man had a thin, gaunt face and scraggly brown hair atop his head. His eyes had been hollowed out, replaced with darkened craters. "Hi, Max."

Startled, Max pushed away, throwing him backward, closer to the volcano's entrance. The light from the beacon shadowed the man's face, but he immediately knew who Calvo had become—his father.

I know what he's doing. He knows my dad would make my anxiety go crazy, but he doesn't know the trials I'd already faced within the crystal cave. I think I can use his ignorance to my advantage.

Walking closer, he feigned a stutter. "D-Dad?"

In the form of Max's father, Calvo held his arms wide open. "Yes, come here, Max. You've probably been wondering where I've been. Let's chat."

Max took small, measured steps, his sword at his side, attempting to convey a sense of vulnerability. Discreetly wiping his hands on his pants, he hoped that his foe took note of the slight movement.

"Wh-where have you been?" He sidestepped to bring his foot toward the edge of the volcano.

With a quick flourish, the man swung his ax, but Max deflected it by raising his sword, knocking his father's arm away. Calvo's body stumbled from the defense, exposing his chest. "The joke's on you, Samael. I've overcome that side of myself."

Max swung his sword once more but missed his target as his opponent's body shifted into another figure.

Who is that?

The boy before him had eyes that were hollow and lifeless, mirroring the trials within the cave. With his sword raised in defense, he braced himself for impact as the figure charged at him with an ax. Max's blade stopped the attack, and he found himself face-to-face with his doppelganger, the Other Max.

The weight behind the ax that had just clashed against him was great. His legs were weak, but his arms remained steadfast, blocking the blade from touching his skin.

"Don't you see?" The Other Max's hollow eyes were crazed. "I am your fears. I am your anxiety. I am one of your many hidden faces. I am part of you."

No, you're not!

Max pushed his sword with all his strength, causing his opponent to stumble backward, nearly falling into the mouth of the volcano. "You may have been part of the old Max, the scared and unsure Max, but I'm stronger now, and you're not part of me." He focused his shapeshifter powers on his free hand to mirror the crystal-infused sword.

Hopefully these two identical swords will confuse him and give me a better shot.

"I'll always be a part of you. You'll now think of me when your anxiety creeps in. When your hands sweat and your heart races, I'll be lurking and waiting to strike."

"Not anymore!" Max swung his shifted hand, which resembled the crystal sword. His hand hit the Other Max's ax and knocked him sideways.

"Did you not think I'd notice that your hand shifted? Come on, Max. I'm not new to this game."

He's going to try to catch me off guard.

The Other Max hit one of the crystal swords, knocking Max's wrist sideways. Without thinking, he threw down his elbow and spun around as if his body was on autopilot. He avoided the Other Max's blow by ducking and raising his shifted arm to deflect it, allowing the correct sword to reach its intended target: his enemy's abdomen.

Chapter Thirty-Five

For a few moments, it seemed as if time had stopped. With the sword sticking out of his stomach, Calvo's thick frame shifted back into his original, muscular body. Glancing downward, his mouth dropped, and his eyes widened once he saw the sword's golden hilt in his tan skin. His calloused hands closed around the hilt of the blade, and a sharp sizzle reached his ears, followed by a growling scream. He couldn't remove the sword.

Max's body froze as if he had turned to stone.

Did I really just pull that off? I need to take full advantage of his distraction to push him into the volcano for the seal to repair.

Max called upon his shapeshifting abilities, envisioning the form of a bumblebee in his mind. In a matter of moments, he vanished from his previous location and was zipping through the air on his buzzing wings.

Calvo screamed in intense pain, violently thrashing his body as if he were drunk. His feet stumbled on the cracked ground, and his strong hands covered his temples. "I can't see! Someone help me!"

Maybe I'll be able to go home with Rylan after all?

Max knew that he needed to lure the man as close to the volcano as possible so he could either latch onto him and descend the depths of the volcano together or get lucky enough to throw him inside alone. Hoping for the latter, he flew to the backside of Calvo and quickly shifted his body into the perfect lure for the villain.

"Sam? Is that you?" Max cooed. The black-and-white striped suit hugged his body tightly, and his eyebrows were tickled by long, black bangs.

Hearing the voice, Calvo stiffened and slowly turned his head to look in Max's direction. His eyebrows twitched as he whispered in a barely audible voice, "A-Ana? Is that you?"

Max smiled and nodded. "I came back for you. Once the gate reopened, I arrived as quickly as possible." His eyes darted to the sword sticking out of his foe's stomach, and he gasped. "Come here and let me remove that sword."

Calvo began stumbling toward him, clutching at his stomach in pain. "All I have ever wanted was to be with you. You'll join me?"

"Of course, Sam, love has brought us back together." As strange as it may be, Max harbored a tinge of guilt for deceiving him, but he knew it was to save the Island of Forever. His breath hitched and sat in his esophagus as he realized he couldn't push Calvo inside the volcano without the fear of it going awry.

I need to know that my plan worked and everyone that I love is safe. The only way to do that is to risk myself and leave no room for error.

Max extended his arms for a warm embrace with the man in front of him, the stripes on his jacket fluttering in the wind.

He forced a smile, noticing the man's breathing becoming increasingly shallow as a dribble of blood stained his lip.

Just as Calvo was a foot in front of Max, his arms opened to embrace. A sincere smile graced his face, and his eyes were full of longing.

This is so weird, but I have to do it.

Just as they were inches away from hugging, Calvo whispered, "Nice try." In a flash, his strong hands forcefully grabbed Max's arms and pushed him to the ground. "Did you think you could fool me, boy? I find it quite impressive that you tried using my emotions against me. Maybe we aren't so different after all?"

As Max's body shifted from the black and white suit to his dirty white undershirt, the thin glimmer of the red beacon behind Calvo diminished. Time had run out.

The sacrifice was over.

The desolate area was filled with the sound of Calvo's laughter as he broke free from his seal. He was surrounded by a thin film of dark smoke, and the only source of light was the sword still stuck in his stomach. He threw his head back and let out a victorious laugh as he stretched his arms high into the air. The cracked ground of the volcano started shaking as if the lava was trying to pound through its sides.

Max sprawled on the ground, at a loss for words or action. Just as the volcano began to rumble, a scream pierced through the air. Calvo barely had time to react before a burst of blue color hit him square in the shoulders, sending him stumbling forward. Rylan's tangled hair flew in all directions as he collided with their adversary. His arms were outstretched, and he was determined to push the man into the fiery depths of the volcano. Both of them sailed through the air, then dropped over the mountain's lip.

Screams penetrated Max's ears as he stood in fear, hoping

that Rylan hadn't sacrificed himself to save him. In the midst of the violent shaking, he spotted a body wearing skin-tight shorts that looked like scales leaning over the volcano's mouth. The rough texture of the volcano's surface dug into the soles of their bare feet as they clung on for dear life.

I'm not losing Rylan.

Running faster than he thought he could, his thoughts swirled at the thought of losing someone close to him once again. He could see Rylan's knees give out, sliding him further into the volcano, leaving only his toes planted into the ground to stop his descent.

Max slid onto the ground and latched his hand around Rylan's ankle. Max was startled to discover that he had been completely deaf to his screams and had overlooked the black crystal chambers emerging from the volcano until that very second. He was too focused on saving his friend.

With both hands around Rylan's leg and with all the strength he could muster, Max pulled. He strained with all his might to pull Rylan out, but it was only when a sudden thought popped into his head that his body shifted. Glancing down at his feet, he witnessed his once skinny legs had turned into thick, hairy trunks, and his arms had gone from being tooth-pick-thin to strong and robust. He wasn't exactly sure what he had shifted into, but he now had the confidence and strength he needed to save Rylan.

He planted his gargantuan feet on the ground and wrapped his hands around his friend's ankles. Max lifted and Rylan's small arms latched around his neck, breathing heavily and slightly winded.

Rylan jumped in his arms out of shock and his eyes were wide. "What the hell are you? A gorilla?"

Max laughed and shifted back into his normal body. "I dunno what I was. I just knew I had to save you." His cheeks became heated, and he raised his eyes to gaze into his friend's bright green eyes. "Why'd you come back up here?"

Rylan detached himself from the protection of Max's arms. Their bodies drew closer until they were inches apart. Rylan lifted his chin to look up at Max and placed his palm on his shoulder, offering a reassuring squeeze. "I knew I had to save you, too. If anything happened to you before I told you..."

Max smiled. "You don't have to tell me anything. I already know."

"You do?"

Max reached for Rylan's arm, which hung limply by his side, and clasped his hand around his fingers to emphasize his point. At first, the touch was gentle, but as their intensity matched, the embrace became fervent. They looked at each other with burning desire, and the rest of the world faded away.

A mischievous smile played on Rylan's lips. "You *do* know." He stood on his toes and pushed himself forward, their lips colliding.

He embraced Rylan, and they kissed deeply, savoring each other's taste. In a way, he was surprised this was his reality because he never thought this would ever happen. Tears poked at Max's closed eyelids, but he didn't care. He knew this was right.

Their lips touched, first gentle and then rough. The pull between them was too strong to ignore, and their hands mapped each other's bodies with a fierce yet gentle urgency. Despite the violent shaking of the mountain they were standing on, Max's mind was erupting with a passion that felt like a dormant volcano reawakening.

One final kiss was all it took to make it completely explode.

The volcano lurched, and a flash of red shot into the sky, startling them. Max and Rylan turned away from one another, the residue of excited nerves tingling on their lips as they gazed at the powerful light reaching into the heavens.

"What's happening?"

Max shrugged. "I think the beacon is reestablishing itself to seal Samael in. Maybe we weren't too late after all."

They watched as the last of the crystal chambers emerged from the volcano, and the beacon grew, beginning no larger than a piece of thread and expanding to cover the entire volcano's mouth.

Max looked behind him and saw the crystalline chambers holding the children scattered around the mountain like shells on a seashore. As the beacon grew, the crystals dissipated like jelly, falling from each of the children's bodies and disappearing into the volcano's dirty exterior, freeing them.

A bright yellow light pierced the sky that was too high to reach, planting itself just above the tree line. A thin, mist-like cloud with purple, blue, and black swirls seemed to be taped onto the night sky, hovering in the air. That area of sky looked like a torn piece of paper or a twisted knot on a tree.

"That must be the portal home." Max pointed. "I didn't expect it to be so high. How're we going to reach it?"

"We're one step ahead of you." Rylan smiled and pointed to a dot on the horizon.

Within seconds, the dot grew closer until he saw Leo, Ella, and Hannah waving to them atop a large pirate ship with the words *The Morgana* painted in gold letters on its hull. The dark wooden ship sailed through the sky until it sat hovering over Max and Rylan. A straw-colored rope ladder unraveled itself in the space between the two.

Max wrapped his hand around a wrung of the ladder and turned his head back to the children and other people lying on the hillside, slowly coming to their senses. He couldn't leave them atop the volcano after saving them.

Rylan followed his gaze. "Don't worry. We instructed the Sofillians to come back up the volcano if they saw the beacon relight. That way, they'd know that Samael has been locked away. They'll be making their way back up here any moment. Don't worry about everyone—they'll be safe. They're safe because of you."

"Us," Max corrected.

Chapter Thirty-Six

"Squawk!" A piercing caw rang from above them. A green parrot sat on the side of the ship, looking down at them with one eye and raising his colored feathers in the air. "Ahoy, ye two! Ye better scurry up this ladder before ye way home closes."

Max glanced at the portal in the sky and prayed for it to stay open until they were on the ship. He was climbing the rope ladder when he saw a small head with a beaming smile looking back at him. Ella leaned over the ship's side, her small fingers outstretched towards her brother.

"Ella, get back in here!" Leo picked the little girl up from the ship's floor. "That's all we need is for you to fall out!"

Max pulled himself up and was greeted with a big hug from his sister. A smile immediately spread upon his face, and her little arms wrapped around his neck.

She's safe. I did it.

He let out a sigh of relief. He was whole again. Max's eyes were wet as he embraced his sister. This whole journey was for her, and it was now ending.

Ella stepped back from Max, her pigtails bouncing with every step. Squinting her eyes and inspecting his face, she poked him in the cheek with her finger. "What's different about you?" Her eyebrow was raised as she stared at him, scanning his face.

Max stole a glance at Rylan. "A whole lot, but to you, I'm still your big brother."

Rylan sidled over to the little girl and ruffled her hair. "Heya squirt, glad to have you back."

A pair of arms flung around Max's shoulders, and a waterfall of blonde hair draped across his neck. "Max, you're safe!"

He turned around and was surprised to see his girlfriend standing there, looking radiant with her hair neatly styled. It bewildered Max how she was able to look as if she hadn't just been kidnapped and held hostage for days. A small lump grew in his throat, and his face paled. He didn't know how to tell her he was a different person, someone who knew what he wanted.

"Hey, Hannah...I think we need to talk when we get home."

She nodded, and a playful look bounced in her eyes. "We do. But just know I'm proud of you."

Max wasn't expecting the reaction, and a fire now burned in his cheeks. His eyes widened, and he raised his eyebrows.

Does she know?

"My heart was so full seeing you two on top of the volcano."

Shit, this'll be an awkward conversation. "Hi, Hannah, you're my girlfriend, but you just saw me kissing my best friend." That'll go over well.

If there was a hole to crawl into, he would have done so at that moment.

Hearing the interaction and seeing Max's face a brighter red than the beacon, Rylan threw his arms into the air. "I can't believe it. This guy just defeated a sociopathic shapeshifter, and yet you can turn him into a blubbering idiot in two seconds." He pushed Max away from her. "The balance is being restored to the Island of Forever, but to reach peak normalcy, we have to go home."

"Full speed ahead," Captain Marris cawed as he rapidly turned the ship's steering wheel to face the portal. "The ride may be bumpy, but *The Morgana* will get us there safe, avast!"

With a wide stance, Max held out his hands, with his palms facing outward. "Come here, everyone, let's hold on to one another. That way, we won't lose each other if anything happens." Everyone nodded and intertwined their fingers with the person next to them, creating a circle.

Rylan laughed. "That's all we need is to get separated in a different world again."

The ship sailed through the air, heading directly toward the pulsating cloud. They cut through the sky with speed and precision until they were inches away. Max looked into the distance, taking a mental picture of the place that had changed him. As his eyes connected with the Great Tree of Hesper standing above the forest and the large castle sitting on a cliff in the distance, the memories of their adventure flooded his mind. He would miss the Island of Forever, though he held a part of it within him now, too.

"We're entering the portal. Hold on, mateys."

The Morgana encountered resistance upon entering the cloud, but the mermaid on the ship's hull pushed through, and suddenly, their bodies were weightless. The ship was engulfed by a vibrant vortex of colors, whirling and twirling endlessly. Passing through the tunnel, they all held on to each other tightly, their bodies shaking and trembling with fear. The quaking was rough, then soon subsided to nothingness.

A vast sea of stars opened before them, twinkling on a

canvas of black. Suspended in the air was a big, bright moon illuminating the darkened clouds, drifting lazily through the sky. Max looked at Leo and Rylan and saw their clothes had changed back into their normal jeans and T-shirts. Looking down at himself, he noticed that his white shirt was still dirty, and his jeans were still cut into shorts.

A whistle came from the ship's steering wheel. "Aye, mateys. We made it back to the Mainland."

Max, Leo, Rylan, Ella, and Hannah ran to the side of the ship and peeked over. From their vantage point, they could see twinkling pockets of lights, each representing a different town below. The ship's hull shifted, and the vessel began to descend.

"Hey, look," Ella shouted and pointed below. "I think I can see our house from here."

Just above the top of a neighborhood, Captain Marris unraveled the rope ladder once more. "Land Ho! We've arrived at your final destination. One at a time, please climb down the ladder. I have to get back to the island before that portal closes."

"I'll go first!" Leo shouted and began making her way down the ladder.

"I'll follow you." Hannah pushed Rylan out of the way, following their friend.

"Aw, why couldn't I go next?" Rylan whined. "That way, I could see up your skirt."

Max rolled his eyes, and Hannah shook her head. "Some things never change."

Max squatted down so that his backside was to Ella. "Hop on and hold tight." He was uneasy about Ella climbing down, so he offered to piggyback her.

His sister jumped onto his back and wrapped her arms around his neck and her legs around his stomach before Max put his feet on the first wrung of the ladder. Captain Marris flew onto the side of the ship and took his pirate hat off his head, crossing it over his chest. "I speak for the entire Island of Forever when I say thank ye for saving our home."

Max nodded to the parrot. "I want to thank the island for everything it has taught me, too."

"Can we come back and visit?" Ella called out.

Captain Marris's one beady eye swiveled to look at the little girl. "Nay, we can't have Mainlanders enter the island, or we will be in this predicament again. If the island calls, ye will know."

"Thank you for your help, Captain."

"Farewell new Hero and Pink Pirate Ella."

Max made his way down the ladder and planted his feet firmly on the pavement. As he released the rope ladder, the ship lifted off the ground and disappeared into the swirling vortex above. The swirling cloud dissipated into nothingness, replaced by the inky darkness of the night. The only sound that was left behind was a far-off squawk.

With their heads tilted towards the sky, the five watched as the ship disappeared into the clouds. "I wonder if anyone else saw the flying boat sailing through the sky and is wondering what the hell it is?"

"Hey, where did my spandex fish tights go?" Rylan whined.

"Why are you upset? There wasn't anything to see there anyways," Leo snidely retorted, elbowing Rylan in the ribs.

The air smelled of fresh rain, and a chill ran through the October wind. They stood in the middle of a street with a towering house to their right and a squeaky gate that clanged every time a breeze passed through.

"He dropped us off outside Ana's house, so we aren't too far from home," Rylan observed.

Ella pointed to a window, and a small light shone through. "It looks like she's awake. Should we stop to say hello?"

Max smiled at his sister, knowing she must be bursting at

the seams to tell Ana about her adventures. "Why don't we visit her tomorrow and get some rest tonight? I have a hunch she'll have some fresh cookies made for us."

Ella opened her mouth wide and yawned deeply as if mirroring the lethargy of her surroundings.

"I'm going to head home," Hannah said. "I just want to make sure my parents know I'm okay. I don't know how long we have been gone, so they may be worried." She rounded everyone with a bunch of hugs, but when she stopped at Max, she kissed him on the cheek. "Call me later?"

He nodded and they separated, Hannah walking toward her house and the rest heading to theirs. As Ana's house disappeared behind them, a sense of comfort and relief burrowed in his body, knowing that she was there and that he could confide in her about the things he'd learned and experienced on the Island of Forever.

Rounding the corner to their apartment complex, their eyes were met with shadows silhouetted in the windows. Different families all under one roof, living their different lives.

"How are we going to go back to normal life?" Leo asked as they neared the path leading to the front lobby.

Max shrugged. "I guess we just have to try to remember everything that happened and use what we learned in our new life." *Our new life.* That is exactly how Max felt. He was entering a new phase of his life, one where he could be who he wanted and where he was not holding himself back.

As they made their way through the dingy foyer, the yellow fluorescent lighting buzzed overhead.

"Can I press the button?" Ella asked as if they all forgot her request every time they came to an elevator.

"Floor 3, please," Leo said to Ella with a wink.

As the metal elevator doors closed, the sounds of cheesy

elevator music started playing through the speakers to mask the wailing of the old elevator as it rose.

"See you tomorrow?"

The elevator doors parted, and Rylan pushed through, slightly nudging Max's shoulder as he exited the elevator. Turning to Leo, he asked, "Wanna walk with me?"

Max was speechless and felt like he had missed something pivotal. He had planned to walk Rylan to his apartment and maybe even give him a hug before saying goodbye. "Everything okay, Ry?"

Is this not how it's supposed to be? Did being home change what we had experienced together? Why's he acting this way?

He shrugged. "I'm kinda bummed about being home, so much happened there and I don't want to forget."

"Then we won't." Max initially thought everyone would be relieved, but understood his friend's distaste after their conversation on the island.

"Yeah, we'll see."

Leo noticed Max's bewildered look and quickly reassured him. "I'll talk to him on our way back. You know how he is, always moody for no reason."

Rylan's comments didn't sit well with him, but he managed to muster a grin, and nod in agreement. "See you both tomorrow."

Max and Ella stepped out of the elevator and turned opposite from their friends. Twisting his body, he attempted to catch one last glance at Rylan, who was steadfast in returning to his apartment. Returning his attention to his sister, they clasped their hands together and walked down the hallway until they reached their apartment door.

"We're finally home."

Max opened the door, and a wave of calm rushed over him. He was home. Lifting his foot, he stepped over the threshold into the apartment. It was the first step he was taking into his new life—the life of a shapeshifter, a brother, a friend. The life of a person who was finally complete and learned to be authentically himself.

It was the first step into a life he could be proud of.

Interested in more adventure on The Island of Forever?
Turn the page for a preview of a free novella that can be read on my website: www.jeremeyharrison.com

The Adventures
of Captain Marris

Chapter 1

"Slow 'er down!" Marris ascended the rope net and his shouts reverberated across the ship, reaching the crew below. "I need to take a look at the map."

His rotund first mate, Knell, exerted all his strength on a few ropes, causing the mast to rotate slowly. "Aye, aye, Captain!"

Making his way as fast as possible to the crow's nest, Marris leaned over the edge of the wooden barrier, listening to the creaking of the ship beneath him. The salty wind billowed around his black jacket, making the silver buttons lining his chest rattle. He desperately clung to the black bicorn hat on his head, determined not to lose it in the wind. The pirate ship slowed its path, and he tightly clasped a tattered piece of paper in his other hand, its edges fluttering in the breeze. With his heart racing, sweat clung to his palms as he grasped the worn piece of paper. His adrenaline buzzed with electricity as the feeling of adventure pulsed through him.

This is the life.

"Knell, get up here!" Marris yelled down to his best friend.

Without delay, he caught sight of a person with a brown bowl cut, their strong fingers tightly gripping the rope ladder as they climbed the crow's nest. "C'mon, hurry up!"

Eventually, two arms heaved onto the wooden landing, accompanied by heavy, labored breathing. "C-Captain, y-you k-know I'm s-scared of h-heights." Knell hoisted himself onto the landing, his brown eyes nervously looking over the side while his knees shook.

"I won't let anything happen to ya, buddy." Marris slapped him on the back and held out the paper. "Here, hold this, and don't let it go." With a swift motion, he reached into his breast pocket and produced a telescope, extending it to its full length.

"Y-you've been q-quiet about where w-we're going, Captain," Knell managed to say over his trembling breath.

"I couldn't let word get out." Marris narrowed his eyes. "Call it a bout of paranoia, but I'll tell you."

Knell's cheeks turned red as he smugly smiled at the man he idolized.

"In your hands is a map that will lead us to the Staff of Melides." His face lit up with a confident smile as he ran his fingers through his vibrant crimson hair. "Don't worry about where I found it; all I can say is that it was a truly heroic discovery."

"I bet it was." Knell nodded, his eyebrows raised. "I was surprised when we found you casually walking along Seashell Shore."

Marris nodded and looked through the telescope, seeing the vast sea before him. "Aye, I know if I'm near water, *The Morgana* will always find me."

"What is the Staff of Melides, Captain?" Knell's cheeks formed a broad smile, causing his eyes to crinkle.

Marris brought his face inches away from the map, his sharp nose almost making contact, before diverting his attention back to the telescope. "There have always been stories of an ancient group whose leader, King Melides, had a staff with the power to turn anything he wanted into solid gold."

His heart skipped a beat at the mere thought of obtaining the fabled staff—all the gold he could possibly want could be his. Dismissing the thought, he focused his attention once more on the map's obscure instructions with frustration building up in his mind.

Why can't I figure this out? We're in the center of the three land masses and the map is pointing me toward the middle. There's nothing here. What am I doing wrong?

He squinted his eye through his telescope once again and sighed. It wasn't uncommon for pirates to make maps that led to a fake treasure. They did it hoping the hunters would get discouraged if they were met with too many dead ends.

I can't be wrong. I'm the greatest treasure hunter the Forever Sea has ever seen.

He pointed to the water. "Knell, do you see anything suspicious?" With a twist of the ring on his finger, he activated its enchantment, granting him the ability to duplicate any item he gripped.

The man took the bronze spyglass in his chubby fingers and put it to his eye. "I-I don't, cap'n."

A voice interrupted their conversation as a pirate from Marris's crew yelled to everyone nearby. "A ship's approaching from the port side!"

"Captain, I-I think..."

"Quiet, Knell." As Marris hurried to the other side of the crow's nest, a sizable, murky shape could be seen lurking in the distance. With the telescope pressed against his eye, he beheld the awe-inspiring image of a magnificent ship effortlessly navigating through the waves, its helm occupied by a determined woman with narrow, intense eyes. "They're following us."

"Captain, I think I found a clue on the map."

"Not now, Knell." With a daring leap, Captain Marris hurled himself out of the ship's highest point, his fingers instinctively gripping a nearby rope. Sliding down toward the deck, he effortlessly swung through the air, and his body came to a halt inches above the gleaming wooden surface of his ship. Marris's voice echoed as he yelled, ensuring his whole crew could hear. "Full speed ahead! We need to lose these girls!"

The men around the deck diligently turned and unraveled the masts, their hands moving purposefully. A moment of silence hung in the air as they waited for the wind to fill the sails.

Gradually, the ship started to sway, moving with the current. Running to the back of the vessel, Marris's heart plummeted as he realized how close the other boat was. The sun illuminated the golden letters printed on its side, causing them to glimmer and catch his attention: *The Pirate Booty.*

"Let's get outta here!" Taking charge, he firmly planted himself at the helm, his hands gripping the wheel with unwavering strength, prepared to guide the ship away from their stalkers

"Sir," Knell ran to him, out of breath and gasping for air, "I-think-I-found-a-clue."

"A clue?" Marris's eyebrows rose. "Why didn't you say so? Where?"

"Look here." Knell held the tattered map to the captain's eyes. "We're exactly where the map tells us to be, but look in the sky."

"A sun?"

"And?"

Marris scanned the document and only saw the drawing of a sun in the sky, nestled toward the right of the paper. He shrugged his shoulders and glanced toward the oncoming ship. "I don't have time for this nonsense."

Knell pointed to the crescent-shaped island on the left side of the map. "The sun and the moon need to be in the sky at the same time."

Suddenly, a loud boom from a recently deployed cannon reverberated through the air. A tremendous splash saturated the ship, startling everyone on board. "They're gaining on us," he said aloud, confident in his abilities as he took his place at the helm. "Losing them shouldn't be a problem for *me*." With an expert swing of the wheel, the ship abruptly turned to the right.

"Look, cap'n." Knell's finger trembled as it stretched to the sky.

"I don't have time to look right now." He tightly gripped the hull, desperately wishing the ship could veer sharply to the right, leaving no time for *The Pirate Booty* to change course and allowing them to pass by undetected. "We aren't getting plundered by a group of girls."

Startled, a bunch of men let out piercing screams as they glanced over the boat. "What the hell is that?"

What now?

Without warning, they were suddenly knocked down by a powerful force as a frothy blue ocean wave surged onto the espresso trim of the deck. Jumping up, Marris's eyes widened as he beheld the aftermath of the collision, the twisted remains of the other ship intertwined with their own. He yelled at the top of his lungs, "What the hell are you doing?"

His words fell on deaf ears as his entire crew and the girls on the other ship had their eyes planted in the same direction. He ran to starboard, and his mouth dropped at the sight before him. Just a few feet ahead, a grand whirlpool swirled and churned with immense power.

The once calm ocean now roared with turbulence, swirling violently to form the menacing spiral of water. A thin foam bubbled in its core as a warning—if your ship entered, it would surely be crushed.

Marris turned to his crew. "Let's get out of this current! Drop all the masts!"

The pull was so strong that the two ships were immediately caught in a whirlpool, spinning helplessly. He saw the women on the other ship scurry around, trying to use every technique they could to extract themselves from the vacuum-like current. They began at the outer edge, then continued their slow, spiraling journey toward the center.

I've led my crew to their death. This isn't what a captain's purpose is.

As they spiraled, he sensed a presence behind him and instantly felt a firm squeeze around his waist. *The Morgana* was sucked into the whirlpool. The front of the ship vanished first, gradually sinking beneath the water's surface as if it had collided with an iceberg.

Marris closed his eyes and held his breath, feeling the anticipation build as he prepared to sink into the watery depths. With the heart of a true pirate, he embraced the notion of going down with his ship, fully prepared to meet his fate with honor.

With each passing minute, the ship rocked back and forth with such intensity that they were forcefully thrown to the floor and skidded across the polished surface.

But then, all ceased.

Silence.

Marris's eyelids opened, and the world around him was dark.

Is this Davy Jones' Locker?

He knew he wasn't going to heaven, so this was the only logical option. Knell was latched around his body, his eyes shut tight. A cavern of wet rocks surrounded him, their surfaces covered in slippery algae and moss that thrived in their cracks. "Wh-where are we?"

The gloom parted, revealing a mesmerizing sight—a lopsided temple nestled in the cavern, its tiers resembling a delicately carved cake. The boat glided through the water without a sound, steadily approaching its final destination.

Knell's grip around Marris loosened, and his voice was quiet. "It's the Temple of Melides. We did it, Captain!"

What dangers will Captain Marris face in the Temple of Melides?
What will happen when he meets his nemesis, the attractive female pirate, Ruby?
How does The Morgana fly?
How does Captain Marris turn into a bird?

Some of these questions will be answered in this novella, which is available for free on my website, while others will be revealed in the future. Stay up-to-date by subscribing to my newsletter on www.jeremeyharrison.com.

Acknowledgments

First and foremost, I want to thank you, the reader, for giving this book a chance. I hope you were able to see yourself in this story and these characters. If you enjoyed The Island of Forever, please consider leaving a review on Amazon or Goodreads.

To my previous publisher and friend, Brittany Weisrock. Thank you for believing in me, I appreciate you for pushing me to make this book the best that it can be. I am so thankful for your guidance, dedication and humor. For a long time, I believed I wasn't worthy of being a writer and I never thought I'd meet someone that makes it a point to prove me wrong.

To my beta readers and editors, thank you for taking time out of your lives to read my rough (**rough**) draft. Your feedback and encouragement helped me shape the book you're now holding in your hands and I am truly thankful for all of you.

Tara, Charlie, and Ramona – thank you for your attention to details and editing this book to be the best that it can be.

M.E. Morgan, thank you for your amazing artistic talent in bringing this cover to life and your assistance in revamping the blurb.

To my friends, family, and LCP siblings who have supported me through this journey, you'll never know what your excitement has meant to me. Whether it's character art feedback or deciding on a particular scene to cut, thank you for being my cheerleaders. Oh, and putting up with me, that can't be easy.

To Erin, Beka, Kirsten, Hannah, and Kait – Thank you for bringing these characters back to me.

To the two teachers who encouraged me to keep reading and that maybe one day, I'd tell my own stories (if I applied myself): Ms. Bean and Ms. Purrington.

To Nag, Yel, and Yem – the three teens this book was originally written for. This may not be the same book you read back in the day, but the message is the same.

Michael, my ride or die, my home. Words cannot express how much I appreciate your unwavering support, humor, and love. Without your encouragement to keep going, I don't think this book would have come to fruition. I promise one day I'll write a character after you...one day.

Lastly, to Harper and Sophie –my writing buddies– for always sticking by my side and reminding me that love is uncomfortable sleeping positions, pug snores, and completely unconditional.

About the Author

Jeremey Harrison lives in Rhode Island with his husband and two pugs. You can connect with him on all social media platforms under @jeremeyhwrites, or subscribe to his newsletter at: www.jeremeyharrison.com

www.ingramcontent.com/pod-product-compliance
Lightning Source LLC
Chambersburg PA
CBHW050007120726
47903CB00006B/1670